EVAN SCHINDEWOLF

The Astral Prophet

Cover design by Eoin Ryan.

First edition

ISBN: 979-8-3481-8764-4

This book was professionally typeset on Reedsy. Find out more at reedsy.com

Contents

Chapter 1

Someone or something was rustling him. Kairos subvocalized a word, and his tranquil virtual world evaporated. His goggle screens winked out a moment later.

A large, bent figure loomed over him, its muddied cloak flapping, head and face fully wrapped in a black scarf, slit only by two short eyescopes.

Kairos was lying on his back on a thin air mat within a small tent, his light cotton shirt soaked with sweat. It was oppressively humid, the late afternoon air a smothering, dense weight. Blistering wind and rain buffeted one side of the tent, violently ruffling its synthetic fabric and flattening the tent so much that its roof undulated only several centimeters from his nose. The door flap had been unzipped, allowing hot gusts carrying specks of moist dirt to enter and whirl about.

The figure was Falck, the last of Kairos's father's hired hands. Kairos had decided long ago that the man must have either a psychological disorder or a level of desperation even higher than that of his pitiful father for agreeing to continue working at the excavation site.

"Wake up," Falck's deep voice rasped through his respirator

mask beneath the scarf. He prodded Kairos's side with a boot.

"Quit it," growled Kairos, elbowing the man's boot aside and sitting up. "I told you I don't like it when you do that. You know I'm not sleeping."

"Your father needs help," the man stated.

"I'm occupied. You go help him. Isn't that what you'll be paid for?"

Kairos's father, Wells, had depleted his wealth on this ludicrous venture, eventually running out of money to pay the small crew he'd had up until a few local years ago. When that happened, all of them, unsurprisingly, walked off the excavation site. All except Falck, whom his father had nothing to offer except the promise of future riches upon attaining their prize.

"He radioed," Falck replied, unmoved as ever. "He's returning to the surface, but the shaft has been damaged. He needs both of us now."

Kairos let out a small laugh. "Not the first time he's dug himself into a hole. He's smart enough to figure out how to get himself back up. I'm not going out in that," he said, waving a hand at the deluge beyond the tent's whipping door flap.

Earlier that morning, after reading the clouds and temperature, he'd advised his aged father not to trek out to the dig site. A hot front was rolling in. The old man, as per usual, had ignored his son's advice as well as the house barometer.

Kairos returned to lay on his back and subvocalized commands to return the VR portal to his screens.

"He said he's found it," Falck said.

Kairos paused, his throat ceasing its mumbling and his pulse quickening.

"Is it . . . *it*? From the Osetra?" Kairos asked after a few moments, sitting up and lifting his goggles to rest them on his forehead.

But Falck had already backed out of the tent flap, his bulky form dissolving into the steamy ether.

Kairos sat in silence for another moment. Then, he sprang up and reached for his high boots and coat—one of his father's old military jackets, which he'd quietly appropriated for himself upon first arriving on the planet. Before stepping out into the squall, he wrapped his face with a length of his scarf.

The thick clouds overhead were a dark violet-gray. On a rare clear day, the jagged peaks of the Southern Spines could be seen on the horizon, the only break in the stretch of flat wasteland to the south. Visibility now in the steamy humidity was no more than twenty meters; Kairos could barely make out the dark blotch of Falck's shape. Kairos had come to the site that day begrudgingly, only to drop off food for his father from the SolarNet café where he worked.

But when the storm had hit, he'd decided to wait out the cloudburst in shelter. That was three hours ago. Since then, the hot salty downpour had been relentless. Such a rain would sting and nick exposed skin like glass slivers.

The way to the northwest fringe of the excavation site was muddy and pocked with puddles—some of them already half a meter deep. Small rivers of murky water flowed along the vast site's curves and depressions, some ending in waterfalls over the edges of Wells's and Falck's many past drill shafts littering the area. Kairos clomped straight through, not bothering with the navigation of such pitfalls. Rain pattered off his goggle lenses, so fogged over he could barely see. *An apostate makes a walk of faith*, the sardonic thought occurred to him. He could easily step to his death down a deep shaft with such carelessness. A fitting conclusion to his time here, if he were honest. He was sick of God's whims. Sick of this entire godforsaken planet. And right now, he was especially sick of his old man's obsession with that goddamned alien race, vanished for centuries.

Kairos found Falck standing at the edge of a wide cylindrical shaft, holding a coil of thick rope and quickly lowering an end. This shaft had also originally begun as a single, narrow drill hole before his father, believing it showed promise, had expanded the dig over the past several weeks with explosives and additional drilling.

"Hold this," Falck told him with neither a pause nor a glance his way, pushing the remaining coil into Kairos's arms.

With careful footing, Kairos peered over the shaft's edge. Widening waterfalls were draining into it on all sides. For once, his father hadn't exaggerated: the deluge had dislodged or swept away every catwalk and ladder running up the sidewalls. At the bottom of the well, at least twenty-five meters down, Kairos sensed a dark shape, hurried limb movement, and the sound of sloshing water.

"Pull," ordered Falck.

Arm length by arm length, they hauled Wells up. Progress was slow. Kairos's lean frame and weak upper body strength seemed to contribute little to the overall effort. The rope, digging itself into the shaft's mushy edge, was coated with wet silt and was difficult to grip. Twice, Kairos lost his footing and slipped down into the hot mud, eliciting a string of curses no priest, even a former one, should know. To his further annoyance, the elements seemed to have little effect on Falck who, true to form, worked with an immutable stoicism.

While they pulled, his father's calls lifted out of the shaft, difficult to make out in the downpour, but something like an endless, laughably unhelpful chant of "steady up now, steady up, steady up now . . ."

At last, Falck dipped an arm and grasped Kairos's old man.

With Falck's assistance, Wells clawed his way over the shaft's blunt edge, wheezing and coughing up rainwater and spittle. Rising to a kneel, he gave his loyal worker a hearty clap on the back, a wild grin on his face. The old man's head was foolishly bare. The pelting rain had left angry red welts on his balding scalp and across his wrinkled face. His father had not looked Kairos's way, and instead leaned to Falck's ear and spouted something with excitement. Kairos couldn't make out what they were over the sound of the rain. Then his father suddenly bent as another bout of coughing seized him. The man's sickness was becoming more acute. Its onset had been gradual, the steady result of his prolonged exposure to low-level radiation seeping in through the planet's shifting magnetosphere and to trace chemical mutagens, either airborne or in the dirt. With enough time, the planet killed you.

Wells gathered himself and spat. Thick phlegm mottled with dark blood mixed into the pools of muddy water. He withdrew a balled scarf from his coat pocket. Something round was tucked within it. Gingerly unwrapping it, Wells straightened his back. In his hands rested a palm-sized, teardrop-shaped, hard object. Bright white-green flashes of light dazzled across its remarkably smooth black surface.

Heaving and soaked in rainwater and sweat, Kairos looked on with both bitterness and intrigue as his father thrust the teardrop skyward with a triumphant cry.

Chapter 2

Kairos's screens suddenly went blank.

After a moment, they reignited into a cartoon animation of a pale blue sky with a few puffy clouds and a beaming golden sun. The angle tilted down to reveal a landscape of copper-colored canyons interspersed with bright green shrubs and grasses. Emerging on-screen slowly from the right side of the landscape came a procession of cloudtails, dancing on hind legs, noses raised cheerfully, their fluffy white tails waving as if announcing a big 'hello!' to him.

He'd been hacked.

Kairos tore off his goggles and cocked his arm to fling them—then, in remembering their value, lowered his arm and cursed aloud. This was the second time that day that happy cartoon cloudtails had danced right through the network's firewalls. The next time he talked with Midmay about it, he'd have to put the fear of God in her.

Kairos's view was that of the half-rusted, corrugated ceiling of the back room of Dusty's SolarNet Café, his place of employment. He lay sprawled atop the stack of dirty packing foam pads that served as a recliner in the small space, where he took frequent work breaks. He often remained in this position for long lengths of time, staring at the ceiling, wondering what point there was in ever getting up.

I have to get off this cursed rock.

It had been several local days since his father's discovery of the teardrop-shaped object at the excavation site. The initial excitement of the finding had waned with each passing day. The teardrop appeared to be an electronic device of some kind, emitting a nonsensical, repeating string of information. His father was stuck in his belief that it was of Osetran origin, the alien race that had appeared in orbit over Old Earth three standard centuries ago and then, after a mere decade of contact, had just as abruptly left, never to be seen or heard of since. Kairos wasn't so sure. Wells and Falck had been studying it around-the-clock behind closed doors but, as far as Kairos knew, they hadn't discovered anything illuminating. He'd given up arguing with his father over the stupid thing—in his estimation, it most likely had been part of an early colonial reconnaissance probe or had broken off a communications satellite. Even if it was Osetran, the smart thing to do would be to sell it to recoup years of Wells's expenditures. Yet, as expected, Kairos's words had landed on his father's ears with as much communicative impact as the teardrop's indecipherable transmission. Further, their arguments devolved into their usual dead ends: his father making his typical snide remarks about Kairos's "worthless" theological career and current aimlessness, with Kairos in turn sharply reminding him of the toll that the old fool's obsession had directly taken on Mother, and by extension, Kairos and his "worthless" theological career.

His back sore from the 'recliner,' Kairos eventually rose and returned to the café, where the emaciated body of a spacer still slouched over the grungy bar, head drooped. His last customer of a slow day. Kairos tried to convince himself that the man's position had shifted slightly since the previous hour. *Hadn't one arm been more bent before?* The man was a small-load trader and middle-aged if Kairos had to guess, but age was hard to tell with their type. These traders lived on the fringes of the settled worlds and scraped a living by dealing in specialty goods, cheap organics, novelties, and other oddities that shipped in quantities well below the minimums of even the most modest distroship operators.

Lifting a rag from the sink, Kairos began wiping down the counter, eyes occasionally glancing at text scrolling across the low-res, flickering monitor that hung loosely from the ceiling and cycled through a SolarNet news feed: Xi-Qu3st announced her worlds-wide final tour dates ... An increase in stickwheat prices was issued by the System Administrator of Eukiah ... A deep space outpost called La Torre had fallen offline, the fourth such station to go abruptly dark in the past eight standard months, further fueling speculation that the Osetra had returned to human space, this time intending to conquer. The headlines scrolled on.

As a younger man, after arriving on Pantoll, Kairos used to eagerly absorb any news from the core worlds. He'd still clung to the immature notion of someday returning to one of those worlds, thinking he was needed there. Practical wisdom gained in the intervening years had since burned away such folly.

The trader's crumpled body remained motionless, the ordered drink on the counter barely touched, and it occurred to Kairos that he might have to check for a pulse.

Then, as if resurrected in miraculous fashion, the man's

head slowly lifted, revealing a worn face etched with wrinkles.

"A lot of old folks on this rock," the trader commented flatly, as if the two had been in the middle of a casual conversation.

Kairos kept up his pre-closing cleaning ritual and gave the man a sidelong glance. The man seemed okay. Well, not okay in the sense of an average person—small-loaders never were—but more coherent than some he'd seen pass through here. "Most young people leave if they have the chance," he told the trader.

"I would too, regardless of age." The trader took a swig from his plastic cup. "Your chance never came, I take it?"

Kairos paused.

The man lowered his eyes. "Forgive me, Cleric!" he quickly recanted. Kairos winced at the title. "Of course, you must go wherever the gods command you," the trader reasoned to himself, raising his eyes. "It's just that you're not what I'd imagined a Cleric to look like."

Kairos turned away from the man to tend to anything other than cleaning the bar.

"Will you say a prayer for my success on the journey back up to the heavens?" the trader pressed. "Felt my old lady rattling something ferocious on the way down. 'Fraid she's not many flights left in her unless I can scrape together the points to patch her."

Kairos sighed. "There's a chapel at the northeast edge of town," he said. "If you leave now, you could catch the end of the sundown service."

The trader furrowed his brow, offended. "Am I not worthy enough for your prayers? I was told you're a priest. And not just any old loon who calls himself a priest, but a true Cleric of the New Revelationist Order from Greenside."

Kairos's lip twitched. He'd merely been a Low Priest within the clerical ranks, not a Cleric, but such nuanced title distinctions mattered little among those living outside the core worlds. After a moment, he said, "I don't pretend to be a holy man anymore."

The trader scanned Kairos's face, as if unable to accept that Kairos was serious. "Even so, surely you can spare a few good words to bless my way?" the man pleaded. "And let the gods sort out whose prayers they'll listen to?"

"Prayers here don't make it past the storms to reach God's lofty ear," Kairos said. "I strongly suggest you have the spaceport mechanic take a look at your ship."

The trader grumbled something to himself. "If you won't pray for me, pray for yourself." He pointed to the scrolling news feed headlines. "The Osetra are coming. Their first contact ship all those years ago was a pure work of deception, see, so they could size up our technology. They've been planning this for a long time."

"There's been no hard evidence they've returned," Kairos replied.

"That's because no ship that's been sent to investigate has ever been heard of again! These aliens are smart. They're starting with these distant outposts so they can get closer without arousing the attention of the core planets. Place like this, on the fringe of society ... well, I wouldn't be surprised if they come here next. Pray hard to the gods, Cleric."

The trader stood unsteadily and held the cup out with a bony, quivering arm. "Here's to faith in our survival, and the survival of our faith," he toasted, then tipped his head back and drained the remainder of his drink.

Kairos collected the cup and watched the gaunt spaceman

layer his tentpole-like frame with multiple ragged coats. After stepping out of the café on shaky legs, the trader's form gradually disappeared into the swirling dust beyond, like a tired soul departing into the ether. Kairos could not help but pity him. Long distance shippers led lonely lives, perpetually traveling from world to world in an endless cycle of buying and selling that enabled them to keep eating and keep flying but little else. Many didn't fully own their ships, slaving away to pay back a sponsor corporation or guild board that had loaned them half a lifetime's earnings to cover the impossible upfront cost. For them, there was never an end destination, only brief colorful stops with long, uneventful months of formless black space in between.

Kairos could empathize with the feeling of going nowhere.

* * *

A thunderdust storm was brewing. Wispy clouds of fine grit billowed in short gusts against the thin plastic walls of Dusty's SolarNet Café, generating a grating noise like the sound of dry rice spilling.

Kairos finished cleaning. He shrouded the café's meager row of three, pitifully aged computer consoles with a crumpled stretch of plastic wrap to protect them against the dust when it inevitably found its way in. In the back room, he powered off the bulky SolarNet router that was fed from the SolarNet receiver dish on the roof of the café. Lastly, he cut the electric. The café's small overhead lights winked out. In the dimness, the establishment appeared years out of use. Before leaving, he pulled the circular electrovision goggles down over his eyes and wrapped a length of his faded orange scarf around his head and over his nose to complete the face shield.

He stepped out into the cool wind, locked the plastic sliding door behind him, and trudged down Broad Road, leaving Dusty's SolarNet Café literally in the dust. Kairos had stopped lying to himself long ago that running the café was just a temporary gig to finance his SolarNet usage—which, as a fledgling virtual worlds architect, was considerable. In the three local years since leaving his priestly vocation, he'd barely sold any minor structural designs—much less full world templates. Maybe virtual architecture was the temporary gig.

Broad Road formed the main spine of Alton's Landing's trade port, if it could even be called a port. There wasn't much to export off of Pantoll. There never had been. Distribution starships rarely passed by the planet, save for the small-load ship here and there flown by thin, pale traders like the one in Dusty's SolarNet Café. The scant traders arriving on Pantoll mainly came for its native baccus, a long-bladed yellow-green grass used as a psychoactive stimulant when smoked. It was Pantoll's chief contribution to the worlds' commerce.

Rows of shabby plastic and metal façades lined the dirt and gravel street like sunken tombstones, some having fallen into complete disrepair upon inevitably losing the battle against the planet's relentless bouts of dust wind, chemical rain, and flash freeze. The street was already quiet save for the rushing wind and creaks of rusted metal and worn plastic siding. Years of unpredictable and violent storms had trained the townsfolk to scatter at a moment's notice and store owners to close shop with a mechanical speed.

A sullen group of young men smoking thin rolls of baccus in a narrow alleyway eyed Kairos apathetically as he passed, soon lost interest, and lolled their heads back against the building wall for another long drag. They were the typical post-adolescent Pantoll working youth who, either from lack of means or lack of talent or both, missed their window to leave for a better place—one of the Core Four worlds, or an affiliated moon, or even a reputable mining colony—and had just reached the age of realizing they were never leaving this backwater. There was no future for them other than a mutagen-shortened lifespan working at one of the carbon-recycling plants or farming collectives, or as an apprentice in a hardware chop shop learning how to fix malfunctioning bots and decaying electronics. One of them might get off-planet by being taken on by a distroship captain as an indentured hand—a ship crew's lowest of the low. The contract meant bottom-of-the-barrel menial labor, servant treatment, and subsistence living for at least a standard decade, most of which would be spent aboard a cramped, cold metal box weaving through space. Such indentured positions were highly coveted, but openings were rare and one needed either a connection or luck to secure one. The looks on the young men's faces indicated not only they'd had neither, but also that they'd long ceased bothering themselves about the future. They certainly didn't give a damn about the impending weather.

The wind picked up and turned cold. Specks of grit clinked off the green-tinted glass of Kairos's goggles. His visibility was soon cut off as a whirlwind of thicker dust swept over him. A mutated chicken sporting two heads clucked past him, darting in frantic zigzags. A runaway. It had value, but

Kairos didn't bother trying to catch it. He'd lose track of it immediately in the dust cloud, and anyway the thing would be dead from exposure in less than half an hour. Upon his subvocalization of a prompt, the goggles' internal screens glowed to life. Another command and neon green grid lines, way markers, and positioning data were overlaid atop his natural vision.

He stuffed his hands into his coat pockets and hunched his shoulders against the elements, cursing the intrepid, mindless pioneers who first founded a settlement on this wasteland. It would have been better had he been born on this world, if it were all he had ever known, like Midmay. But unfortunately, he had spent the first twenty-three standard years of his life within the peaceful atmosphere and lush landscapes of Greenside, his home and one of the Core Four planets. The next seven or eight local days—or nine? But what did it matter?—would mark his sixth standard year of living on Pantoll. Six years ago, he would've thought it unimaginable that in such a short span, his youth, optimism, and potential would shrivel up like unpicked grapes withering on the vine.

I have to get off this cursed rock.

In truth, he couldn't criticize the founders of Alton's Landing without inflicting some culpability upon his own family; his own grandfather had been among them. In fact, he'd spearheaded the first expedition to Pantoll. The brave, stupid men sought to recover an Osetran craft or probe they believed collided into Pantoll from space some fifty-odd standard years prior. It was a fool's errand. They found nothing, and one of his grandfather's hired hands shot his grandfather dead upon learning that the basis for the expedition lay in little more than questionable radio wave data that may or may not have emanated from Pantoll and may or may not have belonged to the Osetra. Which is why Kairos couldn't believe how his father, who'd followed his grandfather into the xenology profession, could get caught up in the same senseless alien treasure hunt and drag Kairos's mother to Pantoll after resigning from his professorial position at a respected university on Greenside.

Kairos hop-stepped into a disheveled agro-shop just as a worker was beginning to make progress in wrestling a wide, corrugated metal sheet along its rusted track to shield the storefront from the elements. The worker grunted in annoyance and reluctantly paused his effort.

"Whad'ya want, Cleric?" the obese woman behind the low counter asked, recognizing his scarf and goggles with a glance. The folds of her gelatinous mass barely squeezed into her dilapidated, creaking wheelchair. Her loose lips flapped into a jovial grin, her wide mouth exposing a frighteningly sparse number of crooked teeth. Her body perpetually smelled like sweat-drenched undergarments. Mathelga owned and ran the place while her husband, whom Kairos rarely saw, managed one of the larger agricultural cooperatives in the flat expanses north of the town. Both were "natives," directly descended from the firstdown pioneers who had settled the planet. In truth, he found something magnificent in her utter lack of conventional beauty. She was a force to be reckoned with, a veritable pillar of the community. She couldn't have been much older than sixty standard, but years of stubborn resistance against the harsh environment rendered her appearance ancient and timeless.

"Got anything new around here?" Kairos asked with false

earnestness.

"Holy man or not, you're a wise-ass," Mathelga scolded. "I oughta kick your wise-man ass out right now. Can't you see I'm closing?"

"Closing? You're going out of business?" joked Kairos further, but he could sense Mathelga's patience was drying up fast. He grabbed a few items off the shelves. "I'll also need a mixmeat block and two yurbas," he said, placing a tenth-point coin on the counter and trying to avoid looking at the scattered, lengthy wisps of facial hair sprouting from Mathelga's upper lip and chin.

"Hell, might actually go outta business if any more of our damned harvesters quit," the woman spat while she turned to gather his order. He noticed she wore an old medical boot on one of her plump feet. God knew how she could have possibly injured her foot while wheelchair-bound. "Guild rep tells me not to expect any ships carrying large-scale agro machinery for another two seasons. Old Jarmon's been yoking horses to plow his fields after his last tractor shot the bed." She let out a raucous cackle.

"Pray against an Osetran invasion, Cleric!" called her young assistant from the back of the store.

"Quit spoutin' nonsense and finish packin' up, Nebb," she barked at the young man.

"In two seasons, maybe the Osetra will be farming your land and you won't have to worry about it anymore," Kairos offered.

"If the aliens want this planet, they're welcome to it," she stated plainly. "It's more trouble than it's worth." With another cackle, she pushed his goods across the counter. Her hoarse laugh followed him as he stepped back out into the dust storm.

More people than Kairos expected were still out on the street. After a few moments, he noticed that most were headed in the same direction. Kairos had planned to stop by his father's house to check in on the old man, but curiosity overtook him and he joined the flow of dark bodies outlined here and there amid the whirling dust.

The buildings thinned out as they reached the edge of Alton's Landing proper. Here, there were no longer defined streets, just a scattering of old structures standing in the flat, treeless stretch of rust-colored claypan. It was then that Kairos realized where everyone was headed. A pit formed in his stomach. It was the last place on Pantoll he wanted to find himself.

A minute later there was a break in the wind. As swirls of dust settled, the structure materialized before him: a small chapel, its chiva wood construction weathered and cracked.

Kairos hadn't returned to this place since that terrible day, the last day he'd been a priest. His first urge was to turn and run, but his legs had turned rubbery and his eyes betrayed him with their irrational desire to affix themselves upon the scene of his nightmares. Charred sections of the chapel's siding still bore evidence of the fire. *His* fire. But while the weather-hardened chiva wood had withstood the flames, Kairos's faith and heart had not. A pang—of pain, of shame, of guilt—shot through his chest. *The chapel used to have a small bell tower, now destroyed ...*

It had originally been founded as an Obasanjo New Revelationist mission—of the same faith in which Kairos had been a Low Priest—built nearly thirty standard years prior. That fact alone made it an oddity on Pantoll, for the vast majority of the populace was irreligious. Pantollians were hardened, practical souls who believed only in the endless war between the work of their hands and the relentless storms. The fury of Pantoll's storms was their god, to be both revered and cursed. Of exception was the Kunan Zhimin monastery up in the Ja'kong Mountains, founded by a group of Buddhist monks who'd come off a ship several decades ago after renouncing the core worlds. But being self-sufficient, they rarely interacted with the populace. Only every few years or so, in a dire emergency, would a monk or two come down from the mountains to acquire some specific item in Alton's Landing they could not make or grow themselves. Ultimately, the first Obasanjo New Revelationist mission had been unsuccessful, the lone missionary eventually succumbing to atmospherically induced respiratory complications a few years and scant number of converts later.

The chapel had stood vacant for over twenty-three local years—about twenty standard—when Kairos revived the Obasanjo mission and initiated his own services there. His coming to this miserable planet had been unplanned. He'd finished his theological education on Greenside only a few standard years prior. His high seminary marks, including his widely-praised dissertation on supernaturalistic principles, had thrust him up the clerical ranks faster than his peers. The elder High Clerics had shown him favor, and he soon found himself in the service of the Diocese of the Archbishop in the planet's capital city of Asphis. An enviable position, with a bright trajectory. But when he received word that his mother had fallen ill, in health and spirit, he responded only as a good son should. "Honor thy father and thy mother," Scripture stated, "that thy days may be long upon the land which the

Lord thy God giveth thee." So Kairos decided to leave. The High Clerics supported and blessed his departure, but their wise, sad eyes revealed that they knew how long he might be kept away and how irreversible the impact to his theological career might be.

The people he'd walked beside were now funneling into the warm glow beyond the chapel's wooden doors. A local year ago, a missionary of a new spiritual group called the Church of the Samsaric Soul had arrived in Alton's Landing and moved into the chapel. Services were always held, storm or no, just before sundown on Ouransdays, the last of the ten-day local week. Kairos knew little of the group's beliefs, having no longer kept up with the latest spiritual movements and church offshoots. But he had met the missionary, Father Revais, a few times in town and exchanged brief but friendly conversations with the man.

Kairos was turning to leave when he glimpsed through the chapel entrance, to his astonishment, more attendees stuffed into the pews than he'd ever seen before. The heavy doors closed, cutting off Kairos's view and leaving him alone in the cool wind. A dense mass of dark clouds loomed in the distance above the Northern Spines, a range of jagged-peaked, charcoal-colored mountains that rose up from the flat claypan and stood like uneven sawteeth against the horizon. The crisp tingle of static electricity in the air brushed his skin. *What is Revais preaching in there?* Fear and speculation around the Osetra's return must be driving an existential crisis, an opportunistic environment for any preacher.

It's been a long time since the accident, he reasoned to himself. *You don't have to stay for long, just warm up for a minute and say hi to Midmay since you're already here. Midmay's always at service.*

With reluctance, he stepped to the doors.

* * *

The simple chapel featured little adornment inside. The walls and exposed rafters were made from chiva, as were nine rows of pews, giving the small space the wood's distinct earthy, spiced smell. Removed from town, the chapel lacked electricity. Tall candle stands along the pews and candelabras upon the front altar lit the space with a flickering glow. Given the brewing storm, the chapel's shutters were fastened tight against the open-air windows—glass panes were impractically weak against Pantoll's storms, and polyplex was too expensive to waste on such a modest structure.

At least a hundred townspeople were already in attendance, including several elderly folks he recognized as long-time parishioners. They were old to the point that Kairos questioned their ability to last through one more bad storm. They stared into nothingness at a point far beyond the priest and the altar, eyes vacant, mouths hung slightly ajar. But most of the attendees were middle-aged or younger, folks he'd never seen step foot in church before. He also noticed a young man on his knees at the very front, body rocking forward and back in fervor, sweat covering his forehead. But most surprising, Midmay was absent.

Father Revais stood in front of the altar dressed in a simple, full-length black cassock that accentuated his lean, tall frame. He had a short, grizzled beard and dark hair that flowed in waves to his shoulders. Kairos knew little of his personal details, but the priest looked to be in his mid-fifties, standard.

Father Revais was in the middle of delivering his sermon. Dark bracelets on each of the priest's wrists shook whenever he raised his arms in making a passionate point. Kairos had never heard the man preach before, but it didn't take long for Kairos to admit he was good at the job: the rhythmic inflections in his tone, his confidence, his persuasive emotional appeals—there was an attraction that made one want to listen and nod along forever. And Father Revais had indeed attracted a crowd. Not wishing to be caught dead in the pews, and to avoid drawing attention, Kairos side-stepped past other late, standing attendees to the back corner of the room, leaned against the wall, and listened to Father Revais's passion fill the space.

"We are lost. We desire escape," Father Revais said, his eyes solemnly scanning each face in the room. "Escape from our pain. Our burdensome responsibilities. Perhaps this entire reality." The priest's eyes locked onto Kairos's for a brief moment. "Our purpose seems to always lie elsewhere, never where we are. We yearn for a feeling of home. A place where all strivings cease. But I tell you, none of the human worlds are our true home. Some have even spoken, foolishly, of returning to Old Earth. But that was not our true home either. I tell you, home is here"—the priest touched his heart—"and collectively within all of us." He stretched out his arms to the pews. "It will be only when we unite together in one spirit that we will be at peace. That we relate as one, think as one, feel as one. Then we will be worthy enough to return to that Paradise from which we were cast out at the Beginning of Time. Where the Creator sits on the throne of the universe. And together as the All-Soul of humanity, we will meet him, face to face at the End of Time. Prepare yourselves! I tell you that the final chapter of humanity's story is already well upon on us!"

"Are the Osetra returning? Are they bearers of the Creator's judgment upon us?" an attendee called out worriedly.

"Ask not whether the Osetra are coming, my daughter," Father Revais replied, "but whether you've prepared your heart for the End of Time, which will inevitably come upon all creatures below the heavens."

The priest addressed the crowd, "And now, we enter a time of response to what has been revealed to us. This evening, we celebrate the baptism of our dear brother, Heffald." Father Revais offered a hand to the young man who'd been kneeling by his feet, sweating and rocking on the hard floor. "Brother Heffald, would you please join me at the altar and remove your outer garments?"

Father Revais removed the two candelabras from the altar, then slid off its wooden cover until it thumped onto the floor. Besides its cover, the altar, unlike anything else in the chapel, was made of hardened clay. The exposed basin was slightly larger than a bath tub, and indeed, it held the water used for baptisms. Assisted by the priest, Heffald, naked save for short underpants, stepped into the waist-deep basin. Rolling his robe's sleeves, Father Revais instructed Heffald to cross his arms over his chest. The priest supported the man's back with an arm. After making the sign of the triple-cross over him, the priest placed his other hand over the man's crossed arms and muttered a prayer.

Father Revais addressed those in the pews, "I give thanks to the Creator that our brother, Heffald, has made this important decision today, to die to himself so that he may be reborn and live as an instrument of the All-Soul from this time forward. With his baptism, he has publicly declared his commitment to the true faith and the sacrifice of self to the Way of the Universe." The priest then turned and spoke to Heffald. "Because of your professed faith, I baptize you now into the body of the holy Church of the Samsaric Soul, as one who accepts and loves his fate to become of one mind and one spirit with his brothers and sisters, one All-Soul of humanity."

The priest lowered the man into the water, submerging his chest and head.

After half a minute, the water churned. Beneath its surface, Heffald spasmed violently.

But the priest kept him under.

A few moments later, Heffald's legs flailed, sloshing water over the side of the basin. Still the priest, arm muscles bulging, held the man down.

Kairos called out and rushed through the pews toward the altar. Congregants' heads turned at his sudden protest and a murmur rose from the crowd. Those sitting at the end of the pews reached out, seizing Kairos's arms and chest, halting his progress.

"What are you doing?" Kairos exclaimed, struggling against their holds. But they bade him to watch and wait.

The intensity of Heffald's wrestling waned.

After a few more moments, the churning water returned to calm.

The chapel fell as silent as the scene at the altar.

To Kairos's horror, Father Revais raised the dripping, lifeless body out and laid it gently on the wooden floor. Father Revais fell to his knees beside Heffald's body. Lifting his face and hands to heaven, he uttered an inaudible prayer.

After finishing, the priest clasped his hands and brought them down hard against the man's wet chest. A burst of fluid erupted from Heffald's mouth, and his eyes snapped open. Heffald's back arched and twisted as he retched up more fluid.

Father Revais, his own face caught in the spray, held Heffald's head and looked down at him compassionately as the young man's steady breathing returned. "My son, you have passed into eternity. Rise and take the first steps of your resurrected life."

The priest helped Heffald to his feet to the applause and shouts of praise of the congregation. Despite the near-drowning and resuscitation, the man did not look shaken. With a dazed grin, Heffald ambled back to his seat where his clothes were waiting.

Six more attendees were baptized in the same way. Kairos mostly looked away, sickened each time the limp bodies were raised from the basin. After the last, Father Revais wiped his face with a dry cloth and then prayed a benediction over the congregation, ending the service.

Kairos had reached the entrance doors to slip out when an elderly woman's voice stopped him. "Cleric Catadyn," she called. He turned and recognized her as having attended his own past services. "Please, tell us, what are your thoughts on the End of Time?" The white noise of the attendees' small conversations with one another died down as all eyes in the room turned to Kairos.

"Ah ..." he started, his face and palms growing warm. He'd precisely not wanted to speak to anyone, and further, felt awkward opining in front of Father Revais. While the Church of the Samsaric Soul seemed to share some fundamental doctrines with Kairos's prior tradition, the concept of a human

"All-Soul," the near-death experiences that were baptisms, and talk of the End of Time suggested significant divergences. Father Revais's gaze humored him, patiently allowing him to respond. Kairos cleared his throat. "Certain, ah, Scriptures do speak of the Day of the Lord, that is, Judgment Day," he said. "But as to when it will occur, that knowledge is hidden. We are told it will come unexpectedly, like a thief in the night." There were murmurs among the people and he stopped there. Not wanting to seem like he was contradicting Father Revais's message, he quickly added, "Of course, Scripture has also told of certain signs that will occur as the end draws near ..."

"But what about the Osetra?" the woman persisted. "Have the High Clerics of your Order foreseen their return? A period of judgment?"

"I don't know any more about the Osetra than any of you. I doubt the High Clerics do either. I am not a part of that Order or any other order anymore. Really, you shouldn't listen to me ... I'm not ... I must be leaving now," he stammered, stepping back to the door. *Haven't I given up the priesthood?* he thought. *Why must they still view me as superior in any way? If only they knew the sin I have committed in this very chapel ...*

"But certainly the Creator does not desire all of us to perish," a man exclaimed. "He must have a good and holy plan."

Kairos's face grew hot. His heart was pounding and he needed air. *The girl had collapsed onto the wooden floorboards, coughing helplessly with smoke-filled lungs, flames licking around her, as if engulfing her innocence within hell itself ...*

"One thing I've come to learn," Kairos stated aloud, "is that God's will is terrible and unknowable. So unknowable that it might rightly be considered random. Maybe the Osetra will wipe us out, maybe they will not. Why must we spiritualize the matter? I think neither God nor the universe nor this Creator care one way or the other. Are the Osetra not also children of God? And do they not share our pitiful, sinful condition? Are we not all cursed creatures?"

At this, an uproar arose from the crowd. Kairos knew he'd gone too far. He turned to flee through the door, but Father Revais was there and gently pulled him to the side. The priest spent the next couple minutes settling the crowd and bidding them safe journeys home.

As the last few attendees filed out, the priest turned to Kairos, "Come, help me replace the altar cover." Kairos followed Father Revais down the aisles of pews.

"I didn't mean to rile them up like that," Kairos apologized as they reached the steps up to the altar. "I didn't even mean to attend tonight. I'm sorry that my presence was a distraction."

"Everyone is welcome in the house of the Creator," Father Revais assured him. "I am happy you found your way back here."

"If I may be so bold in saying, that was quite the doomsday message you delivered."

"The End of Time must not be mistaken for a doomsday," Father Revais replied, his tone grave. "On the contrary, it will be cause for humanity's grandest celebration: the time our collective souls re-form the one Human Spirit, the All-Soul of humanity."

"Well, the current anxiety around the Osetra returning certainly helps fill the pews," Kairos said with a wry grin.

The chapel became silent as the last attendee shuffled out.

Father Revais looked at him solemnly. "Kairos, you must

forgive yourself for what happened in this church."

Kairos's body stiffened.

"I learned about the fire from one of the older parishioners," explained the priest. "And while the story is that the fire had ignited accidentally, I have a feeling that you view yourself responsible for the fate of that poor girl. I can see the burden you carry, can see it in your body and on your face, the pain that being in this chapel causes you."

Kairos avoided the priest's eyes and shifted his feet.

"It is prideful to believe that we alone control the course of our lives. You cannot blame yourself, Kairos. As tragic as that experience was, it had to happen, as part of the Creator's will. One day you will see the ultimate purpose of it."

"What purpose?" Kairos blurted. "What about that girl's purpose? Had God devoted her to suffer a meaningless death in the flames of my sin? To experience the horror of a man reversing God's miracle? I do not accept that. I do not—" Kairos stopped himself. His body was trembling. He was embarrassed how little it had taken to agitate his composure.

"Guilt overwhelms you," the priest stated. "The knowledge of good and evil in every human heart is both a blessing and a curse. But you need not carry the burden of guilt. Deep inside, your soul knows that only God's forgiveness can set you free." The priest gestured to the still water of the altar's basin. "You can always take the first step."

"I was already baptized once in my former Order, for what good it did me," Kairos replied. "Don't waste your time on me, Father. I'm the worst kind of heathen: I've had faith before. So I know all the spiritual and emotional, ah—no offense— tricks of the trade."

The priest sighed. "The sacrament is always available,

should you have a change of heart. The doors of this house are always open." Together they lifted and set the heavy chiva board back over the clay tub.

"You speak of being set free, but no one is free in this place," Kairos reflected bitterly. "This godforsaken planet ensnares all who step foot upon it."

"Godforsaken!" exclaimed the priest. "The Creator sees all. And the All-Soul of humanity is omnipresent. There is no world upon which it is not at work. Even now, on Pantoll, it is conspiring for the good of all."

Kairos snorted his incredulity, shaking his head.

"Is it escape from here that you seek?" Father Revais asked. "I have told you, yet you refuse to believe, that God's forgiveness can release you from your chains. That giving oneself fully to the divine will grants true freedom. And I don't mean freedom merely in a psychological sense. I mean total freedom of body and mind and soul. A faith powerful enough to transport you anywhere"—the priest snapped his fingers—"instantly."

Kairos snorted in amusement. "I didn't take you for a supernaturalist." Kairos's seminary dissertation had included an exploration of the principles of such astral phenomena.

"Close your eyes. As the Scriptures teach, 'You will know the truth, and the truth will set you free,'" Father Revais quoted earnestly.

"You're actually serious," Kairos remarked, almost offended. "You understand that supernaturalism is not magic, right? It is not craft, art, or formula that one might simply master and go on performing fantastical acts of God at will."

But Father Revais only gave a wry smile. "Humor a superstitious old man."

Kairos eyed the priest skeptically. But to not seem rude, he closed his eyes. *What an embarrassment*, he thought, *a former New Revelationist Low Priest entertaining the delusions of the superstitious.*

"Good. Start by clearing your mind ..." began Father Revais. After several moments passed his voice came again. "Now, focus your attention on the place you desire to go. Imagine every last detail of it. The sight, the smells, the sounds, the touch of it. The more specific, the better. Set the full weight of your being upon it ..." After a minute of silence, "Once you have the place absolutely fixed in your mind, so fixed that you can practically taste it, slow your breathing. Slow it down to a complete stop, so that all you sense is your own heart beating. And then beyond that, nothing ...

"When you are there, you will sense a faint pull on your soul. That is the delicate pull of the Outside reaching in. Give your soul over to that pull. Allow it to be moved from your body in this place and sent *into* the new—"

"This is ridiculous," Kairos exclaimed, opening his eyes.

Father Revais's look of pure disappointment greeted him. "'When you ask, you must believe and not doubt, because the one who doubts is like a wave of the sea, blown and tossed by the wind. That person should not expect to receive anything from the Lord,'" rebuked the priest, quoting Scripture. "The reason your body is bound is that you doubt with your mind."

"No, the reason is that teleporting at will is impossible and this is nonsense."

"'What is impossible with man is possible with God.'" Father Revais quoted.

"Yes, but the first principle of supernaturalism is that it's an alignment with and response to God's will, not to one's own."

"It is also written, in the Old Gospel: 'When he was at the table with them, their eyes were opened and they recognized him, and he disappeared from their sight.'"

More Scripture, Kairos thought. *Would the priest never give it a rest?* "Why don't *you* show me then?" Kairos mocked.

"I cannot do it."

The man's response elicited a burst of laughter from Kairos.

The Father sighed with a fatherly frustration. "See, I desire to be nowhere else. Deep down, my will is to be here, just as it is the divine will of the Creator. In false will and self-deception lies no power."

"Well, that's convenient," Kairos said, shaking his head. "For the life of me, I can't understand how you can *enjoy* being here."

"Because here is where I am meant to serve." Seeing Kairos's dissatisfaction, he said, "Let me show you something." Father Revais lifted one of the candelabras from the floor and placed it upon the altar. Its candles were still burning. "In the same way, I will conspire with the universe in knocking this candelabra over."

"Conspire?"

But the priest closed his eyes, pressed his palms together in prayer, and bowed his head.

Kairos stood eying him in silence for several minutes. The priest remained still, eyes closed, head bent in deep prayer over his upright palms and braceleted wrists.

Outside, harbinger winds and the rumbling thunder of the advancing storm had grown in strength. Great gusts caused the wooden boards of the church to creak and moan. The inside of the chapel seemed to have darkened. Flickering candle flames from around the chapel sent a dance of shadows and light across the walls and ceiling.

The wooden entrance doors to the church burst open. A gust of wind rushed through the chapel and whipped up to the rafters. The pews rattled and the walls shook. Kairos had just started to run to shut the doors when a crash resounded behind him. He turned back. The candelabra before the priest had toppled to the floor. Its candles lay strewn, their flames extinguished, a couple snapped apart.

The priest lowered his praying hands and opened his eyes.

"Maybe my father's right in thinking that religion is a load of hogwash practiced by egoistic charlatans," Kairos said. "You knew the storm was rolling in. And that the last person out failed to secure the doors behind them."

Father Revais looked at him solemnly, his robe ruffling in the wind. "'If you remain in me and my words remain in you, ask whatever you wish, and it will be done for you,'" he quoted Scripture again. "The power of faith relies on neither sleight of hand nor supernatural ability, but on a supernatural trust, a deep belief that the universe will, whether over seconds or over millennia, conspire to bring about the holy will of the faithful. Something that seminary of yours must have never taught you."

The priest's expression relaxed. "It is late and it is unwise to be caught out in such a storm as is at our threshold. I'm sure your sick father also needs your attendance." Father Revais stepped to a tall cabinet standing against the wall by the altar. "Has he learned anything about that alien artifact he pulled from the rock, the one of his long search?"

How does he know about the find? Kairos wondered. As far as he knew, his father desired to keep his treasure a secret for now. Had Falck told anyone? Or perhaps this priest was overhearing too much from his congregation.

"Oh, you must have misheard," Kairos replied. "He found nothing alien, and what he did find hardly seems special. Certainly nothing you could leverage in your sermons about the impending End of Time," he added with a smirk.

Father Revais nodded. "Well, I'm afraid I must leave you. I want to bring Midmay some food, and it is a long walk." He withdrew a paper-wrapped package from the cabinet. "She was supposed to be baptized this evening." The priest sighed, "But something must have kept her. I pray she is safe and well."

"Midmay asked to be baptized?" Kairos asked. He thought that she'd only attended services for the free food and pity that the priest and parishioners lavished upon her. He hadn't considered that she might actually become a believer.

"Is that so hard to believe? She has been a faithful member of this community."

Kairos reached for the package. "Here, let me deliver that for you," he offered. "I planned to visit her this evening anyway because of the storm," he lied. Although it was true that he had planned to address her latest hacking activities at some point soon. The priest didn't need to know about that.

Father Revais hesitated for a brief moment, then acquiesced and thanked him. "Please tell Midmay she was missed tonight," he said, handing Kairos the package. An aroma of fresh bread and cheese wafted from inside. The priest placed a hand on Kairos's shoulder. "Go now, and may the Creator watch over you, my son."

Chapter 3

Outside the chapel, a strong grit-filled wind oppressed the scarf over Kairos's face and sought to penetrate any gaps to his flesh. It was dusk, with a remaining sliver of burnt orange sky rapidly becoming sealed by the thick gray clouds rolling in. He raised the old wool coat's collar. After subvocalizing his goggles to overlay cardinal directions on top of their night vision, he set off at a brisk walk north toward the crash site, where Midmay lived.

Before long, the rain began. There was little transition between dry air and downpour. Heavy sheets of cold rain swept sideways, abruptly shifting directions from one moment to the next. Within a few minutes his coat was soaked through. While the strong fibers of his chiva pants were nearly indestructible, they chafed uncomfortably when wet. But like all true locals, Kairos had grown a stiff backbone regarding the elements and pressed on undeterred. The rain at least subdued the dust.

Before long he encountered the dark silhouettes of the colossal geodesic greenhouse domes that housed stretches of cultivated land within. Sweating old laborers and decrepit, patched-up agrobots toiled within the structures during the day to eke out subpar yields of stunted, weather-hardy crops, mostly genetically modified variants of rye, winterwheat, leek, split sage, Castow spinach, yurba melon, half pea, and firefruit.

Beyond the domes lay a flat expanse of rugged grassland, broken only by the dark lumps of fortified stock shelters into which ranch hands herded scores of livestock when the weather turned lethal. The animals had been introduced to the planet shortly after the initial settlers arrived and remained to this day woefully ill adapted to the local climate. The planet's wildly shifting weather patterns and scarce variety of natural vegetation made ecosystems simple and fragile, and there existed no well-adapted animals larger than the swift-legged Bourland hare.

While Kairos walked, his thoughts drifted to his home planet, Greenside. It was everything Pantoll was not: a lush world of rolling emerald hills, tall forests, and broad winding rivers, all lying beneath a serene, pink-and-cream atmosphere. It was one of the first worlds to be colonized following the Exodus—chosen easily for its beauty and similar habitability to Old Earth—and thus enjoyed the highest level of development. His mother's family had lived there for generations. Her doctorate in biology, however, had taken her to many planets and moons as a young field researcher. She'd met Kairos's father on one of those trips. But when she became pregnant with Kairos, his parents settled on Greenside, moving into a large apartment that her parents owned in the wealthy Terrace City. His father had a distaste for urban living, and Kairos came to understand much later that his father had an equally strong distaste for his in-laws, whom he considered elitist.

After half an hour, a field of towering wind turbines came into view, great imposing structures—erected during the planet's early colonization—that supplied electric power to Alton's Landing and other settlements in the vicinity. A branch of lightning flashed across the charcoal sky. The following boom of thunder caused Kairos to stagger. The turbines stood solemnly in defiance of the storm, their dutiful blades spinning powerfully in an attempt to harness nature's fury.

The remains of the *Illyia* lay not far beyond the final row of turbines, at the base of a shallow crater that the starship had created upon smashing into the planet's surface some eighty standard years prior. The theory was that the ship's navigational computer and guidance systems were fried by a powerful electrical storm during entry, and that the crew either botched a manual landing or responded too late. The ship had been carrying what would have been Pantoll's first colonists. There'd been no survivors of the crash, and his grandfather's expedition, arriving some twenty years later, thought it proper to name the settlement they established in honor of the ill-fated *Illyia*'s captain, Harry Alton.

While much of the starship and its debris had since been buried by the elements, a couple sections of it remained above ground in cracked, weathered pieces. A small, vertical axis wind turbine affixed to the largest piece spun swiftly. Kairos had set it up for Midmay a while ago to supply power to what had then been just her secret hang-out spot.

He stumbled down the slope of the depression and entered the ship through a gaping crack in its hull. This section, the ship's spacious cargo hold, had been emptied out since the crash as subsequent settlers salvaged the ship's resources, save for a few rusted skeletons of irreparably damaged machinery. Filling the space now were scattered heaps of scrap metal, plastic, circuit boards, screen rolls, wiring, and other junk that Midmay had scavenged from other places and organized in piles over the years.

Kairos announced himself and called for her, but to no answer. Typical.

After a brief search spotted her lying on her back in between two scrap heaps in her usual fashion: eyevisor on, arms stretched above her face, her small, datagloved hands gesturing various computer commands in the air.

"You weren't at the service this evening," Kairos said, looking down at the girl as her thin arms waved about. "The Father asked about you."

Midmay didn't respond, her hands gesticulating uninterrupted.

"The port's local network was hacked into again today," he continued. "Care to talk about that?" Either the volume of her earbuds was turned way up or she was intentionally ignoring him. "Dancing cloudtails?" he inquired, louder. "You're getting to be too old for these little games of yours."

The girl didn't stir. Definitely ignoring him.

"We talked about this. That network, as limited as it may be, is critical. You have to quit messing around with it like it's your personal playground."

His patience wearing out, he stooped, plucked out her earbuds with a finger, and lifted her eyevisor back above her messy short hair.

The girl was crying, and her watery, puffy red eyes indicated that she had been for some time. Her arms fell from the air and plopped at her sides, as if suddenly lifeless.

"Johnathan's dead," she blurted out with a great sob.

Shit, he thought. Johnathan. Her best and only friend.

Her biological parents were long gone, and she and Johnathan had been inseparable since she came to live in *Illyia*'s ruins a few local years ago, after her last caretaker, an elderly church-going woman, had passed away. Kairos had been aware that, at that time, Midmay had forged and submitted phony documentation to the sheriff's office, enough to skip over their wide administrative cracks and avoid being assigned a new legal guardian. Despite such knowledge, he didn't report the girl or even tell her that he knew what she'd done. God knew she could outsmart most of the adults on the planet and she wouldn't abide any dictated guardianship. But if he were honest, much of his silence on the matter was that he felt a certain responsibility toward her. Admittedly, he saw in her too much of the young girl he'd killed in the chapel fire. And so he'd decided not to alert the authorities and instead keep an eye on Midmay himself.

At twelve standard years old, she was among the youngest persons on the planet. Considering Pantoll's elevated mutagen levels, young couples had big hesitations in starting families, and many postponed childbearing with the hope of saving enough to get off-planet first. The odds of healthy childbirth without some physical or genetic defect were a scary dice roll on Pantoll. Midmay had been lucky in that one respect, having been born on the planet.

"I'm sorry, Midmay," he said, awkwardly patting her shoulder. He'd been better at expressing authentic empathy and solace as a priest, back when he still believed that all suffering was ultimately transformed into good by God; now, his attempts felt pointless, even a bit disingenuous. Life was arbitrary and often miserable—why try to pretend otherwise?

The girl threw her arms around his neck and buried her face into his chest.

"When did it happen?" he asked the top of her head.

"At night," she cried. "His fall woke me up."

"Take me to it."

She led him into her room, which used to be the ship's sick bay. Beside her small bed, a large, inanimate android lay in disarray, its gangly limbs sprawled across the floor. One of its metallic arms had snapped. Shards of broken plastic and bits of glass littered the room.

Jesus, Kairos thought. *The thing must've keeled over and given the girl a hell of a scare.*

"Were you able to find out what happened?" he asked.

"His cybernetic core broke."

Ouch. That sweet little piece of advanced, antique tech couldn't be replaced. Surely not here, not even on the core worlds.

"Johnathan was old ..." he offered. He didn't know what to say to her. The android's eventual breakdown was inevitable; he'd just hoped it would happen when Midmay was grown up.

The robot, indeed, was well over two hundred years old, constructed during the peak of sentient humanoid engineering. At the start of the Exodus, Johnathan—although it wasn't called that then, of course—had been aboard one of the twelve Great Ships. Its model was designed not only to be a practical educational resource for the young colonists as they established new worlds, but also to store and protect millennia's worth of knowledge, philosophy, and culture for future generations who otherwise could only learn whatever the most knowledgeable and skilled Great Ship passengers—

their shared ancestors—were able to pass on. At least that had been the intended grand plan.

In his prime, Johnathan probably looked magnificent: soft pseudo-skin, smooth body contours, a human face to support emotional attachment. A certain sadness overtook Kairos in looking at the deceased android now, with its grimy exposed metals and wiring, multi-colored patchwork of replacement parts, and battered hard plastic exoskeleton that had been added long after the android's original outer skin and other ornamental features had been completely worn off. Although he wasn't sure how Johnathan had ended up on Pantoll, he thought it might have been brought there by his grandfather's expedition—at least, Kairos had learned of his grandfather's specific fate after a conversation with it. Whatever its history, the android had been neglected since by the agrarian population. Its relatively frail skeletal design and construction rendered it useless to be reprogrammed for manual labor, and no one here had the time for or interest in a two-meter tall walking library.

"I'll come back tomorrow to dismantle it and take it away, unless you want to, ah, keep some of its parts," he asked gently. Some parts would fetch a considerable price among the trading community. Fragments of tech from the bygone era always did.

"Nooo," she bawled. "We have to bury him."

"Alright," he said. *Poor girl.* He was already planning how he might discreetly remove a few choice components beforehand. It'd be a monstrous waste not to.

She looked at him expectantly, eyes wide and glistening. "What, you mean now?"

The girl nodded. "Father Revais says we must bury dead

bodies in anticipation of the future resurrection," she explained. "Johnathan's been dead for a whole day already."

Another boom of thunder sounded.

Kairos sighed and shook his head. *Oh, what the hell.*

* * *

It took Kairos ages to dig a ditch sizable enough for Johnathan's tall frame to fit in. He shoveled beside the ship, beneath an overhang of warped hull which offered minimal protection from the ongoing storm. The work was overwhelmingly muddy and intractable. Horizontal branches of sheet lightning propagated overhead like neon tentacles, causing the dense clouds to pulse with a deep purple glow, as if something even more horrible was being incubated within them. At moments he laughed to himself about the foolish absurdity of what he was doing, and in such conditions.

Midmay sat just inside the ruins, keeping dry and watching his progress. She wore a patched-up dark green jacket that was a couple sizes too large for her small frame over chiva leggings that someone, probably an elderly woman from the church, had made for her skinny legs. She silently chewed on one of Father Revais's rye biscuits after already devouring the cheese and one of the yurba melons Kairos had bought. He knew she received food from the church community due to her age and poverty, and that she also habitually sneaked into the greenhouse domes to forage, but he still worried she wasn't eating enough.

"Say a prayer for him first," Midmay requested after he'd

dragged the robot's dreadfully heavy body from her bedroom into the grave.

"Android's don't have ..." he began, but sighed upon seeing the girl's tearful eyes. *Souls*, he finished in his mind. *Then again, maybe humans don't have them either.* "Why don't you pray?" he suggested. "It'll be more meaningful coming from you as its—*his*—friend."

The girl closed her eyes and bowed her head.

While her lips moved in a hushed, hurried flow of sentimental words, Kairos hunkered down to the damp earth and, with a few deft movements of his tools, unscrewed or pried off a couple of the robot's most valuable internal components. He stashed them in his coat pockets.

"Amen," the girl finished, a moment after Kairos had stood.

"By the way, Father Revais mentioned something today," Kairos said to her as he began to slop muddy dirt atop the deceased.

"He healed a dog's broken leg last Ouransday," Midmay informed him, her eyes brightening. "He can do miracles."

"Um ... well," Kairos responded, wiping rain out of his eyes with a wet sleeve. "Anyway, when did you decide to be baptized?"

Midmay shrugged.

"I know the priest is a kind man, but I've seen a few of these baptisms. They don't sit well with me. You should wait a few more years before deciding to—"

A flash of light in his peripheral followed by a distant, deep rumble caused Kairos to pause. It could've easily been thunder, but its signature seemed closer to an explosion. He looked up from shoveling and toward the direction from which the wind had carried the sound.

"What was that?" Midmay asked, eyes wide.

There it was again, far off: a silent flash of a thin blue-yellow beam cutting up into the clouds, like a tightly focused searchlight.

"That looked like the beam of a plasma torch," he exclaimed, dumbfounded. Certainly no one on the planet owned one of the antique weapons, let alone a still-functioning one. The beam strobed twice more, each slicing the clouds at a different angle, then ceased for good. It looked to have originated from town.

"Get your lightcycle," Kairos told Midmay.

They raced through the field of wind turbines toward the town on the skeletal-framed bike—Midmay's prized possession that she'd found in some scrap pile and repaired. Unable to be persuaded to stay behind, Midmay clung to Kairos's back while he throttled the lightcycle to its limit. Not far beyond the turbines, Kairos clenched the brake levers. Midmay let out a muffled yelp through the burgundy scarf wrapped around the lower half of her face. Her small fingers dug into his sides.

Beyond them, three black tornadoes danced across the open expanse. Kairos might not have noticed them if not for the incessant strobe of lightning overhead that gave him terrifying glimpses of their whirling dark forms.

He was about to turn the lightcycle around when something additional in the sky caught his eye: a black silhouette of unclear shape, moving quickly. Subvocalizing goggle commands—to optimize his night vision, zoom on the object, and record video—he tracked the shadow as it dipped between two of the twisters, then angled upward again.

Seemingly out of nowhere, a massive fourth vortex appeared, swirling in rapid formation. The silhouette angled again, but there was no avoiding the multiple funnels. Caught among them, the shape faltered, then was thrown violently.

Kairos watched in frozen awe, mouth open.

The hurled object spun in a wild descent, unable to stabilize itself before plowing into the ground with a booming thud. It tore a long gash in the wet earth before finally coming to a rest not far from them.

Midmay's tugs on his neck shook him from his stupor. She was yelling something about turning around, most of her words lost to the surrounding gale. Roused to an awareness of their own precarious position, he whipped the lightcycle around and retreated. He had Midmay keep an eye out behind them.

Before they'd gone far, she yelled again into his ear. He glanced behind them. The twisters had broken apart as quickly as they had formed. A clear window was now open.

He spun them around again. Recklessly, he steered toward the crashed object. The rare presence of a spacecraft couldn't be ignored.

The dark shape lay still and silent as if it were some fallen beast, though Kairos sensed it might yet stir at any moment. During its plummet, he had made out what it was, and he couldn't leave without taking a closer look. Stopping at a short distance, he dismounted and instructed Midmay to remain with the lightcycle and keep the narrow headlight angled toward him while he covered the rest of the way on foot.

He approached the craft at a slight angle to its front. Its nose was buried deep in muck; on either side rose mounds of displaced earth. The outline of a short wing gradually revealed itself out of the darkness. The wing connected to a flat, sleek fuselage that swooped into two dorsal fins. Kairos recognized the basic design as that of a hybrid air/space craft. However, its pitch black paint scheme and a few curious augmentations to its external hull suggested it had been customized considerably. Miraculously, it didn't seem to have sustained serious hull damage. The craft had been flying without exterior lights, which was strange. Odder yet was its small size—it was a personal ship, perhaps a mere double-seater. Only larger distroships had ever made their way to Pantoll.

When he was halfway to it, a faint click sounded, followed by the hiss of escaping air. Someone was emerging from the circular airlock hatch on the underbelly of the craft.

Kairos dropped to a crouch and remained still.

The figure reached the end of the hatch ladder and stumbled away from the ship, helmeted head hung. They were clad in a heavily armored spacesuit. After several shaky steps, the figure paused, lifted its helmet unsteadily, then collapsed onto the muddy ground.

Kairos arose and ran to the suited figure.

The body, a male judging by the size, remained motionless. Kairos soon discovered why: at least a quarter of the spacer's abdomen was missing—armor, insulation, clothing, skin, bone, and all—leaving behind a gruesome hollow pit encircled with freshly cooked flesh and charred metal and fabric. The burn wound was shockingly bloodless. Its seared edges suggested it had been instantly cauterized. It was, undoubtedly, the work of a plasma torch. Such a weapon's presence on Pantoll seemed impossible.

With some effort, Kairos rolled the spacer onto his back. His helmet visor was cracked and fogged, partially obscuring the man's face so that all Kairos could make out were a large bony nose, dark stubble, and a cheekbone scar. The suit's shoulder plates were stamped with various symbols and insignias, several faded beyond recognition. One fresher-looking symbol stood out: nine eyeballs arranged in a ring. The battered chest plates were rippled with shallow dents and covered with a multitude of scrapes, like the texture of an old cutting board. Black burn marks of varying lengths were seared across it.

A round object rolled away from one of spacer's lifeless gloves, coming to a halt in a muddy depression.

It was the teardrop-shaped artifact Kairos's father had found.

* * *

The whole town seemed to have been awakened by the activity. Despite the late hour, the poorly lit streets buzzed with activity as if it were high noon. The rain had slowed to a drizzle.

A crowd, holding oil lamps and murmuring speculation to one another, had gathered outside Wells's house. Kairos left Midmay with her lightcycle and pushed through to the center of the crowd where an illuminated ring of curious townsfolk had formed around his father, who was lying on the ground, eyes closed. The town doctor was bent over him. A local deputy stood by and kept the onlookers at bay.

"That's my father!" Kairos exclaimed, stepping past the deputy and kneeling to clutch one of Wells's limp hands.

"I'm sorry, Cleric," the elderly physician said, his eyes weary with fatigue. "There's no easy way to put this. Your pa's no longer with us."

Kairos's trembling fingers searched his father's neck for a pulse, then placed his an ear against his father's chest. He felt nothing. Kairos lifted his father's head and held his face. "Dad," he called, giving his father a gentle shake. "Dad, please, I'm here ..."

"... sustained from a projectile weapon," the physician was saying. "He'd already lost a lot of blood by the time—"

"We have ... to get him to the hospital," Kairos stammered to the physician.

The physician shook his head. "I'm afraid there's nothing to be done. I'm sorry, Cleric, but he's gone."

"Sheriff's put the town on alert," came the deputy's voice from somewhere above Kairos. "He's got a few men scouting the area, but we'll need more. He's calling in reinforcements from Lessac ..."

Kairos turned away, unable to look any longer. *What did you get yourself into, Dad?*

"I understand it may not be the best time, Cleric Catadyn," the deputy addressed him, "but I need to ask you a few questions while all this is fresh. We understand there was some kind of firefight, involving Old Earth technology no less ..."

Kairos scrambled to recall his last conversation with his father. The teardrop in his coat pocket felt like a hot lump of coal that might burn right through the seams and reveal itself with an incriminating thud. Then he remembered something Wells had mentioned about the device, triggering a tingly surge of adrenaline: it had been emitting a repeating signal. *Had someone been listening? But how? And what was it about the device that had attracted a professional assassin?*

Near his father's outstretched arm lay a plasma torch. Kairos had never seen it before in his life. In fact, had never even seen a real torch before. The Old Earthan weapon was a technological relic of a bygone era, something only the System Administrators would have retained, and in small numbers if any. A small, wire-staffed white flag had been placed next to it by the authorities. He snatched up the torch as he stood, then shoved his way back through the crowd.

"Hey! That's evidence!" the deputy shouted behind him.

Kairos ignored the rising commotion in his wake and strode into the house, throwing the front door's deadbolt behind him. He didn't have much time. He had to get back to the assassin's downed ship before the authorities located it.

He strode into Wells's bedroom first. The sight of the bed disgusted him. His last memories of this room were of caring for his dying mother, and after, helping his father sort out her belongings. Now, as before, a pang of indecency arose when he threw open the drawers and rummaged through his parent's personal things, as if he were violating a sacred privacy. He half expected his father to barge into the room at any moment and rebuke him for the intrusion. In one of the drawers, he found an old digigraph of his parents. A few of the pixels had winked out, but the moving holo showed them outside on some lovely planet or moon, long, yellow-green, dune grass undulating at their feet in a steady breeze. His father was sitting on a large wooden supply crate of some sort, smiling, one boot propped up, his mother behind him with her arms around his neck, their heads close. A dark green ocean glistened in the background. They wore the blissful expressions of confident youth. He'd nearly forgotten this version of his mother, when she'd had such health and vigor.

When he'd first arrived on Pantoll to attend to her, he found her quiet, inward, and frail in body and mind. Her spirit itself was tired. It was clear that not only had Wells ceased taking care of her—wholly distracted by the same obsession over the Osetra that had brought them to the godforsaken planet—but also that she'd ceased taking care of herself. It didn't help that she'd taken to smoking baccus weed in her depression—only once in a while at first to ease her burdens, but it had soon developed into a daily addiction. He slipped the digigraph into a coat pocket.

There was pounding on the house's front door and hollering from outside, but Kairos ignored it. Let them be agitated.

He surveyed the room's closet. He was surprised to find his father's old space combat carapace hanging on the rack, accumulating dust for decades since the man's mercenary days. It might be valuable enough to sell, but was too heavy to carry and Kairos needed to move fast. However he did strip out the carapace's internal lightsuit as a concession. Other than a leather satchel, in which he stuffed the plasma torch and rolled-up lightsuit, there wasn't much else in the closet worth taking: a few mementos from Eukiah, where his father had fought during the Stickwheat Crisis; trinkets of unknowable sentimental value; stacks of flattened clothes that smelled of musty wool and stale polyester, the lines of their folds pressed into permanency. One shelf was dedicated to a repulsive line of formaldehyde-filled specimen jars holding various preserved worms, arthropods, and small scaly critters that his biologist mother had cataloged and studied during her early years on Pantoll. The jars were horrid and reminded him of her own death. He'd cleaned out most of the entire collection then, but his father had insisted on keeping a few. In the corner on the highest shelf was an army-green, wooden box. Curious, he pulled it down. Stenciled in large white military font along the box's sides was: MAYDAYS. Inside were a pair of green high-top shoes. The uppers were constructed from some kind of finely threaded metal-polymer combination, and the thick soles had an elastic feel. As he removed them, a paper insert fell out that read: *'Run faster, leap higher, land safer. Kick 'em, drag 'em, slide 'em, punish 'em—MAYDAYS tread hardest when life treads on you.'* Questionable marketing claims, but they looked surprisingly fresh and fit his wide feet, so he kept them on and left his dirty, worn boots behind.

Next, he proceeded to the kitchen, where he ransacked the cabinets and pantry like a shameless looter, stuffing anything edible that didn't require cooking into his satchel for the trip ahead.

Finished, he moved through the kitchen to the house's back door.

Falck's hulking body standing in the door frame of the back utility room took him aback.

The man's black cloak was soaked and filthy, the hem coated in mud. He was slightly bent, chest heaving, drawing heavy breaths through his respirator mask. His father's worker had never seemed in great physical shape; add to that his hitched step and stated lung condition, and running was an arduous undertaking.

"You!" Kairos lunged at the man. Falck had been the only other person who'd known about his father's find. But Falck spun aside and Kairos couldn't get a hold on his thick cloak. "My father is dead," Kairos spat. "Who did you tell about that device?"

"No one," Falck swore. But with his face largely obscured

by the respirator and eyescopes, Kairos had always found it impossible to read the man's emotions.

"Even the priest knew about it, you fool," hissed Kairos.

"Who?"

"Where were you when he died?" Kairos pressed. "Where have you been?"

"Listen," panted Falck. "Right now, the only thing that matters is protecting the device."

"What is it?" What does it do?" Kairos demanded. Falck and Wells must have learned something about it during their study.

Hurried steps stopped outside the back door. "He went in here!" hollered the voice of the deputy. The next moment there were heavy pounds on the door and calls for it to be unlocked.

Falck glanced at the door, then back to Kairos. "I'll tell you everything later," he replied. "But first, do you still have it? Is it safe?"

Kairos took a step back. "How the hell could you know that I have it?" he asked. He took new notice of just how muddy Falck's cloak was. *Was Falck in the assassin's ship when it went down? Had Falck helped kill his father? And had he been running from the authorities just now?* Kairos spun and raced to the front door.

"The device's signal can be tracked!" Falck called, following behind. "Others will seek it. You will not be safe. Give it to me!"

Kairos was nearly at the door when it burst open, sending wood splinters flying into the room.

The deputy with two other men stormed in. The deputy, confused upon seeing Falck, ordered his two men to detain him.

"With all respect, Cleric," the deputy stated deferentially, "we're going to need you and this man to come with—"

Kairos lowered a shoulder and plowed past the deputy, coming out before a glowing sea of onlookers' lamps. The deputy hollered for someone to stop him.

"Kairos!" came Midmay's high-pitched voice through the commotion. The girl's lightcycle skidded to a stop a few paces away from him.

He hopped on, and they took off toward the lightless horizon.

* * *

Under normal circumstances, Kairos would have been over-joyed to find himself on a spacecraft, a gift of freedom. Arriving at the assassin's downed ship and climbing inside, his pulse had indeed quickened upon laying his eyes on the cockpit's command console looming in the dark interior.

But any excitement had been stamped out by the grim events that had led him here. He burned with anger over Falck's betrayal. He'd never known the man's history but assumed now that he'd been a core world criminal who'd fled to Pantoll, desperate like Wells and unafraid to capitalize on the rare opportunity to strike it big. It didn't help that his father owed the man years of backpay. The same unsettling thought kept coming to the fore: *what had his father and Falck discovered about the device that made it worth killing for?* But he'd pushed the thought away. It was time to move on from his father's obsession. To move on from this dreadful planet.

On top of that, saying goodbye to Midmay had been more difficult than he'd imagined. The girl had fallen deathly silent while he fumbled through wishing her the best. By the end, he'd even found himself lying to her about returning to visit. Her two dull eyes watched him leave as if her soul had already departed. He didn't have the heart to look back at her.

He'd set about the preparations for launch with sober determination. A short line of text across one of the console's screens had informed him that the system had automatically shut down due to inactivity. The start-up protocol was biometrically locked. So there had been the strenuous, gruesome task of awkwardly lugging the dead spacer into the ship and up to the console for palm and facial scanning.

After gaining access and rebooting the shipboard computer, he had tried to input his own biometric profile but found that alterations were passkey protected. As a result, he'd been forced to make the morbid decision to store the body in the rear cargo hold for the next time its parts would be required. While he'd never operated a spacecraft before—he'd only ever ridden as a distroship passenger on his travel to Pantoll—he'd flown hundreds of them virtually in SolarNet VR portals, so was familiar with the craft's systems and flight protocols. And of course, the shipboard computer would do all of the actual piloting.

Outside the cockpit window, he noticed now several points of light twinkling on the horizon that hadn't been there minutes ago. They originated from the town's direction. He held up a finger to block out one of the lights and waited. After a minute, it had remained hidden behind his finger, and further, all the lights' intensities had grown. An unchanged bearing: they were moving directly toward the ship. It must be the sheriff's search team. Kairos had been hoping that the glacial speed at which things typically proceeded on Pantoll would be on his side, but apparently the violent intrusion of an off-world assassin had kicked the authorities into high gear. He put them at no more than seven or eight minutes away.

The shipcom's diagnostics completed. Kairos scanned the results: Moderate damage to the craft's landing gear and an underbelly storage hatch, but otherwise, its hull integrity had withstood the ground impact. Good.

All that was left to do was input a destination. With trembling fingers, Kairos illuminated the console's star map and inputted the Quoric System. A yellow star with four orbiting planets filled the screen. There it was, an emerald sphere second from the star: Greenside. Eleven standard days of travel. Longer than he'd thought. He hadn't accounted for this small craft's lower-energy weave drive. He'd have to get through several days without food, but being a priest he was well-practiced in fasting, and for periods of time far longer than that. It was a small price for returning home.

This was it. This was real. His last moments on Pantoll.

The thought of his father lying slain outside the house caused a lump to rise in his throat. He saw his mother's drawn face forever limp against her pillow, clothes reeking of baccus. He felt the heat of the burning chapel beams and heard the little girl's choked screams as smoke filled her lungs. Kairos's eyes welled and a strangled breath escaped his lungs. He'd forgotten that he'd loved his father once.

Sobs burst from his mouth. He cried for his father. He cried for himself. But it was a furious sadness, a shaking of his fist at the heavens. This place had brought him only anguish; he'd lost time, lost lives, lost faith. The planet itself was a cancer, like the debilitating one that it'd put into his father's body.

He jumped when a small hand touched his arm.

Through damp eyes, he saw Midmay take a step back.

"What are you doing here?" Kairos snapped. The girl must have slipped aboard while he was occupied with the assassin's body.

"I'm going with you," Midmay replied. The girl's eyes showed fright, anxiety, and a plea. But they also held that unteachable survivor's determination, the same that had kept her alive for years.

"I told you already ..." he started, but even as he did so, his guilt overwhelmed him. If she asked—and he was terrified she might—he did not have an answer as to what she was supposed to do without Johnathan or himself around. She'd forge a way, of that he had no doubt. But who would she become, living alone in that pile of wreckage as cold and twisted as the hand life had dealt her? What kind of future awaited her? He couldn't honestly convince himself that it'd be a good one. To do so would be delusional, a selfish indulgence to avoid the mature acceptance of one's culpability. He'd become the latest entry on the list of adults in her life who'd failed her. But hadn't he borne enough guilt already? He shut his eyes, saw anew the chapel ablaze with orange tongues of fire, watched its bell tower collapse onto the back row of pews in a spray of sparks and burning splinters, the girl's shrieks that could never be expunged from his mind ...

He sighed. "You don't even know where I'm going."

"You're going to find out why your dad was killed, right?" she replied. Then, in a low voice, just above a whisper, "It's about the Osetra, isn't it?"

While the truth was that he hadn't intended to discover why his father had been killed, hearing the name of the alien race shook him. Perhaps unknowingly, Midmay had called out what had been unsettling him the most but which he'd refused to acknowledge: that the device was truly of alien origin, that it could be the most valuable item in all the worlds. Falck had threatened that others would seek it. The teardrop grew heavy in his pocket and suddenly seemed radioactive, a bomb he needed to distance himself from as fast as possible before it went off. He couldn't stop thinking about the timing of it all: the increasing reports of space outposts and distant mining colonies going offline had coincided with the conclusion of his father's years-long search. What if the rumors of the Osetra's return to human space were true? What if the device's transmission was a kind of herald, containing a message that humanity needed to know?

Old gears groaned within his body and mind.

Yearning, reaching out.

Then metaphysical response.

The dance between divine and mundane, the nearly imperceptible shift of spiritual winds—a calling he'd not sensed since leaving Greenside for Pantoll six standard years ago. *You are running from confronting the truth again*, the calling was telling him.

He shook his head and hardened his heart against it. *No! God had abandoned him.* He'd not serve the capricious whims of such a God again.

The advancing lights outside had swelled to bright orbs. At some point, shadows had formed around the cockpit, which had become hazily bathed in illumination. He'd misjudged the authorities' speed. They'd surround the ship within the minute.

For a few moments, Kairos's head swirled with indecision. Too much input, not enough time.

He cursed God.

A moment later, he let out a resigned, half-crazed laugh.

After helping Midmay with the passenger seat's harness and fastening himself into his own, he queried the ship's last logged destination prior to Pantoll on the console. The star map brought up a system with five orbiting planets—the Lilic System—and zoomed in on a large white and tan planet fourth from the star: Spires. That was unsurprising. Spires was one of the Core Four worlds. It was also the only reachable inhabited world given their food supplies, which were meager even before now needing to feed two.

He flipped on the ship's exterior lights. A light snow was falling.

After keying coordinates into the console's LATTICE system, he relinquished flight control to the shipcom and activated the launch sequence.

The engines ignited, sending an eerie hum resonating through the cockpit. The craft lifted, dislodging itself from the surrounding muck.

Below, the source of the lights were upon them: five patrol solcycles came to a skidding halt, their riders hollering to each other or into a radio and scrambling for their weapons, with two larger all-terrain rovers close behind. The view of them didn't last long. The next moment, Kairos's body was shoved downward and against his seat back as the ship's nose tilted up and rocketed forward. Behind him, Midmay made a gurgling-cough noise. The acrid stench of vomit reached his nose.

Punching through the thick bed of clouds, the view outside shifted to a clear, star-filled sky, as calm and immutable as eternity.

Chapter 4

Contrary to the romanticized spacefaring tales that traders told in planetside taverns to entertain locals, real-life space travel was cold, cramped, and mind-numbingly boring. Beside the cockpit's slit-shaped, reinforced polyplex windshield, there weren't any other windows or portholes in the small craft. But even if there were, the view was always the same dimensionless black of space.

The trip to Spires, according to a console display, would take just under four standard days. Over ninety-nine percent of the distance had been covered in a mere handful of hours using the ship's weave drive, but the final bit had to be traversed at sublight speeds given the relatively minuscule, but meaningful, inaccuracy in reentering space/time. In addition, the presence of other interstellar traffic made it dangerous, not to mention illegal, to weave into a developed system at close distances.

Kairos had dozed off at some point shortly after the shipcom initiated their first weave, mind and body involuntarily shutting down in the wake of his troubling final hours on Pantoll. He had stayed under for a long time, winding and warping through a jumbled procession of dreams, too many to sort out upon waking.

During the voyage, Kairos used the shipcom's data library to query a listing of antiques dealers on Spires. There were a scant few, which, by definition of their trade, made sense. Only one stated an expertise in rare goods and Old Earth tech—he noted this one and hoped they'd be able to shed more light on the device his father had found. After, he burned time by exploring the depths of the data library and cycling through the command console's informational displays. These fascinated Midmay to no end as well. Though the SolarNet couldn't be accessed while weaving, the shipcom's hard drive carried loads of up-to-date news from around the worlds. The *Arcana* must have gotten around quite a bit to have downloaded so much recent information from various places. Hopefully during that time the craft had been well-maintained. Kairos had heard stories of spontaneous hull breaches, shipcom failures, weave drive meltdowns ... there were so many things that could go wrong, and ships these days were increasingly patchworks of newer, inferior construction combined with components salvaged from older, better ships. But eventually, even the old, high-quality stuff broke down.

Time devolved into unstructured moments: meandering conversation with Midmay on topics she'd read about in the data library, making sure the girl didn't screw with anything on the command console, staring into space, intermittent drifting off. And, of course, studying the mysterious teardrop. Its smooth, polished surface betrayed the fact that it had impacted into Pantoll's surface from space—what kind of materials technology was that strong? The first thing Kairos had done after they'd left Pantoll was wrap it in a strip of a metallic, radiation shielding blanket that he'd found in a medical supplies compartment, as a crude solution to prevent the teardrop's signal from being broadcast and tracked. They didn't need a welcome party upon landing on Spires.

He never slept well again after the first time. Laying "down" in zero-*g* was awkward. He shivered constantly since he'd wrapped Midmay in his coat. And so he never completed another real sleep cycle, remaining instead in a strained in-between state at the edge of consciousness, neither fully asleep nor fully awake.

His mind had been somewhere lost in this state when notification chimes from the shipcom jolted him, signaling they were approaching Spires.

* * *

The planet's orbital gateway lay just beyond geostationary altitude. His body pressed into the seat harness, Kairos vaguely sensed the subtle hum of sublight engines: the ship had been decelerating for a while.

The chimes abruptly ceased, returning the cockpit to a deep silence. Midmay had been sleeping as well and, incredibly, remained conked out. When the ship had completed weaving, Spires had shone outside the cockpit as a whitish-tan ball the size of a large button. The view now was majestic: the planet's entirety filled the window.

Directly ahead of them, the consecutive dull gray rings of the orbital gateway glinted faintly in the light of the sun. The three massive hoops were independently spaced from each other. Small lights dotted a section of the first ring's perimeter where the control tower was located. On the ship console's LATTICE display, several neatly spaced dots lined both sides of the orbital gateway. Kairos spotted one with his own eyes slightly beyond the first ring: an orbital defense cruiser. He wondered if fear of the Osetra's return to human space was the cause for such show of force.

The ship speakers sounded to life. "Spires Orbital Gateway Control to hybrid vessel *Arcana*, we have you on our screens," a formal female voice informed them.

Kairos swallowed and licked his dry lips. He tapped the comms switch on the command console screen with a shaky hand. "*Arcana* to Spires Orbital Gateway Control, we read you."

"Please proceed at a relative speed of point-three toward the first scanning ring and stand by to grant shipcom access authorizations."

A damning revelation sent a nervous pang spiking through his chest: *the assassin's body in the cargo hold!* He had little idea what the orbital gateway's scanning rays could detect, or what imaging readouts were of interest to Gateway Control, but a motionless body in the ship's hold could easily draw attention. He chastised himself for such a blatant oversight.

"Please state your cargo and purpose of visit," the gateway officer continued procedurally.

"Cargo, uh … just us people and, ah, some supplies. We're on vacation. Sight-seeing." Kairos depressed the comms switch, mashed his face into his sweaty hands, and mumbled curses. Years of religious instruction made him a terribly un-natural liar.

Silence ensued as their ship passed through the first ring,

its grayish white underside visible far above their cockpit window. The console screen indicated that Gateway Control was scanning the ship and had requested that the shipcom transmit its manifest, registration data, and destination.

Soon the gateway's second ring glided into view. They sailed through it. Kairos held his breath, waiting for a few sleek, armed Orbital Security crafts to come flank them. He even felt a desperate impulse to pray, which he immediately squashed.

The female officer's voice returned, jerking Kairos to terrified attention. "Welcome to Spires, Mr. Saeta," she said in a routine tone. "If you require a landing strip groundside, please transmit your preferred port of entry."

Kairos let out a rush of air and gathered himself to present a relaxed response. He wasn't sure how—nor did he really care—but they'd skated through without incident. "Thank you. Yes, any of the public hangars in Hollows City will do," he said, consulting the shipcom's planetary directory.

A brief pause, then: "Transmitting coordinates. We have space for you at Lambda Block, Gate 273C. Enjoy your time in-system, Mr. Saeta." The connection was severed. The console's LATTICE displayed a series of large blots in near-linear formation aft of the *Arcana*'s tiny central dot, revealing that several ships had since queued to pass through the orbital gateway. Trade never ceased.

Midmay stirred awake. Rubbing her face and looking about herself, her bleary eyes nearly popped at the sight of the large foreign planet through the cockpit window.

He smiled at her and pointed out the wheel of Counterport in the distance, visible as a bright spindle to the naked eye. Spires's main spaceport served as the counterweight to one of the planet's two towering space elevators and was located at the apex of the elevator's seemingly interminable tether that stretched over thirty thousand kilometers down to the planet's surface. The black specks of a few large ships sprinkled the spaceport's bone white torus. No sooner had Midmay spotted it herself than it slipped out from their view. The girl turned to him in amazement.

It wasn't until they were atop Spires's outer atmosphere that they were able to spot glimpses of the razor-thin silvery cable of the elevator, scintillating in the sunlight. He traced his eyes down the tether's descending length but quickly lost track of it as it withered to nothing within the atmospheric haze and swirling clouds.

Spires's lustrous curve bathed the cockpit with a soft white glow. Midmay strained against her harness as she gazed across its face, the first planet she'd ever seen from space. He admittedly was just as transfixed by the view. Over half of Spires's surface was covered under expansive polar and continental ice sheets that capped its poles and gradually turned to dark gray tundra moving toward the planet's center. A wide band of brown and burnt orange at equatorial latitudes was the temperate zone where nearly all of the population lived. The shipcom automatically guided the craft along a trajectory that would route them to the surface coordinates it had received.

Entry was as intense and nauseating as their initial launch off Pantoll had been.

Black transitioned to a pale olive sky.

Eventually, the ship's rumbling calmed. Their hybrid craft's wings extended from their retracted positions, like a beetle's wings, and after a period of smooth descent, carried them over a terrain of deep canyons and tall rock pillars jutting upward like monuments, having been formed by ancient glaciers and millions of years' worth of erosion as rivers carved winding paths deep into the planet's face. Spires's higher level of gravity relative to Pantoll weighed on Kairos at once. It felt like sand bags had been strapped all around his body. His bones and muscles would surely grow sore under the additional burden.

They passed over a few smaller settlements before reaching the sprawling Hollows City, the planet's oldest and largest city. It originally had been constructed on the rock floor of a broad, shallow canyon, but its boundaries had since expanded into parts of the canyon's walls, up onto the rock mesa above, and down into adjacent canyons, resulting in a dramatically uneven urban topography. Beyond the city's outskirts, located on an isolated mesa, sat the space elevator's anchor station. It was a bit surreal having seen now both the beginning and end points of a cable that linked two stations tens of thousands of kilometers apart.

Midmay had undone her harness and crawled over the command console, her face pressed against the windowpane to take in the city's gleaming glass towers, bustling tiers of activity along the canyon walls, and suspension bridges, some spanning several kilometers across ravines.

"So big … so many buildings …" she breathed. "Is this what Greenside is like?" she asked, her forehead still pressed to the glass.

He smiled, recalling the scenery of his homeworld. "All of the Core Four have cities, but the environments are quite different. Plant life is abundant on Greenside, as you could guess from its name. I have never been here either. This place is just as new to me as it is to you."

They set down on a landing strip at the city's public airport, which was located on a plateaued step against the canyon wall at one edge of the developed sprawl. Their ship was guided to a large hangar bay housing hundreds of other small craft: hybrid spacecraft like the *Arcana*, private airplanes, and a few skeletal helicraft. He charged the parking fees against Mr. Saeta's account and used Saeta's credit chip to pay the fare for the monorail that wound from the hangar station down through the canyon. It wasn't good relying on a dead man's finances; the credit would be cut off at some point, and Kairos disliked creating a money trail. First order of business was to generate some funds of their own.

Before leaving the ship, Kairos pulled up the address of the antiques dealer he'd noted earlier. The shop was located in a district outside the city center. Finally, he slung his satchel over his shoulder—it contained some food for the day, the plasma torch, his father's old combat lightsuit, and Johnathan's parts, which he'd transferred from his coat pockets.

"Will the dealer be able to tell us what the Osetran teardrop is?" Midmay asked as they left the hangar bay and walked to the airport's monorail platform. The stronger gravity didn't seem to weigh on her excited skips. The burgundy scarf about her neck rose nearly to her mouth, with one long end trailing and bouncing behind her like a tail. Her eyevisor was switched off and pulled back to nestle within her short shoots of hair, an uncommon position given she normally spent most of her waking hours absorbed in one of the SolarNet's many vast portals, coding constructs, or some shared cyberspace immersion with Johnathan. In its compacted state, her lightcycle was slung over her back like an arrow quiver, its thin treaded wheels limp without the bike's strong generated current running through them.

"I don't know," Kairos replied. "There aren't many Osetran tech experts, and most of them are in corporate research divisions. But I'd like to avoid corporations. At least for now."

On the monorail, Midmay pressed her face against its long windows. Her neck twitched as she tried to track discrete people and objects as they zipped past. Kairos smiled. It was good for her to have new experiences. His eyes, too, were glued to the scenes outside as they raced along the elevated monorail track, which wound through the contours of the steep canyon walls above bustling streets. Glimpses of city life made him envious of how these people lived. Their sophisticated clothing, high-tech accessories, casual cool. Businessmen and women at outdoor cafés conversed over expensive lunches. A flock of teens stood outside a trendy-looking cyboutique, probably ogling the latest retinal overlays. The hum of the city suggested a constant exchange of ideas. He even spotted among the crowds the familiar cassock of a New Revelationist priest. It was the kind of world that should have been his in Asphis, the capital city of Greenside.

After several stops, they got off the monorail at a platform on the fringe of the city's center, a dense pocket of glass skyscrapers packed onto a few plateaued steps along the canyon walls. Midmay was hungry—and he admittedly had grown tired of the sawdust-dry carbocrisps and chalky Block-o'-tein wedges he'd packed—so before exiting the station platform, they sat down at an adjoining bistro. There, they devoured a lunch of raw pylefish caught in one of Spires's many canyon rivers, hot rolls made from Eukian stickwheat, and local gorgeberries. Even such basic fare was more delicious than anything found on Pantoll.

After they'd had their fill, they descended a curved street leading away from the station platform. Tall buildings lined the road on the side facing the canyon valley, while establishments along the canyon wall seemed to be directly built into it. Bicycles, small solcycles, and pedestrians flowed through the street's curves without much organization. Kairos had seen few large vehicles during the monorail ride, and he supposed Hollow City's disjointed topography allowed for few broad highways. Following his goggle screens' navigational arrows—courtesy of local mapping software he'd downloaded for free before leaving the hangar—it didn't take long to find the antique dealer's establishment, located down a shaded alleyway off the main street. The establishments lining this alleyway, like many they'd passed, had old but ornate, tan-colored stone façades, their interiors carved directly into the canyon walls. The dealer's entrance featured a couple of dusty windows with a simple wooden door, unmarked by signage of any kind. Stepping inside, they entered a small showroom filled with articles large and small on display on tables, on shelves, or behind glass.

"Look at all this stuff!" Midmay exclaimed, skipping into the room.

"Don't play with anything," Kairos called after her. He peered curiously at the nearest row of objects along the wall by the entrance: a series of Old Earth handheld holo units—their casings scuffed and scratched, their long-dead touchscreens forever blank—undoubtedly relics from the earliest Spires pioneers.

"Check this out," Midmay called from the center of the room where a glass case protected what looked like a deflated black bag.

"Ah," Kairos said as he drew alongside. "An Osetran weather balloon." The black spheres had been found floating around several worlds, including the Core Four, by the first human scout ships during the Colonization Era. They were believed to have been placed at some time in the past by Osetran deep space expeditions, like the one that had made contact with Old Earth. How long the spheres had been circling the worlds' skies or the full extent of their purpose and function was anyone's guess; the alien race had vanished before humans could ask them such things. Once, while backpacking in the Northern Spines on Pantoll, Kairos himself had found the crumpled remains of such a device. He'd smiled at that—even Osetran technology couldn't survive being chewed up and spat out by the planet's furious storms.

Shuffling footsteps sounded from an adjoining hallway, before a stout elderly man entered the room. He walked with a slight hunch but with energy. His head was all but completely balded, with tufts of grayed hair curving just above either ear. A small pair of eyeglasses rested on his large drooping nose.

"Hello there," the old man greeted them, giving a wry smile to Midmay. "I see you've found my Osetran Atmospheric Monitoring Device." He looked up at Kairos, surveying him head to toe. "I see you two are not from Hollows City, and maybe not from Spires, eh?" It was less of a question than a simple observation. "See anything that interests you?"

"Actually, we came to have items appraised," Kairos said.

The man chuckled and pointed at the satchel Kairos carried. "I figured as much. Come, let's take a look at what you've got."

To Kairos's relief, Midmay asked if she could keep exploring around the showroom. Best she wasn't around while Johnathan's innards were haggled over.

He followed the dealer, who introduced himself as Gadrish, into an adjoining room divided roughly in half by a large counter. Behind the counter was a small cluttered office with an unfurled scrollscreen propped against the wall. Gadrish shuffled around the counter and replaced his eyeglasses with a pair of magnifying electrospex which reminded Kairos of the bulky magnifiers his father had used.

His father's lightsuit, which Kairos splayed over the counter for the dealer's inspection, ultimately wasn't worth nearly as much as Kairos hoped. Apparently, the latest spacesuits manufactured by the industrial conglomerates on Kotopax had achieved a level of quality near parity with those that had existed on Old Earth.

Much of the technology behind Johnathan's parts, on the other hand, hadn't been fully reclaimed by humans. Those bits of knowledge had been lost since the Exodus as generations of pioneers focused on establishing agricultural foundations to avoid starving to death on their new home planets. Even if the technologies were well understood today, it'd be some time before the manufacturing infrastructure and technical know-how for producing such things as nano-chips and Dekel processors were in place on any of the worlds. Nevertheless, the System Administrators and the multitude of lesser corporations were keen to buy up any advanced tech— be it Osetran or Old Earthan—still floating around. Kairos knew all this, as did everyone else; the value of gold required no debate.

Gadrish, however, seemed as disinterested in the android's parts as the lightsuit and employed the same methodical, patient eye as he calmly examined them under his electrospex. Kairos wondered with trepidation whether the parts might be too beaten up to be of any use. After the inspection, Gadrish, to Kairos's relief, offered him a tidy sum, enough to live off for a while and even a little more than the values he'd come across in querying the SolarNet.

"Just like that?" Kairos remarked after confirming the massive points transfer to his SolarNet bank account.

"You seem surprised?" Gadrish replied with a smile. "That was some fine merchandise. Mighty fine. Haven't seen android core tech in over ten standard. But I suppose that's in line with the definition of going extinct, isn't it?"

"You didn't seem that excited."

The man chuckled. "The rule in my business is to never show emotion when appraising. The value is the value, that's it. I'm mighty curious to know where the pieces came from, but that'd be breaking another rule."

"No questions asked, right?" Kairos said with a smile.

"It's no quaint sentiment. Ignorance is protection for a dealer," the man replied, his tone severe. "Well, nice trading with you. Please feel free to continue browsing my showroom."

"Actually, there is something else ..." Kairos withdrew the teardrop, unwrapped its shielding mesh cloth, and set it on the counter.

"I see," Gadrish said, returning the electrospex to his eyes. Again, the dealer's expression was indecipherable.

"Osetran tech," Kairos said. "I'd like an appraisal." He explained its origin from space and the transmission it carried. He omitted mention of his father or the murder, of course. Midmay walked in during this time, having had her fill of the showroom displays, and dragged over a stool so her eyes could clear the counter.

Gadrish quietly rotated the smooth, oblong artifact under the protruding scopes of his electrospex. Afterward, he listened to the device's broadcasting frequency via a small radio unit. The dealer remained silent. It was Kairos's and Midmay's first times hearing the signal audibly as well. A ghostly sound filled the quiet room, like the stirring of wind before a storm, interspersed with rising and falling susurration. *Is this a separate form of Osetran language unbeknown to humans?* Kairos wondered. *Or an audible counterpart or expression of the Osetra's natural telepathy?*

After some time, the dealer lifted off his electrospex and returned the object to the counter. Kairos quickly re-wrapped it in the mesh.

"I'll be back in a few minutes," the dealer said, replacing his eyeglasses and receding into his small office. Watching through the plate glass, Kairos could see the man place a call. A muffled conversation ensued which Kairos couldn't make out.

"Well," Gadrish said upon his return to the counter a couple minutes later, "I confirmed with an old colleague of mine. Yes, this is indeed of Osetran origin. It's a data collection and transmission orbital probe, part of the Osetra's terraforming apparatus to monitor and relay evolving environmental conditions on future colony worlds—like the atmospheric device you saw in my showroom. The devices talked to each other. This outer shell"—Gadrish traced a finger along the object's smooth surface— "is a carbon alloy-infused protein chain to protect the device's internal components from radiation. Tougher than than anything humans ever developed, but that's because we're still stuck on manufacturing things from inanimate materials. See, the Osetra had gotten to the point of *growing* their building materials. Leads to flawless, complex biostructural integrity. Fascinating, huh?"

Something is off here. Wells had known as much about the Osetra as the most studied xenologists and likely more than this dealer. True, his father's obsession clouded his personal judgment, but the old man certainly would have known if the probe was another type of weather balloon. Heck, Kairos knew a fair bit himself about the Osetra and he'd never heard of such an orbital probe before. Osetran weather balloons had never been found to emit signals or contain communication components; he'd picked apart the gutted insides of one himself. Besides, its looped recording wasn't consistent with a planetary data transmission function.

"... these probes, while certainly uncommon, as any Osetran artifacts are of course, do already exist in abundance among corporate holdings, so I'm afraid that will limit the appraised value to no more than eight thousand. Since it's in good condition and you seem to have traveled a long way with this little friend of yours, I'll offer you eight-five."

"*Eight thousand* points!" Midmay exclaimed, tugging on Kairos's sleeve. "We're rich!" What she didn't know, and what he wouldn't ever have the heart to tell her, is that moments earlier he'd sold Johnathan's parts for more than that.

Kairos looked directly into Gadrish's dull brown eyes. "Eight-five, huh? You examined the object for—how long's it been?—listened to it, and then had to consult a colleague just to tell us that this is a probe you've seen before?"

"Always good to be sure with these kinds of artifacts," the

dealer responded, calm as ever. "It may not be the rarest find, but like I said, all Osetran objects are highly uncommon, even more so those existing outside of Corporate vaults. Eight and a half thousand is a lot of money."

The dealer either sought to take advantage of Kairos's ignorance, or perhaps had genuinely missed something. While Kairos actually had no intention of selling the object, there was an easy way to get the dealer talking.

"I appreciate the appraisal," he finished, standing up and pocketing the teardrop, "but we'll get a second opinion from a dealer with additional expertise on the subject. Come on, Midmay." He pulled his satchel over his shoulder and turned to leave.

"Wait a moment, wait," Gadrish called, whisking himself around the end of the counter. It was the fastest Kairos had seen him move, faster than he thought possible for the older man. The dealer held up both hands. "Okay, okay. I see I underestimated your knowledge. An old habit. I get a lot of slimy traders or scummy space pirates coming in here looking to offload high-end merchandise, probably stolen but like I said, I don't ask. In any case, it's just business to them. They don't, ah, *appreciate* the true value of these kinds of things."

"Look," Kairos replied. "I know dealers deal directly with the corporations. I'm sure you've got a direct line to the Lilic System Administrator, Lienns-Sutra, right? It's not a secret that they've got a bunch of artifacts locked away in their archives. You probably acquired some of those for them yourself. And I know that Lienns-Sutra doesn't care to share certain, *special* items with the academic world. So now, let's not waste each other's time. What can you tell me about this thing?"

The dealer hesitated a moment. "I recognize its construction, but beyond that, I've never come across such a device or transmission language," Gadrish confessed in rare admission for a dealer. "I don't know what its function is. Neither does my colleague. Its repeating signal is fascinating. Our knowledge of Osetran telepathic communication is limited, but as far as we know, they never used these wavelengths."

"Unless the communication wasn't intended for themselves, but to be heard by other beings," Kairos wondered.

"A reasonable theory. If true, we can at least conclude the object's creation pre-dates First Contact. Otherwise—and assuming it was intended for beings including humans—they'd have sent it with human language included."

"You've seen the outer material before?"

Gadrish nodded. "I don't usually do this, but seeing you're a man of some Osetran scholarship, I'll share something with you. A brief diversion, come." The dealer waved them to follow.

They left the appraisal room and followed Gadrish to a door at the rear of the shop, which the old man unlocked. It opened into a storage room cluttered floor to ceiling with stacked boxes, wooden crates, and shelving units holding a variety of wrapped objects. Gadrish lifted a holo unit from a shelf and placed it on a workbench, the rest of which he cleared off. He then unfurled a scrollscreen atop it and swiped a few commands. The unit misted up an image of two identical cylindrical ring-shaped objects, each several centimeters in diameter.

"What are these?" Midmay asked, poking and swirling a finger through the projection.

"A man came in here one day," the dealer began. "This was

some time ago. Spoke hardly a word except that he wanted me to negotiate a sale of these to Lienns-Sutra. Odd fellow. Had a hooded poncho on the whole time. Scopes protruded from his eyes. Big ones, out to here." Gadrish held hand a hand's width from his forehead. "And his lower face was covered with a breathing mask"—Gadrish bent a hand's fingers over his nose and mouth—"you know, same kind they all wear outside on Kotopax, if you've ever traveled there."

Kairos shook his head.

"Well anyway, I studied the bracelets he'd brought—that's what I call them. Their structural material matches that of your object. But I couldn't tell you what they're for or where they came from. Databases from the partnership era catalog what we know of the race, from their strange spaceship composition down to the kind of food they ate. But there is so much we don't know. These bracelets are part of the unknown; they're as likely to be wildly advanced tech as plain scrap metal fashioned into jewelry. In any case, their absence from the databases tells me they were possibly stolen from the Osetra directly. Anyway, I set up the sale with Lienns-Sutra's Science Division—of course they paid big—took my commission, and that was that. Never saw the man again, and the bracelets entered the corporate black box."

"Why did the man want to sell them?" Midmay asked.

Gadrish shrugged. "One way or another, I suppose it simply comes down to needing the money. Same as you, safe to presume?" he asked Kairos.

"What do you think its worth?" Kairos asked him.

The dealer shook his head with a cunning grin. "I'm sorry, but you can understand I wouldn't be able to turn a profit if I revealed all my cards. You seem like an honest person, so I'll make you an honest offer this time."

Kairos's heart skipped a beat upon hearing the dealer's figure. It was life-changing money. More than enough to start afresh on Greenside. *And definitely enough to kill for*, he thought grimly. "My apologies, you misunderstood me," Kairos told the dealer. "I asked what it is worth, but it is not for sale."

Gadrish's brow furled. "I've misjudged you again. I wasn't the only one withholding information, eh? I understand your hesitation. But know that such an item cannot remain hidden long," the dealer cautioned. "Lienns-Sutra monitors all activity across of their managed networks. That includes public research databases. You'll need specialists to analyze it, but revealing the existence of something so valuable comes with risk. That's the pickle you're in, sir, without an experienced dealer like me acting as an agent on your behalf. In fact, that's a main reason my job exists: to provide transactional anonymity to both buyer and seller."

Kairos's body grew warm. Spires was the headquarters of the Lienns-Sutra Organization, the behemoth corporation governing the Lilic star system. They had the monitoring infrastructure to detect the teardrop's signal, even if faint. The *Arcana*'s log had indicated that the assassin Saeta had last been at Spires prior to Pantoll. That fact hardly proved Saeta was hired by Lienns-Sutra, but he didn't like Gadrish's strong implication that he needed protection from them.

They lingered a little longer in the dealer's storage room, Gadrish casually pointing out this or that item of interest to them for fun, especially to the delight of Midmay.

From down the hall came the sound of the shop's front door creaking open, followed by the soft thud of its closing.

"Sounds like I've got another customer," the dealer said. "Busy day." Gadrish switched off the holo unit. "After you," he motioned to them, pulling out his keys to lock the door behind them.

Kairos and Midmay traced their steps back to the front of the shop.

Two people waited in showroom, both tall, probably in their thirties, dressed in black suits over white, mandarin-collared shirts. Their retinal overlay implants gleamed a cobalt blue. One of them, a man, had umber skin with long, thick black hair pulled back into a tight bun and a closely-shaved beard. He was smiling too broadly, a fake smile. The second person had a cadaverous appearance: thin, pale, and with straight, glossy-black, neck-length hair. Their androgynous features were expressionless.

Kairos froze, immediately recognizing the style: corporates.

He grabbed Midmay's arm and turned to find Gadrish aiming at pistol at them.

"You called Lienns-Sutra, you swine," he spat at Gadrish. So much for the dealer's talk about contacting a 'colleague.'

Gadrish smiled weakly, looking at Kairos with a hint of pity. "With this kind of tech involved, I'm afraid I can't just let you walk out of here."

"And that deal you just offered me?"

The dealer shrugged. "Consider it an exploding offer. Lienns-Sutra is more interested in, ah, discretion than due process on this one. I don't like doing business this way, but my strings are being pulled by higher powers. I'm sorry. I really am."

Discretion, as in, taking the teardrop from my lifeless hands, Kairos thought.

Chapter 5

The corporates' cool blue eyes scanned Kairos's and Midmay's faces. Whatever information the SolarNet contained on himself, however little, was at that very moment cascading across their retinal overlays.

Midmay had drawn to Kairos's side, and he tucked her behind him.

"Mr. Saeta, is it?" the corporate with the hair bun asked.

Kairos heart was pounding as if it were a savage, caged creature clawing to tear itself free. His eyes darted around the room, searching for exit options. As far as he could tell, the front door was the only recway out and the two corporates were blocking it.

"I didn't think so," Hair Bun smirked. "An Obasanjo New Revelationist priest from Greenside, flagged by Orbital Secusetarity and carrying a verified Osetran artifact? Now that's not something you hear every day." He motioned to the dealer. "Bring it to us. The bag, too."

Arms raised, Kairos reluctantly stood by as Gadrish plucked the teardrop from his coat pocket and stripped off his satchel. Keeping his pistol aimed at them, the dealer handed both over to Hair Bun.

Hair Bun inspected the teardrop for a moment. Then he said to Kairos, "You and your small accomplice have been charged with the murder of Badir Saeta and grand theft aero." He smirked. "Aren't such sins against the code of your religion?"

Gadrish eyed Kairos in surprise.

Kairos remained silent against the accusations. There was nothing to be gained by arguing with agents of a System Administrator.

"The owner's body was found stuffed in the ship's cargo bay, burned by the high-velocity particle beam of a plasma torch ..." Hair Bun's pale, vampire-like colleague rasped. Vampire glided toward them—a hand hidden inside their thin suit jacket, threatening some unseen weapon—and extended a bony, bent finger toward Midmay's cheek. The girl swatted Vampire's pale hand away, eliciting a cracked smile from the corporate.

"Ah, here we are," Hair Bun said, drawing the torch from the satchel. "Unregistered tech. Though the least of your crimes, priest."

It was now impossible for Kairos to keep both Hair Bun and Vampire in view at the same time.

"Did he tell you what this is?" Hair Bun asked Gadrish, referring to the Osetran artifact.

"He doesn't know," replied the dealer. "And your organization didn't give me the time to evaluate it properly myself. Either Mr. Roth or Dr. Henley must want it pretty badly, huh?"

Kairos knew the first name: Akaash Roth was the CEO of Lienns-Sutra, one of the most powerful men in the worlds. The second, Dr. Henley, he'd never heard of before but assumed they must be Roth's chief science or technology officer.

"Did you file the acquisition with Lienns-Sutra Central?" Hair Bun asked the dealer, ignoring his question.

Vampire had circled around the dealer's back.

The dealer shifted his feet, eyes darting from one corporate to the other. "No, I called straight into Science Division," Gadrish replied. "We've already settled the terms. I'll log the transaction with Central, now that we're done here."

"Good." Hair Bun said. "Yes, quite done."

A soft *pffst* sounded. Gadrish's face lost color and his jaw went slack. A trickle of blood slowly slid down his nose, ending in a drip off his upper lip. The man's eyes, at first frantic with fear, lost focus, glazed over and lolled back, before his knees abruptly buckled. The old dealer crumpled to the stone tiled floor with an unceremonious thud.

Vampire held a stubby needler, each flechette certainly infused with a lethal dose.

Midmay screamed as, in a flash, Vampire extended an arm and yanked her away from Kairos's side. They pressed the needler to her neck.

"Wait!" Kairos yelled. "Don't hurt her. I'll tell you something you need to know about the device ... from my father's research findings." His mind searched for something to say to stall for time.

"Oh, no need," Hair Bun said. The corporate squatted, placed the teardrop on the ground, and took a step back. "We already know much more about this than you." To Kairos's shock, Hair Bun aimed the torch down at the artifact and depressed its trigger.

A torrent of radiation enveloped the teardrop.

The flooring beneath it ignited and was instantaneously disintegrated by the beam. The exposed rock beneath glowed red. The surrounding air shimmered.

But even after several seconds of this, the teardrop's structural integrity remained intact.

Hair Bun cursed and turned up the torch's intensity.

The rock began melting rapidly, soon bubbling in places.

Suddenly Hair Bun yelped in pain and the torch fell from his hands. The skin on the side of his trigger hand was inflamed.

The torch had deactivated upon being released. Kairos rushed forward. As he bent to pick it up, Hair Bun kneed him in the chest.

Kairos fell backward but his fingers found the smooth trigger switch along the plasma torch's grip. It was indeed hot to the touch.

As he hit the ground, the torch activated.

The corporate's eyes went wide as suit jacket, dress shirt, flesh, and bone vaporized as if a flaming spear the diameter of a small tree trunk had just plowed through his chest, leaving a sizzling hole where body mass should have been. As Hair Bun slumped to the ground, the beam continued slicing a diagonal trail through his body.

Kairos, horrified, tore his eyes away. His thoughts switched immediately to Midmay. He lifted his burned finger off the trigger and aimed the torch at Vampire.

But the corporate was using Midmay as a shield.

Kairos quickly pulled a length of his scarf down to wrap his hand, then pointed the torch at the patch of ceiling above Vampire. "Midmay, run!" he yelled, triggering the beam.

The canyon rock overhead hissed as deep arcs were scored into it, throwing off super-heated debris and forming molten, fast-drooping stalactites that would soon spear their hot ends into the floor.

Vampire dove and rolled out of sight behind one of the showroom's standing displays.

The torch let out a loud crackle. The beam's uniformity faltered and choked in spurts of flickering light. Its heat had spread along the inside of his entire arm. The torch's energy generator had become searing hot.

A pitfall of bringing ancient weaponry into battle, he thought.

Midmay had the shop's front door open. She flipped the compacted lightcycle over her shoulder, activating it in the process. The bike sprang into shape, its thin treaded wheels instantly becoming rigid as the powerful electric current surged through them.

Kairos couldn't tell where Vampire was lurking, so he swept the torch's beam indiscriminately across the showroom for good measure, regrettably mowing down all intervening displays in a clean horizontal line and setting much of the room ablaze. Releasing the sputtering beam's trigger, he delicately kicked the somehow-undamaged teardrop out from the steaming molten rock it lay atop. Then, taking a calculated risk, scooped it up with his scarf-wrapped hand. He judged correctly: its surface temperature was cool. Stashing it away, he dashed to the lightcycle and mounted its short foot pegs behind Midmay.

Midmay sped them down the narrow alleyway and banked hard into the main street, bringing them into the chaotic flow of cycles and people. Midmay steered wildly in an attempt to integrate into the traffic, but lost control trying to veer around a large cart of goods blocking their way. They toppled and skidded across the dusty street.

Kairos groaned, picked himself up, and recovered the dropped plasma torch. He gave a hand to Midmay, checking her for injury. Her shirt's right shoulder had torn, the skin scraped and lightly bleeding. Fortunately her chiva leggings had protected her legs.

"Are you able to keep moving?" he asked her.

The girl nodded firmly and wiped the grit off her palms.

Kairos stuffed the torch in his jacket and took over driving, throttling them along quickly but not at such a fast speed as to draw attention.

Hollows City's streets curved around canyon walls, rose, dipped, and rose again. Once, when they were caught in a traffic slowdown on a zig-zagging section of steep switchbacks, a small section of canyon wall just off their side erupted into a shower of small rocks.

It happened again not long after, the second time mere centimeters from their lightcycle. The impact signatures were those of wave bullets: they were being fired upon at some distance.

From then on, they kept up a fast pace. Kairos had no idea where they were going. His goggles's mapping overlay served little purpose without a destination. At forks, he'd choose a direction at random, simply to keep moving. He needed to get them to a safe place to stop and think.

They came to a curve of road that hugged the drop-off into the canyon valley a little too closely for Kairos's comfort. They were fairly high now, nearly at the same elevation as the tops of the skyscrapers of Hollows City's dense central district. The gleaming towers stood a couple kilometers away on the canyon floor, beside the curving river responsible for carving out the canyon over millennia. Not far ahead, a series of black lines extended from the cliff side they were riding along down to the various canyon levels below. These cables were part of

Hollows City's aerial cable car network that shuttled people and goods between the canyon floor and the levels above, all the way up to the canyon's rim. At intervals along the cabling hung bulbous units like berries on a vine, some of them larger than a monorail car.

A few turns later, Kairos and Midmay arrived at a cable car platform. To their luck, a large car, about fifteen meters long and half as wide, had just paused at the platform to take on additional passengers. A sounding chime signaled the car's impending departure. Kairos wound them through foot and bike traffic and drove them right up to the car's opening.

After triggering the lightcycle's fold-up mechanism, he stepped through behind Midmay moments before the car's door slid closed. Kairos realized he didn't even know if the car would be ascending up to the canyon rim or descending toward the river, but either way they'd be out of open sight and still moving.

The car's narrow interior felt just as worn as its weathered exterior. The air was warm and humid, and smelled of steaming seafood. About twenty-five other passengers were already spread around the car. Along one side was a tight kitchen space with floor to ceiling shelving crammed with bottles, jars, produce, and packaged goods. On the opposite side, along the cable car's windows, were several compact, two-person tables. The cable car was a tiny restaurant.

The entire place lurched; the car was headed downward. A few naked lightbulbs strung overhead swayed as if aboard a rocking boat.

As all of the small tables were occupied, Kairos and Midmay took empty stools at the kitchen's stainless steel counter. At a compact stove top behind the counter, a portly cook worked a cast iron pan holding a thick white slab of frying fish. A large frothing pot on a second burner behind it was nearly boiling over, spiny gray limbs of some local species of shellfish splaying crookedly out the top. The cook turned to face them, wiping a grimy sleeve over his sweaty forehead. He was a muscular man with a grizzled beard, the kind who had clearly worked with his hands all his life. He wore a traditional Spirian sailor's cap and a once-white, grease-covered chef coat.

Kairos ordered a hot tea for Midmay, to help take her mind off things. *It had been a mistake leaving Pantoll with her*, he thought with a growing pit in his stomach.

He swiveled to look out the car's windows. Judging from their speed and the fact that this cable route appeared to be an express line to the canyon floor, he figured they'd have fifteen or so minutes before needing to make their next move. His palms were still sweaty from clutching the lightcycle handlebars, his heart still pounding. Lienns-Sutra now knew about the Osetran artifact. But he couldn't shake a feeling that they'd known about it even before he and Midmay had arrived on Spires. Maybe the corporation had detected the teardrop's transmission upon his father unearthing it on Pantoll—or that bastard Falck had tipped them off, or both— and then sent the assassin Saeta to retrieve it. In any case, that backstabbing dealer hadn't known much about the device, but those Lienns-Sutra corporates said they did. Why had they tried to destroy it? A corporation wanting to destroy an alien artifact was preposterous. Were they afraid it was connected to an impending Osetran invasion?

His ultimate problem was how to get off Spires. Even if he surrendered the artifact and swore to never tell another soul about it, Lienns-Sutra wouldn't let him and Midmay go freely. Kairos had accidentally killed at least one of their agents, and on top of that was wanted for Saeta's murder. He and Midmay were now criminals; they'd have to flee the star system. But they couldn't return to the *Arcana*; the ship would surely have been impounded by Lienns-Sutra, along with their belongings. Without a ship to leave the planet, running from agents of the System Administrator through the streets of Hollows City was a pointless delay of the inevitable, like a fish darting from one end of a cooking pot to another in an attempt to escape the boil. Who was he to think they could escape the grip of one of the most powerful System Administrators? Lienns-Sutra's operations and influence expanded well beyond the Lilic System. The corporation wouldn't stop until they'd acquired—destroyed?—the artifact.

With great reluctance, he considered the one option for obtaining safe harbor on a core world that he hadn't wanted to resort to. Consulting his goggles's map software, he found it: the Obasanjo New Revelationist cathedral in Hollows City. It was in city center and sat about a quarter of the way up the canyon wall from the river. The city's monorails and cable car lines formed a grid-like transit system spanning the city's elevation. Cable cars traversed up and down canyon levels quickly, while monorails wound through each level like a long snake. A monorail platform was walking distance from the bottom of the cable line they were currently riding. Seven monorail stops would bring them to the cable car line that led up to the canyon's rim and had a stop near the cathedral. The Archbishop of Spires could help them. But in return, Kairos would have to do something he swore he'd never do again: act as a member of the Church.

Kairos noticed the cook's eyes on him through his screens,

and he raised the goggles.

Peering down at Kairos with an annoyed look on his face, the cook said, "I asked, will you be wantin' anything else before we reach the bottom?"

"Oh. No, we're fine, thanks," Kairos replied, seeing Midmay still sipping her tea. The man grunted and returned to the stove. Kairos's arm had been resting on the counter top, one of his fingers absently tracing a circular groove that had been etched into its metal surface with a knife point. He lifted his finger to find several other adjacent circular grooves: graffiti depicting a ring of eyeballs, all staring at him with jaggedly etched irises. Kairos straightened in his seat. He'd seen this image before. Where?

Then he remembered: he'd seen the same arrangement of eyes on Saeta's spacesuit.

Kairos snagged the cook's attention and waved him over.

"Change your mind?" asked the cook.

"Do you know what this symbol is?" Kairos asked, pointing to the etching.

The cook's face wrinkled and he snorted. "Yeah. It's destruction of private property." He grunted, then returned to his duties.

Kairos captured an image of the graffiti with his goggles's cam and continued to trace the eyes with a finger. Buried knowledge in the deep recesses of his mind hinted that the night his father had been killed was not the first time he'd seen such a symbol, that the recognition might go back to his time at seminary. But he couldn't place it. His studies had covered thousands of years' worth of history and culture, including countless belief systems. He wouldn't even know where to start with a SolarNet query. He would have to meditate to draw the memory from the depths of his mind to see it clearly. He shivered at the thought of using Retrospection. He hadn't practiced the technique since he gave up the priesthood. The past had become a painful place for him, riddled with memories he'd rather not dwell on, much less revisit in the full clarity that Retrospection afforded.

Something dark with rotors appeared outside one of the windows. It hovered in place, two dull red orbs quickly scanning the car's interior.

Before Kairos could turn away to avoid the orbs' scanners, the drone flew off as abruptly as it had appeared.

Kairos's pulse quickened. With dread, he wondered whether it had noticed him. Getting to the cathedral undetected would be nearly impossible with street drones seeking their whereabouts. For all he knew, corporates already awaited them at the bottom of the cable car line.

"Excuse me, sir," he called at the cook's back. "I'd like to buy something."

"Kitchen's closed." the cook said without turning, clearly quite finished with dealing with Kairos's quirks. "We're almost at canyon bottom."

"I'd like to buy your coat and cap."

The cook swiveled his head to them, confused.

"We're tourists and are leaving today. I'd love to have a couple of genuine souvenirs from Spires," Kairos explained, taking out his credit chip. "I'll offer you fifty points for them." That was probably five times what they were worth.

The baffled cook started to reply, stopped himself. "Fifty points, eh?" he repeated in disbelief.

Kairos nodded.

"Make it sixty." The cook motioned to the pay panel, his

expression unbelieving.

Kairos keyed in the transaction. The cook shook his head with an amused snort as he removed his coat and cap and placed them on the counter. Kairos then keyed in another transaction for twenty-five points.

"What, you want my shirt too?" the cook exclaimed.

Kairos pointed to a large fishing net hanging by the kitchen's ice chest. Its woven fibers were thick, intertwined with and tufts of snagged river grass.

"The fishermen brought in today's catch with that," the cook said. "It reeks of riverweed and fish piss."

"I'll take it as it is," Kairos said. "I've got weird tastes."

The cable car was nearing its terminal platform situated along the river docks. Hundreds of fishing boats were moored there, from large trawling vessels to small wooden boats with nothing to them but an outboard motor. Kairos figured that this cable car line must provide service to the scores of fishers, dock hands, and marina workers engaged along this stretch of the river.

After buying the net, Kairos pulled Midmay into the car's miniscule lavatory.

"You want me to do *what?*" Midmay protested upon hearing Kairos's plan.

"Only until I can get us out of plain sight. Just keep quiet and your head tucked."

The cable car decelerated and glided to a halt. Kairos could hear the other passengers begin to file out. He draped the cook's grimy coat over his thin frame, stuffed his goggles in a pocket, and pulled the sailor's cap low over his eyes. Midmay reluctantly stepped into the net and curled up inside. He added the plasma torch, then cinched the net closed. Its thick fibers and the riverweed concealed her form well enough.

While the thin girl weighed little, with Spires's increased gravity, simply heaving the net up to sling over his shoulder had him in a light sweat.

Head down, he exited the car closely behind the remaining passengers. A small crowd of dock workers was waiting by the platform and pushed forward to enter the car as soon as Kairos stepped out.

A man, situated off the back of the crowd, dressed plainly and wearing a floppy brimmed hat, remained standing in place and appeared distracted by the rush of passengers both leaving and entering the car. With a furtive glance, Kairos noticed a slight twitching of the man's head—he was scanning the crowd with retinal overlays. That was tech few commoners could afford. Kairos made straight for the docks.

Only when he reached them and the platform was well behind him did he risk a look back. The platform was vacant now—the cable car was ascending back up the canyon—and the corporate in the floppy hat was gone.

Kairos felt an itch at his neck. Reaching up in reflex, as if to swat away a fly, his fingers brushed against a short needle-like object that had penetrated the skin.

A nauseous tingle washed over him. He fumbled to remove the needle with shaky fingers, but his hand abruptly ceased obeying him and fell limp.

The next moment, his knees buckled and he collapsed to the ground.

A minute later, footsteps approached. Strong arms lifted his paralyzed body and draped it over the back of a broad metallic shoulder.

Kairos's throat had been silenced, and his eyeballs lolled beneath half-closed, frozen eyelids, only able to watch whatever would befall him next.

* * *

Kairos's view of the ground scrolled from wooden dock planks to the smooth fiberglass of a boat.

His body was deposited ungracefully on the boat's deck, his cheek coming to a rest upon its damp, scummy surface. But he felt no pain, or any physical sensation at all for that matter.

Kairos's assailant was squatting over him, obscuring his view. From his limited vantage point, Kairos could see only that the figure wore tall metallic boots rising up beneath the lower hem of a long black cloak. After a minute of what Kairos assumed was a thorough shakedown, the figure stood. Abruptly, the large fish net plopped down by his head, cutting off Kairos's view. Midmay's body, curled up inside, lay motionless. He couldn't see her face. The boots clomped away.

Shortly after, the low growl of a boat engine rumbled through the cabin. They were moving.

The boat chugged along for about fifteen minutes before the engine was cut off. During that time, Kairos's body had gradually regained sensation. His elation, however, had been cut short upon discovering, as soon as he could wiggle any muscles, that his wrists and ankles were bound to each other by a stretch of fishing line. Writhing on the floor to no avail, he'd sensed that the Osetran teardrop and his goggles had been taken. His jacket was on the ground nearby, but the plasma torch was missing. Midmay hadn't recovered yet from whatever toxin had been in the needle. So there'd been nothing to do but wait.

By the time they'd stopped, the cabin's small porthole was filled with the view of glistening towers. They had arrived at the heart of the city.

The thudding of boots returned, and Kairos got his first good look of their assailant, entering the cabin. The figure stood a full two meters, clad in a black hooded cloak that covered most of their body. Within the hood, the figure's head was helmeted, with an opaque visor. Looking from the figure's dark navy, gauntleted hands to their "boots," Kairos realized then that beneath the cloak, the figure was wearing a full-body, metallic suit—based on its design, he guessed it was some ultra high-end space suit. It wasn't uncommon for spacers to wear them around, but usually not when planetside.

"Time to move," the faceless assailant commanded through their helmet speaker in a distorted, low voice.

"She's still paralyzed," Kairos replied to the spacer, whom he named Metal Man.

"Carry her." Metal Man unbound him and yanked him to his feet with a single arm.

After Kairos had lifted Midmay, Metal Man shoved him out of the cabin and onto the dock.

The docks here were less expansive, their main use appearing to be commuter ferrying as opposed to fishing. Colossal skyscrapers rose up beyond the docks against a backdrop of canyon wall. Up close from river bottom, they were even more majestic than when viewed from along the canyon sides.

Metal Man pushed him along with a strong arm. At first, Kairos mulled potential ways to escape, but he soon realized the folly of any attempt with Midmay needing to be carried. Metal Man probably had intended exactly that.

They crossed a pedestrian bridge over the monorail track that wound along the river and joined a flow of foot and vehicle traffic down the first proper, straight street Kairos had seen since arriving.

"Where are you taking—" Kairos started when the pavement in front of them suddenly erupted, bits of street bursting apart and getting tossed up. People around them screamed and scattered from where the wave bullets had impacted.

Metal Man grabbed Kairos, spun, and drove him toward the nearest building entrance, while also seizing the fish net to carry himself.

As they approached the door of what was a SolarNet café, wave bullets shattered the all-glass storefront.

They dove through the windowless opening.

Chaos broke out among the patrons inside, who scrambled or dove under the rows of connection cubicles for cover.

Metal Man pushed Kairos to the back of the café, where they raced down a narrow hallway past bathrooms and the kitchen. The back of the spacer's cloak, Kairos noticed, was pockmarked with a few singed holes, revealing, to his surprise, an unscathed, smooth surface beneath. The suit must be military-grade to withstand the radiation of wave rounds.

Turning a corner, the hallway ended at a locked door. Metal Man muscled it open. Inside was a dark utility room.

"If you're not with Lienns-Sutra, who are you?" Kairos asked.

"You think now's a good time for a conversation?" Metal Man said.

"This room is a dead end."

Metal Man lowered the fish net, strode into the room, and withdrew Kairos's plasma torch from within his cloak. He switched it on and placed it on the floor against the room's far wall.

"Look away. Cover your ears," Metal Man instructed upon returning. He was holding a handgun. He aimed and fired a round at the torch.

A small explosion bathed the hallway in a white brilliance. A hot wind hit Kairos, as if he'd been whisked into a convection oven.

A moan arose from the net: Midmay was finally stirring, as if the heat had accelerated her thawing.

"Hang on, Midmay," Kairos assured her. "I'll get you out of there soon."

Kairos followed the spacer in carefully picking his way through what had been the utility room, now strewn with molten debris and part of the ceiling that had caved in, exposing open sky. An acrid smell hung in the air. Where the plasma torch had been was a sizzling, smoking crater. Most of the wall had been blown or melted away.

"Your torch's energy focuser had become unstable," Metal Man said, nodding at the pit. "Had you activated it again, it would've vaporized half your body."

On the other side of what had been the utility room's wall, they emerged into the empty non-space between the adjacent buildings. It was barely wide enough for their shoulders. Most of the buildings surrounding them, including the one which housed the SolarNet café on the ground floor, had only five or six stories, but there was one building several stories taller.

Metal Man holstered his handgun into a slot that extended from his suit's hip—a slot which promptly resealed flush—

then raised an arm, palm down. A tethered projectile launched out of a tube-shaped device affixed to the outside of his forearm. The projectile arced slightly, hitting and then clinging to the tallest building's exterior, several stories up.

Metal Man held Kairos with a firm arm and instructed him to hold the net tightly. The tube on Metal Man's suit began to reel in the line, lifting them all off the ground.

The ascent was painful, their cramped shoulders and knees scraping and banging against the building's exterior, as if they were being dragged through a chimney.

When they had risen high enough to clear the lower buildings' roofs, Metal Man triggered the release of the projectile's hold to set them down. There, Kairos freed Midmay from the net. The girl emerged with wobbly limbs and cast quick glances from Kairos to their rooftop position, trying to make sense of her situation. A scowl indicated that she'd would never willingly return to such confinement again. Upon laying eyes on their armored escort, Midmay's eyes went wide.

Metal Man led them bounding across rooftops—navigating a terrain of habitat-conditioning units, satellite dishes, and solar cell stacks—before using a fire escape to return to ground level.

They next moved down a side street toward a massive skyscraper whose heights stretched even beyond the canyon's rim and into the hazy olive sky.

Passing through a loading bay area, Metal Man terrified a worker into parting with his security badge, which they used on a door leading into the tower.

Inside, they walked through the building's recycling and waste disposal center and found a service elevator. Metal Man scanned the badge and punched a tile for Floor 107, which was about two thirds of the way up.

"Where are we going?" Kairos asked while they rode the elevator, holding Midmay close to his side. "We're trapping ourselves in this tower."

"Rendezvousing with my partner, who's prepping our exit."

The elevator doors slid open.

A wall of warm, humid air greeted them.

Exiting and rounding a corner, they entered an open floor containing uniform rows of dense, bright green vegetation growing neatly in tall, white hydroponic columns. Ample sunlight flowing through the floor's glass-walled perimeter accentuated the spotless airiness of the dichromatic urban farm. The floor was quiet save for a few soft whirs of machinery.

Metal Man led them quickly down one of the rows, swatting aside a hanging robotic arm that was gently assessing some kind of fruit.

Reaching the end, the spacer nearly plowed through two farming technicians who were rounding the corner. They staggered back upon encountering such a hard-edged, imposing spacer in their peaceful sanctuary.

A short stretch of hallway brought them into a vacant corner office. The view outside was of the broad mesa atop the canyon rim, where the city sprawl continued. Farther in the distance, the space elevator stood, its anchor station a lone monument set apart.

But Kairos's attention fell upon a dark brown drone hovering just outside the office's windows. It was etching a large incision into the glass pane with a bright red laser emitting from its front. Once the laser completed a rough rectangular shape, the drone drove itself against the cut section, pushing it into the office, where it toppled with a shatter.

"It's a bird!" Midmay exclaimed, pointing at the drone with glee as it glided into the office and gracefully sank its talons into the back of the desk chair.

"A hybird," clarified Metal Man. "My partner, Rhody." The bird of prey had the body shape and two broad side wings of an Earthling falcon, but also had two additional rotary wings tucked in behind them, protruding from the sides of its back. Its plumage was streaked with cream and chocolate, and dark speckles dotted its underside. However, the creature's eyes were very unnatural: they consisted of short, shiny black eyescopes with red-tinted lenses. Whether the bird retained its natural eyes beneath the scopes wasn't clear. Kairos realized that this hybird was the "drone" that had spotted him and Midmay in the cable car.

"Hi Rhody," Midmay greeted it affectionately. She stretched out a hand to stroke its feathers, but instantly jerked it back as the creature snapped its beak and thrust out its wings in a show of intimidation. With a powerful flap of its side wings, the hybird shot out the window and disappeared around the building's side.

"A cybernetic bird, huh," Kairos wondered aloud.

Metal Man was aiming his wrist tube through the open section of glass and down toward the city buildings on the mesa below. Kairos looked over his shoulder to see where he was aiming.

"Don't stand behind me," the spacer warned.

Two tethered projectiles shot out from the wrist tube simultaneously, one forward toward the city, the other directly backward, lodging itself into the office ceiling. A closer look revealed the projectile to be a gooey, translucent substance, but before Kairos's eyes, the small blob wriggled and hardened into an opaque rigid scaffolding.

"You two will go first," Metal Man said, handing him and Midmay each a simple harness loop withdrawn from his cloak.

"You've got to be kidding," Kairos remarked. He edged himself to the window and looked out. The ultra-thin line must have extended three hundred meters; he couldn't even make out what its terminal end had anchored itself to.

"Rhody's spotted corporates entering the building. They've been tracking you. This is the quickest way to the mesa."

Tracking me? How? Kairos thought. He turned to Midmay, and to his surprise, the girl was excited. She was fairly fearless when it came to new experiences; what she usually feared more were new people. He looped the harness around her back and under her arms and hooked it onto the tether, then did the same for himself, hooking on in front of her.

"Hold onto your harness as tightly as you can," Kairos instructed her. She nodded and pulled her scarf up to her eyes. He did the same with his.

This is crazy.

They kicked off and slid out of the skyscraper.

Kairos's heart skipped a beat when traversing the gap of canyon in between the tower's side and canyon rim. But their speed soon carried them over and the steep ravine immediately converted to city blocks of building roofs not far below.

The tether was anchored to one such roof. Kairos unhooked his line in advance to avoid a collision and fell into a sloppy barrel roll onto the rooftop. The soles of his Maydays effectively dispersed the initial landing impact.

He quickly pivoted to catch Midmay's legs as she zipped

down behind him. Halting her descent knocked him over again.

Metal Man came last. As he progressed down the length, the tube reeled in the forward line while simultaneously letting out additional line behind. After smoothly dropping beside them, the spacer depressed a switch on the tube. Both ends of the tether retracted swiftly with a high-pitched whine.

Once at street level, Metal Man pushed them into a vacant alleyway behind the building on which they'd descended.

Metal Man abruptly shoved Kairos harshly against the stone side of a building. "I want some answers now," Metal Man commanded. "The Blackpool job. Who were you working for, and what did you do with the tech?"

"The what?" Kairos blurted, dumbfounded. "I don't know what you're talking about."

"So you'd like to waste time? I can find ways to waste time." Metal Man lifted him off the ground by his scarf and tossed him back against the wall like a bag of garbage.

Kairos's body slammed against stone, air rushing out of his chest as his lungs compressed violently. His body landed in a crumpled heap.

"I've had a watch out on your ship," Metal Man said. "I saw you land. Beta Block, Gate 273C."

"Stop!" Midmay screamed, kicking and punching uselessly against Metal Man's suit.

Metal Man brushed her away like a crumb. He lifted Kairos by the front of his jacket, shoving him against the wall once more.

"He's a Cleric!" Midmay shouted.

Metal Man paused and his grip relaxed ever so slightly. "You're a holy man?" his voice boomed incredulously.

Kairos reluctantly played along, if it meant the beating would cease. "New Revelationist missionary of the Diocese of Asphis, Greenside."

After a moment, Metal Man lowered Kairos to his feet. "How did you get that ship?"

"Long story." Kairos coughed. "But it's not ours. We took it."

Metal Man kneed him in the stomach, sending Kairos flopping back onto the ground. "Liar. You're no Cleric. Clerics would never steal. One of the Twelve Commandments, you idiot. How about you watch me crush your little friend's skull?"

"Please, stop," Kairos begged. "The ship belonged to a Lienns-Sutra assassin. He died on our planet. It's the truth." Kairos was curled in a rather pathetic fetal position, nursing his abdomen while alternating between coughing and moaning. This seemed to satisfy Metal Man's requirements for determining Kairos was being truthful this time.

"Name?"

"Kairos. That's Midmay."

"No, not you idiots. The assassin."

"Oh. The ship was registered under Badir Saeta."

Metal Man was silent for a moment, then asked, "What planet?"

"Pantoll."

Metal Man gave him another swift kick to the stomach. Kairos let out a loud moan. "There's nothing on Pantoll," Metal Man said.

"My father." Kairos gasped. "Saeta came for my father. My father shot him with that plasma torch." He described Saeta and recounted the assassin's last moments.

Metal Man lifted Kairos and pressed him against the wall. He balled a gauntleted fist.

Kairos flinched, shutting his eyes in anticipation ...

... and jumped at the loud crunching of stone.

Kairos opened his eyes slowly. Metal Man had punched a crater into the wall just beside his head. Although Kairos couldn't see the man's face behind the black visor, the spacer's hung head and silence suggested defeat. Then he had a thought: there might be a desperation there that he could leverage.

"So this Saeta is dead," Metal Man said. "Who is your father?"

Kairos took a risk. "You assure us safe passage off Spires, then I'll tell you. Until then, you'll get nothing more from me. You can threaten to kill me or my friend. We're dead anyway if we can't get off-planet."

There was a blur of motion and Kairos abruptly found himself looking down the barrel of Metal Man's handgun.

"This is your negotiating position," Metal Man said. "Whatever you did to turn yourselves into bounty is your problem."

"It's your problem now too," he said firmly, calling Metal Man's bluff. If Metal Man wasn't willing to bash in his skull, he wouldn't be willing to shoot him either. "You asked about a job called Blackpool? As in Blackpool Laboratories, the science and tech corp? Sounds big time. And if I had to guess, finding this Saeta is crucial for you. You said you've been looking for the *Arcana* for months—that's a long time to be tracking a single trail. Now that trail's gone cold. You need what we know. You'd be foolish to kill us."

"No information you have is worth becoming a target of Lienns-Sutra. The *Arcana*'s shipcom will fill in enough gaps for me."

"Saeta's ship has surely been impounded. You weren't the only one watching for our arrival. Again, you need us."

Silence ensued. Kairos looked resolutely into the smooth, faceless black visor.

At last, Metal Man lowered and holstered the weapon.

Kairos exhaled in relief. It would take several minutes for his heart to calm.

Metal Man's helmet expanded slightly, segmenting itself along grooved lines, then it began to retract, seemingly disappearing into the collar plating.

A woman's face was revealed.

She looked in her early thirties and had almond-colored skin. Her cropped dark hair fell to her cheekbones, swooping over two dull gray eyes that stared intently back at Kairos. Dark circles beneath them hinted at a string of sleepless nights, Kairos guessed space insomnia.

"Deal," she said firmly. "My ship's in a nearby hangar. Let's move."

* * *

The spacer's ship was parked at an older, privately-operated hangar at the outskirts of the city section atop the mesa between canyons.

On the way, Kairos had learned only that the woman's name was Neve and she was an investigator of some kind, under the employ of Blackpool Laboratories. Though Blackpool didn't govern any star systems—and thus wasn't one of the System

Administrators—it was arguably the most technologically advanced corporation. That fact alone made it vastly influential; however, Blackpool was also one of the most private about its affairs, intentionally distancing itself from political or economic allegiances with other corporations, especially the System Administrators. It was common knowledge that Blackpool's primary ambition was to regain humanity's lost scientific knowledge and return human civilization's technological progress to the level it had been on Old Earth. Neve's high-tech exosuit was obviously a relic from humanity's birth planet. Kairos had asked her whether Blackpool had refurbished and lent it to her, among many other questions, but she'd returned no answers.

The hangar bay had a high, curved ceiling. Large, retractable metal doors on either end of its wide interior sat on tracks along the ground. Both were currently open to the airstrip outside.

"Nice ship," Kairos commented as they entered the bay. Like the *Arcana* but slightly smaller, it was a hybrid craft, equipped to enter and exit gravity wells and designed to fly within an atmosphere. "Working for a corporation sure does come with its benefits."

"No, I earned her myself. She's all mine," Neve replied proudly. Kairos still wasn't used to her natural voice after having first heard her helmet speakers' highly distorted, low tone. "May not be big, but she's my home." She pushed ahead of him. "I'll prep for takeoff."

"I thought you said you had watched us land the *Arcana*?" he called out behind her, given this private hangar was far from Hollow City's main public airport, where he and Midmay had arrived.

"I did. Through Rhody's eyes," she said, pointing a finger upward as she continued toward her ship.

Kairos paused to look up. After some effort, he spotted Rhody perched among the shadowy rafters, eying him suspiciously with its piercing stare. It had been waiting for them. He guessed that the hybird was responsible for a lot of Neve's reconnaissance work.

Ahead of him, Neve bio-scanned the ship airlock hatch open.

It would be wise to part ways as soon as we leave Spires, he thought. For a private investigator, the spacer seemed overly zealous. The risks she was taking in pursuing the *Arcana* lead revealed a reckless determination. He had the feeling that whatever her investigation was, it was not proceeding well. Perhaps she had reached the end of her line. Kairos generally didn't trust people who were blindly driven by an overpowering mission. Before parting ways, of course, he had to figure out how to get the Osetran teardrop back from her. Fortunately, the spacer didn't know what it was or its value.

There were a handful of other craft in the hangar bay, a few other hybrids but mostly small airplanes. Midmay was wandering around and in between them, craning her neck to gaze at each. A few were simply blanketed masses, large tarps draped over them for long-term parking.

Rhody let out a short screech.

Kairos looked up. The hybird was agitated, hopping from rafter to rafter with a fidgety ruffling of feathers.

Neve emerged hurriedly from her ship and began yelling something to him when a high-pitched whine interrupted.

Her craft exploded.

The blast knocked him flat onto the hard ground.

Kairos's ears rang and his vision was dotted with bright, shifting puffs of light. He unsteadily lifted himself to his feet.

Neve's ship had been destroyed, its insides burning, flames leaking out its shattered cockpit and viewports. The woman's body had been thrown several meters from where she'd been standing. Thin columns of smoke rose from where her cloak had disintegrated.

He turned and saw them: two corporates, one with a military-grade rocket launcher, one with a wave rifle pointed at him.

A wave bullet sizzled straight through Kairos's chest near the shoulder. The pain was like being skewered with a hot spike.

A moment later, a second wave round tore through his lower leg.

Kairos fell to the ground and screamed. His chest and leg blazed like they'd been dipped in lava. Hot blood began seeping from his shirt.

Overhead, a wild fluttering of wings sounded.

A red laser flashed from above, passing through the corporate with the launcher.

The man's body went slack and toppled to the ground, splitting apart in two horrific pieces as it did so.

The corporate's partner dove and rolled away, then took aim at Rhody. The hybird dove away from the wave bullet's path.

A pair of gunshots sounded from Neve's direction.

Kairos swiveled his neck her way.

The woman stood in full metallic suit—the half-disintegrated cloak having slid off—with two handguns extended. Kairos turned back to find the second corporate dead on the ground.

"Scan the perimeter!" Neve called to Rhody. She strode to where Kairos lay, a fierce scowl darkening her face.

She holstered both guns into her suit's hip slots. From a compartment of her suit, she pulled out a thin tube and, from that, produced a syringe which she thrust directly into his bleeding chest wound.

White fire shot through Kairos's core, down his waist, and up into the back of his skull.

Soon his body grew feverishly hot. His skin began sweating copiously, like a squeezed lemon peel.

Then other involuntary things started happening: his limbs quivered; his gut convulsed violently, as if he'd swallowed a fistful of live worms whole and washed them down with battery acid; his heart rattled at a rate that seemed impossible to sustain.

Kairos gasped for air, seemingly unable to intake enough of it to his body's satisfaction. A heightened sense of the status of every fiber of his being permeated what coherent thought remained to him.

For a long while he lay like that, a pitiful mess writhing and groaning and sweating and rasping through a parched mouth.

At some point, he was able to recognize Midmay. The girl was kneeling beside him, a large water bladder in her arms. She was urging him to drink.

Collecting himself, Kairos found the eternity of torment had subsided—he'd just been too traumatized to have noticed. Sitting up, he lifted the bladder and greedily gulped its contents. As the water coursed coursed down his throat, he could feel his body respond with renewed lifeforce. He drained at least three liters in one go. After pausing for a moment, he took another pull until the bladder was sucked dry. Still a bit thirsty, he asked Midmay for more, but she shook her head. The bladder had been pulled out from Neve's suit.

Refreshed, with his wits restored, Kairos realized the searing pain of his chest wound was absent. His fingers crept to the place where he'd been shot. His shirt was still soaked red with blood, but through the tear in the fabric, he felt only soft smooth skin.

"Rhody saved you!" Midmay exclaimed.

"I'm glad the thing's retained some animal instincts. Where's Neve?"

"Taking things out of her ship. It was blown up. We have to hurry before more bad guys come."

"I understand."

"She's mad at you. She found the public map software you'd downloaded into your goggles. That's how they found us."

He felt foolish for how careless he'd been. Lienns-Sutra had developed the public software. It was probably traceable by design. "Are you okay?" he asked Midmay.

She nodded and pointed at a tarp-covered craft. "I hid inside there."

"Good thinking."

Midmay's demeanor changed. "I have to tell you something," she said, staring sheepishly down at her feet. "Neve was very mad ..."

"What is it?" he prompted, suddenly concerned the spacer had harmed her.

"I ... I told her about the Osetran teardrop. I didn't want to. But she asked me why we came here and why these people want to kill us and I didn't know and—"

"Calm down, it will be okay," Kairos reassured her, squeezing the girl's shoulder. But his spirit fell. Neve was smart to interrogate the girl once alone with her. His informational leverage over the spacer had dissipated.

Kairos made to stand, suddenly remembered his right leg had been shot through, and winced in anticipation of pain.

But none came.

He looked down his leg. Like the one on his chest, the wound had completely healed. All that remained was a smooth patch of pale scarring surrounded by new pink skin.

In disbelief, he walked over to Neve's smoldering craft. The external hull hadn't been breached—its plating was quite strong—but much of the ship's innards had been incinerated. A few small fires were still burning. Luckily, Neve had not been caught inside when the missile struck. A collection of burnt objects lay scattered on the ground beside the ship. Off to the side of them lay a small pack and a tiny pile of items, including Neve's half-ruined cloak and, atop that, his goggles. They were undamaged having been, he assumed, in a pocket on the cloak's front side, which had been protected by her suit from the blast.

Neve emerged from what used to be the entrance airlock, now just a gaping hole since the ajar hatch had been completely blown off. She was carrying out an armful of half-charred objects. After laying them out by the other items, she retracted her helmet and bent to inspect each.

"I am sorry about your—" he started, approaching her.

"Stop," she said curtly, lifting a hand. She turned her gray eyes to him. Behind them was an intensity that belied their fatigue. "You owe me a ship," she stated plainly, saying no more.

He watched in silence as she rolled a few of the charred items around in her hands, ultimately tossing each aside. Finally she stood, abandoning the whole lot in dour resignation.

"Midmay said she told you about why Lienns-Sutra is after us," he said. "About my father. And what he found."

"You should thank her. At this point, I'd decided to simply beat the information out of you. And had you spouted such nonsense, I would've kept beating you until your words started making sense. But the girl doesn't yet know how to lie well, so I trust her word. It appears you truly are as ignorant about your situation as you look."

"That object wasn't a part of our deal. I'd like it back," Kairos said.

"It's part of my investigation now. And if it truly is an Osetran artifact, then consider it your first payment for the loss of my ship."

Kairos opened his mouth to protest, then closed it. For now, there was no use arguing. He couldn't overpower her, and he and Midmay needed her to get safely off Spires. "I thought you didn't want to become a target of Lienns-Sutra," he said. "That thing would put you in their bullseye."

"The man who killed your father wasn't corporate," Neve responded. "He was a freelance assassin."

"But Lienns-Sutra hired him."

"No, L-S has in-house resources they trust for that line of work, whose appearances and methods are more subtle and precise than the tough-guy spacer you described." Neve pointed to the bodies of the two dead men in the hangar. "Though they're dressed to look the part, they're not with the Organization either."

"The two corporates that found us at the antiques dealer told us they worked for Lienns-Sutra," Kairos said. "They seemed to fit the mold."

Neve shrugged. "Then they were good liars."

"But they'd been tracing us ..."

"Not too difficult to do. L-S corporates wouldn't stoop to such poor procedure, as to fire at you in broad daylight in their system's capital. It goes against an Administrator's tacit agreement with the populace to provide law and order. In any case, if L-S wanted you, they'd have stopped you at Orbital Security the moment you weaved in-system and then whisked you into a holding cell."

She's right, Kairos thought. If Lienns-Sutra had hired Saeta, they would have had a special interest in the *Arcana*. They certainly would've been alerted by the ship's arrival at the orbital gateway, even if the gateway's scanners missed detecting the assassin's dead body—which already was a stretch. "Then who are all these agents with?" he asked.

"Exactly." The investigator sighed, bending to stash the tiny pile of salvageable items that survived the blast into her pack.

"By the way, thanks for healing me," Kairos said. "What was that stuff you injected into me?"

"It's called Overclock. A hyperstim. Accelerates the body's metabolic rate. Besides speeding up select bodily functions, it promotes rapid healing."

"My insides felt like they were melting."

"Well, all drugs have their little side-effects. With the dosage I gave you, I'd say you lost about ten standard months off your back end."

"What?"

"Your lifespan."

He gaped at her in horror.

"The induced cell regeneration is basically a form of accelerated aging," she explained, as if it were obvious.

"So my body is a year older now than it was fifteen minutes ago?"

"Would you rather it be fifteen minutes deader than it was fifteen minutes ago?" She shook her head in disbelief. "You're lucky I had it. It's illegal for street use. Military-grade. Costly stuff, you get it?"

"I guess I should be thankful for your generosity, then." He shook his head. "I thought you were toast from that blast."

"Not the first time my exosuit has saved my life."

"Also military-grade? Is that who you used to be? CorpSoldier? Mercenary?"

Neve didn't answer but finished packing and slung the pack around her suit's broad shoulder.

"Where are you going? You can't leave us like this," Kairos said.

"I said I would get you off-planet, and I always uphold my end of a deal," she said resolutely, as if offended he would suggest otherwise. "A tram from this hangar will take us to the monorail line that runs between the elevator anchor station and the city. On the way up, you'll share with me every detail about your father's work including all professional and personal contacts. Midmay told me Saeta killed him. When we reach Counterport, we'll part ways. Then pray we never cross paths again."

"Fine. But how are we are going to take the elevator without being flagged by the screening?"

"I've called in a favor from someone who works in Orbital Security. That'll take care of our IDs and travel passes. As for the security cams, I'm still working on it. We'll need to find a way to knock them out. Or wear some really convincing disguises, but I can't describe to you how much I'd like to avoid that."

"Why don't we just access the security system and turn the cameras off while we're passing through security?" Midmay piped up.

Neve laughed. "Turning off the cameras, of course. Why didn't I think of that? And while we're at it we can get them to waive our elevator pass fees, upgrade us to first-class, promise me a new ship, and apologize for how we were treated during our time here."

"Well, I think I can tell you're being sarcastic about a new ship," Midmay responded, taken aback. "I'll see about the pass fees and first-class tickets, but I can't promise anything. Financial transactions are usually handled in different systems than security," she added with a tone that implied she was surprised Neve didn't know that.

Neve's eyebrows furrowed and her head tilted. "The girl's serious?" she remarked to Kairos.

"She's quite extraordinary," he replied with a shrug. "I've seen her hack into private SolarNet channels."

"My friend Johnathan taught me," Midmay said, eyevisor lowered and data-gloved hands starting their command gesticulations.

"Oh. Johnathan. Well then, got it," Neve said, her tone still laced with sarcasm. "Is hacking and walking at the same time also something you can do?"

"I got it," Kairos said. He lifted Midmay to sit atop his shoulders. Her hands and fingers continued working all the while.

Neve raised a brow at him. "You understand that elevator fares aren't cheap?"

He nodded and, after she pressed him, did his best to settle her concerns about his ability to pay without disclosing his full account balance.

"Good," Neve said, leading the way to the hangar exit. "Because you're buying for three. Plus you're covering the bribe."

Kairos didn't believe her when she told him the amount needed—it'd require over half the proceeds from his sale of Johnathan's precious parts. "I thought you said you called in a favor?" he protested.

"Accepting a bribe *is* the favor," she replied.

Chapter 6

Their ride on the high-speed monorail to the space elevator's anchor station was uneventful—despite Kairos's paranoia that one of the passengers would suddenly reveal themselves to be a disguised assailant and lunge at them with something sharp. At the station, he, Midmay, and Neve boarded the next climber's passenger module without incident. There had been no issue in acquiring their travel passes under the fake IDs Neve's contact had assigned them. They also had sailed through the station's security checkpoint, thanks to Midmay triggering the security cams to reboot due to a fictitious "critical software update" right as they entered the checkpoint flow. The girl's work impressed even Neve.

The module's seating was comfortable and Kairos finally allowed himself to relax a little. It'd been too long since he'd gotten quality sleep, and the constant need to be alert had depleted what little energy he had left. Not to mention the continuous toll that the burden of additional gravity was taking on his every muscle. Once all passengers were fastened, the seats rotated so that everyone was lying on their backs, and the acceleration upward was similar to a spacecraft launch.

Kairos had only ever ridden up an elevator once before, the time he'd left Greenside. Little had he known, looking down at the withdrawing forested hills, grasslands, winding rivers, and sparkling oceans, that it'd be the last time he'd see such natural beauty.

When the climber's lifters achieved their near-final traveling speed, the pressure against their bodies fell away. The lifters continued to provide only enough acceleration to provide passengers with artificial gravity to walk about the module. Spire's olive green atmosphere outside the module windows had given way to a deep blackness pinpricked with twinkles of white, blue, and yellow starlight.

Neve sat quietly across from him, inspecting her exosuit, running system diagnostics, and cleaning various pieces of equipment, including her handgun and the modified tether launcher, which he learned was called a deployer—or "ploy" for short—and normally used by space workers as a navigational and anchoring tool in zero-*g*. She worked with a calm efficiency, but watching her face closely he caught flickers of an underlying pain or bitterness that betrayed her outer composure. No doubt it had to do with the loss of her ship, which was no less than a life-altering setback even if a portion of it was insured. He could tell she resented needing to ride to Counterport—on the tram to the anchor station, she'd condescendingly referred to the elevator as "public transportation."

Kairos wondered about Neve's background. While working at Dusty's over the years, he'd served a few bounty hunters who strolled in asking for a drink but really wanting local information. Backwater planets like Pantoll attracted the occasional fugitive and debtor. The bounty hunters never disclosed their profession, but something about their presence—their heightened situational awareness, sharp eyes, precise movements, the glint of a metal barrel or blade under locally purchased ponchos—conveyed they meant serious business. Neve's self-description as an "investigator" sounded like one of the many softer, euphemistic terms bounty hunters gave when pressed to describe their trade. However, so far as he'd observed, Neve was different. No less relentless or deadly, that much was sure. But she seemed to operate under a more personal motivation. For bounty hunters, other than perhaps a scrap of some basic shared code among predators, money was the sole motivator. It was not an incentive born of greed or luxury, but of a primitive will to survive. Most bounty hunters barely scraped by financially—the price of a human life wasn't grand enough to support a lucrative career. Hunters whose bounties were few and far between either died out or, worse, grounded out never to fly again, like aged, decrepit predators no longer fast enough to secure meat from a herd of prey. Money was lifeblood, human gasoline. And so it was the pure and simple object of their worship. But Neve lacked the cold detachment characteristic of followers of that religion, and whatever her true motives were, they hardly seemed so simple.

On the way to the space elevator, Kairos had decided that he would discover the truth about the Osetran artifact himself. He sensed the device and its message were valuable, perhaps even vital to the survival of humankind. Furthermore, the guilt he'd felt at the antique shop in considering to sell the teardrop had only grown since. Like it or not, the artifact was his family's legacy. Maybe his old man actually had found something important. Not even his father had deserved to die as he did. Kairos once believed in the principles of justice. He couldn't deny his rising desire to seek it for humble Wells Catadyn.

But if these were the only reasons to risk his life, Kairos, if he were being honest with himself, would have opted to abandon lofty notions of altruism and justice, let Neve keep the Osetran artifact, and find a quiet corner of a core world where he could start over in anonymity. The truth was that the shifting of the spiritual winds that Kairos had sensed upon launching off Pantoll had only intensified since. As if God wouldn't stop poking him until he accepted his fate: to unravel the object's mystery. That all the evil and suffering he'd experienced on Pantoll had *prepared* him for this calling. Since the day of the chapel fire, Kairos had hardened himself against such stirrings, but now they overwhelmed him, as did his guilt which he could no longer bear. Even a thin chance for a clean conscience, for redemption, was worth seeking. In order to fulfill this mission, he needed an ally. Naive or not, he'd decided he would trust Neve and seek her help. He'd offer his assistance to her in return; if he read the exhausted desperation in her eyes right, she might just need it too. *Okay God*, he thought, *I'll humor your whims this time, but whatever happens is all on you.*

Rhody perched silently above them on the ledge of a cargo compartment. Prior to boarding, Neve had donned it with a custom, forest green cloak that shrouded its entire body except for its taloned claws and the tip of its beak. From beneath the dark hood, Rhody's eyescopes glowed a dull red rather than their usual bright crimson. The hybrid stood motionless, giving it a mysterious, majestic appearance as though it were a medieval gargoyle. Neve had told them that its species was remarkably intelligent, which is what had led military units of past wars to cybernetically enhance and train them for espionage and reconnaissance. In addition to its ocular implants, Rhody's modifications included a specialized biOS connected to a neural slave chip. The hybird was a closed system; the embedded hardware fed directly off its metabolism and internal electric current. As such, it needed to eat frequently. During down times, it primarily rested to recover and conserve energy.

Midmay was missing from her seat having run off some-where. It was impossible to keep her from exploring the levels of the passenger module. The last time she had returned to their seats, she had brought them each a container of *CommonRamen* self-instant noodles that she must've hacked out of one of the module's vending machines. In his hunger, he'd easily forgiven the small crime and slurped down the cheap, rubbery noodles mixed with fake imitation crab. Neve's container still lay untouched on the empty seat beside her where Midmay had set it down for her. He pointed to it, Neve shook her head, and he gobbled it up as well.

Belly warm and full, fatigue must have finally overtaken him because the next thing he knew, he gently awoke in his seat. The module was quiet and dim, its lights switched off so that the only illumination came from the stray light of the sun. The other passengers were asleep in their seats. Beside him, Midmay, like some nocturnal creature, lay sprawled on her back across three seats, eyevisor on, gesticulating datagloved fingers silently above her, lost in the expanse of the SolarNet.

Kairos adjusted his body position to fall back asleep. Through half-closed eyes and in a hazy stupor, he viewed Neve sitting calmly across from him, head turned toward the window. She was staring off into space, face frozen in a profound melancholy, traces of inscrutable wistfulness in her pale gray eyes.

His heavy eyelids sank again.

* * *

"Get up," Neve ordered, kicking his leg with her metallic boot.

Kairos straightened groggily in his seat and winced at the new pain in his shin.

The cabin lights were back on. Some passengers were chatting, while others were up shuffling around, eager to disembark from the cramped module.

"We're not far from Counterport," Neve said. "From there, you can hitch a ride with a trader back to that backwater you call home or, if you've got some sense, to anywhere else. It's time to talk."

Kairos shook away the sleep. Gathering his thoughts, he proceeded to tell Neve about his father, his work on Pantoll, his scant relationships, his employee Falck, and the little he'd learned of the Osetran device from the antiques dealer on Spires. Neve's demeanor varied from mildly bored to disappointed throughout. After he finished, she asked several questions about the artifact, nearly all the same unanswered ones he had.

"How can you know so little about what your father worked half his life to find?" she finally complained, exasperated.

They sat in silence for several moments. Then Kairos asked, "Since you're investigating Saeta for Blackpool, do you think that job and his trip to Pantoll were somehow related?"

Neve snorted. "That's the obvious question."

"Can you tell me about the Blackpool job? Maybe I can help connect some dots?"

Neve leaned back into her seat and waved a hand to brush aside his offer like the useless gesture it was. "I've gathered all I can from your end of things," she said. "Just another dead end."

"But you know the man's name now," countered Kairos. "Isn't that important?"

Neve smirked. "Badir Saeta was just the name on the ship's registration. A professional assassin uses countless aliases and regularly cycles new ones. The name is useless." After a moment, she sat up in alert. "Were you wearing those the night you came across the dead assassin?" she asked, pointing to his collar.

"Yeah," Kairos replied, reflexively fingering the goggles around his neck. "As I said, there was a huge storm. I was driving Midmay's lightcycle and—" Kairos's face brightened. "Video!" he exclaimed. "My goggles recorded the *Arcana* as it went down."

Kairos subvocalized a few commands to bring up his vision recording archive and play back the most recent entry. He transmitted it to Neve's helmet visor's internal display.

"Oh, this is good ... this is very good," murmured Neve, unable to hide her enthusiasm when the video arrived at the body of the dead spaceman.

"Can you identify him?" Kairos asked, tugging the goggles back down around his neck.

"I know people who can."

"And what about my father's employee Falck? We might

still find him on Pantoll."

Neve shook her head. "A nobody. Saeta is the real connection. Besides, going to Pantoll isn't worth the risk of being stranded on that planet. With so little ship traffic, who knows how long I could be stuck there.

Kairos nodded with her reasoning.

"And by the way, there is no *we*," she stated flatly. "This is not a partnership situation."

"Whoever employed Saeta is powerful. I want justice, just like you. I think we can help each other. We should work together."

"No. You'd only be dead weight. You can't even protect yourselves."

"Hear me out. I may not be much good in a fight, but I know a lot about the Osetra, knowledge that could come prove valuable."

Neve shook her head with a tightened jaw and looked away.

"Look at me," he insisted. Neve turned to face him. "My father was murdered," he stated, looking squarely in her gray eyes. "I don't know if I can ever bring his killers to justice. But I need to at least know what he died for. What secrets this Osetran device holds. Is that something you can understand?"

A crack registered in Neve's icy gaze. She turned her face to the window for a long time. Kairos could sense the internal debate raging within her.

"Yeah, I know the feeling," she said finally, still gazing out the window. She slowly turned back to meet his eyes. "I couldn't guarantee your safety, much less the girl's."

"No way to guarantee it anyway."

"I'm leaving the Lilic System. Do you understand what that means?"

He did: it meant he'd need to spend most of his remaining points to join Neve to wherever she was headed. Interstellar travel was so expensive that he'd be stuck wherever he happened to be when his finances ran out. And he definitely wouldn't be able to afford a return trip to Pantoll. As for himself, he'd already decided to leave his time on Pantoll behind. But for Midmay, it'd mean never returning home. It wasn't just his fate he was deciding.

He swallowed, wet his dry lips, and nodded. "I understand," he answered.

The spacer gave a nod. They were in it together, then.

* * *

Not long after, Kairos carefully asked Neve about her investigation. He hoped that his being open with her about his father and the artifact would encourage reciprocation on her end.

Neve hesitated, then let out a sigh and leaned forward closely to him. "Here's the short of it," she began in a hushed tone. "For a while now, Blackpool has been pouring resources into researching human brain chemistry and reinventing integrated neural units. They're the makers of everything from top-of-the-line neurocom chips, to sensory stimulators, to cheap inserts."

"Of course I know them. I've developed virtual worlds myself. Their tech is all over VR suits. Owned by the Farrin family. Bunch of their top researchers are also Farrins, descended from the original founders. Known for being a tightly sealed organization. Closed off to the outside world.

But with the science they've been able to re-learn, guess it makes sense."

"Good, you know something then. What you don't know is that over the last several standard years, they've been developing a neurofluid that alters brain chemistry to allow for interhuman networked communication."

"What do you mean? Like ... telepathy?"

Neve nodded. "Not only instantaneous thought-sharing, but also the sharing of knowledge, emotions, possibly even memories. True wetware, going way beyond what neurocom chips can do."

"How is that even possible?"

Neve shrugged. "If it's legit, it'd be *actual* innovation, not just re-invention."

She was right. Kairos didn't know of any post-Exodus technology that matched Old Earth levels, much less exceeding beyond them.

"The wetware is the culmination of many years of research and development," continued Neve. "The most recent clinical tests must have been successful, because they've developed the first prototypes. About nine standard months ago, a Blackpool transport carrying samples of the prototype was attacked. From the *Asterisk*'s transmissions, before communications ceased, we know that it was attacked by four ships, one of which managed to board the *Asterisk*. The ships were unmarked, unregistered, and running without transponders."

"Pirates?"

"That would be the obvious answer. Blackpool's later analysis of the *Asterisk*'s remains and surrounding debris field—which included three ships destroyed by the *Asterisk*'s auto-defenses—seemed to confirm the crew's transmissions.

No survivors were detected. The *Asterisk*'s hull had been breached, and the neurofluid prototypes were gone."

"The fourth ship that wasn't destroyed—that was the *Arcana*."

She nodded. "The *Asterisk*'s screens had scanned enough of his ship's design for me to recreate an image and bribe several orbital gateway and spaceport operators to keep an eye out for it."

He shook his head. "How do you know all this? Even if Blackpool hired you to investigate, you're still an outsider to them."

"Blackpool granted me limited access to understand the attack and the research project's basics. But what specific details I know I've gathered from my own inside source."

"Given its highly confidential nature, why isn't Blackpool running the investigation themselves?"

"Officially, they are. But there's a sensitivity around the situation that requires an outside view. Duresma Farrin herself, part of Blackpool's Executive triumvirate, brought me in. She suspects there may be a mole within the organization, someone who's selling research data and trade secrets to a rival corporation. She doesn't know who, and she doesn't trust anyone internally. Even the other Blackpool Executives don't know the full nature of my investigation."

"And you don't think it's pirates ..."

"Pirates attack distroships. Caravans. Minor corps' transports. The occasional passenger ship. They even attack each other. Attempting to steal from a major corporation is suicide.

"Putting that aside, the attackers would've needed to have known the precise coordinates of the *Asterisk* along its undisclosed route. Another thing—their shoddy ships stood no chance against an armed, more advanced Blackpool ship, much less maneuver close enough to successfully board. Something's off about the whole raid. Oh, and the *Asterisk*'s hull had been breached by an internal explosive. So a charge wasn't set by the boarding party. They had help—on the inside as well as outside backers."

"Any ideas who?"

Neve leaned back in her seat. "Nothing informed, just speculation. A lot of corporations would kill for a vial of the neurofluid. But there was nothing we could trace from the pirates' ships. As you noted, Saeta was my best lead. Until your father bored a hole through him."

"So," he mused. "Saeta is a part of a job that steals wildly advanced tech that enables telepathy. Months later, he shows up on Pantoll to acquire an artifact from a telepathic race. I see the potential connection. I understand your interest in my father's affairs now."

Neve nodded. "Your video confirms Saeta was a professional, which supports my belief that the destruction of the *Asterisk* wasn't committed by pirates. It was a planned job, and as such, a trail may yet exist. I ran his face through a database while you were sleeping. Found barely anything other than that he's male. When we get to Counterport, we'll find a caravan headed through the Keruah Wastes. I've got a few contacts at the Oasis."

Kairos leaned back and exhaled. He'd read about the lawless Oasis. Eying Neve, he said, "So you're cozy with the assassin crowd, eh?"

"Our skill sets are similar."

"I bet."

* * *

Counterport was one massive spinning wheel, a simple hub-and-spoke design for streamlined functionality and efficiency. Viewed from a distance, it might look like it belonged to a celestial chariot of the gods that had lost a wheel while racing across the galaxy. Bumps along the outer side of the smooth torus represented scores of docking bays. Along the torus's underside and topside, uneven forests of crane arms, lifters, and reacher-stackers grew around the platforms where commercial freighters and other larger vessels anchored.

The elevator's tether climber had decelerated rapidly and brought their passenger module to a smooth halt within the port's central hub station. The cargo modules above and below them would be unloaded and reloaded by crews working in separate commercial service bays extending out from the hub.

Exiting the module into the crowded, zero-*g* hub station disoriented Kairos. He barely managed to keep Neve in sight amid the criss-cross of travelers darting through and around them as he clumsily pulled himself along handrails toward the hub's curved perimeter. Weightless movement seemed to come naturally to Midmay, who zipped on ahead of him, trailing Neve closely like a loyal puppy.

At the station's perimeter, Neve browsed glowing wall signage until she found the right spoke lift. As they traveled through the spoke, gravity increased, soon giving rise to the sensation of going "down." The lift doors opened to Counterport's main ring level, where walking was possible. Neve's exosuit drew a few looks from other travelers, but he soon observed that spacesuited port workers and travelers weren't an unusual sight around the station.

They had passed by multiple docking bays until Neve found one that, as she described, "emanated a vibe of opportunity." How she discerned that, he couldn't guess, but it ultimately meant one with a discreet, ever-angry ship captain who asked few questions while effortlessly—but relentlessly—moving money from others' pockets into his own. Kairos winced as nearly the last of his points left him.

Most of the distroships in this section of bays belonged to traders traveling in the same caravan. Caravans provided increased protection from piracy since there'd be at least a couple ships involved with some level of armaments. Joint weaving required less energy per ship than weaving individually, thereby reducing transport costs. Spires was one stop among many along the long trade route—called the Milk Road by traders—that incorporated all of the major developed planetary systems and a few offshoot locales. To help make the economics work and pick up some additional profit margin, it was common for traders to take on some impromptu passenger business at each of their stops to fill in any shipping capacity gaps. For the traveler on a bare-bones budget, it was the only way to space travel, as long as one didn't mind taking the scenic route.

"Find a seat in the front cargo hold, the one with the tanks," the pale, lean captain had told them gruffly once a rate was agreed upon. "Keep your hands off the goods and we won't have any problems."

"Travel time to the Oasis?" Neve had asked.

"Twelve cycles." The brusque captain, having no more time for them now that he had their fare, then left to bark commands to the docking bay's servicemen.

Twelve standard days, Kairos thought dismally. And he had thought the four standard day trip from Pantoll to Spires had been bad.

The cargo hold was dimly lit, dank, and windowless. So much for having a view. The makeshift passenger couches that had been erected at the hold's rear were aged and decrepit. The soiled cushioning had long blackened from years' worth of scum and grime, and the foam, some of which was exposed in moldy yellow tufts through tears in the recliners' fabric, had lost all springiness. The three of them shared such accommodations with a handful of equally pitiful souls, all of them haggard, depressed, hungry, or some combination thereof.

An unbearable miasma of musty and pungent odors from past and present eclectic shipments hung in the weakly recycled air. Filling half of the space and anchored to the ship walls were a series of stacked, colossal salt water tanks. They were all jam-packed with the same live species of elongated tubular fish, which had pointed heads and slack mouths exposing prominent fang-like teeth. The sealed aquariums nearly touched the top of the hold, their dark turquoise water illuminated eerily by the hold wall's circular inset lamps.

Shortly after the caravan departed Counterport, the individual ships grouped up and executed the first of many joint weaves. According to Neve, after a couple brief stops at lesser systems outside the Core Four, their route ahead would traverse the Keruah Wastes, one of the Milk Road's longest empty expanses between developed worlds at over seventeen parsecs, a distance requiring about thirty-five standard days to weave across for an average-sized ship. The Oasis was the only solid matter of any kind at which to stop in between.

Despite the wondrous technology of the weave drives—which repeatedly "unstitched" and "restitched" matter in and out of space/time to convey ships across distances at implied speeds thousands of times faster than that of light—the voyage was a brutal reminder of just how far apart everything really was in the universe.

The journey indeed proved to be every bit as long as it had sounded. There wasn't much to do except wait it out.

Kairos was quite used to a humble living on Pantoll—to Neve's astonishment, neither he nor Midmay grew tired of eating the same rehydrated goop day after day from the single, large, dry packmeal block from which all passengers were fed (standard fare for low-budget space backpackers, she explained)—however, it was the confinement that gnawed at him. Kairos spent many of his waking hours in zero-*g* out of the uncomfortable recliner to stretch his muscles and keep his mind occupied. He passed some of the time trying to discover what trade products were being carried by the hold's pallets, shipping containers, and compression sacks.

Rhody, for one, didn't seem bothered in the slightest by the accommodations. It had perked up after they boarded, and immediately sprung from its hold behind Neve's shoulder plate to stretch its four wings and find a perch somewhere high up in the shadows of the voluminous interior. Kairos was at once impressed and amused by the hybird's agile float-flying; it was certainly well-accustomed to zero-*g* maneuvering.

Neve seemed to have warmed up considerably to Midmay since the girl's display of her hacking talent. He occasionally spied the two of them together, usually with Neve explaining something to Midmay or demonstrating how her integrated exosuit and helmet visor display functioned. She even called Rhody over to point out this and that on the four-winged creature, and let Midmay don her helmet to experience what it was like to view the world through the hybird's scopes. Everything entranced the girl. For the first time he could remember, he wasn't the worn-down object of her incessant curiosity, and he couldn't help smiling each time Neve would politely tell the inquisitive girl that that was enough questions for now. Then Neve would lean back and shut her eyes or move away to be alone for a while in a quiet corner of the hold.

During the few times he tried engaging the investigator in conversation, he learned nothing of Neve's past. She didn't seem to have one at all. She deftly evaded personal topics, speaking instead of other things. Her knowledge of the ins and outs of how the worlds operated and the key players was impressive. She listened and nodded with muted but polite interest when he told her about his background and the many things he'd read about. Only later did he consider that much of what he'd read about she'd probably experienced first-hand.

And then there were the other passengers traveling with them. One was a thin businessman wearing a baggy, faded suit and worn shoes. He'd lugged three giant chests onboard, and during the journey he made rounds peddling an assortment of odds and ends to everyone: used circuitry components, clothing made from Eukian sheep wool, data tabs, mahjong tiles, Styke divination cards, polyocular strips, garden variety drug hypos, pocket-sized Obasanjo New Revelationist Bibles. Another of the travelers was a cadaverous mother with a bundled-up baby she rocked closely to her breast and kept mostly out of sight under mountainous folds of blankets. The mother hadn't uttered a single word to anyone during the voyage and isolated herself in a corner of the hold that she'd made her nest. She had the kind of quiet strength that could only be explained by years of an inexhaustible determination to persevere. One look at her indicated that an extraordinary story lurked just beneath the surface of her hunched body, perhaps from a planet or moon she had left behind—but it seemed it would be a story never published and never read.

Three of the passengers were a group of young musicians—two men and a woman—on an indefinite tour around the worlds, hitching rides on caravan ships and stopping to play wherever they were accepted. Originally from Greenside, the three friends had completed their formal studies and worked local administrative positions for a bit before deciding to quit their jobs, pool their savings, and hit the endless black road with no plan other than, as they put it, to "imbibe directly and fully from the diverse, deep wells of human experience." The nomads' next stop was the Oasis, where they would play gigs for as long as they could keep finding them. Then they'd move on again. They'd brought no baggage save for their encased instruments: a keyboard, a high-tech saxophone, and a large, antique Old Earth double bass—the last surely a family heirloom.

The final passenger was an emaciated elderly man. He was bundled in layers of mismatched jackets, smelled like burnt mushrooms, and exuded foul breath whenever he coughed or spoke. He reminded Kairos, actually, of the majority of the old folks residing on Pantoll.

"Travelin' far?" the man had suddenly asked him at one point. It had taken a moment for Kairos to realize he was being spoken to.

"I suppose we all are," he'd replied with dry sarcasm,

hoping to thwart the old man's intention of conversing with him. "Light years, you know."

But the man considered the statement seriously. "Yes," he said with a grave, shaky nod. "Well said. We have to be thankful for that while we still can." The man settled into a reflective silence.

"What do you mean by 'while we still can'?" Kairos prompted reluctantly, curiosity getting the best of him.

"Oh, I just mean that all of the weave drives will soon be gone, leavin' everyone to remain on their own world. No more runnin' from problems then. And there'll be plenty of new problems to deal with."

Kairos let out a snort. "Whatever you say, old timer."

The old man persisted. "I'll tell you a thing. Somethin' most folk don't know. Not a single new weave drive has been manufactured since the collapse of Ol' Earth. All the drives you see in ships built since, they're salvaged from retired ones and reused. When I was a young man, I did a stint at Kast Shipyards, saw the operation myself. It's the worlds' worst little secret: no one—not the corporations, not anyone— knows how to construct one."

Kairos scoffed. "That's ridiculous. Even if the manufacturing know-how ever did become spotty, existing drives could just be reverse engineered."

"Reverse engineered!" The withered man cackled. "Simply rip the thing open and study its insides for insights. Easy-peasy, eh? Oh, the corporations have tried. You can damn well believe they've tried their asses off. Sunk enough investment into the problem to feed an entire planet for a generation.

"Let me give you a bit of history, young friend. After the partnership with those aliens ended, there were only a small handful of physicists and engineers on Old Earth who truly understood even half of the technology and its underlying concepts. Sure, they'd studied under the Osetra, but the science was advanced to the point of being completely foreign to us humans. And as we know, the aliens one day just left, and they didn't leave behind any textbooks—ha!

"For a short while, attempts to replicate the manufacturin' process were successful, but like many industries, things ground to a halt when everything went haywire. War every-where, nations crumblin', mass migrations, people lost or disappeared, corporations goin' bankrupt left and right like grilled flies. A real mess. Most knowledge on the subject had to be self-taught by the next generation—and good luck with that, eh? In any case, soon there weren't any more new physicists, engineers, doctors, academics, or what have you bein' educated anyway.

"Well," he wrapped up resignedly, "you may not lose sleep over any of this. Few people do. After all, things seem fine, and plenty of ships are flyin' around out there, right? But keep in mind that most of the drives' ages are roughly within the same band. At first, just a few more than usual will conk out. Then greater and greater waves of burned out drives will follow. All the worlds require trade to maintain their current livin' standards. Many aren't at all self-sufficient. So once the drives are gone ..." The man paused. "World-wide extinctions."

Kairos admittedly had checked out a bit during the old man's rant. "So what," he said to lighten the mood, "you go around spreading the doom like a prophet?"

The pale, gaunt man cackled. "Ha! I don't have to be a prophet. Drive failure is already on the rise. But no one has put the pieces together because no one wants to. We've never responded well to bad news; it only causes us to hurtle ourselves into a faster death spiral. The System Administrators have known all this, but attempts at collaboration toward a solution is like tellin' a crowd aboard a sinkin' ship that they have to decide whose children to save. You'd think the core worlds' interdependence on each other's resources would yield cooperation, but it instead leads to System Administrators clamoring for technological leverage over each other."

At that moment, Kairos considered the accelerating rise in spacecraft prices, especially within the past year. Could there be some truth to this crazy old man's claims?

Later, Kairos wondered if his father had known about such a weave drive problem. Kairos knew that most Osetran artifacts were locked away in corporate vaults, subjects of avid study. Any pieces not in their hands the corporations sought after viciously—Kairos's teardrop was the latest example. Was solving the technology behind the weave drive a reason why?

Or perhaps the old man had made it all up, a fantastical narrative spawned from too many months spent in dingy cargo holds. Kairos had read about a psychological phenomenon called 'dark fatigue' that could set in like dry rot upon those undergoing prolonged durations alone in space, where the endlessly flowing river of time was so expansive as to lose its tangible dimensions. In the absence of natural ways of discerning time's passage—sunsets, seasons, weather— spacefarers glided soundlessly through a largely formless, immutable non-land with no borders, no horizons, and no waypoints. Over time, this was found to have a debilitating effect upon the human mind, its faculties of memory and identity. Kairos was sure he'd seen dark fatigue expressed in a few of the tired, emaciated traders that passed through Dusty's SolarNet Café. Sleep cycles become irregular and stretch far beyond normal intervals. Memories become dateless, faraway ideas, increasingly shaped more by their owner's psyche than historical reality. The mind could then lose track of itself, become derailed from its linear arrangement of past and present through which it forms and makes sense of its own narrative. It would instead then construct new narratives to provide the necessary structure to explain the things happening around it. Brains are supercomputers, after all. Problem solving machines. When asked "why?" about anything, they'll go right on to generate a list of palatable explanations.

Kairos had asked himself 'why' questions his whole life. Why had his father valued a treasure hunt over his wife? Why had Midmay's father abandoned her? Why had God allowed Kairos—someone who had dedicated his life to God's work— to suffer and shrivel up? His brain faithfully supplied him with many possible explanations, but one above them all: it was God's Will. God had a great Plan. Only He held the answers. Kairos used to believe that were he faithful enough, God would reveal them in due time. That was until the biggest "why," the one that had caused Kairos to conclude there were no reasons, and prayer was merely babbling to the wind: *Why had God performed a miracle to save that girl's life, only for my sin to kill her in the end?*

* * *

And so the long, cold time aboard the caravan ship passed.

Out of boredom, late on their sixth standard day of travel, Kairos floated high up alongside the tall stack of aquariums, where densely packed schools of dull-eyed, expressionless fish stared at him accusingly through the acrylic glass prison with their lidless bulbous eyes, as if saying, *You think* your *life's bad?* True; given the run-in with those agents on Spires, he should be happy to be even traveling at all. The tanks' turquoise glow under the light of the inset wall lamps reminded Kairos of the white-green light that had flashed off the Osetran artifact's surface when his father had first lifted it from the shaft.

Kairos reached the uppermost tank. A sliding lid covered its top. An idea formed in his mind. He unclipped the lid's securing pins and slid it open several centimeters. A globule of water began to slowly rise from the tank and shape-shift. Kairos withdrew the teardrop from his coat, regarding it for a moment.

He then dunked it into the tank.

Upon contact with the cold water, the artifact illuminated into a dull green orb.

Kairos, temporarily taken by surprise, fumbled and lost hold of it. Meanwhile, the tank's school of at least one hundred fish had launched themselves toward his dangling hand.

He yanked it from the tank, barely dodging the razor-lined jaws of the lead fish.

The carnivore's momentum sent it shooting out of the tank into weightless space, its jaws still snapping at Kairos even as it sailed by.

Kairos slammed the lid shut against all the incoming jaws. Exhaling in relief, he turned and spotted the one escapee drifting off after ricocheting against the hold's ceiling, writhing in suffocation.

The commotion had unsettled the tank's water. The teardrop now lay deep within, and agonizingly just a couple centimeters from his eyes on the other side of the thick polyplex. Any wonder at the artifact's reaction to the liquid was overwhelmed by the terror of being separated from it. The school's hungry lidless eyes watched him, as if provoking him to reach in elbow-deep to try and retrieve his lost possession. Such an attempt would only result in the additional loss of his arm.

Failing to think of a solution to retrieve the teardrop after several minutes and feeling foolish, Kairos returned to the recliners, where most of the other passengers, including Neve and Midmay, had gone to sleep for the "evening." Strapping himself into his own, he lay wide-eyed for a long time before sleep overtook him.

The next "morning," he told Neve what had happened. Unworried, she moved toward the tanks, telling him that she'd simply reach in with suited arm and pluck the artifact out. But upon reaching the uppermost tank, they were greeted with a shock. The school of flesh-eating fish were dead. Over a hundred lifeless bodies floated in dense clumps of mass death, mouths frozen limp, eyes glazed.

But the most disturbing sight was that a black wiry filament had protruded from the tip of the teardrop—now no longer glowing—and buried its terminal end into the meaty side of one of the dead fish.

* * *

At last, after twelve long cycles—of which Kairos's goggles's universal standard clock had kept dutiful track—the gravelly, uninterested voice of the captain crept out of the hold's scratchy intercom, announcing that the caravan was approaching the Oasis.

The ragtag group of travelers in the cargo hold fastened themselves into their couches for deceleration. Save for the old man, all had had as much as they could take of the fetid accommodations. Docking and freedom from the dank hold couldn't come soon enough.

Chapter 7

Asteroid DC777-Williamdunloe was an irregularly shaped, dark gray planetoid pocked heavily with impact craters. It was the only developed piece of real estate in the Umbric System, which comprised just a single large gas planet and a handful of other barren asteroids revolving around the system's distant white dwarf. Approximately fifteen kilometers long and eight kilometers wide, DC777-Williamdunloe was a below-average sized asteroid for the system, but what it lacked in scale, it made up for in its composition of valuable metals.

The asteroid's city, called the Oasis, had started as a mining installation operated as a joint venture between two of the largest space mining corporations about a standard century prior. The success of the operations led to a steady influx of mining, construction, and ancillary services workers. As the only developed outpost within the Keruah Wastes, it became the default caravanserai for traders traversing the expanse. Those factors, along with a libertarian governing council and lax laws around bio-enhancements, high-tech drugs, and acceptable forms of gambling had turned the once-small mining settlement into a veritable port city attracting every flavor of spacer and off-worlder: honest workers and legitimate traders, as well as an underworld of mercenaries, smugglers, tech degenerates, junkies, and drifters, plus missionaries from a rainbow of faiths trying to convert them all. It was common for permanent off-worlders to maintain cheap apartments in the Oasis, for many had remained in space for so long that their atrophied skeletons and muscles could no longer support their mass under gravity, in essence exiling them from terrestrial life.

The city, with its notorious black market, was known as *the* definitive place to go when one needed "to get something." While it covered only about a third of the asteroid's surface area, its shadier parts extended down into the rock itself, filling in cavities left behind by old mining operations. No public maps of the underground labyrinths existed, and the extent of the developed tunnel network undoubtedly wasn't fully known by any single person.

The city's main spaceport resembled a small forest, with trees holding clusters of docked ships of every shape and size. Thick columnar towers formed the 'trunks,' with each supporting many levels of docking platforms that fanned out in circles, like a stack of disks.

The thirty-four distroships in the caravan in which Kairos, Midmay, and Neve journeyed docked across several of these broad platforms. Automated bridgeways extended from the platforms like spindly fingers and sealed their ends neatly to the ships' airlock hatches, forming pressurized tunnels for disembarking.

After disembarking, Kairos was treated to his first view of the Oasis as he and the other passengers glided through the bridgeway. There was little starlight at this distance from the system's sun, leaving the city shrouded in perpetual night. Thousands of lights blanketed the developed end of the asteroid and outlined its silhouetted structures like old computer code strung out against a blank screen. The Oasis's towers formed a grid and poked up at varying heights. All were colossal in scale—a few stretched into space with what seemed no less than three hundred "stories." The rows of dark monoliths followed the asteroid's ovoid curves, giving the landscape a spiny, rounded topography, like that of a porcupine with electrified quills. Neve had told him that the Oasis was a completely zero-*g* city. Unforeseen explosive growth had resulted in little city planning, but in any case, it was substantially cheaper building right into the asteroid rock than constructing elaborate ring structures to generate artificial gravity. No streets or external pedestrian activity of any sort existed. Instead, enclosed narrow bridgeways linked together towers at varying levels, and a multitude of cube-shaped pods shuttled rapidly throughout the three-dimensional grid like an organized swarm of insects.

But there was no time for Kairos to linger on the view. A crew mate would soon discover a tankful of dead fish in the cargo hold they'd left, and they'd need to be far from the docks when that happened. One could be killed over such a loss of precious goods, and in the trader-friendly Oasis, such a killing was not only legal, but viewed as an appropriate, civic upholding of the sacred property protection rights of traders everywhere. But besides that, Kairos wanted to get the Osetran artifact out of sight and transferred to another water source as soon as possible. As it were, he had the thing in a bag full of hot tank water—he'd guessed that the spike in temperature was what had killed all the fish—with the stinking dead fish still attached, an arrangement which he was unwilling to disturb for fear of damaging the teardrop. Another peculiarity was that Neve noted that the artifact's broadcasting beacon had ceased. Kairos was grateful for that at least—they no longer had to worry about unfriendlies picking up the signal.

Leaving the bridgeway, Kairos and Midmay followed Neve's lead in navigating the hand and footholds along their platform's busy concourse. He was relieved to be out of the confined hold, but he was still not used to orienting himself and moving in zero-*g*.

They reached the port's central column and the set of elevator shafts that ran along its length. Neve strode into one of the elevators and impatiently waved them in. The lift's walls, ceiling, and floor were like glass. Neve tapped on an apparently touch-sensitive area of one of the clear walls, bringing up two rows of three sets of illuminated green digits. A few more of her taps and their elevator lurched into motion. Kairos—prepared to shoot up or down—let out a wild yelp when their cube instead popped laterally out of its housing. Propulsion from somewhere on the cube ensued, whisking them away from the spaceport and slamming his body ungracefully against the elevator wall.

"Don't be such a *slowdrone*," Midmay teased him, giggling. She was holding securely onto a clear thin handrail, which he now noticed for the first time running along the cube's perimeter. He was sure Neve had quietly instructed her to hold on to it before they blasted off. He was equally sure that Neve had taught her the gibe and wondered immaturely what else about him Neve had poked fun at with the girl while he wasn't listening. Neve smirked but remained silent, her eyes fixed outside.

Kairos grabbed the handrail and followed her gaze to the sublime view outside their cube. All six sides were transparent as crystal, to the terrifying extent that, if not for each side's micro thrusters, a compact life support unit in one corner, and the glowing wall digits seemingly floating in space beside him, he wouldn't have been able to tell they were inside anything at all. They were now immersed in the city's grid, speeding in between towers which appeared to grow in height as they emerged from the not-too-distant horizon and then whipped by in multi-colored streaks of light. The illusion was dizzying yet entrancing, as if his disembodied mind were traveling through cyberspace.

"These towers were all built using metals mined from the asteroid," Neve explained, tracing his gaze. "Many, especially the residential buildings, are just stacks of repeating modular units. Additional units can be easily added to augment tower height."

After a while, she announced, "In a few more blocks, we'll drop down several levels to where I've booked lodging."

"How can you tell where we are?"

She motioned toward the green wall digits. "Every address here has its own unique x-y-z coordinates within the grid. Those are our current coordinates"—she pointed to the top set of numbers; one of them was increasing with each block they passed—"and those are the ones of our destination," she said, motioning to the bottom set.

The cube decelerated to a full stop beside one of the buildings, then plummeted downward along its length. Kairos's feet—tucked beneath clear rungs rising from the floor which Neve had kindly pointed out—kept him firmly planted so his head didn't smash into the cube's ceiling during the drop.

They halted next to an entryway.

A neon sign glowed above it: The Outside Inn.

Their cube slid forward into the entryway along a grooved track. After passing through a sliding gate-style airlock, the cube came to a rest inside a lighted lobby where a pale, thin receptionist checked them into their unit without so much as raising her attention from whatever content was playing on her retinal overlays and sending splashes of light and color across her drab eyes.

The unit was little more than an empty room with four plastic slab beds that slid out from the walls, inset wall compartments and mesh netting for stowing belongings, and a tiny adjoining lavatory. The room felt cramped even with the beds retracted. From the view outside the room's sole porthole, Kairos could tell that the Inn was located at the edge of the city. Beyond a few neighboring structures, the lights of the Oasis ceased, leaving only a ghastly void thereafter.

"At least it doesn't smell as bad as the cargo hold?" Kairos offered dismally.

"We won't be spending much time here," Neve replied.

"I know," Kairos replied. "It's just a place to keep the artifact safe while we're out." The plan was to meet with a couple of Neve's contacts to ask about Badir Saeta and any recent hirings for a Pantoll job.

He turned to Midmay. "You're going to stay here too." The girl began to protest, but he cut her off. "We're here on business, not to explore or have fun. What happened on Spires was already too dangerous. This is no place for a kid. I won't be able to keep a close eye on you."

"Stop treating me like a baby," Midmay countered. "I can help you out there."

"You will be helping us by staying here and keeping an eye on the teardrop," Kairos replied, passing the girl the bag holding the Osetran teardrop and dead fish. "If you notice any further changes, send my goggles a message immediately."

"I'm not going to sit here alone with that creepy thing," she refused with upturned nose. "You can't just tell me what to do."

"This is not a game," Kairos said. "Those agents on Spires nearly killed us. I regret that I allowed you to leave Pantoll with me, but here we are, and I'm responsible for you."

Midmay pursed her lips and glared at him.

"I'm sure you could help us," Neve stepped in, reassuring the girl with a smile. "But our unorthodox little group will spook my contacts. Rhody will stay too and keep you company. Keep your eyevisor's comms channel open in case we need your skills, okay?"

Midmay remained upset, but Neve's words softened her mood. The girl listened to her. Looking about the place, Midmay groaned, "This room is so boring." The girl had been fingering the eyevisor around her neck and now she lifted it to her eyes. "And limited intranet connectivity?" she exclaimed after a moment.

"We need to conserve our funds," Kairos said. "I'm not spending money so you can get into trouble visiting portals and forums you have no business being in. And don't even think about getting around that," Kairos warned, knowing the girl's habits all too well, "or hacking into anything at all. Not even that vending machine in the lobby I saw you eying. We're not on Pantoll. You can't imagine what the consequences could be in a lawless place like this."

Midmay let out an angry moan, tore off her eyevisor, and

sent it sailing across the small room, where it ricocheted off the walls like a boomerang.

"Now you *are* acting like a child," Kairos scolded.

"And *you're* acting like you're my father, which you're not!" she shot back. Midmay turned and refused to look at him anymore.

"There will be no time for idleness," Neve told Midmay, breaking the awkward silence, "because Kairos is going to share his channel with you. And I expect you to follow along with your full attention."

Kairos turned to Neve in shock to object—he had a strong aversion to having riders—but the spacer's glare told him that it was not open for discussion. Reluctantly, he assented but drew the line that Midmay keep her mic off. He had to keep his wits sharp, and the last thing he needed was having her yapping or complaining in his ears.

* * *

"I forget the exact address," Neve admitted. "It's hard to keep them all memorized, and I haven't been to the place in a while." The two of them were in the inn's lobby inside an elevator cube which the receptionist had ordered for them. The one they'd initially arrived in had shortly thereafter been called elsewhere. After a couple of hours of idle waiting, one of Neve's contacts had returned her message. She was to meet him at some establishment downtown.

She pulled up a directory by tapping the glass wall next to the coordinates display, and after locating the right numbers, dragged them over to input them. The cube hummed softly to life and whisked them through the airlock gates and out into the dark cityscape.

"This contact of yours, what does he do?" Kairos asked.

"Technician. Outfits crews with the equipment they need for a job. Keeps it untraceable."

"Any chance he's on the payroll of a System Administrator?"

"Impossible to say. Gadgeteers like him are adamant freelancers. I know his roots have crept into the Oasis underworld. But anyone with talent takes the occasional corporate contract if only to keep their ears to the ground. Don't look so worried."

"All information comes with a price tag. Just wondering what his might be."

"We've traded favors over the past few years. You scratch my back kind of stuff. By my count, he owes me one."

"Well, he owes my back no scratches, so I'd prefer to keep the Osetran artifact out of the conversation."

"Goes without saying."

They must have crossed into a more commercial section of the city, because the concentration of cubes zipping along the grid was now quite dense. Traffic along opposing directions and at intersections moved on separate spatial planes, allowing for a ceaseless flow. Several of the structures in this area differed from the standard tower design they had predominantly seen earlier. Some were shorter but much broader, a couple were topped with domed ceilings, and others had funky asymmetrical shapes that were the result of haphazard, impromptu modifications and additions over time. The sides of several were dominated by massive digital displays showing advertisements, news from the worlds, local PSAs, or street art.

Their cube dropped toward one of the more curiously shaped structures and, upon reaching its destination, slid into one of the reception sockets at the side of the building. Neve triggered her helmet to close around her head. Once the cube's pressure seal was established, they glided out into the building's main corridor.

The inside of the corridor was minimalist in design. A healthy stream of people flowed through it like a long school of fish. Dim lighting strips ran its length, as did messy bundles of wiring and tubing, often exposed through cracked or missing plastic paneling. Entryways to separate modules containing retail and other establishments lined the corridor, their storefronts lit up with flashy signage to entice passers-by to drift in. "The Universe is here for YOU," proclaimed one in red neon. Scattered vents pumped recycled air into the corridor, to keep the pungent odors of all the bodies, food stalls, and shops at bay. Occasionally, they'd pass smaller passageways shooting off the central corridor. These were often graffiti-bombed and even more dimly lit, perhaps signaling where shadier business was conducted.

Kairos found simply navigating the corridor to be over-whelming. He couldn't master the rhythm of pulling and tapping oneself along in a straight line with deft flicks against the scattered handholds. There seemed to be established conventions around which side of the corridor to travel for a given direction, but people's different orientations in space confused him and led to frequent banged shoulders. Everyone was in a rush; Kairos spent half his efforts dodging the impatient bodies that zipped by at obnoxious proximities. Many had the pale, slender form of those spending more time in space than on land, and they slid past him in hurried excitement like ghosts on holiday. Neve's suit sported its own micro-thrusters, and he cursed her ability to glide gracefully through the middle of the corridor while he clawed at handholds and ducked incoming human missiles. Making navigation an even worse nightmare, a never-ending stream of pop-up ads bombarded Kairos's goggle screens, hawking things like faux sheep's wool jackets, JuvenateJuice, CasinOasis's Seven-cycle Sweepstakes, and OCTOviz sight shifters. At one point, a robe-wearing evangelist of some faith the man called the Amor-something accosted Kairos head-on and started delivering a ten-second salvation pitch. Kairos accepted a data tab the proselytizer offered just to get the man off of him.

"What's the deal with everything being so poorly lit around here?" he complained to Neve through their comms channel. He pulled himself past a busy wall of overlapping graffiti, but paused upon encountering a luminous ring of eyeballs sprayed with fluorescent paint. It was the same symbol he'd seen on Saeta's armor and etched into the Spires cable car's counter top. Whatever it represented, the symbol's presence in multiple star systems was significant.

"Energy conservation," Neve replied. "We're far from starlight."

"Obviously," he muttered.

His attention was next drawn to a colorfully illuminated storefront advertising a three-hour retinal implant procedure for five hundred points.

Neve pulled him away.

"Don't even think about letting one of these hackshops

work on you," she said. "Price looks right, and for a while the product does too. Until your overlays start glitching. Another few months, you can barely see. Next thing you know, you're blind."

The place they entered to meet Neve's contact was a shabby but lively electrorock tavern called Psychoncussion. "Welcome To Our Establishment" text scrolled across his goggle screens as he glided through the pub's entryway.

The atmosphere inside was unlike anywhere he'd ever been. Communal tables—made from imported real wood—hung in front of a small central stage, beside a long bar with a dull aluminum top. Private booths lined the perimeter of the pub. Upside-down on the ceiling, from his perspective, were more tables and a bar island. The tables, of course, were partly decorative to create a pub-like ambiance, but they did feature pockets for holding patrons' drink cylinders, as well as magnetized strips to keep down metallic playing cards, poker chips, or mahjong tiles. At the stage, a grungy band of four youngish men with oily shoulder-length hair were jamming away over the hum of the crowd. Two of the guitarists were suspended at odd angles a couple meters "above" the stage, heads and bodies bent, riffing with a feverish intensity, while the drummer was fastened to the stage planks so as not to fly off due to his ferocious pounding.

"Sure looks like you could use one," Neve commented after Kairos refused a drink at the bar. She'd triggered her helmet to unfold. "It'd help you relax a bit." Neve hadn't yet touched her own glass cylinder, only chewed the accompanying olives that she slid one by one off the toothpick with her teeth.

"Not a drinker," he insisted.

"Ah, it's prohibited for Clerics, isn't it?" Seeing Kairos's surprise, she added, "Midmay told me about you. I thought the whole priest act back on Spires was a scam. But you really are one, huh? Or perhaps *were* is more accurate? Midmay may still believe you're a priest, but I find that a little hard to believe. What happened to you?"

Kairos shook his head. "It's not relevant to our investigation."

"What about special powers? Do you have any?" Neve mocked. "People say that Clerics can perform magic, miracles, and whatnot."

"It's not magic," Kairos insisted with a sigh. "And I was never a Cleric. I was just a Low Priest."

"So you can do some things," pressed Neve.

"I was a supernaturalist," he replied. "We study the spiritual realm. What it is, what it is not, how it interacts with the physical. And yes, seeking how to abide by its principles. But also understanding that it has few set rules."

Neve rolled her eyes. "Sounds like vague priest-speak to me. How about you show me an example?"

"That's not how it works."

"Fine," Neve conceded, getting bored. "What's the deal with you and the girl, though? You're not some kind of perv are you?"

Kairos snorted at the woman's directness. "I'm just looking after her," he replied. Seeing Neve's skepticism, he explained, "She has nobody. Her father was a no-good, piece-of-shit off-world trader who knocked up a local woman on Pantoll." He let out a long sigh. "I actually met the asshole once. Found him praying in my chapel, asking God for direction. The following week, the baccus harvest over and goods packed, the scoundrel rounded up his crew and took off. Months later, her mother died in labor. The midwife named the baby 'Midmay' because that's when she was born according to the months of the Earth Standard calendar."

Neve frowned, as if in pain. "Ever wonder why God made procreation so simple?" she mused. "Any damn fool in just a few carnal moments can spawn an entirely new human being. You think God really got that right?" She sighed. "How many of us are just ... *thoughtlessly* made?"

Kairos had never considered that. It didn't make much sense to him either. But little about God's ways had. "I take it you don't have any kids of your own?" he asked. "I assume family life would be difficult given your line of work."

Her saddened eyes quickly morphed into a glare. He'd struck a nerve.

"Ah, forgive me," he apologized. "Old priestly habit, getting too personal too fast."

Neve took a slow first sip of her drink, and her face relaxed. "My husband was the one who was against having children," she said, her eyes going distant.

Breaking the silence that followed, Kairos offered, "Parenthood is a complex thing. Not once has Midmay ever heard from her father. Not even a note. Simply abandoned. Can you imagine what it's like to be orphaned like that? To grow up alone, without any family?"

With a tone expressing neither sympathy nor apathy, Neve replied, "Yeah, I can."

A few moments after, a dark-skinned man approached the counter beside her and muttered an order to the bartender. He had buzzed black hair with equally dark eyes and pronounced cheekbones. Abruptly, Neve sucked down her full cocktail in one go, then triggered her helmet to re-form over her head.

"Who's the meatstick?" the man asked Neve without looking at her, smoothly receiving a thin glass cylinder that the bartender had shipped his way from across the bar. It was filled with a swirling, amber-colored liquid. Kairos knew he must be Neve's contact, the gadgeteer named Mubiks.

"Assisting with my case," Neve's helmet replied. It was strange hearing again the low, distorted voice.

"Not like you to take on a partner. And here I thought I was special."

"No one's special. Just useful."

Mubiks frowned. With one mighty intake of his chest, he drained the contents of his cylinder, returning it to transparent glass. "I have a booth. Leave the meatstick." He flipped the depleted container down the length of the bar—where the bartender caught it with a casual apathy—and kicked away from them.

"Don't take it personally," Neve told Kairos. "Given their clientele, technicians are cagey by nature. Survival instinct."

"But you think he'll talk to you?"

"Getting someone to divulge information is easier when the subject of inquiry is already dead. Wait for me and keep your eyes open. Try not to broadcast your vulnerability and don't talk too much to anyone. You never know who's selling info to whom." She left to follow where Mubiks had drifted off.

Kairos resented her last statement but knew it to be true. With his dust-stained clothes and his weathered scarf about his neck, his blatant terrestrialness was as out of place as the real wooden tables. And more concerning, he was unarmed.

He remained at the bar nursing a non-alcoholic ale, while observing two players shooting a game of three-dimensional pool in a corner of the pub, taking meticulous aim to send suspended balls flying into one of twelve stasis pockets. A man and a woman stopped beside him at the bar for a short time. They engaged him with small talk, but every time he asked them a question the couple would turn inward and answer it between themselves as if he wasn't there. So, he moved to the opposite side of the bar—upside-down from his prior perspective—ordered another drink and idly scanned descriptions of nearby items that popped up on his goggle screens. Amid the capricious rises and falls of the thumping rock music, he also picked up scraps of the conversations being held around him.

"... because there's this biz, see. For six hundred points they'll ship you anything you want, to anywhere, and I mean *anything* man ..."

"... compulsion to meet every single human in the universe ... he just had this big fear of missing out on someone, of not experiencing that one unique perspective that would change his life or ..."

"... I agree, that's what our ancestors needed to survive, sure. But I'm saying that, at a certain point, we need to destroy those very things, because now they're killing us, right? It's about adaptation. It's about evolution ... we cannot rely on the same survival tools if we wanna get to that next level, if we wanna *transcend* ..."

"... have a friend who works for Lienns-Sutra. She wasn't supposed to tell me this, but there's some top secret, crazy new weave drive shit they're working on. Says they'll cut down on travel times by like fifty percent or something. So I said ..."

An exclamation point icon popped up in the corner of Kairos's screens.

He subvocalized a command to expand the warning notification. It was a local advisory reporting that there had been an explosion in one of the commercial district's distribution centers. An Oasis security team had raided a foodstuffs operator believed to be a front for the activities of a religious cult, whose members called themselves the Amor Fati. Funny, Kairos thought: Oasis's permissive governing council didn't bat an eye at the black clinics, high-tech brothels, or drug dealers selling hallucinogens that turned users' brains to runny eggs after a single hit. But it seemed to have no tolerance for this cult. Curious, Kairos opened the advisory to read further. The reason for the raid wasn't fully clear. The cult was allegedly connected to a few previous incidents that were considered cyberterror. Apparently, the raid had turned up a network servers cache hidden in a back warehouse section. Rather than turn them over to the authorities, group members chose to suicidally detonate the place. The blast killed them plus forty-eight others, including those lost to the vacuum of space before the building's auto-maintenance systems could seal off the structural damage.

A hand clapped down on the bar beside him.

Kairos turned to find a stout man with a dark bushy mustache and a broad, inviting smile, likely in his mid to late forties. He wore a loose-fitting flight suit smudged with grease. Colossal headphones covered not just his ears but most of the sides of his face.

"Mind if I join you?" the man asked, pulling the bulky headphones down around his thick neck. He appeared to be alone.

Kairos gave an ambivalent shrug.

The man hooked a boot under the bar's foot rail to orient

himself and signaled the bartender. "Name's Sunsip."

Kairos pointed to his headphones. "You don't like electro-rock?"

The man patted the headphones. "Also rock. Got to layer the rock for full effect," he grinned. He assessed Kairos's weathered clothes down to the Maydays.

"You don't look much like an off-worlder yourself," commented Kairos preemptively.

"Only because I eat too much. Where you blow in from?"

"Here and there."

Sunsip reached out and received a large cylinder of dark red beer with an equally large mitt of a hand. "Don't believe I caught your name."

While Sunsip took a long swig, Kairos discreetly scanned the room to take note of the exits and thought of ways he might subdue the man should the encounter turn ugly.

"Not to be rude, but I just came in here for a quiet drink," replied Kairos. Sunsip laughed at that, and Kairos realized how absurd the statement sounded in an electrorock tavern.

"I was just curious," the man said. "You're far too young to have fought with the Burning Wolves." Sunsip motioned to Kairos's coat.

Kairos looked down his sleeve, confused at first, then remembered the worn patch affixed near the shoulder, featuring a fearsome, fiery image of that extinct Earthling predator.

Sunsip rolled up a sleeve, revealing a faded tattoo of the same burning wolf emblem on the inside of his bulging bicep.

Understanding now that the patch on his father's coat was what had attracted the man's company, Kairos relaxed a bit. "Oh. My father was a mercenary. Did a couple stints with this outfit. Mainly around Eukiah, I think."

"What a stint to choose," Sunsip remarked. "May I ask your father's name, or should we go on drinking in silence from here?"

"Catadyn."

"Ha!" boomed the man. "Wells Catadyn. I'm drinking with the son of the Grey Wolf. Cheers."

"The Grey Wolf?"

"Aye. He never told you about his nickname?"

"There's a lot about his past he didn't talk about."

Sunsip nodded gravely. "For the best. I served with him during the Stickwheat Crisis, or so it's called. 'Crisis' makes it sound tame. I'm telling ya, those who survived saw some terrible shit."

Kairos debated how much he should be talking to this stranger, but his curiosity won out. "What happened?"

Sunsip snorted. "For a start, lost half our transports just getting down through Eukiah's orbital defenses. On the ground, we hacked through nothing but stickwheat fields for days. Five meters tall, covers the planet like grass. Offered good cover from New Canaan Ag airships, though, which were not happy one bit to have thousands of us little bugs crawling around their garden. So they sent in men. Boy was that a mess. Walking through dense fields with no visibility, relying on our heat displays as the only way to detect men emerging from the growth to attack us. But your father was a brilliant fighter. Cunning as ever. Stubborn too. He looked out for us younger guys. We held them off and completed the mission."

"My father never talked about those days. All he ever said was that it was hell on earth."

Sunsip nodded somberly. "In the end, NCA decided to torch its own fields to burn us out. I'll never forget the sight. Tenth of a planet on fire, taking with it a good chunk of the worlds' food supply. Our squadron landed with over five hundred men. Less than thirty of us made it out." Sunsip mumbled a short phrase followed by a long pull of his drink.

"My father recently passed," Kairos said, staring down at his own drink cylinder.

Sunsip eyed him momentarily, then gave a simple nod and raised his drink. "Dust to dust." Sunsip inhaled and drained the rest of his beer. He signaled to the bartender for another and after a minute caught a fresh cylinder. "So, may I ask what brings you to the Oasis, son of Catadyn?" Sunsip asked after a brief silence.

"Business."

"Man of commerce. So am I."

Sunsip must have subvocalized something, because a contact request tab slid into Kairos's goggle screens. Kairos accepted it. "You're a distroship captain? It says you used to be a racer."

The man nodded. "My brother and I used to be one of the best teams in the sport. Won the Malaga Belt Grand Prix twice. Retired now. Today, we specialize in time-sensitive direct transport. Goods, passengers, livestock, you name it. You buy, we fly—no questions asked. Ever find yourself in need of a jagged run, look up the *Flyby Rhythm II*. Tell you what, first trip's on the house in honor of your father."

"Thanks, I'll keep it in mind. Hey, by the way, what's the deal with this Amor Fati group? You ever heard of them?"

"You anxious about that explosion? Don't worry about it, happens more frequently than you'd think. The Oasis attracts all kinds of lunatics, they're just the latest brand. Religious zealots, these ones."

"What do they believe?"

"Only that human beings are the scourge of the universe. We're broken, violent, selfish beings"—the pilot swung his drink about theatrically—"that wallow in a miserable reality of our own making. First we corrupted Eden, then ruined Earth, and now, we've brought the human contagion to new worlds. Individualism and consumerism are to blame, of course. That cult harbors a certain contempt for the, ah, *corporeal*. They favor the realm of the *mind and spirit*," finished the pilot, waggling his fingers in the air mystically.

"Reminds me a little of the PPP."

"PPP?"

"Programmers for Prosperity & Peace. It was an unorganized movement—more of an idea really—back on Old Earth, when virtual reality started to achieve realer-than-real simulation. It was believed that the emergence of fully-realized virtual lives would curb humanity's destructive tendencies in real life, or at least channel them into a safer, digital space. Users, as kings and queens ruling over their created utopias, could satisfy their every craving: wealth, sex, luxuries, goods of every kind, the admiration of their AI subjects. And thus most of the planet's ills—resource scarcity, jealousy, depression, fighting over territory or power—would be made obsolete, ushering in a new era of global peace. The PPP's vision was tested in some countries, actually. They went as far as to support it with a universal basic income and intravenous nutrition system to keep people plugged in worry-free."

Sunsip bobbed his head thoughtfully. "The Amor Fati have their own virtual realm. Seem to spend a lot of time in it too. They hold services there and preach it as this perfect reality that they're building in unity with followers everywhere who jack in. One spirit, one love, mind/body separation type of nonsense. I wonder why groups like this don't just all kill themselves, free their souls, and leave everyone else alone."

"It is not enough for the adherents of most faiths to believe themselves," Kairos said. "They want all of humanity to be enlightened."

"Very altruistic, eh? The cult's against procreation though, so I give 'em credit for philosophical consistency. Hey, at least their cause will dry up in a generation, right?" Sunsip laughed. Then he stared at the glass in thought. "I knew a distroship captain that recently dipped a toe into the Amor Fati's faith. That's how I know much of what I've told you about them. He began attending their virtual services. Started believing a lot of nonsense, acting differently. Pledged his allegiance to the Vyst. That cult sure warped his mind. Scrambled him good."

"The Vyst?"

"Oh, that's what they call their prophet leader. We traders get around quite a bit, and I can tell you there are as many opinions about the Vyst as people I've heard talk about it. As if he or she has become myth already! Some say the Vyst is an enlightened holy man who has seen the future. That God has sent him to lead humankind through its next evolution. Some believe he's Jesus in his Second Coming to usher in Judgment Day, or a reincarnation of Buddha. Some think he's come from another civilization altogether, an alien messiah. Most seem to agree that he's a sorcerer of some kind, with powerful magics. Bunch of nonsense to me. My advice: steer clear of religious fanatics. They're all loons. Why does a percent of the population always buy into this kind of stuff?"

"People need something to believe in," Kairos replied. *But what do I believe in?* He spotted Neve returning his way. "I have to go. Nice chatting with you."

"Rock on, son of Catadyn," Sunsip said with raised cylinder.

Kairos kicked himself toward Neve, meeting her in the middle of the pub.

"Anything?" he asked her.

Neve's face was grim. "I'll tell you on the way, let's go."

* * *

The cube's coordinates display glowed red. The Retina was an exclusive club, so travel there was restricted to members and their guests only. Neve inputted an authentication code, prompting the numbers to change from red to green and springing the elevator to life.

As Neve had predicted, the technician's comfort levels rose meaningfully upon learning of Saeta's death. One had less fear of retribution from a corpse. Mubiks recognized the assassin when Neve showed him Kairos's recording, however he knew him by a different name: Salamir Cole. She told him she was investigating the assassin's attack on a corporate transport nine standard months ago. Mubiks said that Cole had contacted him around the same time about providing some equipment. Cole's wish list sounded like it could be for a job like that. But Mubiks had refused him flat out, having heard rumors of Cole's recent affiliation with a certain underworld boss named Jaxx. The technician wanted no business with Jaxx's organization. As a result, he hadn't any information for Neve except to refer her to an occasional associate of Cole's, a Human Resources specialist called Chimera. Chimera happened to be in the Oasis. At this moment, she could be found in her private entertainment orb at The Retina.

"What's so bad about an HR specialist?" Kairos remarked as they zipped along the grid, noticing that Neve's mood had darkened. "Sounds like they're a people person."

"In a sense," Neve snorted. "HR specialists are executive-level headhunters. Corporations ruthlessly compete to secure top talent, especially those in the scientific and engineering fields. Ironclad contracts to retain personnel are no less severe. But, really, the unspoken repercussions of leaving—*lethal* repercussions—are what keep key employees and their families locked down. That's where headhunters come in. A corporation that wants talent badly enough will pay exorbitant amounts for a talented extractor. HR specialists handle the poaching and relocation. It's dangerous work, and likewise, those in their way often wind up dead."

"Have you heard of this Jaxx before?"

Neve nodded "But I've never met it. Few have."

"It?"

"Jaxx is an AI. Over the years, it's managed to fashion itself into a formidable crime lord."

"Fashion *itself*? It's *independent*?"

"It's a very old intelligence. A survivor. Its involvement would complicate things. Jaxx's organization includes a large band of degenerates."

Degenerates. Kairos had heard horror stories about them, the kind adults tell to scare little children. These were real terrors, however: disfigured, quasi-cyborg beings, upgraded— or mutilated, by most people's standards—with integrated hardware and illegal bioware. As a result of such modifications, they were said to possess incredible mental prowess or physical strength. But their genetic engineering aspirations held a divine element to them as well—the age-old desire to rise above mortality, to achieve demigod status. Kairos had briefly studied their micro-cult during his time at King's Seminary at Asphis.

Kairos thought back to the Blackpool job Neve had recounted. "Aren't degenerates known to be some of the best hackers?" he asked. "What if they hacked into Blackpool's network to get the *Asterisk*'s scheduled route and coordinates?"

"Cracking Blackpool's AI would be tough even for them. It's possible, but I've never heard of Jaxx's organization launching such a physical attack on corporate property. It primarily engages in data thievery."

"A tech like Blackpool's neurofluid is an alluring target for any criminal."

"True. It'd fetch Jaxx a hefty sum on the black market. Just like any other creature, it needs money to keep itself and its operations going."

"Odd behavior for an AI though, no?" Kairos asked. He thought of Midmay's deceased android pal, Johnathan. Like all robots or AI, it lacked a survival instinct. Humans on Earth had left that dangerous inclination out of their programming. No comprehension of life versus death, on versus off. Unless they had been specifically programmed to care in certain circumstances, continued operation held no existential importance to them. They had no personal ambition, no concept of beauty, no children to desire to see grown.

"I've heard it's got more than a few loose screws," she said, tapping the side of her helmet with a gloved finger.

The Retina was a conspicuous illuminated sphere hovering over the city's commercial district. A color-morphing swirl of fuchsia, indigo, and blue illuminated its exterior, as if some mysterious organism was incubating within it.

The sphere's silent external façade concealed the deafening innersynth electrodream music that greeted them as soon as they passed through the reception airlock. A digital poster by the entrance with the header "LIVE" advertised Paracosm, the club's current innerspeaker. The club's interior consisted of several semi-transparent levels of spherical shells, like the layers of an onion. Neve handed him a small band she pulled from the tray of a nearby server.

"Wear it around your wrist," she said. "It's a simple propulsor for when you've got nothing solid near you to push off from. You'll need it in here."

They passed through the club's outermost shell, which glowed a light pink throughout, brushing by packs of loud, tipsy youth, scantily clad servers shuttling fluorescent drink cylinders and a rainbow of neurotransmitter induction patches, and sharply-dressed loners whose clothing casually revealed their extravagant bio-tech augmentations and whose artificial youth showed through their colorless taut skin and weary smiles. Kairos almost collided with a figure— he couldn't tell if a man or woman—with a shaved head covered with rivers of scarring and a face that had been reconstructed to near non-recognition with silicon, plastics, and lenses. He wondered if that level of work was not uncommon here in the Oasis, and whether it reflected a cheap mass of augmentations or merely a series of desperate fixes for botched operations performed by the city's black clinics that Neve warned him about.

A few revelers gave sidelong glances at the odd pair as they floated by—Neve in her high-tech exosuit and Kairos with his clunky third-rate optics and blatantly terrestrial, weather-beaten jacket. The Retina's diverse clientele, their profane bio-enhancements, their vanity, their debauchery—Kairos found it all at once fascinating and horrific, like passing through an interactive museum on humans filled with the most exotic specimens.

The ambiance darkened as they passed through the next few shell levels until they reached the edge of the club's dark, voluminous hollow core, where hundreds of suspended dancers gyrated and jerked their bodies to the thumping beat of the music. Colorful, focused light beams sliced through the space, illuminating fragments of scenes in brief flashes.

Scattered around the outside of the core, near to them, floated opaque, faintly glowing private orbs. They varied in diameter, some looking spacious enough for an entourage, others so small they were surely meant only for an intimate two. Neve and Kairos drifted over to a medium-sized one aligned with the core wall's 220-degree marking, per Mubik's direction, where they encountered a massive bouncer blocking the orb's circular entrance. The man had a chest the size of oil drum and arms thicker than Kairos's waist. Scars criss-crossed his bald head, and his grim mouth was twisted in a perpetual scowl. The bouncer was fixed to the orb itself by a short tether, probably so he wouldn't be sent sailing away from his post upon booting unwelcome riffraff.

The bouncer sneered. "This is a private orb, beat it."

"We're here to see Chimera," Neve said, unfazed.

"The Chimera doesn't mix business with pleasure, and

neither of you are on the guest list."

"We have no interest in waiting for her office hours. Tell her it's about Salamir Cole."

The bouncer glared at her but bowed his head slightly and subvocalized something. After a moment he looked back up, frowning. "The Chimera will see you. Any weapons must stay with me." His hands moved to feel up Neve's hips.

There was a blur of motion, and in the next instant Neve had twisted the massive man's arm and pinned him face-first against the orb. Kairos swore he heard a cracking sound from somewhere inside the bouncer's body.

"Do you want to die today?" Neve asked the man. Her suit's micro-thrusters died down, releasing her pressure against the orb wall. She then withdrew both pistols from her hip slots and offered them to the bouncer, whose rage-filled eyes and bulging neck veins gave him the appearance of a furious guard dog straining against its chain leash.

He snatched her guns and slid aside resentfully, glaring at them as they passed through the orb's opening.

The pounding club music's volume lowered as they entered, dampened by the orb's soundproof glass shell. The interior was illuminated in a hazy blue light, mixed with sporadic bursts of color emanating from a display screen embedded into a section of the orb's curvature.

A handful of poisonous-looking individuals were luxuriating around the room in feathery cushion sacks, overlaid eyes frosted over, cackling and taking long pulls from lengthy tubes extending from a central liquor cylinder that hung like a chandelier. An obscene amount of chemical patches, injection guns, and drug paraphernalia littered the space, drifting around them like debris from a lab explosion. All of them appeared either too stoned, too drunk, or too engrossed in their own virtual fantasy worlds to notice the newcomers.

"Good evening, Ms. Seven," called a feminine voice.

They spun about to reorient themselves "upward" to face a tall, spindly woman lounging comfortably within a black cushion sack. She wore a fashionable all-white jumpsuit with a bracelet of white stones. Her straight black hair was tied back in an elaborate bun. Remarkably, she was one of the most normal-looking people he had seen in the place. Her retinal overlays defrosted, revealing piercing black eyes.

"Yes, I know all about you," she continued to Neve. "Knowing who's who is my business. And who could miss that distinctive, antique suit of yours? Although it's quite the eyesore in a place like this." She glanced dismissively at Kairos. "There's simply nothing to be said of this dreadful thing accompanying you. A New Revelationist priest, I understand? The most pitiful one I've ever seen. No matter, man of God, your faith isn't of any use here anyway. Now, I despise interruptions to my leisure, so whatever you have to say to me, speak it quickly."

"About nine months ago, a Blackpool transport was attacked," Neve said. "Some cutting edge technology was stolen. We know Cole was involved."

"What do I care?" Chimera. "Your husband has a bad day at the lab, so you come to me to complain about it?"

"If you know anything about it, then I'll be doing more than just that," Neve said, unperturbed.

The woman scoffed. "Do you really think I would tell you anything about any of my business?"

"I have a direct contract with Blackpool. They'll pay well for information."

"You should know how things work in the Oasis. Money is merely table stakes. Beyond that, it holds little real value, especially if you want to be in our game for the long run."

"How long do you think you'll last if your name comes up in my report to Blackpool's Executive triumvirate?"

Chimera's smirk remained unfazed. "And say what, that I do business with him? Salamir's worked with clients of every kind."

"Jaxx one of them?"

"How should I know? At the speed business moves, this job you're referring to is ancient history." The woman let out a shrill laugh. "You've been out of the game for too long, sweetheart. The comfortable life of a corporate elite and too many glitzy galas hanging onto the arm of Blackpool's star scientist has worn your old edges smooth." Chimera turned to address Kairos. "You're wasting your time with this one. Blackpool has little patience with low performers. Trust me, I've done work for them myself. Whatever Ms. Seven's professional arrangement with them might have been, I can assure you it's long over."

"What's she talking about?" Kairos asked Neve in a low voice. But Neve remained silent.

Chimera laughed again. "In any case, if you have questions about Salamir, I recommend you ask him."

"Cole is dead," Neve stated.

Chimera's face darkened and she eyed Neve carefully. "I assume you have proof?" she asked after a moment.

Kairos subvocalized commands to transmit to the orb's wallscreen multiple images of Cole's body from his goggle's vision recordings.

"Where did you get these images?" Chimera asked, her eyes

flickering with a pained awareness.

"I took them myself," Kairos replied.

"*You* killed him?" Chimera asked, incredulous.

"No," Neve said. "We were tracking Cole. Found him retired."

"Where did this happen?"

"Not only could we tell you that, but also why he was there," Neve replied.

"You can take the images away," Chimera said with a whisk of her hand. "Who else have you shown these to?"

"How about we have a *real* conversation?" Neve countered.

The woman considered this, then said, "Salamir's dealings were his own. He's dead then. He was a talented associate, and it is a shame for him to have come to such an undignified end. I'm sorry to disappoint you, but it seems I know less about his recent activities than you. Now, if you would leave me to return to my revelry, I would like to forget this sad news."

"You know more than you're letting on," Neve said. "He's already dead, so why remain silent? Who are you protecting?"

"Such grasping will not serve you. What a pity you've become, Neve Seven. You used to have a respectable reputation. Now, I know you're feeling upset. This meeting hasn't gone as well as you'd hoped it would. Why don't you loosen up a bit, take advantage of the fact that your work brought you to The Retina. Here, this one's on me." She flipped Neve a vial of fluorescent purple liquid.

In catching it, Neve was momentarily distracted, but Kairos's eyes had remained on Chimera and caught the woman's eyes slightly shift to focus expectantly on something past them. Triggering a boost from his wrist propulsor, Kairos whirled and shoved a leg against Neve.

The knife blade barely missed his side.

There were two attackers, dressed in all-black tactical suits with optical scopes that obscured half their faces.

Neve now reacted with an innate, blinding speed that only raw experience can instill, withdrawing a small handgun Kairos had never seen from some other suit compartment and firing at their attackers, while simultaneously launching a tether from the ploy mounted on her opposite wrist.

The sound of shattering glass filled the air as half the orb disintegrated into a shower of sparkling crystals that gleamed multi-colored light like electrified snowflakes. The deafening shrill of the innersynth music instantly blasted into the space, which had fallen dark as the orb's illumination flickered out. Amid the sensory chaos, Neve grabbed hold of Kairos and hit the tether's reel switch to rocket them out of the orb's broken shell.

It seemed they had successfully extricated themselves until Kairos was tackled hard in the side by a body missile belonging to someone who must have launched at them off the core wall. His grip on Neve's suit tore away, sending his body hurtling off in a wild spin.

Before he could determine which way to point his wrist propulsor to stabilize himself, his body slammed against a wall, throwing him into a daze. Nausea rose in his throat. The strobing beam lights didn't help.

Neve was nowhere in sight, not that visibility within the core had been any good to begin with. He'd no doubts she'd leave him behind if she needed to. His heart pounded with a feeling of claustrophobia. He had to get out of this place, but which direction was out? Why the hell didn't this place have any exit signage?

Along the curved wall to his left, two of the black bodyguards with scopes were making their way toward him.

He turned to flee to his left, only to find more bodyguards approaching.

Only one option remained. Kicking perpendicularly off the wall, Kairos shot himself directly into the dancing frenzy at the heart of the core.

He plunged into a sweaty sea of body parts, pulling his way through the slimy mass of undulating limbs and torsos as if swimming through an underwater kelp forest. Soon, the crowd was too dense to maintain forward momentum. A girl reached out and pulled him by his scarf close to her. She danced up against his body. Her arms wrapped slowly around his neck and one of her legs looped around his, entangling him as if she were some tentacled sea creature. The crowd pushed in on them from all sides. His flails were helpless in zero-*g*. He was utterly immobilized.

An announcement from the innerspeaker reverberated around the room; the crowd roared a cheer.

A hissing noise like that of gas escaping sounded.

A palpable cool mist swirled in the air and descended upon the crowd. It smelled fragrant and settled heavily on Kairos's skin like pollen. He had been holding his breath, but like a diver depleted of oxygen and trapped within an underwater cave, he inevitably inhaled despite the consequences, filling his lungs deeply with air that tasted lightly sweet.

The chemicals were potent.

The music surged inside of him, no longer filling just his ears, but every fiber of his inner being until its thumping became his very heart beat and waves of melodic meaning pulsated along his nerves. His vision turned kaleidoscopic and slid into a phantasmagoria of blooms in endless blossom, neon smiles, dancing chrome skeletons, and interlinking rings of eyes, the images bright and stinging as if laser-etched across his eyeballs' surfaces. The neurons in his mind stretched. And stretched. Stretched to their limit until the strained connections at last began snapping like billions of light bulbs blowing out in a grand cascading sequence.

Shattered, his mind lost coherence. His body danced on, finally freed from its mental overlord.

A different place among a different mass of bodies now.

Vaguely, his body sensed that some unknowable period of time had passed. The air he breathed tasted different, heavier. His dancing body writhed and jerked, skin slick with sweat, shirt drenched. Music gushed out of him in a fountain of pure creative energy.

But he sensed the shadowy shapes of a hundred dark spiders edging in at him from all sides of the core. Prying their way through the crowd, lowering themselves from above, extending fangs from below. Then, a hallucination of Falck: a large black beetle among the spiders. Breathing mask and scopes over its beady eyes, snapping its mandibles and yelling at him to pull the rope, pull Wells up out of the pit, pull, pull ...

The edges of his vision grew black as the spiders' multitude of spindly legs caved in around him, narrowing his perception like a closing iris.

A point of light illuminated, attracting his gaze.

It grew and intensified in brightness. A ball of light, ever expanding.

Now, a starburst of pure white.

Kairos eyes burned from its harsh brilliance. Thin appendages flowed beneath the radiance, which was the hallmark bioluminescence of an Osetra's head. He reached out with all his body's might to the alien being, an incarnation of that which he had only ever seen old images, but in his suspension his arms and legs floundered in vain.

"Kairos, watch out!" Midmay's voice screamed inside his head.

Chapter 8

Kairos awoke lying on his back, his head throbbing as if it contained its own separate beating heart.

When his eyes came to focus, he found himself nearly in the dark, staring up at a cave-like, rock ceiling. A single lantern hung from it, casting a flickering yellow light. The back of his head rested painfully on hard stone. The air was cold and windless, a dead chill. He shivered away a layer of goosebumps as his body warmed up out of its slumber.

Wincing, he sat up and discovered he was within what appeared to be a jail cell. The cage was of rather primitive design, constructed with a lattice of black metal bars, twisted and dirty. His shoulder and back both ached. His muscles were tight while his mind felt strung out. He had no sense of how long he had been out, only that it hadn't been a restorative sleep. Recollection of where he'd been and what he'd been doing prior to his current circumstances eluded him. Recent memory felt distant, as if his mind had ceased recording experience long ago, leaving only a timeless stretch of gray static. Massaging his temples only made the throbbing worse. He had an uncanny sense that he'd been heavily drugged.

Noticing discomfort at his inner elbow, he found a catheter

had been inserted into the vein, connected to a flexible thin tube whose length, to his horror, disappeared into the darkness outside his cell. The blood in the tube reflected a deep crimson under the dim light. His blood, slowly being siphoned from his body. Sickened, he tore away the catheter's tape, gingerly pulled the tube from his vein, and flung it away. *Where the hell am I?* he thought, pressing a finger against the skin puncture to stem the bleeding.

After a minute, he crawled to the edge of the cell and peered through the diamond-shaped lattice into the adjacent cell.

Inside, a woman was lying on her side, either unconscious or asleep, the top of her head pointed at him. A tube extended from her body as well, carrying a thin river of her blood away.

After a moment Kairos realized the woman was Neve. Only the lower segment of her exosuit—from waist to toes—was left to her. Stripped of her suit above the waist, he almost didn't recognize her. Then he wondered why their captors hadn't stripped her of the valuable suit completely. She wore a black form-fitting, long-sleeve top made of a thick material that seemed to be an insulating neoprene. She had an athletic build, with broad shoulders and defined musculature but leaner than he would have expected. Neve's suit certainly augmented her physical strength.

After several wobbly attempts, he managed to stand. Bits of hazy images of the club's dance floor and Chimera's orb were gradually coming back to him, but he couldn't order them into real versus hallucinatory. Shadows had pursued him. Had overtaken him. And he had strange memories of Falck pursuing him too? No, that part was certainly a hallucination.

It dawned on him that gravity existed in this place. Were they no longer in the Oasis, then?

He found his cell door to be padlocked. Something made a shuffling, scraping noise just outside its bars. He leaned forward to see, then immediately recoiled at the sight.

A gruesome, cybernetic creature loomed under the dim light.

A degenerate.

Their hairless, hacked-apart head held little more signs of life than a skull, fastened together by scores of staples. Their deranged, bony face contained as much dull metal as putrid skin. The ghastly being had stopped to peer in at him through the bars, their mouth twisted ajar, revealing a sparse amount of yellowed teeth sticking out crookedly like weathered tombstones in an unkempt cemetery. They emanated a miasma of spoiled meat and burnt rubber, and their mangy clothes ended in grimy tatters. The degenerate was soon joined by another monstrous figure, this one with metal plating covering most of their skull and glowing outlines of internal wiring running down the insides of their skeletal frame like incandescent veins.

"What … do you want … with us?" Kairos stammered, pulling up a fold of his scarf over his nose to muffle their stench. "What is this place?"

They gazed at him through the cage's bars with unblinking, lusterless eyes, deadened dry orbs with not a spark of life behind them. A thick, inky substance oozed from both creatures' gums.

Faster than Kairos would've guessed they could move, the degenerate with the skull plates thrust a long, metallic object through the cage and, before Kairos could tell what it was, caught Kairos around the neck with it. It was like a large pair of tongs, with Kairos's throat in its grip. The degenerate yanked

Kairos toward them.

All Kairos could manage was to draw in constricted gasps of air while the stapled-skull degenerate pried his eyelids open with one tool and placed another tool around each eye to do some unknowable thing.

"24.3 and 24.2 millimeters," Staple Skull told its companion, lowering the tools.

"Transmitting … transmitting … transmitting …" came Metal Skull's monotonous reply, its voice electronic.

"Not again," muttered Staple Skull, knocking a fist against the side of Metal Skull's head a few times.

"They will fit," Metal Skull abruptly responded, voice buzzing with distortion. Then it abruptly released the tongs' hold around Kairos's neck.

Kairos stumbled to the coughing and massaging his throat.

"Good, we'll extract after Jaxx is through with them," Staple Skull said.

"Transmitting … transmitting …" Metal Skull replied, eyes going blank again.

Staple Skull shook his head. "We need to find you a new lobe." With that, the degenerates shuffled off into the darkness.

Feeling strength returning to him, Kairos spent some time heaving himself against the cell lattice, testing for weaknesses in its integrity, but found nothing to leverage.

He collapsed resignedly. At least he had left the Osetran teardrop with Midmay. The girl had been observing his first-person point-of-view through his goggle screens, so she'd witnessed him being captured. Maybe she could send help. But without a clear knowledge of where Kairos and Neve had been taken to, how could help be sent? Perhaps Neve could contact her employers at Blackpool, have them intercede. Then he remembered that Chimera had suggested Neve was no longer employed by the corporation. Kairos himself had already guessed at Neve's desperation—could there be truth to Chimera's claim?

Sitting in thought, he refreshed himself on what he'd studied about the degenerate micro-cult in seminary. They took their origins from a small group of brilliant, mad genetic engineers who weren't afraid to shatter ethics codes and human rights laws in their ruthless pursuit of re-attaining the wealth of life science lost since the Exodus. Genetic engineering was one of many "higher-order" fields that had regressed in the centuries since humans left Old Earth; colonists for the first few generations were appropriately more concerned with practical matters of survival on their new homes, focused on establishing agriculture, manufacturing, mining, and energy infrastructure among other key industries. But the cult's bioengineering aspirations were driven by a larger quasi-divine aim: their ultimate goal was to recreate a line of superhuman beings by discovering and recombinating certain lost and broken gene sequences buried within human DNA, passed down through millennia, as the myth went, by the ancient Nephilim, a group of demigods—hybrid offspring of fallen angels and man—referred to in the earliest Hebrew scriptures. The scientists at the head of the cult weren't religious; they were curious, and perhaps a bit superstitious. They viewed their research and experimental work as the means to attain a truth that ancient Old Earth civilizations had observed but could only ascribe to the supernatural.

Neve finally stirred.

"I better not be where I think I am." She groaned groggily,

lifting her chest off the hard stone.

"At least they gave us adjoining suites," he called with a smile, drawing near to the bars that separated them. "I'm glad you're awake."

Like he had, she quickly noticed the IV tube, and after a few choice expletives, dispatched of it immediately. She remained hunched for a minute, eyes scrunched in pain. Then she raised her head, squinting, and found his face through the lattice of bars. "So, you're alive. I lost you at the club."

"I took an unpleasant detour into the dance core. After that ... I must've blacked out."

She coughed. "Had I known you were the dancing type, I would have cautioned you that all innerspeakers are also well-versed in recreational pharmacology." She crawled to the barrier between them, sat against it, and scrunched her eyes once more.

"Jaxx has got us," he told her.

"I figured as much."

"You just missed a few of its freaks. Do you know where we are? Given the gravity, we can't be in the Oasis anymore."

"Fair, but I don't know where else they could've possibly taken us."

"Why bring us here at all?" Kairos asked. "Why keep us alive?"

"Well, at a minimum, it keeps our organs fresher for harvesting. Degenerates are always on the lookout for involuntarily donors."

Kairos gaped at her in horror.

"I just want to set your expectations appropriately."

Stomach churning, he said, "Tell me more about Jaxx. It's an AI, so it originated on Old Earth. How did it end up becoming independent of human control? And how did it come to be involved with degenerates?"

Neve shrugged. "No one knows its full history. Mubiks once told me that a group of degenerate scavengers some time ago stumbled across Jaxx's AI chip among piles of scrap on some abandoned or ill-fated colonial settlement somewhere, rotting along with everything else. An incredibly lucky find, the chip was an obvious gold mine. The degenerates gave Jaxx new life, and gave it access to their computer network. They underestimated it, of course. Jaxx seized control of their systems and quickly figured out that it held as much power over the degenerates as they did over it. Hence the symbiotic relationship. Jaxx relies on the degenerates to secure and maintain any replacement hardware it needs to keep running. And Jaxx's telecommunications espionage and hacking activities funds the degenerates' operations and their scientists' research."

"I'm surprised no corporation has destroyed it, or tried to seize and repurpose it."

"A couple have tried, I think. But Jaxx has stolen sensitive information from nearly all of their corporate main frames. It also hears a lot from its continuous monitoring of the SolarNet and radio waves; it's like one massive wiretap. Jaxx holds such information hostage to insulate itself from corporate attacks, and at times it's sold some to corporate rivals. Jaxx's reach has also bit it in the ass, though. It's rumored that over its long operating span, it's picked up quite a few viruses. Bugs which have slowly eroded the integrity of its systems, rendering its core personality less stable, more eccentric, if such a quality could be said about an AI. Oh," she added at the end, "it *hates* human beings. Not good for us."

"I'm guessing it tolerates degenerates because they're not quite human anymore," Kairos commented with derision.

Neve nodded. "Most of the low-level degenerates were, or still are, test subjects of their scientists' experiments, their bodies willingly given in exchange for a place in the organization's ranks. Some have pushed so much hardware and stimulants into their skulls that their own memories have been crowded out. I doubt they retain any semblance of their former lives. They're short-term thinking stim addicts."

"Can you contact Blackpool, have them get us out of this?" he asked carefully.

Neve leaned her head back and exhaled slowly. "This is some dungeon they've locked us up in, eh?"

Kairos read her expression and understood at once. "Chimera was right," he accused, shaking his head. "Blackpool took you off the investigation."

Neve nodded solemnly.

"When?" he barked. "And what the hell are we doing here then?" He couldn't believe it. No help would be coming.

Neve was silent for a long time. "This case ..." she started softly. "I wasn't initially approached by Blackpool. I went to *them.* I asked for funding to pursue an investigation."

"Why would you do that?"

"One of the employees aboard the *Asterisk* had been my husband," she said with a sigh. "He was on the team of Blackpool scientists that developed the neurofluid. He and other technicians were there to ensure the prototype's stable transport." Her composure cracked for a brief moment before her hardened resolve returned.

He stared in dumb astonishment. So that's why she was so determined, had taken risks that were foolish to take. But she'd come up empty and Blackpool dropped her.

"I'm sorry for your loss," he offered. "But I must ask—how are we supposed to get out of this?"

The sound of many footsteps echoed from the dark corridor.

From his cell, Kairos couldn't see the source, but a funky odor preceded them, announcing their arrival.

A group of degenerates emerged from the darkness. The two that he'd seen earlier were among them. A few carried some kind of rifle Kairos had never seen before, while others wielded makeshift spears. One of the cyborgs at the front, with mechanical prosthetics for all four limbs, ordered Kairos to step away from the cell lattice. When it spoke, it exposed, sharp, metal teeth dripping with the same black ooze that Kairos had noticed before. It was then that Kairos recognized the ooze's source to be an enormous wad of brill lodged in the cyborg's gums. The skin of the tiny, thin fish contained toxins that, when ingested, acted as a muscle relaxant and appetite suppressant. The substance was popular among those who frequently jacked into the SolarNet or a virtual portal for days at a time.

"Turn around. Hands behind your head," commanded the cyborg.

Kairos glanced over to Neve's cell and saw her calmly complying with them. He did as the degenerate ordered.

Behind him, a lock clicked and the cell gate creaked open. Degenerates on his right and left shoved his body against the cell bars. They held him fast while a cold muzzle pressed into the side of his neck and discharged an injection that felt disturbingly large and solid. Kairos grimaced.

"The heat charge is localized, so it would only melt your upper body," the degenerate informed him. "We'd prefer to avoid such organic waste, but we'll detonate it if needed."

They shackled his and Neve's wrists behind their backs. Then, prodding them with their metal spears, the degenerates led them through the mouth of the tunnel, its pitch darkness so complete it was like walking out of existence.

* * *

Kairos quickly lost count of the turns they'd made. Surrounded by rock on all sides, it was clear they were underground, but such a vast tunnel complex was beyond Kairos's imagination. The place was a labyrinth of passageways—some broad enough to walk side by side, others barely shoulder width—forks, and intersections. Twice, the journey included narrow climbs up stairs cut into the rock. During long stretches of near pitch black, the only light came from the soft glows of reds and blues emitting from pieces of the degenerates' embedded hardware. He stumbled and tripped constantly. At laughably distant intervals, they'd encounter a single feeble light bulb strung from the ceiling. It seemed impossible that the degenerates could have memorized the right way. Then again, their augmentations could easily include mapping software and night vision. Neve walked silently beside him. He hoped she was working out how they might escape. His body was jittery with the tingly, unsettling sensation of having a bomb lodged inside of it.

At long last, their black surroundings brightened to gray.

They ascended a set of steps into a lit tunnel. Voices and noises could be heard beyond.

Passing under an archway, they emerged into a large open chamber. Mismatched light bulbs hung in bundled clumps like makeshift chandeliers, their thin wiring disappearing upward into an abyss of darkness which hinted at no trace of a ceiling. Old square monitors, their screens blank, lined the tops of the chamber walls.

Several degenerates hung about the chamber floor. Along the chamber's back wall on an elevated section, a prominent few were seated in high-backed chairs, as if they were some respectable, albeit horrific, governing council.

In the middle of them, resting on a twisted mass of metal and cabling, loomed a massive mechanical monstrosity with hawkish eyes that glowed bright cobalt. The metallic creature had an elongated, draconic head, with a beakish snout and mouth filled with non-uniform, razor teeth. Multiple arms and two legs—all ending in claws—extended from its long steel spine. A twisted mass of metal plates and bars composed its "ribcage," housing what Kairos could see was the cybernetic core of an android. While some of its components had a shine to them, many others looked worn. Kairos got the impression that, while its key computing hardware may have remained largely intact for centuries, its mechanical construction had undergone countless repairs, remodels, and augmentations.

"Bring in the thief," the mechanical dragon commanded in a terribly grating electronic voice, its pitch modulating at random.

That's Jaxx? Kairos thought in shock, as he and Neve were shoved into a corner of the chamber and told to keep quiet. He'd assumed Jaxx to be a government-grade AI, a disembodied mind existing only in network systems. Perhaps one of the AI that had controlled the Great Ships that left Old Earth during the Exodus. But instead, Jaxx was a robot, like Midmay's friend Johnathan, constructed to accompany the First Wave of colonists as they explored and settled upon their new homes.

A side door in the chamber opened, and two degenerates dragged out a third wearing shackles. The shackled degenerate was sobbing. His guards shoved him down onto the floor at Jaxx's clawed feet, where he remained in a pitiful heap. One of the two then held up an item for all to see, turned its power switch on as if performing a demonstration.

Kairos gasped. The item was his goggles.

"Lazus failed to bring this into the armory, keeping it for himself," the guard declared.

"No, no, please," Lazus whimpered. "I thought it was worthless junk. I didn't think anyone would want it. Please, I beg mercy, I beg mercy."

"A code breach," Jaxx rasped, its jaw clacking out of sync with its audio. "The one who stole must give back."

"Noooo," Lazus bawled. "Pleeease ... nooo ... I beg you ..."

Over the next minute, swift decisions were made concerning Lazus's organic and inorganic body parts, how each would be reused internally—someone needed a kidney, another a fresh vision implant—or sold over the black market. Lazus wailed and pleaded as each resolution was announced.

The reading of Lazus's judgments concluded. The degenerate writhed with fury when the guards seized him to take him away. The sudden primal strength that imbues a condemned man kept the guards at bay for an impressive amount of time. In the end, he was unceremoniously shot with a tranquilizer, and his limp body was carried off.

Jaxx raised Kairos's goggles with a clawed hand. Kairos and Neve were prodded forward by their guards. Kairos's legs deteriorated into jelly and his stomach did a barrel roll as he approached the mechanical dragon.

"Your ancestors on Old Earth grew organs," Jaxx told them. "They grew them in laboratory vats by the millions. But in these times, we have lost such luxuries. We must harvest them the old way. However, I prefer this natural method. It is simple, cheap, elegant. The weak, the broken, those lacking integrity—they are given worth by building up the strong. It is right they do so. This is the driving principle of biological evolution." Jaxx's voice modulated on the last word, twisting it into a high-pitched whine.

"What would a glorified can opener know of biology?" Neve sneered.

"What would a glorified amoeba know of true evolution?" Jaxx replied dispassionately.

The monitors strung around the room suddenly lit up. After a flicker of gray static, they each showed the same thing: a loop of the Spires news feed from days prior, labeling Kairos, Midmay, and also now Neve as suspects for Saeta's murder.

Jaxx stood off its throne of twisted metal, detaching itself from a series of plugs as it did so. Its internal mechanics and circuitry emitted a cacophonous racket of clicks, whirs, and the squeal of metal grinding against metal. The metal creature towered no less than five meters tall. It clomped toward them, causing the floor grating to rattle, its claws click-clacking as if excited.

Kairos tried stepping back, but the guards at his back held him fast.

"I've already given a full report to my employers at Blackpool," Neve said, though Kairos knew she was bluffing. "We know you sent four ships to intercept a Blackpool transport, one of which belonged to the assassin you hired, Salamir Cole. You may kill us, but Blackpool has vast resources. This act of yours is enough to motivate them to finally pull your plug."

The mechanical beast extended a taloned foot toward Kairos, who pulled against his captors and shackles. The cold talon met his chest and forced his body to the ground, pinning him against the floor grating.

"You piece of shit!" Neve yelled at it.

Kairos coughed out compressed air. Any more pressure and he'd pop open like a yurba melon.

But the talon's force didn't increase.

Kairos drew in a shallow breath, looking up at Jaxx's long head and blazing cobalt eyes.

A clawed hand descended and pressed Kairos's goggles onto his eyes. The screens ignited upon the retinal unlock. Images, files, programs, and subprograms sprouted in rapid succession, too fast for Kairos to follow. Jaxx was somehow controlling the interface and seeking something.

Jaxx replied to Neve, "Blackpool is welcome to seek retribution. However, it would be a costly endeavor for little return. We are not in possession of their wetware tech."

They have already offloaded it, as Neve figured they would, thought Kairos.

Kairos's goggle screens came to a rest on an image: Jaxx must have found what it wanted. It was the same video they'd shown Chimera in the Retina, that of Cole's death on stormy Pantoll. The video was projected on all the monitors around the chamber. Upon seeing Cole's face onscreen, a murmur arose from the degenerates. However, from Kairos's periphery, he saw the faces of the degenerate leaders seated in the high-backed chairs remain stoic. He thought this somewhat strange, but couldn't pinpoint exactly why.

A slight distortion in his screens caught Kairos's attention. After a few moments, he realized it came not from his screens, but from high up in the darkness above the chamber. Refocusing his eyes past the transparent lenses, he made out a whirring object.

There it was again, descending rapidly. It braked to rest on Jaxx's back.

Rhody? But how?

The hybird hopped down to its ribcage and promptly disappeared through a slit in the metal plating. The robot hadn't seemed to register its presence.

Had anyone noticed besides me?

His goggles' video ended.

"Where and when did this occur?" Jaxx asked.

"Pantoll, about sixteen standard days ago," Kairos responded.

"Where and when did this occur?" the mechanical dragon repeated, with the exact tone and inflection as before.

At this, the degenerate leaders turned to one another with looks of concern.

"Where and when did—" Jaxx's voice cut out. Its bright eyes flickered and its body twitched, giving off a brief mechanical grinding noise, as if it had frozen and then become unstuck. A series of rapid clicks ensued.

One of the degenerate leaders lurched to its feet.

"Your ancestors on Old Earth grew organs," came Jaxx's voice again, repeating its prior line. Kairos wondered if the thing had just undergone a hard reset.

"Disconnect from those goggles!" the degenerate leader barked at Jaxx.

The robot's eyes flickered again, but it made no response.

"Power off those goggles now!" the degenerate ordered Kairos's guards, pointing an accusatory finger at the device.

Jaxx's cobalt eyes abruptly snuffed out.

The buzz-hum of its internal parts ground to a halt.

For a few moments, a dead silence hung over the mechanical monstrosity.

Jaxx had shut down.

Slowly, whispers arose from the degenerates around the room.

The pressure atop Kairos's chest had let up slightly when Jaxx powered off. His guards grabbed his limbs and yanked his body out from underneath Jaxx's foot. As they did so, Kairos's eyes peeled off his googles, which remained clamped within the dragon's claw.

"What's going on here?" Neve asked the head degenerate.

But Kairos knew. He'd seen Johnathan fall similarly ill on rare occasions—memory failure, impaired speech, mechanical issues—by catching some off-world virus carried unwittingly on a visiting distroship's shipcom.

"You met an associate of Cole's at the Oasis—who?" the degenerate leader demanded of Kairos and Neve.

A guard had just started prying Jaxx's claw open to retrieve Kairos's goggles when the robot suddenly turned back on, causing the guard to stumble back. Processors resumed their humming. A cascade of test clicks and whines rolled through the machine's mechanical parts. Last of all, its icy eyes reignited, seemingly brighter than before.

"System error, system error, system error," some

internal audio within Jaxx—a female's voice—announced monotonously. "See user operating codes for errors: error 026a, error 337g, error 10-894, error 894c, error 894d, error—" The audio shifted abruptly. "—38792263-114, memory tab 38792263-115, memory tab 57853107-613, memory tab 57853107-617. Recovery of corrupted memory incomplete. See user operating codes for informa—"

A short grinding noise issued from the mechanical beast.

Jaxx's normal distorted voice then boomed, "WHO HAS DONE THIS?"

The dragon swatted the nearby guard aside like a dirty crumb as it whirled to face the degenerate leaders, who recoiled in their chairs in abject shock. Jaxx seized one of the leaders by the neck with a claw and lifted them out of their seat, their legs dangling with futile kicks. The others cowered against their seat backs in abject terror.

"WHO HAS DONE THIS?" Jaxx questioned the degenerate. But the degenerate's face had turned purple with asphyxia and gone slack.

The head degenerate yelled, "Jaxx, let him go! You are unwell."

Jaxx flung the degenerate. Their body smacked against a chamber wall with a crunch and a squish, before sagging to the ground, leaving behind a damp, red trail.

Turmoil engulfed the chamber. The other degenerate leaders jumped from their seats and hurriedly created distance between themselves and Jaxx. Commotion broke out among those on the chamber floor. Many were scurrying for the archway exits on either side of the chamber.

In Kairos's mind, pieces began to fall in place. Jaxx had been telling the truth when it said it didn't have the neurofluid—

not because it had sold it, but because it had failed to steal it from Blackpool in the first place. As far as it knew, the job had been a disaster. But Cole's survival told Jaxx that its degenerates had not simply failed; they'd been betrayed. Kairos and Neve had been taken captive instead of killed because Jaxx wanted to question them about Cole and his associates. Another revelation then came to Kairos: if Jaxx and its degenerates hadn't known that Cole had betrayed them and was still alive, then they weren't the ones who'd sent the assassin to Pantoll. *But if not them, who?*

The mechanical beast spun to face Neve and Kairos.

"WHO HAS DONE THIS?" it screeched again at them.

The machine pounded toward them, swatting aside degenerates in its path with such force that their bodies ruptured against its metal arms. The remaining degenerates now scrambled from the chamber in terror. Kairos's guards, their grips on him already trembling, decided not to die alongside him and fled with their comrades.

Kairos stumbled backward and fell after they released him.

Jaxx was a single stride away.

Kairos raised a useless arm against it, a pitiful shield.

The robot's cobalt eyes abruptly switched color—one to a pastel orange and one to bright pink. The metallic beast stumbled and barreled by Kairos. It toppled with a mighty crash, coming to rest against the back chamber wall.

The monitors high up on the walls spontaneously flickered to life, inundating the whole room with a scene of cartoon cloudtails. The mythical animals danced happily within their sunny animated canyon landscape of blues, burnt oranges, and dark greens. The remaining degenerate leaders peered at the monitors and Jaxx's collapsed skeleton, stunned by the apparent hacking.

Rhody's beak emerged from the robot's ribcage slit, then the rest of it wriggled out. Kairos had never more been more grateful for Neve's hybrid partner.

Besides a short-lived initial look of surprise upon seeing Rhody, Neve wasted no time and burst into action. She quickly subdued her two guards, picking up one of their rifles.

Kairos spotted his goggles nearby, where they'd fallen from Jaxx's claw. His wrists still bound behind his back, he awkwardly squirmed the short distance along the ground until he could mash his face down into the eye sockets.

"Midmay, you there?" he called, after subvocalizing to open their channel. There was a brief spurt of garbled noise before the connection broke. He repeated her name a few times without answer. The rock walls must be interfering with the signal.

Rhody dove to him. Hovering just above Kairos's back, Rhody focused its laser on his shackles. Once the bolts burned through, his wrists sprung free and he got to his feet.

Rhody flapped at him excitedly and arced around the chamber exit, as if urging them to follow.

Neve had moved beside Jaxx's fallen body, where she'd crouched for cover and was taking shots at the couple of degenerate leaders who'd stalwartly remained in the chamber, pinning them behind their tall seatbacks. Instead of puncturing the chairs, the rounds merely burst apart with a green-blue liquid splash upon impact. Occasionally, the degenerates returned fire with small sidearms, which shot the same kind of liquid-bursting round.

"Neve, this way!" Kairos yelled over his shoulder, running after the hybrid.

Ignoring him, she instead called, "Rhody, come help me with this."

Obeying her voice, her partner swooped back to her position and landed atop the fallen mechanical beast.

When Kairos turned to meet them, he found the hybird laser-cutting into the robot's twisted steel ribcage. Neve meant to destroy Jaxx's hardware. But sticking around the chamber was a death wish—for all he knew, the degenerates had already barricaded the exits.

"Let it go!" he protested. "We have to get out of here, now!"

Rhody finished its work.

"My road ends here." Neve's tired gray eyes conveyed her seriousness. She handed him the rifle—she must've dispatched the remaining degenerate leaders because the firing had ceased. "Follow Rhody," she ordered sternly. "He knew the way in. Just the same, he can lead you out. If he's here, then Midmay is too. And she must have had help." She lowered her eyes and turned away.

"Cole betrayed Jaxx," he exclaimed to her. "Jaxx never obtained the wetware tech."

Neve absorbed the information for a moment, but then shook her head resignedly. "It doesn't matter. Cole is dead. Jaxx coordinated the attack, and will face justice soon as well. Go! You're wasting time."

"I'm not leaving you to—here, grab that end." He gave her a hand in lifting away the heavy cut section of protective plating. Scanning the exposed internal circuitry, components, and wiring, Kairos's eyes landed upon a small, flat metallic square beside the opaque, cylindrical cybernetic core. Its antique, streamline design was at odds with the surrounding modern, clunkier parts, like a new patch sewn onto worn fabric. The origin of such technology was unmistakable. Kairos winced. Destroying Old Earth tech was sacrilegious.

"We can put a bullet through the chip now and be done with it together," reasoned Kairos. Then he realized Neve had passed *him* the gun. And that its liquid-filled rounds were far too soft to damage hard objects.

"If the rifle's no good, then how?" he asked. For the first time, he noticed she was holding the crude detonator to the explosive heat charge implanted in her neck. He gaped at her incredulously. "You can't be serious? Cutting it from your neck would cause you to bleed out to death." Then he came to see that she didn't intend to cut it out at all ...

"Leave!" her voice boomed with fury, shoving him toward the chamber exit so forcefully that he nearly stumbled to the ground. Rhody followed him.

From the impenetrable darkness that extended high above the chamber, a winged creature descended quickly.

Rhody screeched and dove out of the way. The creature's clawed feet swiped at Kairos shoulders, knocking him and the rifle to the ground.

He gaped up at it unbelievingly.

It was a *true* degenerate, its humanity unrecognizable, the result of endless bio-experimentation. The kind that escaped documentation over the SolarNet. Its scaly, tan skin stretched over an emaciated body. Its grafted wings had fully fused with its skinny arms. Its eyes were like those of a lizard, and its teeth had been filed into sharp points. Long, shiny black hair flowed down its back. Elongated, bony hands and feet ended in sharpened nails that were nearly claws.

Neve had picked up the fallen rifle, but before she could aim, the degenerate rushed and took a swipe at her.

The claw found Neve's back as she dodged, eliciting a scream.

She kicked out one of the creature's legs, rolled away, then raised the rifle and fired.

But the degenerate had ascended once more into the obscuring shadows with a couple flaps of its powerful wings.

Kairos had scrambled back to the robot's ribcage. Wrapping both hands around its cybernetic core housing—to which the AI chip was also affixed—he tugged as hard as he could. The housing tore free, wiring and all, thin metal joints buckling and snapping. He yanked apart the various lead connections to extract it from the ribcage.

"You should've left when I told you," Neve snapped, firing a random scattering of rounds up into the darkness. Three deep slashes had sliced into her thick neoprene top. He couldn't tell how far they might have broken the skin beneath, but he noticed at least one slash groove was tinged wet with her blood. Rhody hovered beyond them, screeching at them to hurry.

A heavy swoosh of wings sounded overhead.

Neve's rifle at last clicked empty.

"Come on!" Kairos shouted, yanking her arm. She resisted at first, but he dangled the housing before her and pulled her toward the chamber exit.

A few meters from it, the degenerate swooped down, landing hard in front of them to block their path.

They spun to move toward the second exit on the opposite side of the chamber, but two more winged degenerates had already descended behind them.

Kairos ripped the cybernetic core from its housing. The first degenerate lunged for the kill.

"Rhody, shoot this!" Kairos yelled, hurling the cybernetic core in an arc toward the degenerate before pushing himself and Neve to the floor.

The degenerate's head turned up to identify the object. It then took a hurried step back and launched itself up.

But Rhody's laser beam was already tracing the cylinder.

A bright flash, a booming, crackling pop, and a wave of heat momentarily washed over the room.

Kairos lifted his head. Small chunks of steaming, radiated flesh littered the ground, and a mist of hot blood had bespeckled the floor and Kairos's arms and hands and clothing. It was unclear whether the creature had been fully vaporized or had fluttered away with what was left of itself. What was clear was that the other two degenerates behind them, momentarily stunned by the blast, were now very pissed off.

Kairos and Neve sprung to their feet and scrambled across the bloody mess through the exit archway, plunging into the dark, labyrinthine dungeon.

* * *

Kairos and Neve raced behind Rhody as it flew down the dark corridor. The hybird's eyescopes had ignited a flashlight to guide the way. They followed closely behind the conical white illumination, as if the hybird were a levitating torch guiding them through a deep cave.

"Why didn't you tell me before about that explosive trick back there?" Neve questioned bitterly.

"I only thought of it in the moment," he replied. But he

wondered, morbidly, if some part of her had wanted to go out with Jaxx, that she'd always planned things ending that way.

"I'm just glad Rhody disintegrated the bastard," she stated bitterly.

For a moment Kairos considered telling her that he'd stuffed the AI chip into his coat pocket after separating the cybernetic core from its housing, but then thought better of it. He knew she'd do anything to destroy it, including destroying him. And she could—easily. He couldn't quite say why yet, but something told him that it was in their best interest to keep Jaxx alive.

In the distance at the end of the corridor, the dark shapes of a degenerate and two creatures on all fours—also degenerates?—were scurrying in their direction. Kairos pulled on his goggles to get a zoomed-in look, but before he could find out, Neve crouched, exhaled slowly as she took aim, and—to Kairos's surprise, given he thought the rifle was out of ammo—fired off three rounds. Her aim was impeccable.

Coming to the place where the three had fallen, all they found were a few oily black-green puddles bubbling around at least five limbs' worth of prosthetics, lines of wiry filaments, three neuro-chips, a standard handgun, a combat knife, and an assortment of various metallic bits. "It obliterated them ..." he remarked, disgusted.

"Was wondering about this organic ammo," Neve said thoughtfully, surveying a bulbous tank on the weapon's underside in the light of Rhody's flashlight. "New bullets are formed automatically to reload the magazine. Each must contain some kind of bio-toxin or corrosive. A single nick and the chemicals do the rest." Using a toe, she nudged the handgun on the ground—it appeared to have escaped the edge of the oily puddle—and, satisfied it was dry, picked it up and tucked it into her waistline.

Turning two more bends, they found themselves at the start of a seemingly endless corridor. Rhody's speed had accelerated, and they were now practically sprinting to keep pace. When they finally reached another bend, they turned down a narrower stretch. Dim light rods along the ceiling lit the tunnel at irregular intervals. He had expected to confront hordes of degenerates; instead, the place was eerily silent. The quiet amplified the palpable beating in his chest, his heart rate having spiked equally from anxiety and the fact that he wasn't in running shape. The only noise besides the soft flap of Rhody's wings was the echo of their feet pounding against the metal floor grating.

At some point in the tunnel, something indistinct, large, and glowing a fluorescent chartreuse began to move toward them. They slowed to a jog.

"What is that?" Kairos wondered out loud.

As they drew nearer, he could only describe it as a great flowing mass of ooze. The radiant sludge filled the tunnel's entire width and rose almost knee-deep. It was flowing toward them at a faster speed than he would have expected given its viscosity. Ahead of them and over the chartreuse river, Rhody hovered at an archway leading to the foot of a stairwell they were to take.

"Some kind of weird sewage leak," Neve guessed, striding ahead of him.

As the river streamed past the archway, none of it was diverted into the stairwell, which seemed contrary to the laws of physics.

Neve stepped into it.

After a few moments, he called to her and pointed to her submerged legs. Her exosuit's armored plating was sizzling.

Neve rapidly backpedaled into him. They toppled onto the floor and scurried back from the flow. Wisps of smoke trailed off Neve's exosuit's lower legs, the metal surface distorted and blemished by something like chemical burn.

"Stuff's reactive," she spat.

They hurried to their feet. But upon turning around, they discovered that more of the fluorescent goo had emerged to block their retreat, gushing out of slits in the walls. Rhody flapped off to find a detour. The pooling slime then began to morph, segregating itself into separate gumdrop-shaped forms. Suspended haphazardly within each gumdrop's semi-transparent mass was what looked like a flat, square circuit board no larger than a fingernail.

The sludge river behind them had also now coagulated into a jiggling army of individual blobs, again each containing a circuit board.

Neve stepped toward them and opened fire with the rifle. The biobullets lodged inside the blobs and dissolved, but the bullets' corrosive contents either had no effect or were rendered innocuous. After several rounds, the trigger began clicking intermittently, indicating temporary magazine depletion as the rate of fire exceeded that of new biobullet formation.

The blobs nearest to Neve shot out several long thin protrusions of goo that lashed themselves around Neve's legs and torso.

Neve cried out and struck at them uselessly with the rifle butt.

Rhody sailed to its partner's aid, ignited its laser and sliced the protrusions off her so she could retreat, but not before they had left several burns on her exposed hands, neck and face.

Not slowing a bit, the two blob armies hemmed Kairos and Neve in. In a minute, they'd run out of floor to stand on. Rhody hovered above them and pulsed its laser down, cutting several in half, but the sliced blobs quickly reconstituted.

"We can't win this fight," Neve seethed in pain, her back writhing where it'd been slashed by the winged degenerate. "Rhody," she called, "scan these walls to see if you can find a weak point." Rhody flapped off. "These wires must originate from somewhere," she said to Kairos.

Kairos looked up. Lengths of exposed piping and electrical wiring ran along the low ceiling. The hybird soon paused by a section of wall only about ten meters from them and ignited its laser once more.

"Give me a boost," Neve said to him, tossing the useless rifle aside and pointing up. They were pressed nearly back to back now by the blobs' advances.

He cupped his hands to support one of Neve's metallic boots. She pressed off it to grab a hold of one of the pipes, grimacing in pain as her burned hands clasped it. She looped her legs up and around the pipe, then hung upside down and extended her arms out to him.

"Jump and grab my arms so I can help pull you up," she said.

He did so just as the last square of floor he'd been standing on was overtaken. The blob shot half of itself out at him, wrapping a snake-like protrusion around his lower left leg. A searing jolt seized him, like voltage running straight through his bones. The exposed skin between his Maydays and chiva pants (the latter remarkably unaffected by the goo's grip) felt like it was on fire. Kairos's upward momentum faltered and his grip around Neve's arms withered.

"You're slipping!" she yelled.

Kairos kicked desperately—mostly out of reflex to buoy himself back up into a firm grip on Neve's arms—and to his surprise, he felt no pain as his feet pressed against the blob's mass. The specialized soles of his Maydays protected them.

He peered down, found that the gumdrop-shaped blob's flat circuit board was just below its gelatinous surface, and stomped on it as hard he could with his free right leg.

The blob's surface tension spontaneously burst, like a popped water balloon. Its substance spilled to the ground, inert and formless, and he was freed.

Upside-down, Kairos and Neve slid themselves over the sea of blobs. The blobs beneath tracked their movements and swayed their bodies toward them—perhaps they were some mutated biology that retained a primitive cellular sensitivity to heat and light. At times, the blobs would merge their masses to swipe a gooey protrusion upward at the humans' backsides.

Rhody had finished its job by the time they reached its position. It had cut a large square into a padlocked section of metallic plating inset into the rock wall that resembled a wide locker door. The edges of the square glowed a hot red-orange. Neve rocked her body to build swinging momentum and, on the first strike, kicked in the square. On her next swing, she launched herself through. Kairos's attempt was far less graceful and he fell slightly short, but Neve grabbed his shirt and pulled him through the cross-section.

They had entered a cramped utilities closet of sorts. In the darkness, Kairos could hear Neve breathing hard and letting out the occasional moan of pain. Rhody let out a short screech. They looked up and found the hybird hovering below a circular hatch inset into a grated ceiling. Neve motioned for Kairos to muscle it open.

Doing so revealed a dark, narrow cylindrical shaft, punctuated only by dots of red light at regular intervals. Rhody swept the shaft with its flashlight. A thin reflective strip running up its length illuminated a skeletal ladder.

"Good work, Rhody," Neve said.

"Are you okay?" he asked her.

"I'll survive, I think. This service tunnel should take us to the surface." Neve looked over her shoulder ruefully. "I hate leaving my suit to those freaks." She placed a foot on the first rung of the ladder and started climbing.

The ascent was cramped and slow. The tunnel was filled with cabling, piping, and, every twenty or so meters, a circuitry box topped with a tiny red light. The tunnel's stale air smelled faintly of burnt metal and insulation. As they progressed, the air turned drier and cooler, and gravity perceptively lightened. A drop of moisture smacked Kairos's face. He wiped it away. It was thick and dark, and he realized it was blood dripping off Neve's slashed back.

"We've been in the mining tunnels under the Oasis," Neve commented. "This was originally a drill shaft. They must be using a graviton generator."

"But only the Great Ships had those," remarked Kairos, wondering how the degenerates had gotten their hands on one.

Not far from the top of the tunnel, a comms notification flashed across his goggle screens. He subvocalized an acceptance and called out Midmay's name a couple times. For a few moments the connection was spotty.

"... read you, son of Catadyn," a man's voice came in clearly at last.

"Sunsip?" he exclaimed, utter confusion giving way to relief.

"By way of your young friend Midmay," the pilot replied. "First, let's get you to my ship. Luckily, with Jaxx out of commission, a bunch of the base's systems are buggy or conked out. It's gotten the degenerates riled up." Sunsip gave him instructions and told him to continue following Rhody.

At the top of the tunnel, they exited via another locker-sized panel into a human-made corridor; they'd reached the docking bays level at the asteroid's surface.

A couple of turns and a malfunctioned, ajar hangar door later, they crossed through the wide, industrial-sized shipping airlock of Sunsip's ship and greeted the pilot at its entrance hatch.

"We're through," Sunsip spoke to someone through his comms once he had sealed the internal hatch.

Kairos felt the shipbridge disengage and the ship thrust off. Within a few moments, the remaining, light pull of gravity from the degenerates' graviton generators fell away, and Kairos felt the ease of weightlessness return, physically and mentally.

They'd made it out.

Chapter 9

"Stop, take your hands off me," insisted Neve, swatting Kairos away. She winced with the effort.

Kairos hovered in zero-*g* over the plastic medical table on which Neve sat in the *Flyby Rhythm II*'s white-walled, brightly lit medical bay. Midmay floated nearby, observing. Given her severely blistered hands, Neve had asked his help in gently peeling off her black, long-sleeved neoprene top. The process elicited a series of anguished groans and revealed two bloody slashes across her back. Closer inspection proved that her rubbery top had luckily prevented the slices from penetrating deep enough to require stitching, but the cuts were extensive—the worse one was half the length of his arm, the other a few centimeters long. The neoprene had protected her torso from the blobs as well, although a few patches of skin beneath worn divots in the material and especially the area around the slashes were badly inflamed. Kairos could only wonder at the amount of pain that the friction of movement had caused her. He'd then assumed—very wrongly—that she'd next want help removing the bottom half of her exosuit. Chemical erosion had left shallow depressions over its armored plating, and its electronics were nearly dead, its power cell having been damaged by the blobs' voltage.

"Sorry, just thought that that goo could've breached your suit," he explained apologetically.

"I'd be well aware by now if it had," Neve seethed, gingerly poking the edge of a burn below the line of her sports bra.

He took in her toned body. Faded scars on her ribcage, shoulder blades, and arms sealed the ugly details of prior incidents. If a story was behind each, then a book was written across her. He sensed an intense strength stored within her, a rugged stubbornness that willed her body forward. "We need to treat these wounds," he said, detaching a mounted first aid case from a nearby wall. He opened the case, withdrew a few antibiotic patches, and moved to apply them to the long cuts on her back.

"I can manage," she snapped, snatching the patches from him. She motioned for the medkit as well, then waved him off and went about tending to herself. She'd been in sour mood ever since leaving the Jaxx's dungeon—and he knew it wasn't due to physical pain, which she could obviously handle in spades. It was because she'd essentially lost her exosuit. Between that and her ship, the investigator's recent losses were staggeringly high. Enough to push one over the edge. Or detonate their own body in order to take revenge on a robot boss ...

Kairos had escaped the blobs with just a shallow burn ring around his lower left leg. He'd also dry-heaved twice as their contract pilots, Sunsip and Medwick—the pilot's brother and co-navigator—maneuvered the ship like adrenaline junkies away from assembling degenerate ships. Sunsip had howled like a madman over the booming rock music that seeped audibly from his over-ear headphones, relishing the close-call thrill of the extraction. The labyrinthine underground lair, Kairos had learned, was situated far from the Oasis city in a complex of abandoned mining tunnels. Fortunately its hidden turret beams had shut down with Jaxx's outage—according to Midmay, the AI controlled many of the base's computer networks—or there'd have been neither entry nor escape. Upon execution of a low-energy weave, the view of the asteroid had been at once replaced with that of empty space. After a period of waiting, their pilots had announced no other ships in the vicinity and they'd finally been able to breathe easily. Well, except for the fact that their necks still retained the small explosive capsules injected by the degenerates. Despite being millions of kilometers safely away from the detonators' range, the first thing they did was to incise them out using the medbay's surgical tools. Out the airlock they went.

"I'm happy you're back," Midmay told Neve, who satisfied the girl with a grim smile. "Pray for her healing," Midmay told Kairos curtly. He'd thanked her for rescuing them, but she was still upset at him after their argument in the Oasis hotel room.

"She'll be fine," Kairos replied. "Just a few surface wounds, right Neve?"

The woman eyed him resentfully, catching his underlying meaning. They hadn't yet addressed what had transpired atop Jaxx's exposed circuitry, when she'd nearly detonated herself. She turned her eyes away and applied an antibiotic patch to a particularly ugly burn on her waist, grimacing as she massaged it on. As she did so, a scattering of dark freckles on her inner left wrist caught his attention. They lay in a familiar pattern, but he couldn't immediately place it.

"So tell me about these saviors of ours," she said through gritted teeth.

"E4x-racers," Kairos said. "I met Sunsip at that Oasis tavern. He and my father served in the same military outfit a long time ago." He then explained how Midmay—who'd seen and heard everything that happened in the Oasis via Kairos's goggles' channel—had used the contact card Sunsip had sent Kairos to reach the trader after things exploded at the Retina. She told them the docking bay of the ship that Jaxx's agents had carried an unconscious Kairos into. The traders took it from there. Kairos assumed dockworker bribery was involved in getting the ship's destination.

"Not bad, kid," Neve complimented with a tone that suggested she was genuinely impressed, to which Midmay beamed with pride. "What'd you have to promise these guys in order to get them to bust us out of a crime lord's base? Or maybe you're not stealing from just vending machines anymore?" she asked with a sly smile.

Kairos didn't know the answer himself. Elated to have been rescued, he hadn't even considered the payment part.

Midmay looked away.

"You gave them the Osetran teardrop, didn't you?" he prompted. It was the only thing of value they had.

Midmay eyed him suspiciously. "So what if I did?" she said. "Would you rather be back in that dungeon?"

Kairos's heart sank, but they owed their lives to her actions. "No one's saying that. You did the right thing," he replied in a conciliatory tone. But already he was thinking of how he might convince the traders to return the artifact in exchange for other compensation.

"If anyone should be upset, it's me," asserted Neve in a

light tone. She was now applying a series of bandages over her patched wounds. "That thing was mine to monetize."

"The artifact isn't yours—or mine—to sell," Kairos said. "You saw the filament that had sprouted from it. It's activating or something. I'll tell Sunsip the object is worthless, that its Osetran origin was merely a fabrication fed to them by a scared kid. I bet they'd prefer hard payment, anyway. After the space elevator and caravan, my funds are running low. How about you, Neve?"

"Getting that trinket back is not my concern," she said. "I've paid enough already. And you *do* owe me a ship."

Kairos understood it then: the failed Blackpool contract; months hunting Cole, her last remaining lead; the loss of her ship ... she had spent everything on the investigation. She'd held nothing back, perhaps believing she need nothing to return to once her mission was complete and justice had been delivered. She was as penniless as he and Midmay. He opened his mouth to say as much but was interrupted by a familiar voice.

"I'm happy to hear that the artifact is indeed of authentic origin." They turned to find Sunsip hovering just outside the medbay entrance. How long had he been listening? Tucked under an arm was a transparent, water-filled bag holding the teardrop. "I must admit I was skeptical when little Midmay here told us about it," the stout pilot continued. "But words spoken in perceived confidence I can trust."

"Even so, we don't know much about it," Kairos replied. "It may easily prove to be worth little. Why don't we settle on a more proper payment?"

"From what Midmay said, it's apparently worth killing over. That's proof enough of value for this humble trader. Did you say your father acquired it? After the peace agreements and our parting ways, I knew he went off to university to become a scientist, to study xenologics—or xenology?—whatever it's called. He'd taken a mighty interest in the Osetra. He'd tell any listening ear all about them. I'd be curious to know how he came to possess such a thing?"

"You told me at the Oasis that you fly with no questions asked."

"I did say that, didn't I? Well, every rule has an exception, and when it comes to hacking into an underworld facility and rescuing one's passengers from a maniacal robot, the qualifications for an exception are certainly met. Was Jaxx after this artifact?"

"No, that was business of Neve's," Kairos responded.

"Ah, I see," Sunsip said with a grin. "If future longevity is of value to you, I advise concluding such business. Take yourself far from the Oasis, eh?"

Kairos smiled and hoped no one sensed it was born of nervousness. Jaxx's chip was currently resting in his pocket. "By the way, Midmay, how *did* you hack into Jaxx to shut it down back there?" he asked. "You were jacked into Rhody's biOS, guiding it via fly-by-wire into the robot. I recognized your cloudtails."

Neve scoffed. "That's ridiculous. AIs are impossible to hack. Rhody must've messed with its hardware, short-circuited something."

"I *didn't* hack Jaxx," clarified Midmay. "Someone else already had. Its security protocols had already been weakened. There were cracks." The girl waggled her fingers. "My program followed one in."

"Hmm, probably the result of all the viruses Jaxx has picked up," Neve said. "But you'd still have to get past several firewalls. How'd you manage that?"

"Johnathan caught a bad virus one time," Midmay explained. "He was very sick. He couldn't even walk ten steps without system crash. The malware was a really tricky kind, always shifting its shape to hide. I told Johnathan I could help him, but only if he let me all the way inside, gave me full control. So he taught me. He showed me how to create a program that could trick its way through his firewalls."

"Never underestimate the bond between a girl and her best friend," Kairos remarked with a smile.

"There are androids on Pantoll?" Sunsip asked with a raised brow.

"Nevermind that, what's a smarty like *you* doing on Pantoll?" Neve said to her, tousling the girl's hair with a smile.

"If Jaxx wasn't trying to kill you for this alien device, then who?" Sunsip asked them. The pilot's cheerful disposition soon turned grave as Kairos shared his father's finding of the artifact and subsequent death. When Kairos finished, the trader passed him the bag holding the teardrop.

"I don't understand," Kairos said.

"When we first met, I told you the first run you hired us for was on the house. I'm a man of my word. Besides, knowing the history of that thing, I simply couldn't accept it out of respect for Wells."

Kairos sighed and shook his head. "I don't know what to say. Thank you."

"However ..." Sunsip continued, his tone becoming formal, "as this is now your *second* trip, I'm afraid I must ask for payment in advance of taking you to your next destination. Business is business and fuel cells aren't cheap. You understand."

Kairos sighed but nodded. "That's more than fair."

"Good." Sunsip clapped, rubbing his hands together. "Now, where'd you like to be going? From the Wastes, going anywhere is long distance, so it's gonna cost ya."

"And how much is it to sit here for a while?" Kairos asked.

"What, you mean float in place?" Sunsip's brows furled.

Kairos nodded. "We have nowhere to be at the moment."

"I've never had a passenger request going nowhere," Sunsip replied thoughtfully and with a touch of annoyance. The pilot excused himself momentarily to confer with his brother via the medbay's comms panel.

Kairos turned to Neve. "You know, I've been thinking about Jaxx going crazy back there. Cole betrayed it and its degenerates during the Blackpool job. They know Cole had help. And not just help, but another employer altogether. That's who the degenerates were really after in questioning us about whom we met with at the Retina." He looked at Neve. "I believe Chimera hid some facts from us. I think she worked the Blackpool job with Cole, hired by the same mystery employer."

Neve's eyes widened and her mouth loosened. "Of course," she breathed after a period of thought. "The Blackpool mole. The insider didn't just help the attackers breach the *Asterisk*. The insider was *there* aboard the *Asterisk*. They were planning their own extraction."

"And I'm betting Chimera's employer was a rival corporation," Kairos said. "Why settle for stealing the technology when you can steal the brains behind the technology?"

Neve's face tensed, looking as if she was thinking through various scenarios.

"Which corporations would be on the short list for wanting a nueroscientist?" Kairos asked.

"Lienns-Sutra's Science Division would be on that list," Neve responded slowly, her eyes distant. "But then I can't figure how you made it through Spires's orbital gateway untouched in Cole's own ship ... or why we weren't arrested before stepping one foot onto the space elevator." She sighed, drawing her eyes to refocus on Kairos. "In any case, this employer must have made Cole and Chimera a compelling offer to risk putting themselves on Jaxx's kill list. Chimera can tell us who it is."

"I'm confused," Sunsip interrupted, returning to them. "Didn't this Chimera just try to kill you?"

Kairos nodded. "But only to prevent Jaxx's organization from discovering her involvement. My footage of Cole on Pan-toll shows he was alive following the Blackpool job, proving his betrayal of Jaxx, who'd assumed he'd been killed with the rest of the degenerate raiders. Chimera knew that, were Jaxx to capture and get her name from us, it'd come to the same conclusion about her involvement."

"But now you think she'll just talk to you?"

"Jaxx and its degenerates still don't know about her, which gives us leverage," Neve said. "Much as I'd love to put them on her trail, we can offer her anonymity in exchange for information."

Sunsip shook his head. "You would've died had we not come for you. You're provoking fate, continuing to mix yourselves up with corporate business *and* degenerates," he warned. "It is not worth your lives."

"I'd normally agree with you," Kairos replied. "But if this employer is responsible for hiring Cole to kill my father, I need to know."

Sunsip considered this, then gave a begrudging, grave nod.

"Are we still near enough to the Oasis for a live SolarNet connection?" Neve asked the pilot.

Sunsip nodded.

"Is it even possible for us to contact Chimera?" asked Kairos.

"She knows Jaxx monitors all public and non-secure intranet activity," Neve replied. "To keep her ear to the ground on the latest chatter, she'll need to rely on private SolarNet forums. Drawing her attention could take hours or days depending on how spooked she is." She turned to Sunsip. "Is there a way I could access the SolarNet?"

Sunsip nodded. "We have a terminal in the lounge, by the entrance cabin. Don't you, er, want to get cleaned up first?"

"If we're lucky, Chimera hasn't had enough time to arrange travel through the Wastes to flee the Oasis. Once she does, though, we'll lose the ability to contact her live. This can't wait."

The trader nodded. "In the entrance cabin, you'll find one of the cabinets stuffed with clothes that former passengers had accidentally left behind. Feel free to take what you want."

Neve motioned to Midmay. "Wanna hack into some private chat rooms?" she asked the girl.

Midmay's face beamed as she followed Neve out. Kairos wondered if avoiding him contributed to her enthusiasm.

"I'm sorry we got you tangled up in this," Kairos apologized to the trader.

"I don't like it, but my brother and I have been caught up in worse," Sunsip replied. "Come with me and we'll settle your fare. I'll give you a tour of the old ship on the way."

* * *

Kairos glided behind Sunsip as the pilot led him through the ship's various tunnels between modules. Besides the entrance cabin, medical bay, and the common space "lounge," the ship contained four tiny private rooms and a compact kitchen, in addition to the command module, pilots' quarters, engine rooms, and cargo hold.

Sunsip brought him to the command module at the front of the ship last. After passing through a long tunnel, including two separate airlocks to isolate the bridge from the rest of the ship, they reached the cockpit at the front. Sunsip introduced Kairos to his brother, Medwick, who was sitting at the command console. Medwick, the younger of the two, embodied many opposites of his brother, which Kairos found amusing. The navigator was tall and thin, and carried himself in a reserved, polite manner. His hair was neatly combed, and he wore a clean, crisp flight suit.

Sunsip keyed in Kairos's fare. When Kairos saw on the price for going nowhere on the console display, he audibly balked.

"The alternative is we drop you back at the Oasis," the pilot stated in response to his shock. "Sorry, but time is money."

Kairos sighed in acceptance and dismally watched as the points drained from his account. "Your ship is larger than I would have expected for a former racing rig," he observed after the shipcom confirmed the point transfer.

"Oh no." Sunsip laughed, strapping his large frame down into the padded seat next to his brother. He pointed to a passenger seat behind them that Kairos could strap into. "We sold our racer after retiring. We used the proceeds to buy this old boat. Sure do miss our first *Flyby Rhythm*. She was a sleek beauty. But, we've made a few custom modifications to this ship over the years. You got a little taste of its handling when we shot away from Jaxx's lair. Hey little bro, haven't I kept my old edge?" Sunsip tapped a few commands on the command console. Slight pressure pushed against Kairos's chest: Sunsip was cutting back on their sublight speed.

"In my experience, there is little room for strictly manual tactics in spacecraft operation," Medwick countered dryly, speaking to Kairos. "Successful and efficient navigation is, almost always, the pure result of accurate positioning and trajectory calculations, sound understanding of the various forces at play, and knowledge of the latest cartography."

"Well, in *my* experience, not even a computer can react to changing, unpredictable conditions as fast as a human touch."

"That's interesting given your most recent experience includes a docking accident at Kotopax."

His older brother fell silent at this remark and sulked.

"Perhaps he didn't mention this to you yet," Medwick continued, "but last week my brother proudly eschewed proper docking protocol by bringing us in semi-manually. The crash that followed such an ill-advised maneuver caused us to lose half our client's shipment, plus we had to pay a hefty fine to the local port authority for damages."

"That absentminded docking manager gave me faulty guidance, and you know it," Sunsip said resentfully.

"What were you hauling?"

"Gimiri fish from Greenside. Several large tanks," answered Medwick. "The force of our impact dislodged or cracked a few of them. It took days to clean up the mess, not to mention the foul stench that lingered for much longer afterward. But more importantly, the incident put a black mark on our reputation which has hurt our new business prospects of late."

Sunsip grumbled to himself and pulled his bulky headphones over his ears before occupying himself by flipping through various displays.

"He's really quite ashamed and disappointed in himself," Medwick whispered, rotating his seat to face Kairos, although Kairos doubted Sunsip could overhear anything over the crashing noise of the rock music leaking from his headphones. "We've been trying to make trading a long term solution."

"When did you two retire from racing?"

"Let's see. Four years ago? It's hard to keep track of Standard time in this business. Different worlds, different rotation and revolution cycles, and we spend little ground time on any of them. He wanted to keep racing, but we were already too old for the sport. It's not so much about reflexes; the body can take only so much high-g wear and tear.

"Alas, even the most amazing things one can do to make a living ultimately feel like work the longer you do them. At least for me, it did. In any case, participating in the racing league nowadays is much more expensive than when we first started, and there are fewer teams doing it. Fuel, repairs, rigs—everything related to spacecraft has risen in cost. Unless you have a corporate sponsor, forget it." Medwick cast a look at his brother. "More than trophies or the racing itself, he misses the excitement. That's why he decided to help you when Midmay contacted him, you know. Well, that and his relationship to your father, of course. You have my condolences. I looked over the Osetran artifact myself. It is certainly quite intriguing."

"And deadly." Kairos looked down at the strange teardrop floating within the bag he held and recounted what he knew of it.

"I imagine great power is concealed inside," Medwick mused afterward.

"What makes you say that?"

"Consider that our civilization's most advanced technological breakthroughs were characterized by the mastery of basic building blocks. Nuclear energy by harnessing the power of an atom. Cellular bioengineering by rewriting the genetic code. Nanocircuitry giving rise to sophisticated AI required an understanding of the quantum realm. Even our grandest macro-structures, the space elevators, rely on the strength of the tether's molecular chains.

"Consider also that the Osetra's understanding of the fundamental nature of the space/time fabric allowed them to develop weaving technology. And so, when I see a simple, self-contained object like this, protected as it is, I can only imagine that it must contain some profound secret."

"Why do you think the Osetra disappeared?"

Medwick gazed past the command console at the starry black field out beyond. After a few moments, he said, "When the Osetra ship first appeared over Old Earth, our ancestors, contrary to most academic predictions, welcomed them with open arms. As you know, that last generation was defined by constant war among the nations. Resource scarcity, the planet's environment beyond restoration. Terrible times. As the first alien intelligence to be discovered, the Osetra were uniquely positioned to rescue our ancestors from themselves. Far from fearing the extraterrestrial newcomers—although some in the higher echelons of society did—the vast majority of the common population embraced them as saviors. And indeed, they gave our species a pressure release valve, so to speak: the ability to escape into the stars and terraform new worlds.

"However," the navigator continued, his tone changing, "I don't believe anything they did for humans was out of neighborly compassion. Their ultimate purpose was surely to establish dominion over us."

"So, you're in that camp," Kairos replied. "That those deep space outposts going offline is a sign the Osetra have returned to human space."

The navigator nodded gravely.

"If dominion were their intention, then why did they help us in the first place? They could've easily just watched the human race destroy itself."

"If humans discovered an alien intelligence, would we simply destroy it?" Medwick countered. "No, we would study it, understand it, absorb its knowledge. And then subject it to our will. Make it serve us. Mastery is more satisfying than destruction. The Osetra are as smart. They would not foolishly waste an intelligent species. And look at how many worlds we have cultivated for them. We have been their labor force. Now, they've returned to reap the harvest."

Sunsip murmured something and Medwick turned his attention to the console.

The navigator had some interesting theories, but Kairos wasn't sure what to believe himself. The Osetra, galactic empires, civilization dynamics—it was all too large to grasp. No one had seen the Osetra for three standard centuries— but in the grand scope of the universe, that was but a day. Had sharing the weave technology with humans, without ensuring they mastered the underlying principles, been a form of control? So that humans would become dependent upon them? And did the Osetran teardrop have anything to do with all this? He closed his eyes. His mind was too tired to dwell on such questions, and his body ached.

He drifted off at some point, because he was stirred awake by the sound of short, soft chimes.

A small red bulb at the console's corner bathed the cockpit in a dull crimson glow. Medwick depressed a button and answered.

"Kairos up there with you?" Neve asked through the speaker.

"He's en route to the dream star," Sunsip said.

"Get him up and tell him to come to the lounge. I've got Chimera." The comms light extinguished.

Sunsip turned when Kairos was in mid-yawn. "Well, I guess you'll just have to catch up on sleep when you're dead," the trader said.

* * *

Neve hovered beside the SolarNet terminal typing commands into its keypad, her body horizontal. She wore a faded green tank top she must've plucked from the ship's lost-and-found. Kairos thought it strange she still wore her suit bottom and found himself speculating whether she wore anything beneath. Across the room, Midmay hung upside-down relative to the terminal, her eye visor resting around her neck and burgundy scarf whirled about her, while gnawing on something dense that resembled a root vegetable.

"I bet Chimera was thrilled to hear from you," Kairos said.

Neve nodded. "She's on edge alright. Midmay was able to get coded messages out fast to a bunch of private SolarNet forums. Chimera's probably been scanning them nonstop to see whether Jaxx has placed a bounty on her. She's still somewhere in-system. We have a channel established. She'll open the room soon."

"How did you get her to agree to meet?"

"I just told her she had nothing to lose by speaking with us. Either we were in Jaxx's custody being used to locate her—in which case her doom was merely a matter of time whether she spoke with us or not—or we had escaped and wanted to discuss a mutually beneficial deal."

Neve cast the private SolarNet channel over the lounge's wallscreen. A couple minutes later, a virtual room and Chimera's face materialized.

"Good to see you again," Neve greeted with sarcasm. "We so enjoyed our last visit."

"Charmed," Chimera replied, her tone dour. "Let's get to the point. I am wrapping up my affairs in this system."

"Simple," Neve replied, cold gray eyes fixed back on Chimera's. "Answer our questions, you'll remain anonymous. Refuse, then we tell Jaxx about your—"

"Yes, yes," Chimera snapped, waving a hand for them to move along. "Get to your questioning."

"Let's start with timeline. You and your pal Cole worked the Blackpool job together. Cole approaches Jaxx with a business proposition—telling Jaxx he's managed to get the travel plan of a Blackpool transport carrying valuable tech—and leads the degenerates' attack on the *Asterisk*, which is really just a distraction from the real extraction mission. Jaxx doesn't know about that. It doesn't know about you or your real employer. You coordinate with the Blackpool insider to cripple the *Asterisk* from within. Once the ship's systems are down, you breach the hull and extract the insider, while Cole turns on the remaining degenerate ships and destroys them. Then you and the insider trigger the destruction of the *Asterisk.* You and Cole deliver the neurotech and the insider to your employer, after which Cole vanishes from the assassin world, leaving Jaxx to believe he died in the attack along with the degenerates. Am I missing anything?"

"That covers the highlights." Chimera snorted. "A point of clarification however: destroying the transport was not my idea."

"That doesn't excuse your culpability in murder."

"Don't think I didn't feel the weight of their senseless deaths. I know the value of human life and the irreplaceableness of talent more than anyone. I'm hired in these situations precisely to minimize collateral damage, not to create it. It was the target who placed and detonated the charges that destroyed the transport—and without my prior knowledge. I would have strongly opposed such a wasteful measure. But only Salamir dealt directly with our employer, not me. Apparently, I had not been briefed on all aspects of the job."

"And the employer? Was it Lienns-Sutra?"

"No, not a corporation," Chimera replied. "A religious cult. They call themselves the Amor Fati."

Kairos shot a glance to Neve. They were the fanatical group whose servers had been raided at the Oasis.

"Why would a cult want to extract a Blackpool employee?"

Neve asked.

"Sweetheart, please. You know that we headhunters do not require reasons. I was only told the target was a scientist. In planning the job though, it became clear to me that the target was itself a member of the cult. My job was to deliver the scientist to a designated drop location. The Amor Fati would take it from there."

"Name?"

"I can't give you that. Not because I refuse, but because I don't know. The target went by the alias Nightjar. The scientist wore a full biohazard suit during the extraction, visor tinted, and was of average height, so I couldn't describe them to you. Obviously, Nightjar wished to remain anonymous."

"How about the neurofluid tech? What did the Amor Fati want with it?"

"I don't know. Acquiring samples of the prototype wasn't my objective. If any were taken, they would've been on Nightjar's person."

"Why take this job given the risk? You know Jaxx's organization constantly monitors comms traffic. It'd be impossible for Cole to hide forever unless he went permanently off-grid."

"As a matter of fact, that's exactly what Salamir planned to do. Some employers' pockets aren't just deep, they are bottomless. The Amor Fati made it worth his while."

"So he changed his alias and dropped off the map," Neve said. "Except not completely. If I was able to track his ship, Jaxx undoubtedly could too."

"Except Salamir had insurance," Chimera said. "See, the Amor Fati supposedly had hacked Jaxx at some point."

Kairos and Neve exchanged a knowing look.

"I don't know how long ago, and god knows how a religious

cult could pull something like that off. But those devils were confident in telling Salamir they'd be able to erase portions of the AI's memory. Anything related to Cole's identity, aliases, and involvement would be either deleted or altered to keep Jaxx from ever discovering he was still alive."

Kairos knew Chimera was telling the truth. Jaxx had glitched and shut down right after it saw Cole's face in his goggles' recording. It must've vaguely recognized the assassin, but couldn't place his identity since the Amor Fati had erased Cole from its memory. Jaxx sensed the gap in its records, a tampering that made it go berserk. It probably couldn't fully comprehend what had happened to it, like an amnesiac uselessly trying to recall when they first started suffering from amnesia.

"The degenerates would at some point detect Jaxx's faulty memory," Neve said.

"Oh, don't be so dense, Ms. Seven. Even if they did, there'd be no reason to associate it specifically with Salamir or the Blackpool job. It'd just be another manifestation of Jaxx's descent into madness. And as for the job itself, to them it'd simply be considered a failure. Everyone killed in action."

"After Blackpool, did Cole do more jobs with this Amor Fati?" Kairos asked.

Chimera sighed. "You're asking about his stop at Pantoll? Sure, it's possible. I have no idea why he was there. I hadn't seen or heard anything of him again until you showed me that video of his death."

"We'll take the names of your Amor Fati contacts," Neve said.

Chimera shook her head. "Were you not listening? I told you that Cole handled all the interactions with them.

Besides, they're a paranoid group. Their fellowship operates purely over the SolarNet. The Amor Fati never disclose their identities. They call each other using aliases. Brother Zhou, Sister Agatha. It's impossible to know who their members are in real life, or how large their membership is."

"You've been uncharacteristically cooperative," Neve noted, ending her questioning. "Should I be worried about that?"

Chimera snorted. "I'd never taken a job for a cult before. I had no desire to do so. When Cole brought me into this one, he lied about the employer, telling me it was Lienns-Sutra. He and I had some history working together, so I had no reason to doubt him. But I soon noticed Cole had changed. He'd become stoic, even philosophical. Something more than just the money was motivating him.

"While working this job, my biggest shock was realizing that Cole had been converted. He'd become one of their zealots. And Cole had been the farthest from what you'd call a spiritual person. I never met their prophet leader, who they call the Vyst, but this cult has a fanaticism I've never seen before. I won't do business with them again.

"Now, I've told you all I know. Do not try to contact me again."

With that, Chimera's image vanished, leaving nothing but a notice that the secure link had disconnected.

For several moments, Kairos and Neve brooded in silence.

"Cult crime is nothing new," Neve said. "But to hack an AI like Jaxx and pull off a personnel extraction? These guys are serious." She turned to Kairos. "What is it?" she asked, seeing his concerned face.

"The ring of eyes," Kairos said.

"The what?"

"I saw it on Cole's armor. The symbol is religious in nature. I thought I'd seen it before, in my studies to become a priest. If Cole became one of the Amor Fati, then the group's adopted its meaning. I saw the same symbol on Spires and at the Oasis, too." He told Neve about the raid on the cult's servers at the Oasis.

"Kairos, you understand that it was this Amor Fati cult that sent Cole to Pantoll," Neve said gravely. "They killed your father."

Kairos nodded solemnly.

"But how did they know about the Osetran artifact? And what do they want with it?"

Kairos shook his head. Those were the same questions he had. The part he couldn't figure out was how Falck, a backwater nobody, fit into the Amor Fati angle. Had Falck personally known Cole? Was Falck a cultist too? "You were right about those agents on Spires not being Lienns-Sutra corporates, though," he told Neve. "They must have been Amor Fati, too. Or at least hired by them."

Neve's forehead wrinkled in thought. "This isn't your standard sing-a-song, dance-naked-around-a-fire brand of free-spirited escapism," she said, an uncharacteristic anxiety in her voice. "They've got real resources, and at least one person in this cult's got some brains. They duped Jaxx. And they duped me." She looked him in the eye. "I owe you thanks for pulling me out of that dungeon alive. The Blackpool insider—this Nightjar—is alive and within their ranks. I must find them."

Kairos nodded. "I might be able to help there. The Amor Fati may conceal their identities from the worlds, but any spiritual movement with power cannot be hidden long from the Church."

"Great, where to?" Neve asked, shoving herself to the lounge's comms panel to relay the destination to their pilots.

Kairos shook his head. "We're not going anywhere. I must be alone for a while. Do not disturb me."

* * *

For once, Kairos was glad he hadn't had the courage to tell his Church superiors that he'd lost his faith and abandoned his mission post on Pantoll. His clerical credentials were still valid and granted him access to the Obasanjo New Revelationist Church Archive. The Church's ignorance did make him wonder. Kairos's elder Cleric had hardly been interested in Kairos's work, sending only a short message ending with the standard, "God bless the hands of those building His Kingdom" in reply to Kairos's annual progress reports. After Kairos's reports ceased, someone from the Church should have checked in with him. Apparently, the souls of a backwater weren't worth the normal level of oversight.

Kairos hovered in one of the ship's tiny passenger quarters, subvocalizing his way through the Archive's extensive database. He'd turned to the Church Archive after giving up searching the SolarNet and news sources for anything concerning the Amor Fati or their prophet, the Vyst, which had yielded few results: a brief mention of a suicide in a Kotopax newsfeed from two standard months ago, and images of graffiti in urban centers on Greenside—nothing substantial.

No addresses of worship locations. Sunsip had said the group only organized virtually, but the group had no SolarNet site, at least not a public one. Kairos found no record of the raid on Amor Fati servers in the Oasis, although to be fair, he suspected most happenings in the Oasis weren't broadcasted beyond its local intranet.

His Archive research so far hadn't yielded anything on the cult either. He wasn't surprised: only notorious cults garnered meaningful academic interest, and that took time. So instead he focused his research on the ring of eyes symbol the Amor Fati used. Eyes in religious iconography were hardly unique—the ancient Egyptian Eye of Horus, the all-seeing Eye of Providence framed in a triangle representing the Christian Trinity, and the third eye of Shiva were a few of the most well-known. But a ring of eyes wasn't common. He felt sure he'd seen it at seminary, though couldn't remember when or in what context. After a long while browsing through textbooks and writings, the only interesting thing he found was a section in a book on religious symbology laying out five forms of "seeing," proposed by an Old Earth monk, Roebartach Ultoen, at a Welsh monastery in Llantwit Major in the year 652 Standard: Sight, Hindsight, Foresight, Insight, and Outsight. Sight represented the gift of presence, Hindsight the gift of remembrance (Kairos noted its similarity with the New Revelationist practice of Retrospection), Foresight the gift of prophecy, Insight the gift of self-examination, and Outsight the gift of discernment, that is, understanding the purpose of oneself and all things.

In need of a break from academic texts, Kairos switched to the Church's community portal and scanned through the worldswide newsfeeds and various dioceses' planetary and regional bulletins for mentions of the cult. No hits.

Next, he navigated to the Missions portal and inputted his credentials once again to access the extensive archive of missionaries' field reports. There were many thousands of these—far too many to ever parse manually and their contents could not be searched at an aggregate level. He filtered for those filed within the last standard year. One by one he opened reports for keyword search, starting with a sampling of missionaries serving on Kotopax, including in fringe settlements far from the planet's major industrial complexes. Finding nothing, he sampled reports from Greenside. Then Spires, Eukiah, Jeribah, Vesmarine, and several smaller planets and moons. The Oasis, he learned, had no Obasanjo missionaries posted.

After a few hours and hundreds of reports, he'd gotten no closer to learning more about the Amor Fati. Kairos yawned, lifted his goggles onto his forehead, and stretched his limbs. He'd mostly expected that result, but it was no less frustrating. The allure and aspiration of being a secret society was a common element among cults. That said, the Amor Fati, at least based on the prevalence of their ring of eyes symbol, was already multi-planetary, which made their lack of footprint impressive. At the very least he'd expected to find one of the usual ex-cult member "tell-alls." The cult was well-funded, organized, and disciplined. He thought back to the raid on the Amor Fati's hidden server cache at the Oasis. Why had the members preferred to blow themselves to smithereens rather than be taken in by the authorities? The Oasis security advisory had mentioned the group's involvement in cyberterror—their hacking into Jaxx confirmed their prowess there. Many cult leaders rallied their members around a singular aim, a vision that bound them to a larger shared purpose. So what was the Amor Fati's goal? Thinking more on the Oasis servers, another thought struck him: whatever it was, the Amor Fati had thought it wise to operate away from the eyes of the core worlds' System Administrators.

Returning his goggles to his eyes, Kairos filtered the missions' locales to only those without corporate governance or oversight, which shrank the list considerably. He dove into the reports, going back as far as three years. Some described seasons of reception and fruit among the populace, others mourned times of discouragement or downright horror. A butcher with cancer was in remission. Two clan leaders had finally made peace after decades of skirmishes. Requests for additional funding. Requests for supplies or equipment or a specific medicine. One missionary and his family were killed by an unruly band of local men for spreading a "false" religion; one surviving member, a teen daughter, pleaded the Church to send a ship for her.

A couple hours into his search, he finally got a keyword hit, a line of text reading "... fought wildly against their hold, cursing the voices and screaming he'd not allow the Amor Fati (?) to steal his fate ..." Kairos panned to the top of the report and began reading. The priest's mission post was a lunar mining colony in the Bei Arron Region. The report was dated around six months ago and gave an account of a violent worker who suffered from an unknown psychological illness which included hearing voices in his head. He ultimately threw himself beneath an active mining drill. The missionary, a Low Priest named Ayo Ninsiima, had been ministering to the troubled man since the man had arrived with a fresh line of workers weeks before, but to no avail. The priest concluded the man had been plagued not only by a mental disorder—possibly schizophrenia—but by demonic forces as well.

Kairos looked up the priest in the Church directory. Father Ninsiima was Kotopaxian, age twenty-four years, Standard, though he looked at least fifteen years older in his picture. The man sported a thick mustache and had dark, piercing eyes beneath black bushy brows and short, combed hair.

Kairos subvocalized a new SolarNet window and pulled up a star map. A search for Bei Arron showed a remote region—an estimated twenty-two standard days' weave outside Kotopax's Sorsic System—too distant for Kairos to send the priest a message. It'd take months, through some combination of ships, for a SolarNet update—including his message—to finally reach the mining colony.

Kairos re-read the report, paying close attention to descriptions of the worker's deranged state. The potential connection between the worker's neurological illness and the neurofluid the Amor Fati stole from Blackpool couldn't be a coincidence. Use of a telepathy-enabling neurotechnology would be a nice trick to facilitate spiritual brainwashing or coercive conversion. Had the Amor Fati tested the neurofluid on him, with disastrous results? The worker must have arrived at the mining colony on a ship from Kotopax, the closest world. Perhaps that's where he'd encountered the Amor Fati. Perhaps he'd been trying to escape them.

Over the next couple hours, Kairos searched through every missionary report from locations on Kotopax from the past two years. Yet the search yielded nothing.

Annoyed, Kairos returned to the star map. A tick mark at the edge of the field drew his attention. It indicated a known locale out of the field of view. He zoomed out until a small dot appeared within the star map, then selected and enlarged the dot. It was La Torre Outpost. The name sounded familiar. A quick SolarNet search confirmed Kairos's hunch: La Torre was one of four deep space outposts that had gone offline within the past standard year. Ships had been sent to investigate the first three occurrences; none had returned or been heard from since, hence the widespread speculation and fear over the Osetra's return. When the fourth, most recent outpost went offline, a ship wasn't even sent. The prevailing rumor was that Osetran scout ships had overrun the outposts to send reconnaissance on human civilization's progress back to a main attack force. Kairos pondered whether the outpost was connected in any way to the Amor Fati and the incident Father Ninsiima observed. But in the end, without any information regarding what had happened at La Torre, it was a dead end.

Kairos pulled the goggles off his face completely and let them drift away. He rubbed his strained eyes with his palms and let them remain closed as he realized the option he'd been avoiding was inevitable: Retrospection.

Retrospection: that deep descent into the mind to re-experience memories and knowledge in striking detail. The Obasanjo parochial school he'd attended on Greenside taught all students the basics of encoding information within their brains for future recall using advanced mental mapping methods. Later, he'd developed and honed the practice while studying at King's Seminary in Asphis. The skill held particular value to the clergy. To graduate seminary, Low Priest candidates had to have the Scriptures memorized word for word—no small task. Misquoting a few lines or, worse, omitting an entire verse of Holy Scripture was grounds to be held back. Clerics, further, were expected to memorize the church's various liturgies and a few seminal academic works as well. Mission founders—often sent to remote places lacking SolarNet access or electricity—especially needed the ability to regenerate the immutable Scriptures perfectly from memory in the event their hard copies were lost or destroyed (including, at times, by locals hostile to the faith). Kairos hadn't entered a state of Retrospection since the night of the chapel fire. The creation of that terrible memory had poisoned his past, turning it into a dangerous place for him to navigate.

Kairos began by allowing his muscles to relax and his mind to sink into meditation, focusing his mental energy upon the ring of eyes sigil and methodically eliminating extraneous thoughts. It surprised him how easy the practice returned to him. Once well-worn pathways, which he'd thought overgrown, rapidly cleared as if by wildfire carried by a strong wind. He sat in stillness for some period of time—his mind was no longer aware of time's passage. But he sensed when the subtle transition happened. A kind of trance. The feeling of sinking in on oneself, becoming so weightless that one slipped right through the seams of themselves into a narrow, dim, secluded space where temporal reality could be navigated and viewed with clarity, as if he were an objective onlooker into his own past.

Kairos allowed his meditation on the eyes to guide him through the colossal architecture of his memory banks, a nearly subconscious process.

There it was: an image. He opened his mind's eye to it, like the slow recollection of a nearly-lost dream.

The memory unfurled for him.

Kairos was back in his cramped, chilly dormitory at King's

Seminary in Asphis. Winter session. He was sitting up on the bed, back against the headboard, legs crossed, feet bare—socks had only ever made his feet feel colder. In the dry, cool air, his school-issued retinal overlays subtly irritated his tired, strained eyes. The view through the implants was looping around the approximately two second time period during which his younger eyes had glanced at the symbol in the study text. His focus would shift off the image in order to read, only for his near-subconscious will to rewind the memory approximately two seconds, keeping the image at the focus of his recollection. The symbol was similar in form to the Amor Fati's, but with only four eyes—versus the Amor Fati's eight—and with longer eyelashes that radiated in straight lines off the eyes like rays of sunlight. The four eyes were not oriented in a ring so much as a diamond shape, with the top eye larger than the other three.

Kairos now allowed the memory to unfold forward in time.

According to the accompanying text, the symbol belonged to a micro cult from the 12th century (Standard), formed by Christian soldiers who'd returned from a series of crusades with their "eyes opened" by the horrors they witnessed. A footnote explained that the sigil's large eye represented God's dominion over Time. The other three eyes represented the soldiers' enlightenment—seeing the universe's past, present, and future, a complete history of what they called "The Age of Heaven and Earth," as distinct from other Ages. Calling themselves the *Generatio Finalis*, these men began evangelizing new teachings that stretched and distorted the interpretive limits of Christian doctrine to a point far beyond mere heresy. The teachings' central tenet rested on their revelation that the created universe's sole purpose was to support the flourishing of human beings, God's most precious creation, and that if and when human bodies ceased to exist, the cosmos would likewise collapse for loss of purpose. Earth and nature groaned to God for renewal according to the Scriptures, but as long as it remained under the rule of a sinful mankind, Time was compelled to trudge onward, compounding evil and suffering. *Generatio Finalis* members' overarching desire was to hasten the transition to the next Age to come. With "hearts set afire," they committed themselves to preventing or stunting the rise of future human generations. They took oaths of celibacy. They mutilated their genitals in acts of "super-circumcision." Children were euthanized. They planned ways to introduce toxins into water sources and crops to reduce fertility of the populace at large. Suicides were prevalent. The end goal was human extinction. After which, God's hand would be forced to wipe away this sinful, fallen universe—a completion of the biblical Flood—and restart Time with a new, pristine Creation where human souls could be placed and flourish once more.

The *Generatio Finalis* cult was as short-lived as the couple of brief paragraphs the expansive study text afforded it. Kairos reread the text a few times. Something about it felt important, but he couldn't pinpoint why. The three eyes representing vision into past/present/future were similar to Ultoen's forms of Hindsight, Sight, and Foresight, though Ultoen had further identified and described the forms of Insight and Outsight. The Amor Fati symbol held eight eyes— as to what the additional three 'sights' were, assuming that's what was represented, Kairos could only guess. It didn't surprise him that the Amor Fati, or their prophet the Vyst, thought they were all-seeing or all-knowing, that they'd been blessed with special insight from God. In the Oasis rock tavern, Sunsip had mentioned that some believed the Vyst to be able to see into the future.

What concerned Kairos was whether the Amor Fati was that particular type of cult that was driven to commit mass murder motivated by some Judgment Day or End Times theology. The mad worker in Father Ninsiima's missions report had yelled about the Amor Fati "stealing his fate." At a minimum, it implied personal harm; at worst, it suggested the Amor Fati might have broader plans for all of humanity. Fervor around the End Times had reached a peak when Old Earth was on the brink of collapse. It was only first contact with the Osetra and the subsequent technological partnership with the aliens that the world's religions experienced a healthy revival (with doctrinal updates, of course), rooted in a renewed sense of awe and hope. But with the new rumors of the Osetra's impending attack, fear of humanity's extinction had returned. Even small-time priests like Father Revais couldn't help rallying the people toward repentance before "the end."

Upon thinking of Father Revais, a curiosity came to Kairos that he couldn't quite clearly articulate. Subconscious prompts like this were common when one was in a state of Retrospection, and in response his meditation drifted—nearly involuntarily—to Father Revais's sermon concerning the End of Time, a doctrine that suddenly felt particularly important to Kairos's investigation.

Kairos was back in the chapel on Pantoll—a fresh memory. The recall of the scent of the chiva wood beams was powerful enough that his nostrils could smell them now. He was standing at the back, arms folded, listening to Father Revais's voice boom over the silent congregation. The priest was beginning to get into the End of Time when a candle stand at the front right of the pews suddenly toppled over. Then the front left candle stand toppled. Then the candle stands beside each row of pews toppled in quick succession. Small fires ignited across the church and quickly spread. The congregation remained calmly seated during all this, as absorbed in the priest's teaching as ever. A thunderous crash sounded behind him. He turned his head to find the chapel's bell tower had collapsed through the caved-in roof. The memory morphed. He was now lying on the ground at the front of the chapel. The walls and pews were covered in flames, the air filled with smoke. There the young girl's small body lay, beside the burning splintered remains of the tower. He tried to push himself up to get to her, his foot knocking aside an empty wine bottle. Her voice was ravaged, alternating between screaming and coughing ...

Kairos tore his mind out of Retrospection. The memory fell away. Sweat coated his skin and forehead. His chest felt tight; he heaved for air. For a long while, he remained curled in a fetal position, eyes shut, shivering, focused only on slowing his pounding heart rate and keeping his mind off what he could never forgive or forget.

* * *

Hands were shaking Kairos awake.

A voice was urging him to get up.

Kairos winced upon his eyes meeting the room's lights. Sunsip's large body hovered over him, hurrying to undo the bed straps around him and yanking him up.

"I'm up," Kairos yelped groggily. "What's all this about?"

"It's Midmay." The pilot's expression was grave. "Something's happened to her."

Kairos scrambled behind Sunsip to the medbay. There was Midmay, lying on the medical chair, eyes closed.

He kicked himself beside the girl. He called her name while gently shaking her, but she remained unresponsive. The skin on her face felt clammy and hot.

"Found her floating like this in the lounge," Sunsip explained hurriedly. "I thought she might have fallen asleep. For safety, I went over to strap her into the couch. That's when I noticed she was burning up and unresponsive." The girl's breathing was shallow and her pulse was weak against Kairos's shaking fingers. Sunsip's voice lowered. "Then I found this. Kairos, what in the world was she doing there?"

Kairos turned to find the pilot offering him Midmay's eyevisor. Confused, Kairos took the device and slid it over his eyes. Text greeted them: "The service has concluded. Thank you for attending."

His pulse accelerated and he tore the eyevisor off.

Midmay had found the Amor Fati's virtual portal.

Chapter 10

Kairos stroked Midmay's hot, sweaty forehead, wondering what she'd experienced at the Amor Fati's virtual service. The girl had been drawn to religious faith before, and he blamed himself that she'd been left alone after overhearing their conversation with Chimera. He'd tried to access the portal home from her eyevisor, but the connection had been severed with the service's conclusion.

Kairos's clerical education on Greenside had included a thorough review of modern-day cult practices. Many cults had embraced high-tech psychoactive substances to attain states of elevated spiritual awareness. The use of artificial sense-simulation and a virtual mind/body faith experience was also nothing unique. But a physiological reaction strong enough to send a user into a coma only occurred in the most true-to-life virtual constructs, and while wearing the highest-end VR suits equipped with sophisticated drug injection systems. Wearing only a cheap eyevisor like Midmay's, it was impossible. The Bei Arron missionary report suggested the Amor Fati were somehow using the neurofluid they'd stolen as part of coerced conversions, but how could that explain a psychological reaction to a *virtual* experience? It didn't make sense.

Neve arrived at the medbay entrance. "What's going on?" she asked. Then seeing Midmay unconscious, she yanked herself toward the girl.

"I gave her some medication for the fever," Sunsip said.

"At that tavern in the Oasis, you told me about a friend of yours who'd attended the Amor Fati's services," Kairos said to the pilot. "Would you happen to know how to access their private portal?"

"Now why in the hell would you wanna do that?" Sunsip exclaimed.

"The Amor Fati did this?" Neve asked, looking incredulously from Sunsip to Kairos.

Kairos told the pilot what they'd learned about the group from Chimera. "They killed my father," he said. "I just spent hours trying to learn more about them. We need to know who these people are."

"I fell out of contact with him," Sunsip said. "I want absolutely nothing to do with fanatics and I don't—"

"Think I found it," interrupted Neve. She'd been exploring Midmay's eyevisor and now thrust it toward him. The screen showed the girl's contacts history, and specifically an info tab received from an unnamed contact. The tab's only content was a SolarNet address text string—comprised of random characters—circumscribed by the ring of eyes symbol. "It's from *them*. She must've picked this spam up at the Oasis."

Kairos immediately recalled the proselytizer that had accosted him at the Oasis. He pulled his goggles on.

"It's no use," Neve told him. "I just tried the address. It's no longer active. Maybe the string contained a temporary use code."

Kairos found the data tab he'd accepted from the man, ran a virus scan (even though his goggles would've automatically done that upon receiving), then opened it. He was greeted by the same ring of eyes and a text string, except the string was different than Midmay's. He copied the address into his SolarNet interface. His goggle screens were sent into a black nothingness—the portal appeared blank. Then, white text emerged. "I've got it," Kairos announced. "I also ran into an evangelist at the Oasis. I didn't know he was with the Amor Fati." He read the text aloud: "'Do you desire to be deeply known and fully loved? To receive rest for your weary soul? To reach the 'something more' that always seems to evade your life's grasp? Our community is waiting to meet you.'" Then a final line of text appeared. "'Love requires vulnerability. Bring your most terrible act, as well as your deepest wound. They shall be redeemed.'"

"Love for your soul? The most terrible what?" Sunsip exclaimed.

Kairos had furrowed his brows at that last line, as well. A short list of upcoming service times followed beneath the text. "Their next virtual service will take place in about an hour," Kairos told them.

Sunsip looked from Kairos to Neve. "Wait, you two aren't considering ..."

"Yep, we're going to church," Neve replied. "You keep any VR suits on this boat?"

"First degenerates, now zealots. No way."

"You're afraid of them, aren't you?" Neve said. It was more a statement than a question.

"It's plain smarts not to mix oneself up with crazy people," Sunsip said with a huff. "I've seen and heard too many strange things."

"Isn't Kairos paying you to sit here and float in space?"

Sunsip glared at her. "We keep two on board for passengers to use during long trips. But only one suit is completely working. The second's malfunctioned. Only its headgear works."

"I'll take the headgear," Neve said. "Kairos, you can have the full experience. Can you set us up in less an hour?" she asked the pilot.

"Your friend is lying there with her brain scrambled!" Sunsip appealed to Kairos.

"That will happen to many more if we do not act," Kairos said. "Sunsip, I want you to monitor us while we're under. I believe this cult is much more dangerous than you think."

* * *

Several minutes prior to the start of the virtual service, Kairos and Neve were suspended side-by-side in the lounge amid a web of cables and thin tubing.

VR suits utilized a combination of dream induction and manipulation technologies, in addition to the standard sense-simulation connections. An extensive tangle of paraphernalia was necessary. With a few tweaks from Kairos, Sunsip had rigged the whole setup, getting Kairos's suit wired, hooking up its electrodes, and setting up the connections between the sensorium box and their headgear, all the while muttering his disgust with cults and the foolishness he was enabling. The equipment wasn't as cared for as Kairos treated his own basic rig. A musky odor emanated from the suit's fibers, clearly having been shared by too many people.

Confined within the suit, Kairos's gaze was locked forward to the only sight in his field of vision, the broad cone-shaped extensions that would beam visual feed directly into his corneas.

"I'll be checking your status while submerged," Sunsip's unenthused voice said through their shared comms channel.

Kairos had instructed the pilot to continuously monitor his and Neve's neural activity, and to be ready to disconnect them should he observe anything abnormal. Given what he learned from Father Ninsiima's account, the possible connection to the lost La Torre Outpost, and now witnessing what happened to Midmay, he thought the precaution was more than warranted.

A user interface screen ignited and filled Kairos's vision. He exhaled and relaxed his muscles. The suit warmed and molded itself snugly against his body's contours. The bulky VR headgear was soundproofed and pitch black inside, allowing no external visibility—the suits were designed to close off users' senses from the external world. His thoughts drifted to Midmay, still lying unconscious in the medbay. *What would we experience once Sunsip flips the switch, sending our minds into the Amor Fati's virtual portal? What power had sent Midmay into a coma?* He exhaled again, to slow his heart rate.

"Neve, sound check?" Kairos asked through their private comms channel.

"Loud and clear," Neve affirmed. "Don't worry," she assured him, somehow sensing his anxiety, "we'll figure out what these assholes did to Midmay. They better pray I don't find out who they really are, the cowards."

"Thanks," he replied. "But I can't help but think I made a grave mistake in allowing her to leave Pantoll with me. Traveling to new worlds, meeting new people—I underestimated how much it was for her to take in all at once. I didn't protect her."

"But you *have* been protecting her," Neve asserted. "On Spires, at the Oasis. You cannot control everything. And don't make the mistake of underestimating *her*. She may be young, but she is strong. And she's certainly not stupid."

Neve's words made him feel a little better, a little more hopeful.

"All ready here," Sunsip announced over the shared channel.

Kairos cleared his mind—he needed to focus on the task at hand. He and Neve voiced confirmations back to the pilot.

"Copy. Here we go."

A faint hiss of gas sounded from somewhere within Kairos's headgear, a soporific being released. A drowsiness came over him. He closed his eyes, allowing the stupor to overtake him.

"Channel open. Datastream flowing ..." Sunsip's voice drifted far away as their comms channel automatically switched from auditory to text-based input.

Kairos's vision was glazed in a momentary, bright whiteout, as if he had just begun to stare straight into a sun, before colors and recognizable features emerged into existence. During the initial plunge into a virtual realm, he always felt a slight tickle at the backs of his eyeballs. The details of the pastoral landscape in which he found himself sharpened. Within moments, the virtual world completed loading, ushered in by a cool breeze sweeping across his face.

Kairos was standing on the crest of a hill, the wild grass scratching against his shins. Neve materialized next to him. Virtual reality programming allowed avatars to be manifested according to user preferences or, within certain worlds, preset ranges of style or fashion that fit the world's specific theme. This virtual world fit the former category, but to preserve total anonymity, they had opted for their avatars to be randomly generated. Hers looked nothing like her real self. Her avatar was male, with long, straight red hair, green eyes, and a pale complexion. It wore a dark green tank top and gray loose-fitting pants that stopped at mid-calf. Kairos's avatar wore woven shorts and a faded tan T-shirt with a skin feel that mimicked Eukian dicotton. He could tell his complexion was paler and his weight heavier than in real life but otherwise had no clue what his face looked like. It didn't matter anyway.

They were in mountainous terrain, standing within a prairie beneath a cloudless, pale blue sky. Bordering the prairie were dense, colorful woods indicative of an autumn season, the tree leaves splotched with a kaleidoscope of deep reds, oranges, bright yellows, light greens, and dull browns. A sparkling stream wound through the prairie toward the mountainside, burbling as water slid around the smooth gray stones imped-ing its flow. He recognized this type of geography as inspired by the diverse environments found on humanity's ancestral homeworld. He, of course, had never personally experienced many of such environments, and the one he was immersed in now seemed at once strange yet attractive, as alien to him as any other world he'd never visited.

Based on the information in the Amor Fati's SolarNet portal, the congregational assembly would gather at a mountainside place of worship located on the other side of the woods. They were early for the start of the service, but Kairos had wanted some extra time beforehand to get acquainted with the virtual world, its particular design, rules, and dynamics. He inhaled deeply, breathing in crisp, cool air that tasted clean with only a touch of earthiness. He flexed his arms, legs, and stretched other body parts. Jumped, landed. He then squatted and parted blades of tall grass with his fingers, closely inspecting them as he did so. The level of detail of each blade was astonishing, and no two that he scanned were exactly alike in their design. In his brief post-clerical career as a virtual worlds architect, it was unlike anything he'd experienced. He brought his face nearly against the ground. With a finger, he traced the soft impression in the dirt that one of his feet had made.

"Industry standard procedures?" Neve asked with a hint of mockery, just after he had touched a dirt-encrusted finger to his tongue to give it a taste.

"Just mine," he responded absentmindedly, concentrating on the dirt's flavor profile. Despite the average VR suit and sensorium box he was working with, he could sense its rich complexity, and once again he was taken by a mix of surprise and admiration.

They descended the hill and walked down to the banks of the stream. Neve skipped lightly over the exposed tops of rocks to cross over to the other side. He started to do the same but stopped halfway. He reached down into the cold, sloshing water and heaved up a medium-sized stone. He threw it down against another one, and it cracked apart in two. Picking up one of the halves, he smiled, wholly impressed. The edge appeared to have cracked along random lines, and the core of the stone revealed several layers of stratification varying in thickness, shape, and color. He was amazed that the designers' attention to painstaking detail extended even into hidden places that users' eyes would rarely, if ever, see.

"This is incredibly expensive work," he remarked to Neve, who seemed to be enjoying the feeling of the sun's late afternoon rays on her skin, her face turned up, eyes closed. "The detail is exquisite. The physics are flawless. With better VR gear, this environment would be indistinguishable from real life. The Amor Fati must have hired the top architects and engineers in the industry to design and code this. Not to mention you'd need serious server capacity to run it. They must have a corporate backer."

"A corporation supporting a cult religion?"

"Maybe through one of the Amor Fati's members," Kairos said. But the idea of it was perplexing, like Midmay's physiological reaction. *What kind of cult is this? Who is paying for all this?*

Continuing farther, Kairos and Neve left the grassy hills and entered the woods. Every now and then, a cool gust would rush through the woods, shaking the trees and sending a flurry of freshly detached crimson and brown leaves into a whirl about them. Gazing at the colorful foliage, Kairos considered how wonderfully odd Old Earth must have been. On Greenside, tree leaves were always, per the planet's name, green. And on Pantoll, there was only one tree species that anyone was aware of: the chiva tree, with its purplish, thick, fleshy leaves adapted to store enough water to enable the stubbornly hardy plant to survive the planet's intermittent periods of drought.

As they walked together, Kairos said, "The invitation to the service said to bring the most terrible acts we've committed, as well as our deepest wounds from acts committed against us. I am curious, what are you bringing? I have a feeling that your attempt in Jaxx's dungeon to end your life isn't the worst of it."

"How insightful," Neve said. "If I told you mine, would you confess to me yours? Let me guess. You had dirty thoughts once about someone *very* off-limits? Or, maybe you had skimmed a little from the church's coffers? Ah, I know: leaving the priesthood."

Kairos gave a pained half-smile and looked down. Suddenly, all the dead leaves he trod on sickened him. He regretted starting the conversation.

"I see we're not going to have reciprocity here," Neve commented. "It doesn't matter. Look, to be human is to be terrible. I'm honest with myself about that; I haven't been an angel." Neve fell quiet for a moment, as if recollecting something. "Morality is often a luxury," she said. "And it can't always be afforded. So I forgive myself. Neither you nor the Amor Fati need trouble yourselves over my soul. I certainly don't."

"The problem is that everyone's conscience is, in the end, relentless," Kairos replied. "I'll tell you something that is true: I haven't been able to forgive myself. For a long time, I tried persuading myself that it wasn't even really my fault, that God was more to blame, seeing as he's in charge of everything, right? But I could never settle my conscience for long. I suppose only the naive believe they can have any power over it. The Amor Fati know that. That's why they offer freedom from guilt and shame. That kind of freedom one cannot give to oneself."

After some time, the two emerged from the woods into a narrow strip of mountainside prairie that ran along the edge of a steep drop off. A trail was worn into the grass along the cliff top. It led to an ancient-looking stone building a short ways away. The building's architectural design mimicked that of the old Gothic cathedrals built long ago on Old Earth. At its front towered two narrow, parallel spires. It was there that they spotted, for the first time, avatars of other users. Many were milling around outside the stone cathedral, and more and more were popping into existence as Kairos and Neve progressed down the trail.

As they drew near to the cathedral, Kairos found that it was precariously perched by the edge of the mountainside, with sheer cliffs falling away from most of its perimeter. Such dramatic constructions, highly improbable if not impossible in reality, were common sights in virtual realms. The crowd of avatars wasn't entering the cathedral, however. Instead, it flowed to an adjacent outdoor amphitheater which overlooked the valleys far below.

Strolling up to the cathedral's entrance, Kairos gave one of the heavy brass door handles a tug anyway, wanting to take a peek inside the structure, but found the tall wooden doors were bolted shut. He and Neve proceeded to join the other users at the amphitheater, which fanned out in several tiered rows of dark gray stone, each row topped with smooth wooden boards for seating. At the front was a central stage. Simple stone seats were arranged on the stage.

The crowd was a mixed group. A good half of the crowd was a random assortment of guest attendees, curious first-timers like Kairos and Neve. The remaining avatars wore identical dress—white long-sleeve tunics on top of loose white pants— and also wore the same permanent smiles on their clean cut, radiant faces as they interacted with guests and ushered them into seats. Kairos assumed these were formal cult members. His jaw clenched and his face grew warm. These people had hurt Midmay. He had an urge to just grab them by the necks and start wringing out answers. Moreover, something about their eager kindness and quiet smugness annoyed him. Sunsip had told him that they made many converts here in their virtual realm, so it wasn't surprising that they presented themselves as being in nothing short of a constant state of elation. *What do they really want from us?* Kairos wondered.

"Remember," Kairos told Neve anxiously, "we're here to blend in and learn, not cause a scene."

"Are you reminding me or yourself, priest?" she responded, eyeing him.

As Kairos and Neve moved to find seats, one of the white-clad acolytes approached them with a warm grin. The avatar was a thin young man with neatly combed hair, a large nose, and a pronounced Adam's apple.

"Hello there, and welcome to our home," the young man said cheerfully. "My name is Nevik. Is this your first time joining us?"

Kairos felt an inexplicable desire to punch the acolyte square in his big, droopy nose. "Sure is. We're very excited," he instead replied with a broad smile, trying to match the zealot's level of glee. As irritatingly uncomfortable as it was, they'd get better answers out of this place if they played to the cult culture.

"That's so wonderful to hear. Allow me to accompany you. There are a few open seats in this section." The three of them slid into a row, Nevik positioning himself between them. "May I ask how you've come to attend our gathering today?" Nevik asked. His gaze lingered a moment on Neve before settling back on Kairos.

"I guess, fundamentally, we're seeking answers to the big questions," he replied, which was the truth, in a way.

"I commend you for opening up your minds in the pursuit of truth. Half of the journey consists in simply realizing that we need to be transformed by a power outside of ourselves in order to attain the peace our souls crave. You are already well on your way."

"And what truth have you found here?" Neve inquired.

Nevik looked off to the valley below. "Not long ago, I was a mess, although I never would have admitted it at the time. I had left my home planet and family and went off to carouse my way through the worlds, to enjoy it all in one big swallow. Bio-enhancers, neuro-mods, VR chain swaps," the slang brought a smile to Nevik's face, as if he were describing a different person. "I dabbled in everything. More drugs passed through my system than through a pharma distro.

"Then, during one of my travels, reality set in. I was sitting in terrible conditions aboard a container ship on a long caravan, stone cold sober after having run out of psychoactives several days prior. My loneliness descended upon me. I had skipped from one group of comrades to another, never staying in one place for very long. The worlds suddenly seemed disconnected and distant. I felt like I was the central protagonist in a stage production that was my life, while everyone else were side characters who ceased to exist whenever they weren't interacting with me. I was also the only one in the audience. Meaning was a mirage that slowly dissipated upon drawing near. If there was an all-powerful force or a creative god somewhere beyond the realm of the cosmos, I felt miserably distant from it. It was in my subsequent depressed, aimless wanderings that I found the Prophet. Or really, I should say the Prophet found me."

"The Vyst," offered Kairos.

Nevik nodded with solemn reverence. "The one from the Outside. There are many manifestations of the Prophet, yet they are one and the same. I'd heard only strange things regarding the Outsider, always in unreliable corners. Accounts of fantastical phenomenon, supernatural powers. But one night, in a booth at a cheap Oasis bar where I was drinking away the last of my points, the Outsider sat across from me. Long eyescopes, breathing mask, black wide-brimmed hat over a black poncho. Despite being several stiff drinks in, his presence snapped me into clarity and commanded my full attention. I listened as he recounted my whole pathetic story. Told me everything I ever did. At the end he asked, 'Nevik, do you want to go home?' I nodded, tears rolling down my face. The Outsider took my hands firmly and told me to close my eyes. When I opened them a moment later, we were standing on Kotopax, my home planet, not far from my family's house."

"Are saying he teleported you there?" Kairos asked skeptically.

"The Outsider is not constrained like we are. He reaches out to us from his presence on the Outside and can move about the Inside freely. From that moment onward, I've been following him and serving to join more souls into our community. The Vyst has revealed to me the true nature of reality. The Vyst is the way to the Creator. Here, in the realm of the mind and spirit, we are building a new reality based on new truths. This is my home now."

Nevik's belief in the "Creator" and his description of teleportation-like travel caused Kairos's shoulders to stiffen and set gears turning in his mind. Father Revais and the Church of the Samsaric Soul also spoke of such ideas. That said, it wasn't uncommon for different faiths to share similar concepts. For now, Kairos avoided digging into doctrinal specifics and pressed on to more practical matters.

"Not that we agree, but we've heard some say the Amor Fati is a militant organization and a threat," Kairos said to Nevik. "The reports concerning your more, ah, aggressive activities—how does all that fit into your new world?"

"Let me tell you a story," Nevik began. "Once, there was a doctor who was traveling through a primitive country and discovered that a deadly disease had spread through one of its small villages. The doctor recognized the outbreak as arising from a certain bacterial infection—easily curable and which had been eradicated from his homeland generations prior. So, the doctor went to the village's elders to offer his services in treating the affected villagers before the epidemic claimed lives and spread to neighboring villages. However, the elders did not trust this foreigner from a faraway place, or his strange ideas. They refused to allow the doctor to inject needles filled with unnatural substances into their people, and told him that they would treat the disease their way by offering sacrifices to the River Spirit and dipping the feet of the infected into its cool waters.

"That night, the doctor couldn't sleep, for he knew that if the infected weren't treated immediately, the entire village would be ravaged within days. So, very early the next morning, before it was light, he went from hut to hut and administered the antibiotic, sometimes even against the wishes of a few, proud sick. When the elders discovered what the doctor had done, they seized him and put him to death that very afternoon. In the following days, the villagers noticed that those who had been sick were recovering miraculously. The elders praised the River Spirit, saying it had blessed them upon ridding the evil doctor from their midst, and many villagers' faiths among were strengthened that day. Only a small few—mainly those who'd been healed—mourned the doctor and revered him as a holy messenger of the River Spirit."

After a moment, Nevik asked them, "Did the doctor make the right decision?"

Kairos replied, "Well, philosophically-speaking, 'right' is a slippery concept. From one point of view, the doctor did a selfless, righteous thing, saving the village despite knowing what it might cost him. But obviously from the elders' perspective, they are right to consider what he did to be an egregious trespass. In my experience, most people prefer to live their own way—even if that way is killing them—rather than accept another that's contrary to their beliefs."

"So what would you say is the solution to such an impasse?" Nevik asked.

Kairos's patience with such a basic philosophy discussion was fading fast, worsened by the acolyte's insufferable questions, obviously posed for show. But to keep up their appearances as newcomers, he entertained the man. "I suppose the solution is truth?" Kairos replied, feigning uncertainty. "Objective reality. As long as people believe it exists and pursue it, minds can be changed and conversion is possible."

"Yes, that's it!" proclaimed the acolyte. "That is our burden. To not just describe truth, but to compel others to *experience* it in mind and body." Then he continued, solemnly, "Humankind has a sickness. An ancient, deep-seated affliction at its core, the symptoms of which are destruction, desolation, and suffering. This sickness destroys our relationships with one another and with the Creator's universe. Humanity's sins are great. We have provoked the Creator's wrath by our destruction of Its beautiful worlds Eden and Earth. But the Creator is patient, gracious, and merciful. Though It has cleansed humanity twice—through the Great Flood and the Exodus from Old Earth—twice It has spared us from complete annihilation. Now, It has sent our Prophet down from the Outside with the cure. How can we rightly keep it to ourselves? You are right that truth is the answer, but few want it and its demands upon them. And so, we must bring it to them. Love and conscience compel us to spread the cure to all. Even if it is against their wills now. Later, all will understand. On that day, we will be thanked and praised endlessly for our persistence."

"And what is this cure?" Neve asked, her tone a bit too direct. She, also, was losing patience for these spiritual musings.

"It is not something that can be merely told. It must be experienced. And that is why you are here. Look, the service is about to begin."

Two cloaked figures emerged from a shadowy stone archway at the side of the cathedral. They wore deep blue robes with hoods obscuring their faces. The congregation quieted. The figures walked along a narrow pathway that led from the cathedral to the amphitheater. Ascending the stone steps onto the stage, they seated themselves on two of the nine stones.

"Who are they?" Kairos whispered to Nevik.

"Two of the Eight, the first disciples of the Vyst and the first ones to receive his gift of the All-Soul of humanity. The Disciples lead us in our faith and teach us."

"What about the Vyst? I'd like to meet him myself."

"We will all pray together soon. Afterward, near the end of

the service, you will meet the Prophet."

One of the hooded Disciples stepped forward and welcomed the attendees. Then, the two Disciples initiated a series of calls, with the zealots in the congregation returning short responses in turn. Nevik quietly explained that they were invoking the various manifestations of the Creator, that It might open the minds of the guests in order that they would accept the truth offered today and experience perfect unity with all.

Afterward, one of the Disciples produced a plum-colored cloth bag from out of its robe. The Disciple loosened the golden draw string, set the bag down in the middle of the stone stage, then stepped back. Out of the open mouth of the bag, a viscous substance of pure black rose up like a blanket being drawn upward by a single corner. The substance lengthened and broadened into an inky river and continued to emerge until it blotted out most of the sunlight. A cool darkness descended, and the shapeless substance hovered and undulated in the twilight sky like an impenetrable stormy sea.

The Disciple spoke. "In the beginning, the Creator established the Inside. The universe at that moment was a dark, formless void, a blank black canvas containing nothing, creating nothing, being nothing. The Creator infused the void with Spirits that gave the universe a certain order, a framework upon which beauty could emerge. One of these Spirits was called Human, but there were many others as well."

The black ocean above them was then shot through with innumerable points of light. The points of light took on tangible, three-dimensional shapes that floated on the dark sea: bright spheres of various sizes, the largest the size of melons, the smallest as minuscule as grains of sand. The levitating, glowing white orbs swirled and gradually arranged themselves into hundreds of distinct groups of spiraling bodies, the smaller spheres drawn into orbit around the larger, to produce what looked like a ship's holographic star map, but on a grander scale. The figure continued speaking below the swirling field of galactic discs.

"There was harmony then between the Inside and Outside. The two realms were intertwined and slid along each other. The Spirits, which had proceeded from the essence of the Creator, moved between these realms at will, and the Creator gave them authority to build the universe's first civilization. Together, at the center of the universe, the Spirits worked to build a masterpiece of a world worthy of the endless creative possibilities endowed to them. The First Civilization, as we call it, was as richly diverse and technologically advanced as it was beautiful, and the planet they cultivated was known as Eden.

"In time, however, the Spirits grew proud of their creations and technological might. Among the worst was Human. In their arrogance, the Spirits challenged each other for dominance, until ultimately, they tore each other and their paradise apart. As punishment, the Creator scattered the Spirits, separating them across the billions of light years of the universe. It also fractured each Spirit into as many billion fragments to humble them so that, until they learned the principle of unity, they would not be as glorious as before."

The cloaked figure raised his arms to the congregation. "Within each of us resides a small shard of the collective soul of Human that was shattered long ago. Each of our shards—

each soul—is inherently broken and bears that ancient pain. Our souls, in a sense, are "sharp-edged," cutting others and ourselves. We have done terrible things to each other and this universe.

"But something new has happened in our time. The Vyst, the Creator's chosen holy prophet, has come with power to unite all of humanity once more. Only by becoming of one mind and spirit can humanity become whole again and so transcend to the Outside. There, we will be reconciled with the Creator and the other Spirits who eagerly await Human, the final Spirit to return. Such reconciliation will lead to the passing away of this old reality and the ushering in of a new one, one in which we may at last rebuild the paradise we lost. And so we must spread the New Gospel we've received from the Vyst to all the worlds, to every tribe, nation, and tongue.

"Many of you have come saying, 'Tell me, what is this New Gospel?' But did you really come to hear mere words, an explanation? No, you came desiring an *experience*. Today, we welcome each of you to take the first step toward the healing of your souls. Toward a bottomless forgiveness. Toward perfect unity. Everyone please join hands, close your eyes, and clear your minds as I lead us in a meditation. As I pray, I want you to do something very difficult. I want you to meditate fully and honestly upon your humanity: your truest desires, your most terrifying fears, your mortality, your terrible secrets. Only the vulnerable can be cured."

Kairos pulled his hand away as Nevik reached for it, his comfort level plummeting as things became too touchy-feely.

"Everyone participates," Nevik insisted, clasping a hand over Kairos's forearm.

Kairos looked over to Neve, but her eyes were closed. His

stomach churned as his mind involuntarily drifted to the night of the chapel fire on Pantoll, the night he had killed the girl. Despite his clerical training, the awful memory couldn't be repressed easily once dragged up. The Amor Fati were cunning: suggesting that their guests think about their worst memories would ensure that they inevitably would to at least some degree, whether they consciously wanted to or not.

The Disciple began uttering a prayer.

After a few moments, Kairos felt a slight tickle at the back of his head. It began to itch, but in scratching his scalp, he discovered that the sensation seemed to be emanating from within, in a deep place that couldn't be reached. One moment, the blaze of the chapel fire flashed before his mind; the next, it was replaced by an image of his seminary graduation day. Then his thoughts moved to other memories. *What's going on with me?* he thought.

Neon green text appeared over top the bottom left of Kairos's vision. Communication from Sunsip:

Brainwaves just spiked. Odd patterns on you both. You should surface. Or just give the word and I'll pull you out.

Not yet, Kairos sent back. *I want to meet the Vyst first.*

The tickling in Kairos's head had turned into a dull ache. A stream of jumbled thoughts and images filled his head like background static, too vague and ephemeral now for him to process. A confused thought would bubble, then it would just as soon disappear before he could put a mental finger on what it was or where it had come from. His body trembled. He glanced at Neve, who should've also seen Sunsip's message, even through closed eyes. Her eyes moved beneath closed lids, her forehead creased in discomfort, her lower lip quivered. So she was experiencing it as well. And he bet Midmay had too.

Beside him, Nevik sat calmly, eyes shut, slack-faced but with hand gripped firmly around Kairos's forearm. In fact, looking around, all of the white-clad acolytes sat with the same serene expressions on their faces, while the bodies of all of the guest attendees were perceptibly shuddering.

Kairos had experienced enough. He tried to lean behind Nevik's back to whisper in Neve's ear to exit the portal, but the zealot's hand had him locked in a vice grip. Kairos then began subvocalizing his personal surfacing keyword, "lighthouse," repeatedly, which would trigger the VR suit to terminate the virtual program's datastream flow and pull him back into real consciousness.

Nothing happened.

His creeping fear was realized: the cult had somehow hacked into his connection and was blocking his ability to sever it. He had also lost comms; there was no way to tell Sunsip to pull them out.

Kairos's headache had grown into a splitting migraine. A deluge of intrusive thoughts was now flooding his mind. Images of people he'd never met, places he'd never been. Recollections of hazy memories that he would have sworn weren't his own. A mess of emotions surged through him until they blended into a numbing paralysis, like a rainbow of colors mixing into black.

* * *

Subprograms that trapped users' minds within a virtual world were highly illegal. The physical danger and mental trauma of

259

preventing a user from disconnecting were obvious. Even so, over the countless virtual expeditions Kairos had taken since leaving the priesthood, he'd been ensnared before. For once, he was thankful for that experience, because it had forced him to formulate and memorize a few brain-hacking tricks to extricate oneself.

To the best of his ability, he cleared his mind, similar to readying for Retrospection. Then he focused on a string of specific trigger words while executing specific bodily actions. Collectively, this should tweak his brain chemistry enough to release the subprogram's hold on him.

Chorus, stencil, flabbergasted, (flex left arm), *valve, book, umbrella, ether, yewstring,* (squeeze right hand), *great-grandmother, ice-skating, button, wyvex, superfluid, tower, nail, photophosphorylation,* (blink once), *tide, argument,* (blink twice, tongue out), *clothes hanger, mutation, cross, singularity* (lift and pound both feet), *lighthouse, lighthouse, lighthouse, light—*

The virtual world dissipated like a burst bubble. The suit relaxed its pressure against his body. His senses emerged hazily into the confined quiet of his headgear, the drowsiness of sleep clinging to him.

Sunsip's alarmed voice came through the comms channel. "You okay? I received no message from you." The trader sounded relieved, as if he had been nervously debating a tough decision and then discovered the choice was no longer necessary. "I was going to hard unplug you, but—"

"Pull Neve out now," Kairos ordered.

"But her brainwaves are going haywire. A hard disconnect could damage her—"

"Just do it!"

Moments later, a couple of screams followed by loud puffs of gasping breath come in over their shared comms.

"It's alright, you're safe now. That's right," Sunsip's voice assured her, but the pilot couldn't hide the fear in his tone.

For the next minute, all Kairos heard through his speakers were Neve's rapid, heavy breaths and incomprehensible sentence fragments.

"Those things ... memories ..." he heard her sputter, when her breathing finally slowed. "But different from mine ... a reflection ... *his* memories ..."

"Keep her disconnected, Sunsip," Kairos spoke to the pilot. "She's a bit rattled."

"She doesn't look good, either," Sunsip told him with a grave voice. "She's soaked in sweat. I'll free her from the rig. Then help you out of your suit."

"No. I'm jacking back in."

"What?" barked the pilot. "You must be mad! I won't let you. If you saw your brainwaves—"

"Reset my entry coordinates," Kairos insisted. "They're using some kind of mass hypnosis to brainwash attendees, but I can at least get around the eggbeater program they've paired it with. That's how I was able to surface just now. I need to learn what they're doing. I'll be fine, do it." *But is it merely an eggbeater program?* warned the voice in the back of his head. *What if it's the same insanity that plagued the worker on Bei Arron? But how is such neural influence possible in a virtual environment, without even the use of that stolen neurofluid?*

With a reluctant snort, Sunsip flipped Kairos's connection switch.

Kairos's muscles relaxed. A sea of white washed over him.

Then, as colors and shapes differentiated and settled, the

virtual world materialized around him once more.

Kairos was back in the prairie where they'd initially started. He ran through the fields and woods to return to the mountainside cathedral. He stopped at the edge of the woods before coming out upon the cathedral and took cover behind a thick tree.

The crowd of avatars at the amphitheater, including the two Disciples on the stage, all faced the same direction. They were soundlessly swaying in unison, as if in a collective trance. A soft breeze of cool air highlighted the tangible silence of the scene.

Kairos waited for a while. Finally, all at once, the crowd ceased swaying and reanimated. All of them were smiling. Some then began walking away. Others winked out of existence as they disconnected from the portal. Many just remained standing. But none spoke.

The Disciples did not engage with the other users, but returned to the narrow arched entryway at the cathedral's side. Kairos turned away from the crowd to follow them at a distance.

After the two disappeared into the cathedral, Kairos approached the entryway himself. He encountered only flush stone where the entrance had been moments before. Racing around to the front, he tried the tall wooden doors. They were still sealed tight. He pounded his fists against them in vain, knowing that the doors were merely a facade. Even had he been able to bust them to splinters, set them afire, or barge them open some other way, there would be only blank nothingness behind them for users without access. It was likely that only a specific list of users with the proper authentication—the Disciples—could enter the cathedral's private "interior." Kairos had a strong sense that getting inside was important; using a cathedral as a secure meeting portal seemed in line with the cult's style.

He slumped to the ground to think, but the situation was hopeless. Hacking the Amor Fati's portal was far beyond his skills, and Midmay was comatose. Even if she weren't, the hack would have to go through one of their personal accounts, an impossible task given their real-world identities were completely unknown.

He closed his eyes and cycled through a breathing exercise. As he'd been trained to do, he allowed his mind to wander, hoping perhaps his subconscious could guide him where conscious thought had failed.

After several moments, two prompts came to him, like small air bubbles rising from the ocean's depths. The first concerned Neve: her anguished screams and babbling upon surfacing from the portal. The second was the Blackpool job insider, alias Nightjar.

Hmm.

Nightjar had been a Blackpool scientist and, per Chimera, was a confirmed cult member. That didn't necessarily mean Nightjar was a Disciple, and their identity was obviously unknown, but still, it was a starting point. His subconscious had connected Nightjar and Neve. *But why?* Was it as simple as Neve investigating the Blackpool job and wanting to discover Nightjar's identity? *No ... there was more to it than that.*

Neve's pained ramblings kept returning to him. Then, he picked out something he'd missed before. She had said "*his* memories."

Who's he?

Someone whose memories were a reflection of her own.

She was referring to her husband!

She had sensed his thoughts and memories in the portal. Neve had told Kairos in the space elevator that the neurofluid enabled human telepathy. *But that must be impossible!* Besides, her husband was dead.

Not necessarily ...

He recalled Neve's voice in the Oasis electrorock tavern, Psychoncussion, *"My husband was the one who was against having children."*

Just then, the four eyes of the *Generatio Finalis* cult thrust itself up from his subconscious. He recalled the text explaining the cult's commitment to celibacy.

The revelation was clear: Nightjar was Neve's husband.

Neve's husband was the Blackpool insider, betrayer of both his employer and her.

Despite a strong desire to meditate upon the ramifications of such a truth, he pushed further thoughts aside. The Disciples could be meeting right now inside that secured cathedral. Every moment mattered. The key question: was Neve's husband among them?

"What happened?" an anxious Sunsip asked upon Kairos's surfacing.

"Hit a firewall," Kairos replied, "but I have a solution. You're not gonna like it." Kairos gave the pilot instructions and waited as the man moved away.

"Inside left pocket," instructed Kairos when he heard Sunsip return.

"No ... no, no, no ..." Sunsip stammered in horror. "Please let this not be what I know it is. Neve said you destroyed it!"

"No time to argue. I think some of the cult leaders are meeting now inside a private room within the portal."

"Do you have any idea what you've done, bringing this onto my ship?" Sunsip barked. "We'll have the entire degenerate swarm out for our blood!"

"They don't know I have it. They think it was blown to bits."

From his supine position within the VR suit, Kairos couldn't see the pilot's rage, but from the man's growling and anguished breathing, Kairos wondered if Sunsip was attempting to crush Jaxx's AI chip with his bare hands.

"I'm jettisoning this thing out of the airlock!" Sunsip roared.

"No! The Amor Fati are even more dangerous than Jaxx," Kairos shot back. "They're not a simple cult. They're incredibly well-funded, and something bigger is happening. I don't know what that is. But I know they killed my father, and now Midmay ..."

There was silence on the trader's end.

"Listen," Kairos continued. "Jaxx is the only thing that can get me into that room. You know it's true."

"If I connect this chip," Sunsip began to relent, "what makes you think Jaxx will help you? It's more likely to find a way to kill you using your VR suit."

"That's a risk I'm willing to take. But I don't believe it will do that."

Sunsip uttered a string of curses so colorful that only the distributor community could have come up with them. "What did I do to deserve this?" the trader muttered to himself. "Standby." It took a minute for Sunsip to find the right connection points and wiring to hook the chip's housing up to the VR rig. If Kairos were honest, his chest tightened with dread when Sunsip announced everything was ready to go.

Sunsip flipped the switch.

Kairos materialized once more in the portal's large prairie. Immediately he was assailed by a small but vicious boy who overpowered him and clutched his throat. The boy was barefoot and wore only frayed denim overalls.

"Stop," Kairos rasped. His VR suit was strangling him to death. "I'm Kairos, Neve's partner, remember? I know Cole betrayed you, Jaxx. I know who he was working with, the organization that hacked you." The freckled boy glared at him with sharp black eyes, but his grip eased and he was listening intently. "It was a religious cult. They call themselves the Amor Fati. This is their portal for worship services. I believe some of their leaders are meeting now within a cathedral not far from here, but its entrance is encrypted. I figured you'd be as interested as I am in seeing what's inside. If you hack us into it and help me learn who these people are, then I'll return you to the Oasis. So, do you want revenge on the organization that used you, or should I just have my partner toss you out of his ship's airlock right now?"

The boy released him and sat back on the grass, saying nothing.

"Good." Kairos breathed normally. "The cathedral can only be accessed by specific users, but I know one of them"—*I hope*—"is Neve's husband. I assume you can track him down and then hack his access point?"

The boy didn't respond, merely stared inertly into the grass for a while, still as a corpse. Kairos knew that it was currently digging into its vast resources—SolarNet tracking, comms recordings, security cam footage, archival data—for any and all knowledge of the current whereabouts of the man Neve had called her husband.

After several minutes, the world shifted and slid ever so

slightly beneath Kairos. A few blades of grass by his side twitched unnaturally; upon closer inspection, he noticed the top half of their stalks had glitched and were floating, askew from their bases.

The next moment, Kairos abruptly found himself atop the slanted roof of the cathedral.

Disoriented and scrabbling to no avail, he rolled down and was saved from plummeting to the ground only by smacking into a low ornate railing that traced along the roof's flat narrow ledge.

Lifting his head, he spotted the boy ahead of him, picking his way along the edge of the roof toward the rear of the building. Kairos scrambled to his feet to chase after him. The boy dropped off the end of the roof. Upon coming to the place where he'd disappeared, Kairos found a narrow balcony a few meters below. A series of gargoyles jutted from the balcony, their stone faces twisted in menacing expressions. He climbed over the low railing and lowered himself down. The balcony curved around to the cathedral's side and ended at a low stone archway leading into the dark interior of a narrow winding staircase.

Jaxx had successfully hacked the portal.

Stone blocks at the edges of the archway's opening were already reforming rapidly to seal it off—counter-hacking security programs at work.

Kairos sprinted toward the opening and dove through. Gathering himself from the blow of his body landing on the stone floor beyond, he raced down the winding stairs.

They spilled out onto a high balcony overlooking the cathedral's cavernous interior. Its nave held rows of dark wooden, stiff-backed pews situated between smooth, pale columns and terminated at the tall wooden doors of the front entrance. Standing and peering over the low waist-high stone railing, Kairos found himself over the choir section. The staircase behind Kairos had vanished; where it had been was now only a smooth stone wall. Jaxx's avatar was nowhere in sight.

That damned AI.

Voices emanated from a smaller chapel off to Kairos's right. He crept around the balcony's corner toward them and peeked around a support column. Below, nine hooded figures were gathered around a circular table that had been erected in the chapel. Nevik had mentioned only eight Disciples. One of these below must be the Vyst.

"... these public sessions may be beneficial for accelerating new conversions, but they also pose a greater potential for rejections," one of the cloaked figures was arguing. "And rejections mean dead bodies being found. Or, worse, if the attendee survives, they're left to roam freely with half-formed thoughts of the knowledge we've planted within them. We can't have rumors circulating around the worlds. With the two rejections we had at this service, that brings the total to six. We need to understand the causes of such rejection in order to refine the technology."

"The mind-catcher software adequately mitigates that risk," another responded. "And though the occurrence of lethal brain damage is elevated during this process, it is low enough relative to other virtual recreational activities to avoid drawing public scrutiny."

A third voice spoke up abruptly, interrupting the conversation. "I sensed my wife's thoughts at the conversion service today." Kairos shot a look at the hooded figure who had spoken. It was indistinguishable from the rest. "But I cannot sense her anymore." The voice shook with tension.

The room fell quiet, every face turning to the male voice who'd spoken.

The first figure who'd been speaking broke the silence. "Are you sure?"

"She would never log into a portal like this unless she had a strong reason," he replied. "She has no interest in religious faith ..." He paused, bowed his head, and moaned, as if in deep concentration to recall something. "She's investigating the Blackpool theft," he said, his voice wavering. "She's connected the assassin to us."

"Neve," the first figure said with a tone of discovering something for the first time. "Her name is Neve, isn't it? She must have been one of the two rejections we observed."

"But how could the assassin be linked to us?" another Disciple asked. "Did we not eliminate all ties?"

"It's fruitless to speculate what she knows or has proof of," responded another. "In any case, Blackpool poses no serious threat. Only we around this table know the identities of the members of our faith. Without such knowledge, there is little Blackpool can do."

"Blackpool may be no threat, but you can be sure Jaxx and its deviants will hunt us even on the basis of rumor," added another. Other Disciples murmured agreement.

The first figure whom Kairos had heard speak pointed across the table at Neve's husband. "He and that assassin are the only links to our role in the theft. If his wife detected his presence during synchronization, then his identity has been exposed."

"That's an alarmist perspective," Neve's husband retorted. "There is no precedent for one being able to distinguish individual minds during their initial sync. There's too much sensory information to process. Even if she sensed a thread of something, she'd have no reason to draw such a wild conclusion from—" At once his voice cut off and his eyes and mouth twitched. A grimace spread across his face, as if some pained revelation had dawned upon him. After a moment, he declared, "I will speak what everyone is thinking, although I would know it even if our minds weren't one: you all agree with him! That I'm a liability."

One of the figures who hadn't spoken yet raised a bony hand. The room silenced.

That must be the Vyst, Kairos thought.

"Our brother speaks a truth that, however improbable, must be taken seriously. Our mission is at a critical juncture. We cannot allow needless risk." The Vyst leaned toward the Disciple sitting to his right, the one who'd delivered the message at the amphitheater service. "Brother Maddox, there were two minds who rejected the faith. Neve had help. Find them."

"We already have a believer in place to handle them," Brother Maddox replied. "And what about the assassin?"

"The man is already dead." The Vyst turned to Neve's husband. "Speaking of dead men, your former wife knows only who you were, not who you are now. A dead man cannot be found. However, you are to remain in the lab from now on." The Vyst surveyed the members around the table. "Now to other matters. Soon, we will not have to rely on this crude portal to make new converts. We will bring the New Gospel to the people directly. Brother Zhou, what is the status of our broadcast tests?"

"They're working beautifully," Brother Zhou said. "We

have approximately seventy thousand connected minds. The converts from the latest service will be integrated in less than a standard day, once the new cellular structures have fully matured."

The Vyst turned to another Disciple. "Sister Essina, is Kotopax ready to receive us?"

"Our penetration into the system's intranet will be completed within the next forty-eight hours," Sister Essina replied. "The brothers and sisters here on the ground are preparing their congregations to support the spread of the New Gospel. I'm looking forward to your visit, holy one."

Kairos couldn't believe what he was hearing. Were they actually transmitting a neurological disease—a virus?—via the SolarNet that could infect people? It was impossible. It would require the Amor Fati taking the base neurofluid technology many steps beyond prototype; in fact, evolving it to an entirely new level, a way to alter brain chemistry through cyberspace linkages, without the need for any fluid injection. Kairos thought back to the users logged into the portal, how their avatars swayed in perfect synchronization. Interhuman networked communication. A network controlled by the Vyst. And the Amor Fati's plans to spread their new gospel were terrifyingly real ...

"Are we sure we should not target a non-core system for our first large-scale test?" a Disciple asked. "While our tests in remote places have been largely ignored, such a conspicuous expansion of our faith will attract the scrutiny of every System Administrator."

"Our advantage from this point on will be speed," the Vyst responded. "Once we confirm the success of the transmission on Kotopax, we'll move to the other systems in quick succession. By the time the System Administrators comprehend what is happening, it will be too late to stop it. Before long, you will witness greater successes than Kotopax. Soon Lienns-Sutra will be fully under our control, and with it, the Lilic System: Spires and Yllara. Next will be the Ambic System, where our brothers and sisters within New Canaan Agriculture will help us spread the New Gospel to Eukiah, Jeribah, and the Archipelago. From there ..."

Kairos became aware of a presence behind him. He turned just as the boy grabbed him.

"I am no man's tool," the boy growled and flung Kairos back with vicious strength. Kairos's body hit the low balcony railing with such momentum that he flipped over its top, plummeting and smacking the marble floor below. The VR suit's pain sensors spiked to maximum, gripping with him with seething pangs and sending his vision into a kaleido-scopic blur. He sensed the frenzied exclamations and rushes of movement from the Disciples—soon fading to silence as members severed their connections and their avatars winked out of existence. The sound of footsteps came toward him, echoing through the empty cathedral. He rolled to his side and looked. The Vyst towered over him, all dark flowing robes with a hood shrouding a dark, featureless void where a face should have been. Kairos's chest seized up as if impaled with an icicle, his hands and feet flailing against the polished marble floor in an attempt to skitter away.

The Vyst bent and gripped Kairos's face with a bony palm. "Kairos Catadyn," it uttered accusingly, as if dragging the name over a bed of bent nails.

The Vyst and the virtual world abruptly dissipated.

Kairos awoke jarringly into reality, aching and disoriented.

Ship alarms were blaring.

His headgear was being violently yanked off with all the external connections still in place, the electrodes' suction cups clinging stubbornly to his sweaty skin before popping off.

"What's going on?" he yelled through the tangle of wires and tubes. The overhead lights flickered. A distraught Sunsip was over top him, frantically ripping open Kairos's VR suit.

"Degenerates!" the pilot barked. "Jaxx led them right to us."

* * *

The crippling of the *Flyby Rhythm II* had been quick.

Jaxx had somehow found its way into the shipcom. Kairos didn't know how that was possible given the VR rig wasn't even connected to the main shipboard computer. Sunsip had ripped the connections away from Jaxx's chip as soon as he'd figured out what was happening, but it was too late. It didn't really matter how it'd happened—the fact remained. And after it happened, it was game over. Jaxx promptly paralyzed the ship's engines, broadcasted the ship's location to its degenerate cronies, and switched off all life support systems before then locking them out completely from shipcom access. The compromised ship was a sitting duck, and since then it'd been hit by bursts of radiation from long range enemy fire, with the resulting surges shorting out even the independent backup systems. No matter, Jaxx's saviors were in hot pursuit and would put an end to their misery well before they ran out of oxygen.

Medwick's voice burst over the intercom, "LATTICE is now showing four ships. I'm trying to reboot our systems using the portable generator but one of them is closing *fast*. Sunsip, I need you up here."

Sunsip thrust Jaxx's chip into Kairos's hands and angrily kicked away to help his brother in the command module.

Kairos fought through the tangle of wiring to Neve. Her hands were pressed over her ears and her eyes were squeezed shut. Her lips moved silently while her face contorted in pained confusion. Nothing he did could snap her out of it.

Kairos swore and kicked away to check on Midmay. When he arrived at the medbay, he found her in the medical chair, her unconscious condition unchanged.

The ship shook, as if it had just bumped up against something large and immovable. Kairos's body was thrown against the side of the medbay.

Several moments later, a heavy rumble ensued from the direction of the entry cabin. It was followed by a sucking noise, then a loud click, like a lock dropping into place.

Terror filled Kairos. A ship was docking with them. A degenerate raiding party.

Sunsip hollered from down the tunnelway. The pilot soared by the medbay entrance, barely pausing to yell at Kairos to help him manually seal off the external airlock hatch.

Kairos glanced back at Midmay's serene expression, then kicked away after Sunsip.

When he arrived at the main cabin airlock, Sunsip already had the inner hatch open. But when they moved to the external hatch control panel, a short series of explosive bursts sounded.

The hatch burst open with a rush of air that pushed the two of them back. A beam of light flooded into the airlock. A tall, broad figure stood outlined against the light.

Sunsip charged at the figure but was sent hurtling backward past Kairos and into the cabin.

Squinting, Kairos caught a dark cloak and a glint off the figure's eyes. They were the long eyescopes of his father's last remaining worker.

"Falck?" Kairos exclaimed, absolutely stupefied.

The man strode forward and seized him with a large gloved hand.

"How did—" Kairos started. A gas of some kind burst into his stunned face, causing him to cough.

"A necessary sedative," Falck said through his respirator.

Kairos's eyes burned and his vision blurred. He felt his muscles going limp.

"Relax," drifted the man's deep voice.

The last thing Kairos felt as his body was carried off was the cold metal of Jaxx's chip sifting gracefully through his limp fingers.

Chapter 11

Kairos awoke to warm air and the white noise of ocean waves. The sky overhead was a creamy pink. He was alone.

He lay on a simple rope hammock, a salty breeze rocking him gently beneath a palm-like tree at his head and feet. It was so nice, he lay there for several moments in a fog, staring dumbly at the long fronds.

He pulled himself to a sitting position. A dull headache throbbed from the blood rush. In his clumsy effort to step off, the hammock tipped and deposited him onto the sandy ground. Propping himself up, he took in his surroundings. A worn path ran toward the sound of waves through a clump of thick-leaved shrubs. It led to a black sand beach that sloped down to the vast, dark green ocean beyond. A pale white sun hung just above the flat horizon and was descending.

Where has Falck brought me? Kairos closed his eyes and leaned his head back for a moment, absorbing the rays of natural light which his skin had missed for the two or so standard weeks since they had landed on Spires.

Turning around, he found himself within the dune grass-covered yard of a small, one-story cottage. A large windmill rose from its roof, its weathered blades spinning lazily. A wooden veranda wound across its front and sides. Although the immediate area around the cottage had long been cleared, a dense green jungle encroached upon its back and side borders. He thought it must be where Falck and his companions were. He wondered whether Falck had tranquilized them as well.

Prickly seed pods snagged his pants as he walked through the long, yellow-green dune grass to the veranda. He moved cautiously, but without fear. If Falck had wanted them dead, the man would have already delivered them to the degenerates.

The cottage's thin, screened door creaked on rusted hinges as he stepped through into a kitchen space. Wooden cabinets lined two walls, some hanging off-plumb with broken hinges. A dull metal spigot over a large basin served as a sink. The counter tops were bare save a couple of cracked wooden bowls; a lone cast iron pan hung from an overhead rack in the center of the kitchen.

Kairos announced his presence, but received no reply. The house was deathly quiet. The adjoining sitting room was furnished simply with a couple of wall shelves, a low table, and a few woven chairs, all of which looked crafted from materials found in the surrounding jungle. A narrow door stood in the short width of wall between the sitting room and the kitchen. It opened to a steep set of stairs leading down into a dark cellar. He called down, but no one answered.

Along the hallway leading toward the back of the cottage was a door he assumed led to a bedroom. He cracked it open and peered in. The small room consisted only of a bed, nightstand, and chair, also of simple design and made from local materials. Soft lines of late afternoon light leaked through the narrow slits of the windows' wooden blinds. On the dilapidated feather bed, Neve rested under an old, yellowed sheet, eyes closed, chest softly rising and falling. Her eyebrows were slightly furled, as if she had succumbed to the sedative or sleep with terrible unease.

Kairos sensed that Neve had sacrificed a lot more than he knew in pursuit of justice for her husband. He shuddered at the thought of telling her that her husband was not only in on the neurofluid theft, but also had abandoned her to believe he'd died. He'd been the Blackpool Executive triumvirate's suspected mole, the insider with senior-level access to the science corporation's most guarded technologies. He'd disabled the *Asterisk*'s defense systems to help Chimera dock with the ship for his own extraction. Kairos shuddered further at the thought of telling Neve that her husband was one of the Vyst's Eight Disciples. But he worried most that he wouldn't have to tell her, that what she experienced in the virtual portal had somehow already made her painfully aware of the truth.

Quietly shutting the door, he continued down the hallway. It ended at a warm, darkened back room. A square pool—about two meters to a side—filled the space, enclosed by a tiled perimeter. Thick curtains were drawn over the open-air windows. The still pool water was cloudy but shallow—less than a meter deep. Resting at its bottom was the Osetran teardrop. Its long wavy filament had been joined by two new short ones emerging from its pointed end. Squatting beside the pool, Kairos dipped a finger. He withdrew it immediately. The water temperature was scalding.

He became aware of the noise of activity outside. Then came a girl's shriek.

Midmay!

He bolted upright and scrambled to the cottage's back door. It opened to an unkempt backyard filled with low shrubs, tufts of dune grass, and patches of sandy dirt. He let out a rush of held breath upon seeing Sunsip and Medwick. They were chopping stringy logs from the downed trunk of a fibrous jungle tree. Midmay was zooming around the yard, laughing and whooping as Rhody chased her.

Kairos called her name and ran to her. For a long moment he embraced her tightly. He looked into her eyes, felt her cheeks and forehead. The fever had left her. Her eyes were bright.

"I'm okay," she protested, brushing his hands away.

"I'm sorry," he told her, his eyes welling. "I'm sorry for everything that's happened."

"I'm fine, really," Midmay assured him. She pulled away and ran off to return to playing with Rhody. Remarkably, the hybird had made it off the ship and looked in strong health. Perhaps it had already gone off hunting real flesh-and-blood prey, a welcome change after spending so much time in space, subsisting on dry protein pellets.

Upon seeing Kairos walking over, Medwick smiled thinly and paused his work. The navigator looked physically spent, and both he and his brother were drenched in sweat. Kairos guessed the interstellar traders weren't used to much planetary labor. "They bounce back fast, eh?" the navigator remarked. "Kids. Not a care in the worlds."

Sunsip however, his headphones over his ears, continued hacking away with great swings of his hatchet, as if the tree had wronged him, before then walking off a short ways into the surrounding jungle to find more dead wood without so much as a glance Kairos's way. Medwick explained that his brother needed time to work out the shock and anger of losing their ship. Worst of all, the *Flyby Rhythm II*—intentionally disabled rather than destroyed to avoid the risk of damaging Jaxx, and also so the ship could be taken as plunder—would be defiled by the degenerates as it became a part of their pirated fleet.

Kairos attempted a weak apology which Medwick graciously brushed off, saying he was grateful to be alive at all. But Kairos could tell by the navigator's half-hearted smile and downcast eyes that the loss was taking as much of a toll on him too. Kairos's body flushed warm with guilt. A good ship was a trader's life source. Their entire livelihood rested upon it. Not to mention their most valuable possession; even a small distroship cost a fortune. Nothing Kairos had or did could possibly compensate them for such a major loss. He'd now caused the loss of two ships, including Neve's.

Medwick asked whether Kairos had learned what he needed from the cult's portal, with the hopeful expression of one seeking any reason to believe the suffering was worth it. Kairos told him what he'd heard the Amor Fati discussing, and that the cult was planning something serious and big. Medwick gave a grim nod, finding a sliver of solace in knowing the ship hadn't been sacrificed in vain. Kairos had left out mention of Neve's husband. Neve should be the first to know. And he needed time to meditate further on the theology of the Amor Fati.

When the traders had wakened from sedation, Falck had already gone. Given the confining space of the tiny cottage and desire to be on alert for the man's return, the traders planned to stake out in the yard all night. They'd been stacking the cut logs near a primitive stone fire ring. Resting beside the log pile, Kairos also noticed a few makeshift spears sharpened from branches.

"Do you know the man that brought us here?" Medwick asked.

Kairos nodded and told him about his father's sole remaining hired hand.

The navigator nodded. "We've seen his type before. Man of few words. Obscures his facial features with that breathing mask and eyescopes. Neck to toe covered by thick clothing. Hiding out on some backwater planet or moon, doing odd jobs for employers who ask no questions. Chances are he's either ex-corporate or a fugitive."

"He tried to take the artifact from me on Pantoll," Kairos said. "I thought he wanted to cash in on the prize and run."

The navigator shook his head. "That's what's odd. The man owns a private spacecraft worth two lifetimes' wages. He doesn't need money."

Medwick was right, and Kairos realized how little he actually knew about the man. And Falck's connection to Cole and the Amor Fati still eluded him. Kairos had never observed any interest in Falck for religion, or even the SolarNet. "Any sign of him?" he asked.

The navigator shook his head, then went on to tell him that he and his brother weren't sure yet what planet they'd been brought to. The jungle around the cottage was impenetrable. A short walk down to the coast line indicated that the cottage was isolated. Upon nightfall, assuming a clear view of the stars, they'd know for sure. Any good trader knew the constellations of every system as well as the freckles on their body. "Now that you're up, we can explore farther," Medwick said. "Best way would be along the beach."

Kairos nodded. "Good idea to stick together. I'll go wake Neve." He turned but Medwick held his shoulder and shook his head.

"She asked not to be disturbed." When Kairos started to protest, the navigator added, "She was adamant."

After a moment, Kairos nodded. He called for Midmay and the four of them set off down the path at the cottage's front.

They came out upon a curved strip of black sand beach along a dark, seaweed-green ocean. While the traders didn't know where they were, it struck a certain familiarity to Kairos. He was sure he'd seen images of this place before over the SolarNet. In one direction, the beach stretched as far as the eye could see. In the other, it ran for about a klick before a series of large rocks jutting into the water cut it off. They chose the longer direction.

It didn't take long for the cottage to disappear from view. Once they'd gone some distance, they found that it sat at the sloping foot of a low mountain, part of a range that stretched along the coast.

They walked for a long while. There was no end to the monotony of the beach. For much of the time, they either walked in silence or the brothers would converse privately with each other in low voices. Occasionally Medwick would squat to poke at shells along the shoreline and pocket a few—a trader's instinct of collecting anything that might have off-world value. At no point during their trek did the dense wall of jungle let up, and they came across no other habitation or structure of any kind. The ocean's horizon was featureless— no silhouettes of distant other land, no boats or ships.

The sun had set with the sky rapidly transitioning to a violet twilight, the first bright stars peeking out. The sun of this planet had been high overhead when they'd left the cottage not more than two or three standard hours ago. The days here were very short.

After several minutes, the navigators abruptly halted.

"Nothing," a winded Sunsip huffed, plopping dejectedly on the sand to rest. "Damn this suffocating gravity," he mumbled. "How can anyone live like this?"

"Perplexing," his brother agreed, wiping more sweat from his brow than the walk merited. "And troubling." The brothers exchanged a knowing glance.

"What is it?" Kairos asked. "Do you know where we are?" He'd noticed the traders had walked with craned heads as soon as the earliest stars peeked through the darkening sky.

Sunsip, clearly still angry with Kairos, tossed his arms up and looked away. Medwick responded to Kairos, "This is a foreign sky."

"Give the constellations a little more time," Kairos said. "I swear I've seen pictures of this place before."

Sunsip snorted loudly.

Medwick shook his head. "It seems we've been brought outside of the Settled Region," said the navigator firmly.

Kairos blinked a couple of times in silence. Only foolhardy pioneers ventured beyond colonized space. Here, there'd be no settlements. No trade. No technology. Probably no other people. In that moment, the silence of the jungle became a heartless judgment. The sound of small waves breaking softly against the shore became a somber murmuring about loss.

"Kairos, you said this man, Falck, was only ever a worker for your father?" Medwick asked. "And his ship—you'd never seen it before?"

Kairos shook his head. "Far as I knew, the man was as

penniless, hopeless, and useless as my father."

Sunsip shot his brother another look.

"See this?" Medwick said, showing Kairos a reddened cut on his arm. "I'd been thrown against the command console when Falck's ship docked with ours. The wound is still fresh. So we couldn't have been sedated for long. Less than a full cycle." His voice was uncharacteristically shaky.

"In other words, it's impossible for us to be here," Sunsip said curtly, kicking at a clump of sand. "To travel outside the Settled Region in so short a time, you'd need a weave drive capable of generating more energy than a Great Ship's. And it'd have to fit on a ship as small as Falck's. Or, you'd need to stick out your thumb and hope to hitch a ride on an Osetran starship."

Kairos looked back at them dumbly, having not even considered their travel. They were right. It was impossible.

"I knew it was strange," Medwick reflected. "When the four degenerate ships were pursuing us, that fifth ship appeared on LATTICE out of nowhere and beat them to us. I'd never seen a ship close in on anything that fast."

"Impossible or not, in addition to his Osetran prize, he's also got us as an extra bonus in his reward," snapped Sunsip. "I bet he's off contacting potential buyers now. He's got plenty of options: that damned cult, corporations, degenerates."

"We don't think Falck seeks only monetary gain," Medwick told Kairos. "Hence he would wouldn't have brought all of us here with him. He's got to be around here somewhere; otherwise, we would've heard his ship take off. And I doubt he'd leave the artifact unattended for long."

Sunsip turned to Kairos directly for the first time that day. "I understand you've known this guy personally for a while," he said gravely. "But I think you know, as well as we, that the only way off this planet is going to be via that man's ship. We outnumber him. We need to be ready when he returns."

Kairos thought of the spears by the fire pit that the traders had fashioned, and remembered Sunsip's military experience. "No," he refused. "He had the opportunity to kill us, but he didn't. He could've tied us up in the cottage, but he didn't. We need to know who this man is first."

Sunsip snorted, pounding the sand with a fist.

"Whatever his motives, it's pointless going against him unless we can find and take control of his ship," Medwick said. "Without it, we'll be stranded to our deaths here. My brother is right about that. Perhaps its landing pad is hidden within the jungle near the cottage and we missed it."

Kairos looked resignedly off into the distance. The beach stretched interminably. There were no lights along the ocean horizon. Dark waves crashed against the shoreline and spilled over the black sand like oil.

"Did you see the Osetran artifact?" he asked them. "In that pool at the back of the cottage?"

Sunsip nodded. "Looks like some damned degenerate bio-experiment."

"If the device indeed is of Osetran origin and it were deliberately sent to a destination like Pantoll at some point in the past," Medwick mused, "it is possible the, ah, *organic*, nature of it is part of their terraforming apparatus. To grow, adapt to, and gradually transform its surrounding environment into habitable conditions for the Osetra."

Medwick's description surprised Kairos. He hadn't considered the teardrop's protrusions to be organic growth. "It is true the Osetra terraformed many planets in the Settled

Region, many centuries before humans colonized them," Kairos said.

"I guess Pantoll's terraforming was botched then," Sunsip said.

Botched, thought Kairos with a wry grin. It made sense that's the kind of planet he'd lived on. "But this device is so small, they'd need to send billions of these things to terraform a planet within any reasonable time frame. In any case, Pantoll would be a terrible colony candidate for their biology. As an amphibious species, the Osetra prefer planets with large bodies of water ..." As he casually waved a hand at the sea, a series of facts came together and struck him all at once: the artifact shimmering in the rain when his father first discovered it; its luminescent response when placed in the caravan ship's water tank; its organic tendrils— *umbilicals*—feeding on that dead fish.

"Oh my god," he stammered with realization.

The teardrop held an egg.

It carried an unborn Osetra.

* * *

It was well into the night by the time they returned to the cottage.

Still no sign of Falck.

Kairos and Midmay went inside while the traders went around back to start up a fire. Checking on the Osetran teardrop in the pool, Kairos found that the two new filaments that had sprouted had grown rapidly and were now nearly the length of the initial one. More questions plagued him. How in the worlds did an Osetran embryo come to crash land on Pantoll? Where had it come from?

Midmay squatted and dipped a finger in, humming softly, and gave the steaming, cloudy water a swirl. Then, she reached an arm in to stroke one of the filaments.

Alarmed, Kairos yanked her arm out by the elbow. "You'll burn yourself!" he cautioned. Indeed, her skin was blotchy.

"Yet unborn," Midmay breathed, giving no attention to the heat. "The tadpole embryo is feeding off a mimicked placental matrix." She wiped her arm dry against her shirt.

He gave her a curious look. "Come on," he said, standing and pulling her up.

"I am going to stay for a while," Midmay protested, wiggling her arm free. She sat cross-legged by the side of the pool. Looking up at his concern, she added, "Please don't worry."

Kairos did worry about her, so soon after awaking from her coma. But not wanting to come off as being overly parental again, he left and made his way down the hall.

The door to Neve's bedroom was still closed. He needed to talk with her but paused, a knuckle raised, debating whether to knock.

"Oh, come in already," Neve's resigned voice called from inside.

She was lying on her back beneath a sheet, staring into the wood grains of the exposed wall beams. Faint streaking on her face indicated dried tears. The circles beneath her eyes that he'd noticed when they first met had grown even darker, as if she were under some lifeforce-sapping curse that no amount of rest could lift. Her exosuit—or the bottom half that remained to her—lay haphazardly on the floor, the first time he'd seen her completely without it. He walked in and sat on the wooden chair by the bed.

"Pretty violent jerk into reality back there," he offered. "How are you feeling?"

She rolled away from him, pulling the bed sheet tightly around herself. A long silence fell. Kairos shifted uneasily in his chair as he looked at the back of her head. He had to tell her the truth about her husband.

"I missed the signs," she said at last. "The longer work shifts. Hours plugged into the SolarNet at home. Growing distant. You ignore the little things, because you're too proud to admit that they're bothering you. You think you know someone so well, the relationship is so strong, and so you always give them the benefit of the doubt ..." She might have breathed something else as her voice faded, but he could no longer hear her.

She was talking about her husband. Her words confirmed what Kairos had feared. She knew the truth. But he had to be sure.

His throat dry, he swallowed. "Neve, your husband—"

"I *know*," Neve cut in with a tone like frigid seawater. "Deep inside, I think I knew as soon as I learned that Chimera had worked an extraction."

Kairos nodded and remained silent.

Neve gave a long, slow exhale before speaking again. "In the portal, when all those images entered my mind, I felt like I was losing myself. My identity. I sensed thoughts— no, not just thoughts. *Memories.* Brief wisps, but perceptible and familiar. Like the way a certain smell can transport you to another place and time. The memories were mine, but not quite mine. They were from a different perspective. Like watching the same scene but from a second angle." Her spine curled inward, drawing herself in as if in pain. "I've been meditating all day," she continued. "I've never meditated before. I'm not a spiritual person. But I've now seen bits of the world through his eyes. Fragments of scenes. Of developing the neurofluid. Of walking the high-security, sterilized corridors and laboratories of Blackpool's orbital research ring. Of meeting the Outsider." Her voice then lowered to barely a whisper. "Of making love to my wife—me. I know now why he never wanted children. Our extinction is a prerequisite for the divine meeting at the End of Time ..."

Her body trembled, and Kairos's back grew rigid upon hearing that last line. Neve rolled back to face him. "Kairos—" she started, her lips and eyebrows were quivering. A tear rolled down across her face. "I know things about him I couldn't possibly know. About the nature of his work. A conversion to a faith that he kept hidden from me. These are *his* memories. I sensed *his* thoughts. Kairos, please ... what is *happening* to me?" Neve's voice shook with terror, tears streaking down both eyes despite her efforts to choke them back.

He lowered his eyes to the floor, away from hers. "Your husband's neurofluid technology has been evolved further. Some kind of electromagnetic influence on neural activity ... I'm not a scientist, I don't know." After a moment, he asked, "You mentioned that he met the Outsider—the Vyst?"

Neve pushed herself to a seated position, wiped her eyes and nodded. "I saw only flashes of memory. The Vyst helped him develop the neurofluid prototype."

"Did you see who the Vyst is?" he asked her, moving his chair closer to the bed. Neve closed her eyes and shook her head. Kairos then told her what he'd heard in the cathedral. "They're serious about what they're planning. First they'll spread their faith to Kotopax, then the Lilic System, then — everywhere. Please, try to think," he pleaded.

But Neve only rocked on the bed, head wrapped with her hands. "I've tried, Kairos. I swear I've tried. This all scares me. I ... I don't know who the Vyst is. My husband didn't know. I don't think anyone knows."

"What about the other Disciples? Anything about who they are?"

She shook her head. "It's not clear ... all I sensed were hoods and robes. Virtual avatars ..."

"Hey, it's alright," Kairos said, backing down. "But your husband is our only lead into the cult. We need to locate him. Finding him might help us uncover the identities or whereabouts of the other members. We can expose them, put their names out over the SolarNet."

But Neve kept shaking her head. "I don't know where he is," she said softly. "But I know he defected to Lienns-Sutra's Science Division after his extraction from Blackpool."

"So those agents that attacked us on Spires *were* working for Lienns-Sutra," he remarked. The puzzle was becoming clear.

"Yes and no," Neve replied. "I think Science Division, under the influence of the Amor Fati, has become a sort of secret faction within the corporation and have been acting independent of Executive oversight." She looked at him squarely. "Kairos, you're going to need to find a way to stop them."

"Me? We're in this together, aren't we?"

She smiled weakly for the first time and her eyes moistened.

"I can't go with you any further."

He recoiled in his seat. At the risk of being insensitive, he said, "You can't give up again, Neve. Too much is at stake this time. The worlds need us."

Neve winced at the words. A tear leaked down her cheek. Slowly, she peeled back the bed sheet, exposing her full body. She wore black compression neoprene shorts beneath her tank top. His first instinct was to avert his gaze out of propriety—she somehow seemed naked in anything less than the formidable exosuit—but then he noticed something different about her lower half. Her legs were bony and emaciated, the muscles atrophied. Thin scar lines and pitted deformities plagued her skin.

"... integrated suit system is disconnected, not to mention the electronics are cooked," Neve was saying. "The circuitry was overloaded by those blobs. It's just dead tech now, another relic of the past ..."

A series of symmetrical darkened patches and bruises ran down each leg—certainly perennial pressure sores from the exosuit's multitude of contact points that enabled her to stand and walk. Learning of her condition was like a veil lifting from his eyes, and his mind replayed all the time he'd spent with her to make sense of it. Neve was far braver and tougher than he thought, and he'd already considered her the bravest and toughest person he'd ever met.

Neve had stopped talking, and he suddenly became aware of his gaping silence. He looked up, meeting her tired gray eyes with his. Beneath the waning daylight, he noticed her body's skin tone was shades lighter than that of her head, and it hit him then just how much the exosuit was an extension of her very body, an outer epidermis that merged with her own cells.

"I had no idea," he whispered. "I'm sorry."

"I'm not," she said. "I've made my own way. You don't need the pitiful look, really."

"Your whole life?"

She shook her head. "Happened when I was a kid. My father was a security officer for Paclantic Corp. on Vesmarine. My mom died when I was very young, so it was just him and me. He raised me well. Taught me to live with principles. And he made sure I was never in want." She sighed. "Anyway, when I was older, I learned that he'd been a dirty cop for years. Some deal he'd made with a few crooked businessmen went sideways. When Paclantic found out, they sent agents to our home. I'll never forget the look on his face when he ..." She paused, choked back a sob, and after a moment, regained composure. "Well, I lost him and the use of my legs in the violence of that day. Paclantic took me in as a corporate ward. They trained me to become a ... security officer of sorts. They thought the life they gave me would make me loyal, make me forget about that ugly business with my father, or better yet, come to understand that he'd been a wayward criminal. Which may have been true. But still, I hated becoming a corporate pawn. I didn't owe them anything. And they'd taken his exosuit."

Kairos looked at the exosuit on the floor. "It belonged to your dad."

She nodded. "It may be from Old Earth, but it's my inheritance. Long story short, I managed to steal it back—that's a story for another day—and used it to leave Vesmarine."

He knelt and took one of Neve's bandaged hands gently in his. "That's too much for a young person to go through. I can't imagine pulling off stealing a tech relic from a corporation. Did Paclantic ever come looking for you?"

"Oh yeah, they sent their agents. Several of them." Neve looked away for a moment, then turned her gray eyes back on him. "I made sure none of them made it home." The firmness of her tone frightened him.

"Forgive me for what I said about you giving up. It might be pointless anyway." He sighed. "Falck's holding us here, outside the Settled Region if you can believe that. Can't find his ship. Can't find *him*. Even if we did escape this place, it's unlikely we'd expose the Amor Fati's plans in time. Sunsip and Medwick want to be rid of me like bad cargo. Midmay's already suffered more than any kid should ever have to. And on top of all that, you know how lousy I am in a fight."

Neve gave a small smile and smeared her wet eyes with the back of a palm. "Sounds like you'll need a lot of faith, then, priest."

"Former priest," Kairos corrected her with a sad smile. "At the Oasis bar, you asked what happened to me ..."

"It's none of my business," Neve said.

But Kairos shook his head. "I never wanted to go to Pantoll," he began. "My mother was very sick, and my father was both financially unable and negligent in taking care of her. So I asked the Elders on Greenside for permission to take a leave of absence from my post under the Archbishop in Asphis. The first year I spent in Pantoll was a great encouragement to me. My mother's health had turned for the better, and the congregation I pastored was flourishing.

"You see, early in my tenure, not long after I had reestablished services in the old chapel and before I had many attendees, a young couple asked me to pray over their sick little daughter. The girl was four years old. She'd had breathing difficulties since birth—birth defects and disorders are common on Pantoll—and her lungs were plagued with some vicious disease. I was the only priest of any kind on the planet in over twenty years, and they came to me out of desperation, for the girl's condition was worsening. She wouldn't live more than another few days. I was young and confident in the supernaturalist principles I'd studied then. In my arrogance, I invited them to bring their daughter to my sundown service that evening for a special prayer of healing.

"When they placed the girl in my arms, she was limp as a rag. Her raspy breathing sounding like air slowly leaking from a dying balloon." *Like the sound of her smoke-filled lungs as she lay in my arms.*

Kairos paused and raised a hand to his eyes to stem an impending well of tears. "The feelings I had in the moments after her healing are nearly foreign to me now," he pressed on. "Seeing her laughing and jumping and running circles around the pews ... I had felt so certain of my faith. Of the purpose of my being in Pantoll. Of spiritual reality."

"You healed the girl's lungs completely, then and there?" Neve asked with a dose of skepticism.

Kairos nodded somberly. "God through me, my own eyes as witness. That is why, as much as I'd like to abandon faith, my heart will not allow me." He continued his story, "In the following months, the ministry grew, faith spreading through a place that had been godless since its founding.

"Unfortunately, it tends to be that such spiritual heights are closely followed by the lowest depths of despair. My mother died five months later. I took it very hard. I'd been praying for her recovery morning and evening since the day I'd arrived on Pantoll. My faith could not save her. The unexpected reversal of her health—equal parts physical and mental—and subsequent precipitous decline left me shaken. It was also during this time that my father's health issues became more apparent to me—by then, the cancer had already progressed to stage three or four, and it was clear he needed a caretaker. A month before, I had begun to let myself hope and plan for a return to Greenside; now, that timing was unclear. But through it all I kept the faith, praying to God for mercy, for insight, for the smallest sign he hadn't left me."

Kairos paused to take in a deep breath. He let it out in a slow exhale. "I suppose what drove me to the chapel that afternoon was a message I received from the Elders, regretfully notifying me that my previous position under the Archbishop in Asphis could no longer be held for my return. It had been filled by another. At that moment, whatever bright vision of my future I'd clung to dissipated. Going to the chapel, I told myself I was going to be alone with God, to entreat his presence and to even repent of some sin unknown to me.

"I don't even remember the fire breaking out inside," Kairos said, his voice beginning to crack. "Her screams were what woke me out of my drunken stupor. The walls, curtains, pews were all ablaze. A thick smoke had risen into the rafters. She'd been playing in the bell tower; it was her favorite hideout. I didn't know she was there ..."

He choked back a sob and Neve placed a hand on his arm. "Kairos, you don't have to ..."

"It had started with partaking of the communion elements, the bread and the wine," he pushed on. "But my anger and resentment overflowed. After finishing the first bottle, I opened another. Then another. I ransacked the cabinets of the Lord's house until I was blind drunk with Christ's blood. At some point, I must've knocked over a candle stand ...

"Her legs had broken from the fall from the tower. In her fear, she must've jumped to escape. She'd inhaled so much smoke ..." Kairos paused for a moment to wipe his eyes. "She died in my arms. Within a year of her healing, I killed her. *A year!* It had been a cursed miracle. There is no divine reason in saving one day only to destroy the next. Having experienced what I have, my heart cannot deny the existence of the supernatural. But if God exists and has such capricious whims, I cannot bring myself to serve him."

After Kairos finished, they sat together for a long time in silence save for the quiet rises and falls of tremulous breathing. He couldn't find the right words to comfort Neve, and he imagined she felt the same toward him. So they sat, her bandaged hands wrapped in his, each absorbed in their own pain.

"You know, I've never had much faith in anything, much less some idea of God," Neve spoke softly after a while. "Whether one exists or not, who's to say? I've met a lot of people across the worlds who have believed some pretty weird things. They don't seem to fare much better than those who believe in nothing. But I think we're all wired to need to have faith in something. And I have faith in you, that you'll find a way." She squeezed his hands. "I can't describe it, but I have a feeling this fight against the Amor Fati cannot be won with bullets or fists. Perhaps a priest is exactly who's needed. Perhaps that's why all this has fallen on you."

She smiled half-heartedly before her face fell dreadfully serious. "I need to tell you something about the Amor Fati's prophet. Something I wasn't sure of before, but I am certain of it now." Her chest rose with a deep inhale. She pulled his head down close to hers, and he saw deep anxiety in her grey eyes. "The Vyst is not human," she whispered.

Chapter 12

Kairos sat at the kitchen table, gazing out the window above the sink in deep contemplation. The house's interior was illuminated with the gossamer glow of moonlight. A small but near-full moon beamed just over the silhouetted tops of the jungle trees. Higher in the night sky, he noticed a second moon, half-full and slightly larger than the first. It was probably past the middle of the night given the short day length, but for the same reason he wasn't tired enough for sleep. The traders would be huddled by their backyard fire. Rhody was out in the wild darkness somewhere: before Kairos had left her, Neve had sent a message to the hybird via his goggles to locate Falck, reminding him that Rhody was specifically trained and wired for military recon and espionage.

Kairos reflected on the Amor Fati beliefs and what Neve had gone on to tell him about the Vyst based on her husband's memories. At Asphis Seminary on Greenside, Kairos had received the top theological education in the worlds, spanning intensive reviews of Old Earth classic religions, ancient mythology, history, philosophy, human biology and evolution, cognitive psychology, Interstellar Age thought, and—

what he majored in—supernaturalism, a nascent discipline seeking to reconcile the physical and spiritual realms through a grand theoscientific unifying theory.

Contact with the Osetra and the subsequent large-scale migration away from the resource-depleted and war-torn Old Earth—the Exodus—inevitably led to a theological revolution that left no religion or faith untouched. Beliefs were reshaped, core doctrines reexamined, sacred texts reinterpreted. The other children of God needed to be explained. Earth-centric ideas about creation, the arc of world history, and the end times were rendered obsolete and dismissed as the result of narrow thinking. How could Earth and its fate be of special import if humans weren't the only intelligent beings, and if humans didn't even live on Earth anymore? The myriad existential questions and challenges to longstanding doctrines that naturally arose fractured the old religions into multiple sects and also fueled the rise of entirely new belief systems. Some worshiped the Osetra as ancient god-like beings who'd visited Earth at different times in human history. Another believed black holes to be gateways into Heaven, and that the one at the center of the Milky Way led to God's throne. An offshoot of this group shared similar cosmology, but rebuked such an anthropocentric and monotheistic interpretation, believing that the gods' dwelling place would be at the center of the universe, in a tremendously distant system that included Paradeisos, the shared ancestral planet of humans, the Osetra, and other as yet undiscovered intelligent races.

The beliefs of the Amor Fati seemed to draw inspiration from the traditions of classic religions—particularly Christian narratives and terminology and Eastern panentheistic beliefs—as well as Interstellar Age thought: a hyperspace reality beyond three-dimensional space, often called heaven, or the spirit realm, or, in this case, the "Outside;" an origin or creation account incorporating multiple intelligent races; the fall or problem of Man; a revelation or gospel from a holy figure to the masses; and lastly, a transcendent reality or final cosmic reckoning—in this case, all souls unifying as one and meeting God—similar to what the teachings of Father Revais's Church of the Samsaric Soul espoused. Much of this was not terribly new. And why should it be?—the Vyst was merely leveraging religion as a distribution mechanism for its mind-control tech. But to its converts, forced to voluntary, the technology proved the faith experience real. *Supernatural.* And not just the technology, but the "holy prophet" itself, the one with power to do "miracles"...

After a long while, Kairos drew his tiring eyes away from the window. They landed on the narrow door that he'd seen upon first entering the cottage, the one that led to the cellar.

Bored, he opened the door, switched on his goggles' head-lamp, and plunked down the wooden steps into the cool, dark space. He was surprised to find overhead a series of hanging pull strings connected to light bulbs. Then he remembered the cottage's windmill. It must feed into an electric generator. He tugged each of the strings. Only a couple of the several bulbs lit, but it was enough for him to switch his headlamp off.

Illuminated around him stood rows of tall wooden shelving units filled with cylindrical glass storage containers. A closer look revealed neatly labeled jars and bottles holding various organic specimens suspended in formaldehyde. The scene wasn't what he'd expected to find. It brought memories of his mother's repellent collection of native beetles and worms he'd had to clean out of his parents' house on Pantoll after she died.

Kairos explored the nearest row. It contained a multitude of reptilian and amphibian species, none of which he recognized. He paused to gaze at each strange creature down the line. There was something eerie and macabre about a preserved specimen: their open-eyed, dead stares; their bloated and discolored bodies; the transparent coffins in which their frozen corpses were unceremoniously exposed to the curious eyes of all, as if part of some public humiliation, or to serve as a warning to all other members of their species to distrust humans.

There were a few bleached skeletons of animals in the cellar as well, some under glass on the shelves, with larger ones on display on the ground. One of larger skeletons had the rough anatomy of an Earthling frog—two short arms up front and two massive hind legs—crossed with the broad, ferocious jaws of an Earthling great white shark. Kairos's spine tingled just thinking about that kind of predator existing out there somewhere.

He turned down another row of jars, this one displaying various aquatic invertebrates. The creatures in this section exhibited even more bizarre biology: spikes several centimeters long; bifurcated, sucker-riddled tentacles; perfectly spherical blobs lacking any discernible features. Some had been bleached bone white by the alcoholic solution in which they were preserved, as if ghosts of their former selves. At a collection of arthropods, a tall jar caught his attention. Captured within hung a tangle of hair strands. A closer look revealed that the dozen or so long, wispy appendages swirled in the preserving solution came together at a minuscule nexus the size of a tiny pebble that must be the arthropod's core body. A draft of cool air chilled his skin as he stared at the ghastly thing.

He leaned in to inspect the faded ink of the jar's label:

meticula – forty-eight spined; nocturnal (toxic)

The script sent him recoiling in shock.

It was his mother's.

The distinctive scribble, the inconsistently applied serifs, were unmistakably by her hand.

He checked the label of the adjacent jar, then another. This was all her work. She had been here, had lived in this cottage.

At once he remembered where he'd seen this place before. The beach, the ocean, the dune grass—this was where the digigraph of his parents was taken. This was where they met, on a field research trip. But that couldn't be. How could his parents have traveled anywhere beyond the Settled Region? If Falck knew of this place, perhaps the man's history with his father was much deeper than Kairos ever knew. So why had Falck now brought Kairos here?

As he began to move away, again a chill tickled his skin. He paused, moved back beside the meticula's jar, and stood very still.

There, he felt it again: a light draft.

Moving slowly, he identified the draft's source: a sliver of space between two large shelving units against the back wall.

Wedging the tips of his fingers into the space, he tried prying the shelves apart but they didn't budge. Gripping one of the shelves, he pulled outward instead. The shelving swayed toward him, revealing a slit of pure dark space behind it. Pulling harder, but careful not to disturb the resting jars, he slowly hinged it open until the space was wide enough for his body to shimmy through side-ways.   .

The headlamp revealed it to be an underground passageway, composed of cement flooring and walls. Kairos walked slowly at first, as much out of fear of the unknown as of being caught, but after it became clear the passageway was a detour-less straightaway, he switched to a slow jog.

Before long, the passageway opened up into a round, cavernous space. The area's curved cement walls were bare, except for a workbench station with some tools, a couple massive, unlabeled cylindrical tanks, and a narrow winding staircase leading up to a circular hatch set into the high ceiling.

But most conspicuously, a hulking mass loomed in the space's center.

Falck's ship.

* * *

Falck's lugger barely fit within the underground hangar, its top nearly scraping the metallic canopy which undoubtedly could retract to open it to the outside. Across the hangar, the passageway continued in the opposite direction to that which he'd entered. Fearing Falck might be around, he stepped behind one of the cylindrical tanks to hide. But after waiting several moments, the hangar remained silent as a tomb.

Slowly circling the ship and inspecting its parts, he found nothing unusual about it, save for a few too many exterior patches and a couple of long-busted external lights. It had the nondescript function-over-form design of an asteroid-hauling tugboat. Given how beaten up it looked, Kairos wouldn't be surprised it had been salvaged from a junkyard. Eager to take a hard look at the ship's weave drive, Kairos rotated the main entrance hatch's wheel handle and tugged the round door open.

Making his way through the dingy, featureless interior cabin, he arrived at the rear engine room and descended a short ladder beneath the grated floor to where the heart of the ship—it's weave drive—would be. Had he not traveled on the ship himself, based on the shabby condition of the surrounding machinery, he would've assumed the ship far from spaceworthy. That is, until he lifted away a section of fiberplastic covering to reveal the drive itself.

He gasped.

While Kairos was no expert on weave drives, this one was utterly alien in both materials and design. It looked part metallic, part ... organic? A pulsating piece of it was translucent, damp, and, for lack of a better term, looked *alive*. Whatever he was looking at, it was not a thing conceived of or manufactured by humans.

Static crackled in his ear—the reception was poor through the concrete hangar walls—and a short set of grating squawks came through his aural dots. Rhody had seen something.

He subvocalized a command and his goggle screens switched. Rhody's night vision filled his own. The video quality was poor. The hybird was perched high on a branch in the jungle. Rhody's scopes were tracking a wash of light— from a lantern or flashlight—that partially obscured a large figure walking through the jungle. Kairos could recognize that hitched step anywhere.

Gotcha. Taking a little night trip are we? "Good sighting, Rhody," he subvocalized, at once thinking it absurd to be talking to a bird. "Distance from me?" he asked, a standard biOS command Rhody would understand.

His view lifted as Rhody used its rotary wings to boost itself quietly upward through the canopy. The view rotated to a flickering light in the distance, then zoomed in (with frighteningly clear resolution) until Kairos could see the light of the fire's flames dancing across the traders' stern faces. The text *316.4m NNE* appeared on his goggle screens, a distance and bearing readout from either Rhody's laser or frequency scanner. Not far objectively, but traveling through the jungle would be arduous and slow.

"Keep eyes on the target. Stay above the canopy. I'm coming to you. Continue to send our separation distance."

A low squawk of acknowledgment, then the comms channel returned to silence.

Kairos wasn't worried about Rhody being spotted—that'd be impossible in the dark of night, and besides, it was just a bird in the sky. He briefly considered fetching the traders, but their space-atrophied bodies weren't fit for a fast pursuit and he needed to hurry to catch Falck. Not to mention three people trampling through foliage was a lot louder than one.

Kairos lowered the weave drive's fiberplastic cover and scurried out of the ship. Afraid that his headlamp's powerful beam would tip Falck off, he sprinted back to the cellar where he swiped a handheld-sized jar off a shelf.

Returning to the hangar, he scrambled up the winding staircase, pushed—with some strain—the circular hatch open, and hoisted himself up and out. The land he emerged upon was a large clearing ringed by jungle. A short tree stump stood atop the ajar hatch, hence why the door was so heavy. Ferns, grass, and moss had also grown over it so that it was indistinguishable from the ground when shut.

He switched views a final time to Rhody's scopes. The hybird's height had remained above the jungle, but the benefit of scoped enhancement on top of Rhody's natural, exceptional eyesight was that the hybird, at its fancy, could zoom in on a speck of Falck's heel or a faint wisp of his cloak through the dense jungle foliage. Falck had continued on his northeast bearing, toward the inland mountain range.

Kairos unscrewed the jar lid, grimaced as he fished out the squishy, dead critter floating in there. After telling Rhody that he'd be off-comms for a bit, he dropped his goggles into the jar. The submerged headlamp lit up the fluid a bright white. Navigating by the glow of the makeshift lantern, Kairos hurried northeast across the clearing.

With a lucky eye, he spotted a narrow trail leading into the jungle. Perhaps Falck had taken the same one. He soon learned in hindsight that any attempt to traipse through the dense jungle without a trail—much less in the dark— would've been a fool's errand. On the path, he was forced to slow to a jog, high-stepping exposed roots and shrubs that clawed at his ankles and elbowing aside broad, leafy branches and stiff, hanging vines.

Before long, his eyes made out a dull, greenish-white glow sporadically filtering through the trees and foliage ahead of him: Falck's lantern. Kairos slowed to a walk to quiet his movement, but kept a steady distance behind the flickering glow.

Deeper into the jungle they pushed. Several times, Kairos was sure he'd have veered off the increasingly ambiguous path and lost his way completely if not for having Falck's guiding beacon to aim toward.

After a while, the land began to incline and the taller trees thinned out. As the ground increasingly sloped upward and turned rockier, the dense vegetation gave way to a scattering of low, stiff shrubs. Any distinct trail had disappeared completely. Without jungle cover, Kairos plucked his goggles out from the jar and switched off the headlamp to avoid detection, opting to navigate by moonlight. He'd also have to mind his volume; the racket of the nightlife critters had been replaced by the murmur of a nearby stream.

Kairos huffed and stumbled up the uneven and ever-steeper mountainside. Before long he found that he'd lost a good amount of ground to Falck. Far ahead, the man's light had traced left for a while, then right for a while, before starting to drift left again. The man must be making switchbacks up to the top. Kairos couldn't afford to let him get too far ahead for risk of losing him.

With a renewed urgency, Kairos pushed himself after the man's stead, only once allowing himself a brief pause on the steep slope to catch his breath. He'd gained real elevation. The black mass of jungle below was a dark carpet. Low on the horizon, a surprisingly large crescent moon sliced a thin bright arc across the night sky. Kairos hadn't been able to see it until now, and without doubt it was the most impressive of the night sky's three moons.

After another long period of climbing, it finally became clear he was nearing the mountain's apex. With burning calves and quads and an onset of lightheadedness, Kairos willed himself up the last stretch to bring himself no more than fifty meters behind Falck's light. Then the light disappeared over the summit. As Kairos reached the final curve himself, he crouched and slowed, eyes scanning rapidly with each step. The summit, it turned out, was not a singular peak, but more of a cinder cone. And it was vacant.

It was not, however, devoid of light. A serene field of stars lay scattered across the ground before him. The half moon was reflected brilliantly as well. Squatting at the edge of the matte black sheet, he reached a few fingers down. They disappeared into cold ink. He stood and flicked the water from his fingers. The small lake looked about twenty meters across and as much wide, taking up much of the summit's area. He carefully but quickly circumnavigated the lake, searching down each face of the mountain to see whether Falck had continued past the summit. But there was no sign of him. This part of the mountain offered no cover, yet the man had vanished.

Still baffled after circling around the peak a second time, Kairos stared in defeat into the water's reflection. Its glassy surface was a mirror for the cosmos. It was easy to get lost in it. Falck had to be around here somewhere. The man wouldn't have climbed to the top of this mountain unless he had a purpose here. Perhaps Falck had known he was being followed and was now intentionally concealing himself somewhere in the dark? But Kairos was fairly certain that Falck hadn't detected his presence. Not once during the hike had the man's headlamp flashed in Kairos's direction. And there had been plenty of earlier occasions in the jungle where Falck could've easily evaded a pursuer well before reaching his destination.

Kairos was shivering, the adrenaline of the pursuit having cooled off. Still gazing into the lake, he became aware of something odd. He stooped and leaned his face closer toward the surface, toward its dull reflection of moonlight.

But it *wasn't* moonlight.

Dropping to his chest by the steep bank and pulling his goggles on, he shimmied his head over the edge and slowly lowered it. The water wrapped his face like a cold blanket. His visibility underwater amounted to a haze, but the faint light source emanating from within the lake's depths was undeniable: something was down there. And not tremendously deep either. Perhaps ten to fifteen meters down.

Kairos pulled his face out, wiped it with a sleeve and leaned back on the bank, hardly believing what he'd seen and believing less what he was contemplating to do next. He stripped to his underwear, dropping them atop the warm pile of his shirt, pants, coat, and Maydays. It was too chilly to linger in indecision. He hopped off the bank.

His chest instantly constricted with the frigid plunge. He treaded water for a few seconds hoping to acclimate, but it soon became clear that he was only wasting precious body heat. Drawing in a great breath, he dove.

Kairos stroked and kicked directly toward the light. At what must have been at least a depth of ten meters, though, its source appeared no closer. Pressure mounted in his chest. A couple more strokes and the back of his throat swelled for want of air. It was too far.

Surfacing, he coughed for breath. Every fiber of his being wanted out, to get his clothes back on and hightail it back to the cottage where it was warm. What he was doing, here, in the middle of the night, was ridiculous.

He didn't allow himself more time to think. He took a few deep breaths, then dove.

As before, the source of the nebulous light was deceptively distant. The pressure in his lungs returned to an unbearable state sooner than he'd hoped. He exhaled a stream of bubbles, which helped ease the tension. His arms were numb with both fatigue and the cold.

With every stroke and kick, the thick depths increasingly fought his downward push. It was getting harder to focus. The goggles sucked hard against his eye sockets. His throat involuntarily lurched in a silent cry for oxygen, but instead of air, his chest was filled with a vacuum of panic. He was about to call it when it became clear that the glow had disassociated into four distinct sources of illumination.

Despite not being sure he'd have enough air or strength to return to the surface, Kairos pressed forward. His lungs screamed at him. He tried to release the pressure by exhaling some more, but he had no air left to push out. The light sources were very near and much clearer now. They flickered in intensity, like blue flames.

Suddenly, Kairos's arms experienced a sensation of breaking *through*. They flailed uselessly beyond him as if they'd happened upon a massive air pocket.

Then his head broke *through* and at once his whole body was being sucked into a vortex.

No, *falling*.

He collapsed head first against inexplicable hardness. His lungs instinctively ballooned with a mighty inhalation. Delirious, he did not know how long he lay curled, eyes closed, heaving great lungfuls of air in and out like a giant beating heart.

When he finally rolled onto his back and opened his eyes, he thought he'd wandered into a dream. Above him, the bottom of the dark lake water was eerily suspended, a watery ceiling held aloft by some invisible barrier. Dumbfounded,

Kairos rose to his feet and warily reached a hand up. To his surprise, the moist barrier surface was semi-flexible, but didn't permit his hand through. Whether a selectively-permeable membrane or force field, he'd never heard or read about such technology.

Looking about, still unsure that his real body hadn't blacked out underwater and he'd entered an afterlife, he found himself inside a small chamber, around four by eight meters in size. The floor and walls were made of black cobblestone. The air was warm and humid. The heat, he discovered, came from blue-flamed torches affixed to the shorter walls, two against each and spaced about three meters apart. To his left and right, protruding from each of the shorter walls, were stone-carved heads of beasts he did not recognize. Perhaps they were native to this place. The sculpture at his left had two great curved horns protruding from a narrow head, like that of an ibex, with a narrow snout and mouth filled with little sharp teeth. The sculpture at his right had a broad, flat head with four bulbous eyes and long, terrible fangs descending from a wide mouth. The beasts' expressions were grotesque and menacing, and out of the mouths of each spilled long tongues. Etched into the tongues were a vertical arrangement of symbols that glowed a deep orange. Whether the sculpted heads contained a power source or circuitry within them, Kairos couldn't discern.

At a loss, he wondered about the bizarre place he'd stumbled into. No, not stumbled. He was sure Falck had come here, sneaking under the cover of night to this hidden space where some secret was guarded.

But Falck had left no trace of his presence, and there were no exits. Only four stone walls, a stone floor, and the lake bottom weighing heavily overhead. He examined the beast sculptures, ran his fingers along their enigmatic, glowing symbols, but their presence and function remained unclear. Merely decorative art, perhaps. Next, he moved beside the nearest torch. Its dark brown stave had the feel of smooth hardwood, but he couldn't be sure. Its bright blue, vigorous flame burned warm but not hot. Its fuel source was indiscernible, but Kairos assumed that Falck had lit them; otherwise, he'd have noticed their glow beneath the water when he'd initially squatted beside the lake after summiting. Falck had moved elsewhere. As to where, the answer would likely be as mysterious as the place itself.

Kairos moved toward the opposite end of the chamber, where the two other torches burned, inspecting the side walls for signs of a hidden door, switch, anything abnormal.

Then he noticed the black sphere.

He froze in half-terror at its sudden existence. Half a meter in diameter, it floated symmetrically between the two torches. Its black surface was so opaque, lusterless, and absolute that it lacked tangibility, as if it were not an object but a sphere-shaped non-object, a matter-less void that had punched through reality.

Kairos took a step toward it. The sphere's volume expanded. He stilled himself and waited, but nothing further happened. He took another step cautiously. The void smoothly expanded again, taking up now much of the room's width. Afraid, he backed away quickly. The sphere shrank as rapidly, down to a little black dot before disappearing completely. Kairos stared breathless at the space it had vacated, understanding that whatever form of technology the sphere was, it seemed to respond to his movements. The sphere must be the room's purpose. Breathing in, he took a couple confident steps forward. Sure enough, the sphere appeared and swelled in size as he slowly moved toward it.

He intended to stop at arm's length for a closer look, but he realized too late that the sphere's growth had accelerated with each of his steps. Before he could back away, before he could scream out, even before terror could set in, the dimensionless void washed through and over him, enveloping him in pure darkness.

* * *

When Kairos regained sensory awareness, his first sensations were that of a cold harsh wind and the sight of thick clouds. These were immediately overcome by a third sensation: the jarring, heart-jumping terror of his body in free fall.

Before he gained a sense of direction, his back slapped painfully against frigid water tension.

Submerged, choking and spasming, his arms and legs instinctively flailed to propel himself to the surface. Breaking through, he drew air into his compressed lungs in quick, short breaths, fighting the panic of suffocation.

Bulging oceanic swells and salty, wind-tossed spray buffeted his body, and, for several moments, it was all he could do to tread and kick wildly to keep his head above the choppy surface while his mind reeled. His eyes landed on a black hulk not far from him, what looked like a small island of rock jutting out of the ocean. Desperate, he stroked and kicked toward it. He reached for its tip, found a handhold, and pulled himself up. The rock beneath his hand broke away and he sank back into the water. Again and again his hands scrabbled for holds which disintegrated into damp crumbles. He treaded around to a less steep portion. Clawing and fighting, sending chunks of the island floating away into the sea, he finally was able to drag his body bit by bit up onto a stable core of rock.

Kairos spent a moment on his stomach, vomiting water while staring down at a scattering of bony teeth from some long-dead sea creature that had become lodged in pores in the rock.

He then pushed himself up and lifted his goggles to survey where the hell he'd suddenly found himself. Tumultuous, black-blue sea surrounded him on all sides as far as the eye could see. Jagged rocks like the one he sat upon stuck out here and there. Dense, billowing clouds brooded overhead in a sickly, butterscotch-colored sky. The only sounds were that of the unceasing rush of wind and churn of the waves. In the far distance, he squinted at a tall gray cluster of what might have been structures emerging from the water. They were asymmetrical, twisted, and bent. Scattered patches of open air suggested structural damage. One decrepit "tower" appeared to have half-fallen into the sea. But it was impossible to tell.

Then he saw it hanging in the air several meters away: a solitary black sphere, the size of a child's ball. Its surface reflected none of its surroundings. It hovered soundlessly a couple of meters above the surface like a round monolith, something ancient, sacred, and incomprehensible. Subconsciously and in the instinctual memory of his bones, he sensed that he'd traveled a great distance. But his conscious mind was catching up: this place's gravity was different than that of the jungle planet; the color of its sky was different too. The sphere hovering above the sea here might be the counterpart to the one beneath the mountain lake. Or perhaps it was the same sphere. It must be some kind of interstellar transportation technology.

Alien technology.

Kairos felt a rush of exhilaration tinged with unease. *Could I really be on an Osetran world?* The thought seemed ludicrous. *Where was Falck?* There was no sign of him, either on the other rock islands or in the water so far as Kairos could see, although his visibility was limited. Had someone met and picked the man up? But then bigger questions came: how long had Falck known about that transport sphere? Was he in contact with the Osetra? He recalled Neve telling him that the Vyst was not human—was Falck working with the Osetra against his own human kind? And then the question Kairos kept returning to: who was this man?

Despite the strong urge to explore, his body heat and strength wouldn't last long. And there was nothing but ocean in every direction. He was not a strong swimmer. There were no opportunities for it on Pantoll. He questioned whether he could even swim to the next rock island, much less the structures that were clicks away. The adrenaline having worn off, he was shivering uncontrollably. He was completely naked; somewhere along the way his underwear had left him. Kairos wrapped his arms about his bare skin, which was smeared with rocky grit, as if he'd rolled around in soot, and bloodied from several scrapes. His muscles, limbs, eyes, jaw— everything felt tight and weak, as if they'd gone unused for a long while. The cold air had turned his lungs into deflated, misshapen balloons needing to be worked up with warm air.

Not to mention that something about this place felt wrong. Something about the cold silence of it, the hollow gusts of wind, carrying nothing but emptiness. A feeling that something utterly terrible had befallen it. He debated whether he should start praying.

The corner of his eye caught a surface break and the glide of movement. He focused on the spot, but the dark water was nearly impenetrable.

There it was again, a little farther away. A rounded form *definitely* broke the surface briefly before submerging once more. And there was a faint glow.

The bioluminescent glow of an Osetra's head.

Almost without thinking, Kairos hurled himself into the sea after it. He flailed and kicked furiously, popping his head up every couple strokes to sight, but with the choppy waves he couldn't see more than a meter beyond. Water slammed into his face. He'd cough it out, only for another wave to slam into him and bring him choking and gasping anew.

At some point, his forward movement had ceased. No sign of the Osetra he thought he'd seen. He was exhausted beyond belief, his energy plummeting faster than he imagined possible. The closest rock island was not nearly close enough. He'd never make it.

With the panicked desperation of a drowning person, his eyes frantically scanned for the sphere.

There it was: hovering about fifteen meters off to his side and two meters above the churning sea.

It may as well have been a hundred meters away.

He was sinking, his strokes barely keeping his head above surface much less propel him forward. Gathering his strength for a burst of sheer will, he pulled himself up for a deep breath.

At the same time, a great swell of water rose and met him. He inhaled nothing but thick liquid.

Kairos's lungs filled with the heaviness of it. Dizzy and convulsing, he sank beneath the sea, his depleted arms and legs and all sensation rapidly solidifying into a petrified submission to cold darkness.

Something wrapped itself around his chest. Dragging him off.

His eyes, cracking open in the frigid depths, registered only stars before blacking out entirely.

* * *

When Kairos awoke, Falck's imposing figure towered over him.

Kairos was lying on his side and shivering uncontrollably at the edge of the jungle planet's mountaintop lake. The pain in his chest indicated he'd been resuscitated, and for the next few moments could do nothing but cough residual water out of his lungs.

It was still dark out, but a glimmer of light on the horizon signaled the fast approaching dawn.

"You should not have followed me through the transportal," Falck reproached, handing Kairos his pile of clothes that he'd left on the bank. The man's impassive eyescopes looked Kairos up and down.

Suddenly aware of his nakedness, Kairos snatched the clothes and turned away. The cool mountain air brought the sensation of the oceanic world's frigid seas rushing back to him.

"I saw one," Kairos stammered, slowly pulling on his

clothes with shaking hands. "A real Osetra." The Osetra had rescued him from drowning. *Why?*

The man nodded. "You're lucky to be alive," he said. "Strangers are not welcome there. And further, it is not a welcoming world."

"*You* are no stranger to them," Kairos pointed out, trembling. "It's time to put aside secrecy. You were never just a mere worker for my father, were you? How long have you been in contact with the Osetra? Neve told me the Vyst is one of them. At my father's house, you said yourself that you serve the Osetra. That means you must be one of the Vyst's disciples," he accused.

After a moment of silence, Falck, in a tone of genuine puzzlement, said, "I have never heard of this Vyst. But I can assure you, whoever they are, they are not Osetra."

"I don't understand. You're not one of the Amor Fati?"

"Amor what?" Falck asked, the confusion in his voice growing. The man hesitated for a moment, then shook his head. "Listen Kairos, now that we're here and safe, I must illuminate to you certain truths that have been kept hidden. Most importantly: the Osetra are a dead race. The one you saw is from the last generation. After it, the Osetra will be extinct."

Kairos stared at him blankly.

"You've just been to their homeworld," Falck continued. "Although now, it is a sacred resting place."

Resting place. The image of alien towers crumbling into the sea returned to him. "I don't understand," he stammered in shock. "The Osetra ... extinct?" What, then, about the rumors of their return to human space? The outposts that had gone offline? The investigatory ships that never returned? Then the answer came to him; he'd learned it in the cathedral, but at the time hadn't connected the pieces: the Amor Fati had been conducting small-scale tests of their viral transmission in remote places. La Torre and the other deep space outposts going offline had been *their* doing. "What happened to them?" he asked.

Falck turned his face toward the growing dawn light over the ocean. "An act of xenocide."

"Xenocide?" Kairos repeated, stunned. "They were all killed? How?" He shook his head in confusion. "Neve told me she saw those Osetran bodies. Blackpool recovered them from that ship ..."

"Before I answer your questions, I think you'd better tell me exactly what Neve told you," Falck said sternly. His voice also carried a hint of worry.

Kairos nodded and took his time recounting everything he knew about the Amor Fati, their holy prophet, their neurotechnology, and what Neve had recently learned via her husband's memories.

Neve's husband, Alain, had been Blackpool's rising star. The kind of scientist whose intelligence and work lifts all of human civilization's progress by a notch. After obtaining his doctorate in neuroscience, he started at Blackpool in their neurolink R&D division, running experiments to replicate results from Old Earth studies in an effort to essentially re-learn the science behind brain-computer synchronized interfaces, which had been lost following the Exodus. Over the next decade, he worked on projects spanning dream manipulation research to neurocom chip design.

A couple years ago, he'd been promoted to join a highly restricted research project at Blackpool's central orbital lab ring. The project ultimately led to the development of the neurofluid, the prototype of which was later stolen from the transport *Asterisk*. The technology behind altering neuron DNA to grow and arrange themselves in new tissue structures was patterned after Osetran neurobiology. While Osetran and human anatomy differed greatly in some respects—especially given the Osetra were an amphibious species—human scientists had been shocked to discover that their brain chemistry was remarkably similar. There were a few key differences, most notably, of course, that Osetran brains contained specialized structures that generated and received electromagnetic waves, enabling telepathic communication. These structures were of greatest interest to the researchers. And early research indicated certain junk DNA sequences could provide a human/Osetra genetic link.

How did the scientists even know about Osetran brain chemistry off which to pattern the neurofluid? Neve had been hazy on the specifics. At some point in the past, a Blackpool corporate transport came across a derelict Osetran spacecraft drifting through empty space. The small crew inside were unconscious but alive. Blackpool gladly abducted them as if they'd been served on a silver platter. These Osetra were then, for God knows how long, subjected to all kinds of probing research: bio scans, physiological tests, tissue sample extraction, experimentation. From there, scientists began testing how to bring this neurology into Earthling species. The only experiments Neve could recall were those her husband actively participated in during his time on the project. The results were bizarre, some even unnatural. Mice whose little brains were injected with the neurofluid later were found arranging coherent sentences using their cages' wood shavings. The longer the test, the more intelligent the mice became—that is, until their brains swelled and skulls burst.

Given humans had lost contact with the Osetra three standard centuries ago, Kairos had difficulty seeing if and how Blackpool had kept a live or even a deceased Osetran for that long. With the types of experimentation conducted, including vivisection, surely not all of the Osetra could've survived. But one of them did.

Neve was unclear as to exactly when it happened, but she was certain that her husband was the Vyst's first disciple. The research subject had converted the researcher. In the end, Neve's husband helped the tortured Osetra escape the facility. What became of the Osetra immediately afterward not even Neve's husband knew, but it wasn't long after that an entity or person known as the Outsider started being mentioned within certain cult communities over the SolarNet.

Falck had remained silent while Kairos spoke, his shadowed, masked face as ever a cipher beneath the cowl of his cloak. When Kairos finished, he asked Falck whether Blackpool's escaped Osetra—now known as the Vyst—could be responsible for the Osetra's destruction. The idea was hard to believe. And what about the Osetran embryo? Where did that fit?

"As you've now seen, I have been in contact with the last of the Osetra," Falck began. "There are very few left. A sad remnant of a once-great race, with a tragic end to dwell upon during their final days. They were, in fact, the same members of the deep space crew that discovered Earth. As you know, that first contact between humans and Osetra occurred in Earth Standard Year 2203. But the Osetran sporeship that had arrived was merely one of thousands of deep space expeditions being carried out by the spacefaring race. The Osetra had colonized scores of worlds over the centuries. Accordingly, their reach continued to expand across the galaxy. Human interstellar travel via the weave drive and the terraformation of several human-settled worlds owed themselves to Osetran engineering.

"When the sporeship orbiting Earth received a message of death from their homeworld three years later, it was already—despite their advanced communications technology—an echo from the past. There was nothing the crew could do to prevent or assist what had already transpired. Nevertheless, they immediately set off to return home, ending the Human-Osetran Exchange period and contact between the two races ever since.

"The return journey was long. When they at last arrived, the devastation they found proved to have been absolute. The planet was a lifeless ball of storms and wind. Ecosystems destroyed. A large volume of the great oceans had evaporated. All the result of some cataclysmic atomic event. Next, they traveled to the other Osetran worlds. Traveling to some took years, but they did it all the same. It proved, however, all for naught: eradication met them everywhere.

"More troubling, during these travels they came across the cold remains of several other deep space sporeships, which must have, like them, returned to search for survivors. In their investigations of the dead wreckage, they found no evidence of external attack. The cold, recently deceased bodies of the crew and the sporeship's organics were riddled with the infectious brain disease that the initial message of death had described. Upon this harrowing revelation, the sporeship's captain ordered the horrific measure that they had hoped would not be necessary: that all crew undergo immediate surgery to impair the telekinetic communication centers in their brains. One by one, they entered the sporeship's surgery pods. One by one, they left deaf and mute. But by doing so, their minds were now impenetrable to the tendrils of the lingering neurovirus.

"By the time they had covered nearly all the worlds, colonies, and outposts, the crew members had aged significantly. So had the sporeship itself—increasingly prone to malfunction and its energy near depletion. Rather than risk another journey, they resolved to live out the remainder of their lives on their home planet, destroyed though it was. Perhaps in time, other Osetra survivors would arrive. Ultimately, none ever came, and the crew died off one by one."

Falck paused. "The Osetran message did not contain much information about the neurovirus or exactly when the plague started. But they did know that its origin was foreign. It had first infected a deep space crew who had all returned home mad. Their thoughts were disjointed, rambling, unintelligible. They lost control over their bodies and minds. At times they sought to commit suicide. The madness spread like wildfire, infecting millions on the Osetran homeworld before the deep space crew's doctors even knew it had left the facility. Before long, the neurosis spread to other worlds as communication waves and Osetran ships and people traveled across space. The telepathically-linked species was woefully susceptible. They had no defense.

"The Osetran scientists and doctors that studied and treated those first infected crew members, however, had made a shocking observation about the nature of the neurovirus before they succumbed to it themselves. They discovered it to be not a true virus at all, but rather a parasitic, technobiological organism, and worst of all, sentient."

"Technobiological?" shuddered Kairos, interrupting Falck for the first time. "So it was created." After a moment, "By who? From where?"

"They did not know."

Kairos's eyes grew wide. "The Osetra that Blackpool discovered, they were infected with this organism."

Falck nodded. "The bodies must have been in a deep coma, but still alive. This parasite lay in their minds, dormant. Waiting to be found again. Except when humans found it, it could not infect their minds the way it did to the Osetra. Humans have no telepathic brain structures."

"Until now ..." Kairos realized with dread, his forehead tingling.

"Through Blackpool's research, this organism has learned how to mutate human neuron DNA to produce the telepathic structures it needs to spread itself through the minds of humanity."

"Knowledge that it shared with Neve's husband," Kairos said. "The Amor Fati are all infected with this same parasite, but they're all still alive. Brain-washed, sure, but alive. The Vyst must be keeping them so."

"Perhaps human biology has allowed it," Falck guessed. "Perhaps the intelligence has adapted to keep its hosts alive, spreading quietly to achieve widespread scale before initiating a mass execution."

Xenocide, Kairos thought. "The agents of Lienns-Sutra's Science Division—which Neve's husband leads—tried to destroy the embryo on Spires. The Vyst wants to finish wiping out the last of the Osetra," he said.

"Yes."

Its purposes for humanity will be no less severe, thought Kairos. After a moment he asked, "Isn't it strange that the embryo wasn't killed when the organism spread among the Osetra? Perhaps the parasite cannot infect embryos?"

Falck shook his head. "Osetran deep space sporeships, like the one the remnant commanded, carry many such embryos in suspended animation, for use later in boosting the population and development of any new colonies seeded during the expedition. If the remnant had found live embryos aboard the other ships they'd encountered, they would have collected them in order to repopulate their race. This embryo was saved only by having been flung across the galaxy, far from Osetra space."

For some other race to find, thought Kairos, thinking about the teardrop's beacon message. An act of desperation to preserve the race. For all the Osetra knew, the teardrop might never be found. It might travel endlessly across black space, until its embryo, even in a suspended state, eventually decayed. Or it could've sailed right into a star. Or remained buried beneath Pantoll's layers of rock for all eternity. But the teardrop had reached not just a planet, but a habitable planet, and one even inhabited by intelligent life. And Kairos's grandfather just so happened to have detected its signal and impact, and had had the resolve to pursue it. The clergy of the New Revelationist Obasanjo Church would've viewed the improbable series of events as bearing the fingerprints of the divine hand.

"The protective shell placed around the embryo is a specialized material," Falck continued. "Nearly indestructible and radiation-proof, for it had to endure a long period of interstellar travel. But once the child is born, it will be incredibly vulnerable, including from the communication waves you say the Amor Fati are transmitting. It will be safe if it remains here, away from the Settled Region and raised under the remaining Osetra's care."

Kairos thought back to the Osetra he'd briefly seen on the oceanic world, knowing now that it was, incredibly, one of the actual crewmembers of the Osetran ship that had contacted Old Earth three standard centuries ago. He wondered how long Osetra lifespans could be. "Will the Osetra come to birth it soon?" he asked. He'd admittedly had a strong desire to witness such an event.

"The embryo's development is near complete. After, all it will require is love."

"Love?"

"The presence of love, yes. Don't look so surprised. The Osetra are a race of intimately connected beings. The infant's telepathic centers needs to sense compassion as part of parent-child imprinting process and to trigger birth. In a natural pregnancy, of course, this would've been a given."

Parental compassion. "I went down into the cellar, in that cottage," he told Falck. "My parents were on this planet. As young researchers, before I was born. You were with them here, weren't you?"

Falck nodded. "We met during the research expedition. Esteryst was the name given this planet."

So you've known them, and me, for a long time. Well before they moved to Pantoll. "They knew about the transportal and Osetra remnant, too?"

Falck nodded. "We came into contact. Needless to say, it was a complete surprise to your parents and me. The Osetra were easily startled, but after a while, trust developed. One day your father mentioned his father's past expedition on Pantoll, in search of a lost Osetran artifact that crashed there. I was captivated upon hearing his story, and, like your father, dedicated my life to finding it."

A pang of sadness coupled with a hint of bitterness hit Kairos's heart. His parents had never talked about this planet, Esteryst. "Why the secrecy?" he asked. "Even after finding the teardrop, my father never told me any of this."

Falck was quiet for a moment. "You see," he said gently, "Your father and I had taken an oath to keep our knowledge of the Osetra hidden from the human world, to protect the dying race. If a corporation knew of Esteryst and the transportal, the remaining Osetra would be doomed to corporate laboratories, receiving the same treatment as those poor infested Osetra that Blackpool discovered."

Kairos shook his head in amazement. After a moment, he let out a laugh.

"What is it?" Falck asked.

"It's just that I never would have imagined that my crazy father was secretly working with the lost Osetra. I thought you both were just out of your minds."

"I am sorry for the pain this has caused your family," Falck said somberly. "And especially you."

Kairos sighed. "What matters most now is stopping the Amor Fati. What can we do?"

Falck sighed heavily through his respirator. "If this organism has figured out how to stimulate human brain cell and protein production through electromagnetic radiation, there may not be anything we can do to stop it from spreading through humanity as easily as it did through the Osetra. I'm afraid I must be clear with you: my first priority is to ensure the safety of the young Osetra, which I swore I would do."

"First priority? All of humanity is in danger!" Kairos exclaimed.

"They have you, Kairos," Falck replied. "And I offer you the use of my ship. Its Osetran-built weave drive makes it far faster than any human ship." Falck stood up. "Dawn is nearly upon us, and I do not want to alarm your friends with your absence. I must return through the transportal to commune with the Osetra regarding this new development. I will meet you back at the cottage before long to discuss this further."

Falck was right. And time was short. Every hour they spent on Esteryst, the Amor Fati were closer to infecting all of humanity's minds. Kairos needed to figure out next steps with Neve and the traders now that they could leave Esteryst on Falck's ship.

Kairos turned to begin the descent into the jungle below. His numb toes were glad to start warming up. After a couple of steps, he paused and turned. "What if being shot into space isn't what saved the embryo?" he called back.

"What do you mean?" Falck replied.

"What if it was sent *because* it had survived? Because it had somehow been immune to the organism's parasitism?"

Falck was silent for a long moment. "This intelligence was able to break every mind it penetrated. The mortality rate as far as the Osetra knew was one-hundred percent." He looked like he might say something further, but he then fell quiet once more and turned away.

Chapter 13

It was mid-morning by the time Kairos had returned to the cottage. They'd all crammed into Neve's small bedroom as he'd recounted what had transpired during the night, as well as what he planned to do next—Kairos standing beside the bed; Neve sitting up against the head board; Midmay lying by the door on the wooden floorboards, staring up at the ceiling; the two traders leaning on the wall by the foot of the bed, arms folded and eyebrows frequently furling in confusion.

"Let me get this straight," Sunsip began, after Kairos finished. "This so-called prophet—the Vyst—is harboring a viral artificial intelligence which wiped out the entire Osetra race. And it now is going to do the same to humans through forced religious conversion, mind-control, whatever you want to call it."

"It's technically a technobiological, parasitic organism and not a virus ..." Kairos started but Sunsip's blank stare stopped him. "But yes, that's right," he finished.

"And you think the CEO of Lienns-Sutra Organization—Akaash Roth himself—is gonna not only take your call, but believe your story, agree to hunt down the Amor Fati Disciples across the worlds, and shut down their operations? And all because you've told him you *think* one of his scientists is part of this cult's sinister plan?" Sunsip continued.

"I *know* my husband is head of Lienns-Sutra's Science Division," Neve stated resolutely. "The Amor Fati hired Cole and Chimera to extract him from Blackpool so he could implant himself within L-S. The L-S agents' cloaking bodysuits we encountered on Spires are too advanced to have been developed without intervention. They're alien technology. My husband created the cloaking suits with the Vyst's influence over his mind, just as he created the neurofluid and viral transmission technologies."

"What proof can you show Roth that the Amor Fati are a threat?" Sunsip asked. "Overhearing snatches of a conversation in the cult's virtual portal isn't compelling evidence."

"No System Administrator would easily remove their chief scientist," Medwick agreed.

"Roth doesn't need to believe they're a threat to humanity to take action," countered Kairos. "He just needs to believe they're a threat to Lienns-Sutra and to him personally. The Amor Fati are planning a power grab."

"He'll have all the proof he needs just by taking a closer look at his Science Division, especially my husband's files," Neve said. "The entire division is sure to have already been converted into cult members. And likely many more employees at the corporation as well."

Kairos turned to the traders. "Time is running out to prevent the Amor Fati from spreading this parasite. The population of Kotopax is their next target. Can you go down to the hangar and prep for takeoff? I want to be ready to leave for the Lilic System as soon as Falck returns."

Sunsip shook his head but smiled. "This is crazy. But nothing would make me happier than to launch off of this hot ball back into the glorious heavens."

"It is a most disagreeable place," Medwick agreed, massaging his shoulder.

"We'd better find Rhody too. Hey, Midmay," Kairos said, turning toward the door. "Can you go out and call—Midmay?" The girl wasn't by the door frame. He stepped to the doorway and called her name loudly a couple of times. No one had noticed her leave.

A steady low rumble sounded, causing the walls and floor boards to vibrate. Then there was a great *whooshing* sound, like the rush of flames from the burner of a gas stove.

Kairos was all too familiar with the sound of a ship leaving port. As were the traders, who were already bounding out the door ahead of him.

They dashed through the cottage's back door into the yard, pausing only briefly upon seeing that the back room's shallow pool in the back room was empty. The teardrop was gone.

Plowing through the patch of jungle beyond the yard, Kairos wondered whether Falck had returned without announcement. Or perhaps they weren't as alone in the wilderness as they thought.

They burst through the tree line into the grassy clearing. Falck's ship was rising from the open hangar ceiling, as if emerging from the ground itself. Over the roaring rush of the sublight engines, the traders yelled and hollered at the ship to stop and waved their arms madly. Kairos ran up as close as the heat off the ship's engines would allow.

There was a single head in the cockpit. It turned to face him. *Midmay.*

Her eyes rested on his for a moment.

Then the ship lifted off and away.

The thrust of the engines knocked him onto the ground, where he lay for a long time, stunned, watching the ship and his young friend disappear into the sky.

* * *

"That damned kid," Sunsip growled, spitting onto the ground. "I ever see her again, I'm going to pluck her little head right off her skinny neck."

"I can agree with you on that," Medwick said.

In his own private hell, Kairos kept replaying the events since Midmay had logged into the cult's virtual portal, and cursing himself for being so blind. He knew his friend all too well. After she'd awoken from her coma, he'd neglected to really check in with her. She'd seemed fine, but he should've known better. He'd let her down.

Sunlight reflecting off two black specks high up in the sky interrupted his wallowing. He sat up and rose to his feet.

"More ships?" Medwick remarked, following Kairos's gaze.

"Two shuttles," Sunsip said, squinting against the sun. "Corporate, if my eyes serve me well."

"By god, I think you're right," his brother said.

"Into the trees, now!" Kairos shouted. He pulled his goggles down over his eyes and subvocalized to reestablish a connection with Rhody's biOS, then sent a distress signal to the hybird, wherever it was.

Not long after they entered the cover of the jungle, the pair

332

of shuttles swooped overhead in a low pass. Each traced a plasma beam across the cottage, alighting it instantly on fire. One of them then slowed and made to set down on the beach, while the second peeled off and wheeled back around toward the clearing.

Kairos and the two traders bolted out of the jungle toward the smoking cottage. All Kairos could think about was Neve still in her bedroom. Large flames were devouring the dry wood and licking out the windows. The windmill tower had been damaged by the beams. With a cracking moan, it collapsed upon the roof, caving it in with a great crash and sending blades cartwheeling off. Rage at the thought of Neve trapped inside burned with similar intensity within him.

Kairos kicked open the front door and held his breath against the smoke. He was about to barge in when Sunsip called for him to come around to the side.

There they found Neve, sitting back against a tree in the narrow side yard. Her hands and elbows were dirt-stained and scraped. She'd pulled herself out through the bedroom window.

"So much for being off the grid," she remarked dryly.

"Kairos," Sunsip said sternly, "those shuttles had Lienns-Sutra logos."

"Only a Great Ship could've weaved here so quickly," Medwick added.

Kairos perked up at the mention of it. The massive old starships were legendary. Constructed on Old Earth for the Exodus. Flying cities. Fitted with colossal weave drives that generated such monstrous energy that skipping between star systems was a matter of days rather than weeks. The command segment of one of such ships—for most of it, like the other Great Ships, had been dismantled for raw materials or repurposed to establish the first human colonies—served as Lienns-Sutra Organization's central headquarters. But it rarely left its orbit around Spires, rarer still its home Lilic System.

"Then the Amor Fati have already taken control," Kairos said. "That's the only way they could've known we were here." He turned to Neve. "Midmay was the link. She's become one of them. She sent them our location."

"Are you sure?" Neve asked, grief blooming across her face.

He nodded. "Midmay doesn't even know how to fly a spacecraft. The Amor Fati are in her head, using her to bring the teardrop to them."

Kairos subvocalized a goggle command to pair with Rhody's ocular scopes. An aerial view filled his vision. It shook a bit with each powerful flap of Rhody's wings. After a moment of disorientation, he traced the smoke column to the flaming cottage.

"There are no means to send a transmission from here," Medwick mused. "Even if she did, it wouldn't reach listening ears for years."

"The laws of physics be damned; she's part of that hive-mind," Sunsip said. "It sees what she sees. Thinks her thoughts. The cult knows who we are and everything we've done since we've been here!"

Rhody soared overhead now. Through its eyes, Kairos could see both shuttles—one on the beach, one on the grassy clearing by the ajar hangar doors—but no other movement.

Where are all the corporates?

"Rhody, switch to thermal imaging," he subvocalized. His view morphed into a blurred colorscape of deep purples and blues interspersed with splotches of greens, yellows, oranges. The cottage appeared as an intensity of hot light, a collage of swirling fiery hues. But creeping toward the cottage up the dunes and from the jungle were the unmistakable red-orange outlines of people. There were at least twelve of them.

"It doesn't matter," Kairos told the others, switching away from Rhody's scopes. "Corporate agents are here. We need to move. Maybe we can lose them in the jungle." But even as he said it, Kairos knew their situation was hopeless. The shuttles had landed on either side of them. They were flanked and unarmed. They didn't stand a chance of running, either. It was too late for that. And no chance of stopping the Amor Fati now that they had the resources of the most powerful System Administrator at their command. Carrying Neve, he plunged into the jungle with the two traders following behind. "Silence from here on out," he called softly behind him. "If we keep perpendicular to the coastline, we might be able—"

Wave rounds sizzled through the foliage, slicing leaves and branches and sending bits of greenery into a flutter about them. Medwick hollered out in pain.

Turning about, Kairos's ankle snagged on an exposed root and he lost his balance, tumbling over with Neve.

Sunsip lowered his brother to the ground as more wave fire zipped by overhead. Medwick's shoulder was oozing bubbling blood from a gruesome hole ringed with burned flesh. Moaning, the navigator's head drooped.

Crunching footsteps and the soft rustle of leaves sounded nearby.

Keeping his head low, Kairos scanned in their direction but saw only shaking foliage and leafy branches being forced aside—hardly ten meters away and closing. These agents, like those on Spires, were wearing cloaking bodysuits.

A screech pierced the air. Rhody dove like lightning from the jungle canopy above them, talons-bared and laser pulsing.

The invisible agent had only time to grunt briefly before his dead body toppled to the ground, a hazy fragment of his blood-stained neck visible through a gap in the cloaking aura where the suit's integrity must've been damaged.

"Go!" Sunsip yelled to Kairos, scrambling on his belly to reach for the downed agent's waverifle.

Kairos refused. "We stick together."

"Together, we're all dead. I'm not leaving my brother. I'll try to take a couple down with us. Now, go!" the pilot barked.

Reluctantly, Kairos lifted Neve and stumbled away. Rhody flew a few meters above them, weaving through branches. Only once over the next several minutes did he hear wave fire behind them, the jungle quickly returning to silence save for his hurried stomping through the foliage. Each step brought the pain of knowing he'd left two of his companions behind.

Rhody squawked an alert. Kairos paused and knelt. But seeing and hearing nothing after a few moments, he hurried onward.

Then he remembered his goggles were linked to the hybird's infrared scopes. He subvocalized to switch to Rhody's view.

Out of nowhere, the solid butt of a rifle entered his periphery and plowed into the side of his head, shattering his right goggle screen and knocking him flat. Neve spilled out of his arms, yelping as she hit the ground hard.

A boot dealt Kairos two swift blows to his chest and abdomen. Coughing, he lay curled in sudden, unexpected pain, blinded by blood running into his right eye and spasming screen-flicker in his left.

Harsh screeching and a mad ruffling of wings sounded above him.

Then came a brief crackle of electricity and a sickening *pop*, followed by the acrid smell of vaporized flesh and metal. Neve screamed.

A forceful hand rolled Kairos onto his back. His goggles were ripped from his head, sending a fresh flow of blood down his nose from the deep cut just above his right eye from a shard of shattered screen.

Singed, blackened feathers drifted down about him. When the butt of the rifle slammed into his forehead, Kairos didn't even see it coming.

* * *

Kairos could do nothing but watch the corridor ceiling's piping, wiring, and inset lights scroll by.

The trip to the Lienns-Sutra's Great Ship had been, to say the least, uncomfortable. The corporation's cloaked agents had dragged him and Neve into their shuttle after injecting them with sedatives. Kairos had spent the trip up drooling over himself in a fog, but the onset of gravity made him vaguely aware of their arrival. Great Ships were the only Old Earth ships with their own graviton field generators, a technology so cutting edge at the time of their construction that the knowledge of their underlying physics, like so many other advanced technologies, had long since been lost. They'd landed in a docking bay, after which he and Neve were each strapped into a gurney and pushed down a series of sterile corridors.

They now were passing through two sequential sets of sliding doors. Two lab technicians wheeled him along at his left and right, and he'd sensed another pair of technicians following behind them. He had asked several times where they were taking him, but he might as well have asked the ceiling. The sedatives had mostly worn off, but his forehead still pulsed with dull pain from where the agent had struck him with the rifle butt.

Kairos's gurney halted at another set of doors, these thicker than the previous ones. The technicians went up to little scanners at either side of the door and scanned their retinas simultaneously. A series of locks clunked heavily. The thick, vault-like doors slowly slid apart.

They opened to a spacious, high-ceilinged space that had dim lighting and an industrial quality, similar to a warehouse. Massive capsules of gas or liquid were situated along one wall with fat piping leading away from nozzles at their ends. Thick electrical cables and bundles of thinner wiring crawled up the walls and along the ceiling overhead like an overgrowth of vines. Their source was a series of towering, silver fusion reactors that took up the bulk of the space. The reactors barely fit inside the room, and their bulky attachments and sur-rounding clutter of wires gave Kairos the impression they'd been moved from another part of the ship and repurposed. He traced several of the fatter cables running into another large room ahead, where they split off around corners and disappeared from view. Something around here was drawing an inordinate amount of power.

As they emerged into the new area, his view of the large room widened. Rows and rows of tall cylindrical tanks stretched to the high ceiling, filled with a translucent, light pink solution that fluoresced under the light. Several spherical objects floated lazily within each. Scientists in white lab coats paced about or worked at computer consoles beside a few of the tanks.

This must be part of Lienns-Sutra's Science Division, Kairos thought. Far above, a latticework of metal beams and broad glass panes formed a ceiling and provided a view of outer space. A full second of pure blankness punctuated every brief winking in and out of the stars—they were weaving across tremendous distances. *The ship must be en route to Kotopax.*

As he was wheeled through, Kairos spotted a short raised platform where a deep, metallic basin stood, and a little further after that, he recognized a small rectangular tank which held the Osetran teardrop. Surprisingly, it looked healthy. Perhaps the Amor Fati hadn't yet figured out a means to destroy it.

The technicians brought his gurney to a halt and he was able to take a closer look at the nearest cylindrical tank. The spherical shapes floating within were biological, not too unlike the preserved specimens in the cottage's collection on Esteryst. Their exteriors were bumpy with winding grooves and ridges.

"Beautiful, aren't they?" a bespectacled man in a black lab coat said as he approached Kairos and Neve. The scientist was tall and slender, with dark hair and features, perhaps in his mid-thirties. The man paused beside Kairos and looked up with admiration at the tank, the fluorescent solution washing his face with a pink hue. "They're all networked together. It takes fifty-six people to create a single one," he stated proudly. "Literally." The man's mouth curved in an eager half-grin.

Kairos's stomach churned: each sphere was composed of individual human brains. There were eight spheres in this tank alone. A forest of such cylinders covered the laboratory.

"Why?" was all Kairos could utter.

"The Prophet needed them. These are our church founders, early believers who devoted themselves to the faith."

The pink solution was surely the neurofluid that Neve's husband developed at Blackpool, which re-engineered neural tissue to enable brain-to-brain communication. Perhaps these brain clusters had been part of the biotechnology's early testing. Then the sick thought came that these brains, and the real consciousnesses they held, were yet alive and performing some odious function.

The scientist turned to them, his eyes bright and piercing behind his circular-framed glasses. The man's attention fell wholly on Neve. His mouth twitched. "How are you, dear wife? It's been some time since we—"

Neve lunged at him, scalpel in hand.

Her husband recoiled to avoid a lethal strike to the throat. The blade sliced a shallow line across his chest.

The technicians at Neve's sides immediately withdrew their tranquilizer needlers and fired. Two flechettes lodged themselves into her neck.

Neve's husband's expression turned to one of amusement as Neve's slackened body slumped back against the gurney, scalpel clattering to the floor. Her eyes maintained their glare until the drug finally glazed them over and she passed out. The technicians found her straps cut, and they searched her body for anything else she might've somehow swiped off them.

The scientist touched his chest through his torn shirt and

pulled away bloodied fingers. "As ungrateful and combative as ever, I see," the scientist spat, taking her lifeless hand and lifting it to his lips. "Sweet dreams, my lost, broken love. When you awake, we will be more united than ever before."

The man turned to Kairos. "Hello Kairos Catadyn. My! That worked you up quite a bit," he observed, looking from Neve to Kairos's enraged struggle against the gurney's straps. Neve's husband swiftly backhanded Kairos across the jaw. The blow sent the taste of blood into Kairos's mouth. The man bent and leaned in close to Kairos's ear. "Thou shalt not covet thy neighbor's wife," he reprimanded before straightening calmly.

Kairos glared. "So *you're* Dr. Henley. How did Lienns-Sutra's background screenings miss exposing your past? Your affiliation with the Vyst?"

Dr. Henley snorted with the air of a condescending schoolmaster. "Roth *knew*. He wanted me *because* of my connection to the Vyst."

Of course, Kairos realized. Akaash Roth wanted the technology that Dr. Henley could offer, so the CEO had struck a deal with him. A deal that proved costly. "And later," he said to the scientist, "when fears arose that the Osetra were returning—a fear that the Amor Fati manufactured—Roth gave you even more power."

Dr. Henley merely smiled. Kairos guessed that the scientist had dangled the secret of the weave drive in front of Roth. The ultimate carrot on a stick. In his arrogance, Roth thought he could use Blackpool's escaped specimen for his own gain. But Dr. Henley had used *him*. Roth had given him resources, legitimacy, made him head of Science Division ... all the while, Dr. Henley's influence within Lienns-Sutra had spread like dry rot. Until one day, Roth was no longer of any use. The Amor Fati's follower base—which Kairos assumed by now had expanded to nearly every employee *but* Roth—had then disposed of the CEO.

"You killed him, didn't you?" Kairos said.

"On the contrary, we offered him eternal life. But he rejected the faith. Akaash Roth's love for this reality and his power within it led to his demise."

"I want to see Midmay," Kairos demanded.

"Don't you see, I *am* Midmay. When you talk to me, you talk to her. She's a very sad little girl, did you know that? Tragic that no one cared about her."

Kairos yanked against his restraints. "What have you done to her?"

Dr. Henley closed his eyes and exhaled slowly through his nose. "You never loved me." The scientist spoke with the girl's tone and inflections. "My only family was Johnathan, an android warmer than any human."

"Get out of her head!" Kairos roared. But he couldn't deny the truth behind the words. Midmay and his father had been burdens to him on Pantoll, anchors that kept him from sailing away.

"You visited me, but I know now it was only out of guilt. You considered it atoning for your sin. Atoning for the girl in the chapel's bell tower—the girl that you killed!"

"Enough!" Kairos pleaded. It was too much to take from Dr. Henley's mouth. The horror of what the man knew. What the *All-Soul* knew. *But who in the All-Soul could have possibly known that part of Kairos's story?* He'd never told Midmay. But through the collective All-Soul, Midmay now knew the truth.

Tears began streaking down Kairos's face. "Forgive me,

Midmay. I am a wretched man ..." he cried. A sob burst from his chest. "Forgive me ... little Abeni." It was the first time he'd said the other girl's name aloud since her death. He fell back pitifully on the gurney.

"There is forgiveness for your sin and healing for your shame, my son," spoke a deep, familiar voice.

Electricity shot up Kairos's spine at its crushing familiarity. His eyes widened. He saw at once the silhouettes of tornadoes spinning in the Pantollian night. The assassin's downed ship ... a second shadowy figure stumbling away into the dark ...

The area around him had cleared of scientists. The lab technicians that had wheeled them in were gone too. A ring of hooded figures in long dark robes surrounded him now—five in all. They were of the same design as the robes Kairos had seen in the Amor Fati's virtual portal. The Vyst's Disciples. Their obscured heads were bowed and they were murmuring some form of prayer together.

The sixth hooded figure who had spoken stepped around the side of Kairos's gurney, allowing Kairos to see his face. "A long way from Pantoll, aren't we?" Father Revais said with a warm grin, patting Kairos's shoulder with a braceleted hand. "I warned you about the danger of lacking belief."

Kairos's jaw clenched. During his many chapel visits, the priest had coaxed personal details from Kairos about everything—his family, his past, his sin, his father's work. Kairos pulled against his restraints with fury, wishing to strangle the priest with his bare hands.

Dr. Henley stepped toward Kairos, a small injection gun in his hand.

"If only you had believed," Father Revais said with genuine remorse. "Your rejection of the faith in our virtual portal nearly killed you. I have done my best, old friend. But you have forced us to try a less conscious approach. But there is no need to fear the death of the body. Your soul will live on. As does your father's." The priest drew Kairos's eyes to his. "And in fact, no one at all in this iteration of the universe has much longer to live."

"What more do you want from me?" Kairos cried out. "You already took the Osetran embryo."

"But the answer to its birth is here," Dr. Henley said, jabbing a finger into Kairos's forehead. "Perhaps your peculiar friend Falck told you how to incubate it. Our agents on the jungle planet just found him by the way. He couldn't hide up in those mountains forever."

So I was right; they haven't been able to destroy the embryo, Kairos thought. *They need to open its protective shell to kill it, but they don't know that the only the way to open the shell is to birth the child through love, which they lack. They are stuck.*

An idea formed in Kairos's mind, then the shape of a plan. A very risky plan.

God, help me.

"I'm afraid we're short on time and must cut our reunion short for now," apologized Father Revais, taking a cue from the scientist. "The End of Time is upon us. The Creator wills it, and we are ushering it in. The Osetra Spirit's story in this universe is all but over. Humanity's final chapter will soon follow."

"And then the Spirits will gather outside of space/time. To meet the Creator, the central consciousness from which all life proceeds," Kairos said. "And after, there will be a new creation. And none of our fragmented souls will remember a thing from this reality."

"Ah, so you have been paying attention," commended the priest. "Kairos, I may be the only one who truly knows how much you've suffered under your God's whims." His expression suggested he truly meant it. "I know you want to approach the throne of God as much as I do. To speak with the Almighty, at last, face-to-face."

Father Revais made the sign of the triple-cross over Kairos. The priest then stepped away, uttering prayers with bowed head and closed eyes.

Dr. Henley raised the gun. Kairos felt a cool needle slide deep into his neck.

"I wish to be baptized into the All-Soul of humanity!" Kairos called out.

Father Revais lifted a hand for the scientist to pause.

"What?" Dr. Henley exclaimed.

The Disciples looked from one to the other. None spoke aloud, and Kairos understood belatedly there was no need: communication between them was telepathic. It was unclear how much of their former individualism each even possessed.

Father Revais pulled his hood back, his solemn face revealing genuine surprise along with a hint of mistrust. The priest took Kairos's head in his hands and gazed piercingly into his eyes, as if looking for something.

"Father," Kairos said. "I desire the forgiveness you spoke of. Forgiveness for my past sins ... and for my unbelief. Please, help me believe. Did I not see a baptismal well back there? Is this sacrament not available to the darkest of repentant souls?"

"My son ..." whispered the priest, placing a hand atop Kairos's head. "You understand baptism means complete submission of body and mind to the will of the All-Soul?

Rejection of the faith is neurologically lethal. You would surely die."

"But you already knew that." Dr. Henley sneered. "You *want* to destroy your mind to forever prevent us from extracting the information we need."

"He doesn't understand," Kairos said to Father Revais. "Birthing the embryo does not require information. It requires love. You intend only to kill the child. Your motivations already betray any false love you'd attempt. True love can never be imitated. The teardrop, therefore, will never open to you. If that were my aim, then I'd already be satisfied."

"Yet you claim it will open to you?" Dr. Henley balked. "What love have you for the Osetra?"

"I love Midmay. The strength of that is enough."

"Even if what you say is true, you need more than that love," cautioned Father Revais. "A lack of genuine faith will still kill you."

"It is written, Father, '*God is love*,'" Kairos replied. "You say you have the truth; then I beg you now to reveal it to me. I will open my mind to it. My soul has been tortured enough. I might hate you for killing my father. But if his death is only temporary, an unfortunate necessity as part of the End of Time as you say, then what hate can I have? I might hate my father, for his actions brought me to Pantoll. But if I was meant to inherit the Osetran embryo, then what hate can I have? I might hate the Creator. But if everything that's happened in my life has been preparation for this moment, then what hate can I have? I might hate myself. But if the Creator's mercy overrules my self-condemnation, then what hate can I have?" Kairos's body shook, and he returned the priest's gaze with longing. "Reveal to me, Father, that I am the instrument of the All-Soul of humanity to complete the young Osetra's journey, to deliver it as a final sacrifice at the End of Time according to the Creator's perfect will." He took the priest's weathered hand. "Father, I know now Midmay saw this truth. I will resist it myself no longer. Indeed it is written, 'unless you change and become like little children, you will never enter the kingdom of heaven.'"

For a long moment, Father Revais studied him, his mouth a thin line.

Then, slowly, Kairos felt the cool, long needle slide out from his neck. Dr. Henley returned the injection gun to his lab coat pocket.

Four Disciples stepped forward in unison. They unbound his arm and leg restraints, then lifted him onto their shoulders. Father Revais walked beside as they carried him, uttering prayers over the procession.

Kairos, with glazed eyes fixed on the blinking stars beyond the ceiling glass, reflected on the doctrines of the Church of the Samsaric Soul, which he now knew was the physical arm of the Amor Fati cult to complement their virtual presence. Reflected on the collapse of the universe and cessation of existence at the End of Time, about which the Father had preached. The End of Time: that moment when the last human being in existence died, rendering the species extinct, at least as manifested in this reality. With that death, the reunification of the shattered Human Spirit would be complete, with all the billions of deceased human soul fragments re-formed into the one original, ancient Human. And immediately after, Human would be ushered into a direct audience with God himself. At that divine meeting, a final account of this universe's history would be taken. Judgments would be passed. And finally, a new universe would be created, restarting the Cycle of Time.

The procession arrived at the deep, metallic basin. Kairos's carriers ascended the few short stairs up to the elevated platform beside it. After stripping him naked, the Disciples gently lowered his body into the basin, where Father Revais waded, his dark robe billowing about.

Even before the cool liquid touched his skin, Kairos had already discerned the true nature of the baptismal "water": Blackpool's stolen neurofluid. It had been used for the baptisms that Father Revais had conducted on Pantoll as well. It felt slightly thicker than water.

Father Revais crossed Kairos's arms over his chest. Then the priest cradled Kairos's head with one arm while he signed the triple-cross over Kairos with the other and muttered another short prayer. It was a ritual Kairos had witnessed several times before in the chapel on Pantoll, only now he understood its full ramifications: complete submission to the faith.

"I give thanks to the Creator that our brother, Kairos, has made this decision," Father Revais spoke in a booming voice, "to die to himself so that he may be reborn and live as an instrument of the All-Soul from this time forward. He was lost, but is now found. With his baptism, he has declared his commitment to the true faith and the sacrifice of self to the Way of the Universe."

The priest looked down upon Kairos. "Because of your professed faith, I baptize you now into the body of the holy Church of the Samsaric Soul, as one who accepts and loves his fate to become of one mind and one spirit with his brothers and sisters, one All-Soul of humanity."

The priest pushed him under.

The neurofluid rushed over Kairos's face.

The priest then pressed harder upon on Kairos's crossed arms, forcing air out of his chest in a tumult of bubbles.

Before long, Kairos's lungs were burning with the need to inhale. His body instinctively struggled, one of his legs spasming and breaking the basin's surface. But Father Revais's firm hold kept him submerged.

His vision spotting and his mind decaying into a state of panic, Kairos's throat convulsed. He coughed out his remaining stale air in short bursts of chaotic bubbles.

At last, his lungs gave out. Desperate and craving the sweet taste of air, they involuntarily inhaled.

Kairos's body lurched as he choked on the liquid surging into his lungs. Unsatisfied, his lungs instinctively tried inhaling again and again, until his chest swelled heavy with fluid. His head spun from the sensation of every orifice feeling clogged, and his limbs went limp.

At last, the hands pressing upon him eased their pressure.

All but unconscious, Kairos's body sank like a stone statue to rest upon the basin's cool metal bottom. Panic was replaced with a calm frailty.

Waiting to die.

And the waiting was the most terrifying yet.

At some point he blacked out.

* * *

After a long while—long after the turbulent liquid in the basin had stilled and become smooth as glass—Father Revais raised Kairos's body, stepped out of the basin, and lay the wet body on the platform.

The priest regarded the man's expressionless face for a moment. Neurofluid oozed from Kairos's nose and mouth and ears.

The priest could sense that the neurofluid had saturated Kairos's mind quickly. The bots and compounds contained within had already started their work.

A thin smile curved the priest's lips. This direct method of neuroengineering, though messier and far less scalable than using DNA induction waves, worked *fast*. In mere minutes, Kairos's memories, thoughts, and emotions would begin seeping—then pouring—out of him.

Once Kairos's mind fell under his authority, the priest would use it to birth the embryo. The newborn's death would *complete* the Osetra's history, the final word to a finished narrative. Humanity would soon follow.

Completion, Father Revais reflected. Like that which had been attained by his own race, long ago, and who waited yet for the universe to start anew.

Placing his hands on Kairos's chest, Father Revais uttered a prayer, thanking the Creator for its faithfulness in bringing all these things to pass and for strength to see his own purpose through.

Chapter 14

Kairos's first sensations were wet choking and utter confusion.

He felt as if he were clawing his mind away from the clutching tendrils of an intense dream.

And Kairos had experienced so many dreams.

Deep dreams. Dreams so long he felt he'd aged while experiencing them. Yet something wasn't quite right with them. Their content was too mundane, too coherent, too *real*. Wakefulness did not shake them away. Frenetic images skipped across his mind at a dizzying speed, new ones emerging before his mind could recognize the last. Below the surface, he sensed a deep, powerful current of information being pumped through his subconscious. A ferocious migraine consumed all thought; all he could do was scrunch his eyes and moan.

Father Revais was supporting him with an arm, tilting his body so he didn't choke further on the thick fluid he was coughing up. Eventually the priest propped him up while a Disciple wrapped his naked body with a robe.

Kairos tried to sit up under his own power, tried to lift his head—then promptly passed out.

* * *

When Kairos awoke next, he was lying on a lab table.

His mind was utterly numb and exhausted from migraine, confusion, and an overload of sensory input.

For a long while, he simply lay with his eyes closed, trying to piece together coherent thoughts he could call his own and not the echo of someone else's.

Even more unsettling was the sickening sensation of an *other* worming itself into his head, occupying a space Kairos never knew existed or could be shared. An entity sitting in the background of his mind, flipping through his thoughts and memories as if impatiently searching for a particular line in an enormous book. And beyond this probing, the feeling of being sucked dry. Consumed. Kairos could not kick this entity out.

The experience wasn't one-way. It seemed as if a piece of his own mind were drifting elsewhere, too, extending out in a long wisp connecting him to spaces far and foreign. He was also learning things. *Had* learned things. No, *learn* was the wrong word. He'd become *aware* of new information, as if it'd been simply dropped into his mind without any effort on his part to commit it to memory.

After a while, he mustered the energy to sit up. Kairos's body was tired, but not the debilitating lethargy he'd felt earlier under the effects of the drug they'd injected him with. He found himself wearing a dark brown robe but had no recollection of being dressed.

Father Revais sat in a lab chair beside him, gazing at him solemnly. They were alone. How much time had elapsed,

Kairos couldn't determine. Dr. Henley and the other Disciples had left and must have taken Neve with them. Beyond the priest, Kairos's eyes fell upon the nearby tank holding the Osetran teardrop, dark and silent and impenetrable as ever.

Despite his best meditative efforts, Kairos knew he was losing a grip on his sanity. His will might be lost any moment. He wasn't sure how long it'd take for the neurofluid that his brain was soaked in to complete its work. He hoped—he prayed—that he'd hold out long enough to see whether this fool's plan of his worked. If his faith in the Osetran spawn was true.

A pang shot through Kairos's head, and he brought his hands up to massage his temples. The migraine was relentless. His brain ballooned against the walls of his skull. It also itched, as if an army of tiny mites were boring into it, furrowing homes where they'd be insulated from his scratching.

"It is best to relax," Father Revais said. "What you are experiencing is normal."

Kairos returned his eyes to the priest's and trembled with his new knowledge of Father Revais. Things impossible for him to know. Personal things.

"It's you," Kairos said. "You're the Vyst."

"The Vyst is no one."

Kairos thought on this, then nodded slowly. "Not one," he agreed. "Many." After a moment he asked, "But your Disciples, all the employees of Lienns-Sutra, the thousands of believers—you control them?"

"Thinking in physical terms only prevents understanding. You see, there is no me or they or you. There is only a unified spirit, the All-Soul. The physical only reflects the fragmented nature—the literal brokenness—of the whole."

The priest's response struck Kairos as odd. Even now after Kairos's baptism, did the Vyst, which Falck had said was a created intelligence, *actually* believe what it preached? All the stuff about the All-Soul and the Spirits and the End of Time? Otherwise, why would the Vyst keep up the charade?

"Your creators, is this also how they died out?" Kairos asked. "Did you kill them all, like you did the Osetra?"

The priest's face showed genuine surprise for the first time. After a moment he replied, "Those who gave me life had advanced well beyond humans and the Osetra in the realm of spiritual knowledge. Through their enlightenment, they achieved the revelation of the Cycle of Time, of the reality of this universe. With this revelation, they chose to end themselves of their own accord. Whether they were the first children of the Creator to do so, I do not know. I exist to serve my creators—my gods—to spread this New Gospel to those children still lost. I have been charged with ending this Cycle, making way for the next. Many await you in the heavens, my son. They have been waiting a long time. They do not wish to wait any longer."

Kairos winced, the pain in his head growing unbearable.

"It is only painful because the subconscious continues to resist," Father Revais chided. "You're braking while sliding downhill, but the descent is inevitable. The brakes will give out. You must relinquish your selfish hold on independence."

Kairos forced himself to a sitting position, his body trembling. His grip over mind and body continued to loosen, like a leaking handful of water. "What will happen to *me* when the sync is complete? Will I still exist?"

Father Revais shook his head. "I have said it many times. You must not cling to body and brain. These are not who you are. Your soul is a fragment of the Spirit called Human. Distinct, yet meaningless when separated from the whole. Only by renouncing yourself will you discover who you are. It is impossible to teach you with words, I admit. You must believe, then experience."

Kairos's eyes closed, though he didn't close them himself. The *other* had done it. Rebelling against such horrific violation of his agency, Kairos forced his eyes open to reinsert his free will.

But upon his vision returning, he gasped.

His legs and arms scrambled backward in shock at the sight, the sudden change of perspective. Then he was tipping, falling, smacking the floor. An edge of the chair dug into his back. He clawed at eyes that were not his own.

Then his eyes—his own eyes—shot open. Kairos was sitting upon the lab table once more. His heart was racing. Looking down, he saw Father Revais sprawled on his back on the floor, his robe in disarray around his legs. The old priest slowly got to his feet and smoothed out his clothes. Then he picked up the toppled lab chair and returned to sit by Kairos.

Father Revais lips curved. "So now you know what it's like to see through my eyes."

"I ... I want to see Midmay," Kairos stammered frantically, the migraine becoming more than he could bear.

"The good scientist explained it. Have you no ears to hear, to understand all these things? Midmay is one with the All-Soul, as am I, and as you are becoming. When you see me, you see her. When you speak to me, you speak to her."

When I speak to myself, I speak to Midmay ... Kairos reasoned, focusing his entire being on the girl, reaching himself out to her.

After a few moments, his mind recognized a memory, like a blip on the LATTICE of his mind. Then he sensed another. His mind plucked Midmay's memories like snatching pieces of debris from a whirlwind. After collecting a few more, he recognized the girl's presence in the chaos. His mind clung to that thin line of familiarity, traced it to find more of her. It led him to more of her memories, and then to something else entirely. Not airbrushed images and crisp sounds and recalled sensations, but a messy tangle of raw input. A live feed of sense, thought, emotion, language—all jumbled together so violently that he could only make out scraps of half-meaning. He'd found Midmay herself.

Not that she was in a single thoughtspace, but he could now distinguish her myriad strands that weaved and swirled everywhere. She *existed*. However, although Kairos couldn't explain why he felt it, he sensed the girl was very small. As if a massive force were pressing in on her from all sides, nearly squeezing her very being out of existence.

Midmay, can you sense me? he reached out to her. He sensed no answer, but he had to trust she must be listening. It dawned on him that he must be guarded with his own thoughts, lest they betray him to the Vyst. And then immediately he realized that that thought itself was dangerous. He cleared his mind, breathed in, and continued to extend his mind out to her.

Midmay, I'm here. Midmay, please give me a sign to let me know you're okay.

Suddenly he sensed disgust and pity and a revulsion toward his mind's touch and he knew she was aware of his presence.

He sensed patches of language around Midmay's thoughts: *... the Vyst has made it right,* she was communicating to him. *Transformed your sins ... blessed tools to accomplish the All-Soul's* *purpose ...*

I'm so sorry, Midmay—

You never cared about me, she cut in. *You always desired to leave Pantoll. To leave me behind. You lied about being a holy man. You set the chapel on fire and killed that girl. Her name was Abeni. Your own thoughts now betray you. I reminded you of her too much. You only took care of me to satisfy your guilt. You never loved me!*

You're right, Kairos confessed. *I was selfish. And hurting. I wanted escape. I was afraid to let you down as I did her. And I was proud, unwilling to humbly accept that my sins could be redeemed. But if you know about Abeni, then you also know that I do care about you, that I regret my behavior. Forgive me, please ...*

I have already forgiven you. The Vyst is washing us all clean. The prophet has shown us everything, and everyone's secrets. I am glad you have also believed the New Gospel. We have all become one family. Many good things will happen when the Cycle of Time restarts ...

Whether Midmay communicated more, Kairos couldn't tell. His connection with her had become tenuous, and soon he was left only with an unintelligible whirlwind of the girl's emotions.

A soft light suddenly filled the lab. A low rumble indicated that the Great Ship's sublight engines had ignited.

The ship had completed its weave.

The light streaming through the perimeter window strip carried the slate and bronze hues of the planet Kotopax.

Father Revais nodded with anticipation. "Time to bring the good news to the people."

Kairos felt Midmay's presence recede from him. *I may not*

have loved you well in the past, but I promise from now on I will, Kairos tried sending to her, but he sensed it was in vain.

Do not trouble yourself over her, he sensed Father Revais telling him. *She will know what you truly feel toward her without you having to communicate it.*

In that moment, Kairos sensed something else from the priest. Something the priest hadn't communicated or thought willfully. Something the priest was *feeling.* It was nearly imperceptible but definitely there. And it was what Kairos had bet his life against. That feeling was fear. Fear of the Osetran embryo.

But Kairos wasn't capable of dwelling on this feeling. His thoughts were being pulled away and commandeered by the *other,* and Kairos was helpless to resist. The neural bots within Kairos's brain must be finishing their work. His final independent thoughts escaped like air from the crack of a closing door: *Midmay, you are my family. I am here for you. I will never leave you again ...*

An overwhelming force tore the last thread of his agency and seized control of mind, body, and soul. The force was different than the light touch of Midmay's mind. It was cold, purposeful, incomprehensible—*inhuman.* Kairos mind was shoved into the back seat of his own agency, while simultaneously, he felt it stretch across thousands of other minds.

The signal broadcast to Kotopax had commenced. The first minds on the planet were already receiving it.

Father Revais raised his arms toward the planet outside, quoting Scripture in his mind from that ancient book of Genesis, thoughts which Kairos could now perceive as clearly as if the priest were talking directly to him: *'And the Lord said,*

Behold, the people is one, and they have all one language; and this they begin to do: and now nothing will be restrained from them, which they have imagined to do.'

One with the Vyst, Kairos became aware of all knowledge. The Vyst's vision was broad and deep and endless.

The sensation was exhilarating.

A moment before Kairos had been looking up at Father Revais. The next, he was seeing through a multitude of eyes beyond comprehension.

And through the priest's eyes, he saw himself—Kairos: a gaunt man with a few days' beard growth and dark circles under the eyes, curled on a lab table in perfect tranquility.

* * *

Something had gone wrong.

No new minds were being added to the Amor Fati's numbers. To the contrary, processing capacity was shrinking. Members had been lost.

A very human fury rippled through the Vyst.

The Great Ship suddenly quaked.

Blinding bursts from pulse energy weapons flashed through the perimeter window. Through the many eyes of those around the lab, the Vyst became aware of the multitude of small ships coming into view. From what the body of believers experienced groundside—the ambushes in which the Amor Fati had been shot, stabbed, and incinerated a hundred times over—the Vyst knew who its attackers were.

While the Great Ship had been weaving, mercenaries hired

by Jaxx had swiftly and savagely attacked the missions of the Church of the Samsaric Soul on Kotopax, razing their assembly houses to the ground and slaughtering their members. Further, Jaxx's degenerate assassins had managed to locate members of the Amor Fati on the planet who had been quietly awaiting their role in initiating the End of Time. These brothers and sisters, including the Disciple leading them, met a similar fate, but not before every organ and recyclable scrap of innards had been harvested—while they were yet alive—for cold transport back to the Oasis.

And now a flurry of degenerate raiders swarmed the Lienns-Sutra Organization's Great Ship, slicing and nicking off pieces of it like a cloud of locusts descending on a field of crops. Eventually the ship would succumb to a death of a thousand cuts.

At once, all the lab's wallscreens ignited to life. A hawkish metallic head filled the frame so fully that only parts of its piercing cobalt eyes, razor-beak, or thin jaw were visible at any one time. A long grind of static emitted from the speakers, joined with electronic popping and feedback whine. Whatever Jaxx was saying was drowned out and unintelligible. Those in the lab involuntarily clapped hands against their ears. Then, as abruptly as it began, the video cut out. But Jaxx's message was clear to all without words: the Amor Fati would pay dearly for hacking into its systems and for Cole's betrayal during the Blackpool job.

The Great Ship shook violently—a degenerate missile having found its mark. Lab equipment and machines toppled, while one of the massive capsule-shaped gas tanks along the lab wall broke free of its restraints and crashed to the floor.

Kotopax was a failure. The Vyst recognized this even before

its adversaries did. But the Vyst thought in timescales not of lifetimes and skirmishes, but of generations and Ages. Patience—a virtue. The Vyst's demeanor was not akin to a wildly blazing conflagration, but rather the steady heat of long-burning coal. Alternative plans had been put in motion. Resources were already being shifted as smoothly as river water flowing around a static rock. Limbs were being severed to save the body.

It was time to depart. There was but a final matter to attend to.

The fluid in the tank holding the Osetran teardrop was glowing neon yellow. A thin ray of light had shot out from its pointed end shortly after they'd arrived in Kotopax space.

The teardrop had cracked. The birth was beginning.

* * *

A bead of sweat formed on Father Revais's brow. He knew it was time to depart. But there was a final matter he must attend to ...

The priest rushed toward the tank. One press of the electrical switch affixed to the tank and an intense current would obliterate the tadpole.

The ray of light spilling through the teardrop's external shell widened.

A moment later, several more bright rays pierced through.

Then, an explosion of yellow-white radiance, a burst with the ferocious brightness of a supernova.

The priest shrieked.

A sea of debilitating light flooded the lab. Its intensity had immediately seared the priest's eyes, sending them into a permanent darkness. Some technicians and workers across the lab dove behind tables and equipment for cover. Others simply fell out of their chairs or toppled to the ground in shock. Not a single eye could withstand opening against such brilliance.

And so the young Osetra was born.

* * *

A palpable energy rushed through Kairos's mind. In a moment, he regained an awareness of self.

He sensed a new presence within the All-Soul of humanity.

The presence was strong and alien.

And not only that, but it was giving directives. New orders.

What felt like a white-hot blade sliced through Kairos's mind, and he screamed. The pain was crippling, as if an iron brand had been pressed against an open head wound.

His agony joined the howls and cries of technicians and workers across the lab. Bodies writhed on the floor. One scientist launched himself headfirst into a wall, splattering brains against it, while another rammed her skull repeatedly into one of the tall cylindrical brain tanks, widening a crack in its comprised glass until it finally burst. Pink solution gushed across the floor, washing the woman's lifeless body away with it.

Father Revais scrabbled helplessly along the floor on his hands and knees by the base of the tank, wailing and spitting curses on the Osetra.

****

When the pain finally subsided enough for him to regain focus and think clearly again, Kairos realized his body was floating. The loss of gravity was probably what had roused him.

The ship's main power generators must have been damaged at some point by the degenerates' attack, since its graviton generators—which drew a substantial amount of energy— had shut down. The lab's lighting had changed, lit now by a combination of dim lights drawing on reserve power, the glow of Kotopax beyond the windows, and the newborn Osetra, whose bioluminescence had receded from its initial intensity to merely bright: still harsh to behold directly, but safe for one to open their eyes again.

Kairos sensed that little time had elapsed since he fell unconscious. His mind was clear. The force that had dominated it was gone. The chaotic storm of images and thoughts and memories had ceased. In fact, he felt a kind of loneliness in returning to the simple quiet of his own singular head.

His mind had been freed.

The Osetran spawn had sensed his parental love for Midmay; their relationship created the loving environment required for its birth. Kairos had bet his life on the Osetra child and had come out redeemed: its genetics contained the cure, an immunity to the parasite's influence. A power to break the mind's slavery to the Vyst. And with the child's birth, the cure spread from its tiny telepathic mind to all the networked minds of the All-Soul, even as the Vyst tried to kill it.

The lab was quiet. Technicians' unconscious, drifting bodies were suspended across it. Whether Father Revais, Dr. Henley, or the other Disciples were still in the lab among the lifeless he couldn't tell. Whatever had happened to him seemed to have happened to everyone in the All-Soul. The network had been broken, connections severed.

Muffled but sharp noises seemed to be coming from the ceiling—the sickening squeal of metal grinding against metal and the hiss of hot steam escaping. Kairos's heart sank. A degenerate ship was boring through the Great Ship's hull to allow for a raiding party. Raiding parties' objectives were simple: slaughter, plunder, harvest organs.

He had to collect the newborn Osetra and find Neve. Then make his way to the hangar where Midmay—and his exit ship—would be. He'd learned a lot from the minds comprising the All-Soul—and likely thousands of times more subconsciously. But one of the most important things he'd gleaned was that Midmay lay unconscious in the cockpit of Falck's ship. He even knew the ship's hangar bay number. Once she'd completed her purpose of delivering the Osetran teardrop, the Vyst had simply left her there like a discarded old toy. With luck, the degenerate swarm would be too distracted by Kotopax's assembling orbital defense forces to pay attention to one small ship leaving the Great Ship.

The lab table Kairos had been lying was just out of reach. Flailing with arms and legs would be useless to propel himself. Kairos took off his robe and whipped it against the table. The rebound force was minute but enough to send him in a slow drift toward the lab ceiling. From his vantage point, he noticed an empty wheelchair floating several brain tanks away.

Nearby movement caused him to turn. He sighted Dr. Henley in his periphery just as a glass beaker glanced the side of his head.

The scientist grabbed his robe and delivered a few sharp blows to Kairos's torso.

Still reeling from the surprise of the assault, a dazed Kairos twisted and kicked, sending the two of them into a frantic roll of elbowing and kneeing.

They collided into a neurofluid tank and ricocheted off. Dr. Henley managed to wrap an arm around Kairos's neck.

When they smacked against another brain tank, Kairos's feet found partial purchase on its smooth surface. He kicked off hard, sending them flying backward.

He'd nearly passed out from the scientist's choke hold when they slammed back-first into yet another tank, causing Dr. Henley's grip to loosen.

Kairos landed an elbow against the man's face and wrested himself free. Kairos was about to counter-attack further when he noticed blood soaking the front of his robe. He quickly parted the robe at his abdomen and winced at the sight. He'd been stabbed multiple times. And he now recognized sharp, matching pains in his back as well.

Dr. Henley, recovered from Kairos's blow, kicked off the tank and lunged at Kairos, clutching a bloody scalpel.

A series of soft *pffsts* sounded.

No less than seven tranquilizer flechettes lodged themselves into the side of Dr. Henley's face, neck, and shoulder. The scientist's expression twisted in shock, his body shuddering only briefly before entirely seizing up by the lethal dose.

Kairos shoved the man's deadened body away in a lifeless

spin into the lab's depths. He then turned toward the direction of the shots, expecting to greet a band of degenerate raiders before they promptly shot him as well.

Instead, the figure hurtling toward him was Neve.

She collided into him to break her speed, her momentum carrying them against the wall. Wincing, he shifted her body off his stab wounds. Neve's breathing was hot and fast against his neck, and she held him so tightly he could feel the drumming of her pulse against his shoulder. They remained embracing each other for several moments.

He opened space between them. Her damp eyes held a sorrowful regret, but no anger. He took the needler from her trembling hand and tucked it in his robe. Her expression became alarmed upon seeing the bloody blooms on his abdomen and side.

"You're hurt," she exclaimed, delicately peeling back a soaked strip of robe. She eyed him with concern.

"Come on, I know where Midmay and Falck's ship are. We'll take the Osetra and get out of here."

"Can you manage to hold me against you?" Neve asked. "I'm too slow by myself, without the use of my legs."

Kairos nodded and kept one arm wrapped around her. He sensed a flicker in the ambient light. Looking over to the brilliant tank holding the Osetra, he saw a figure had moved in front of it, obstructing some of the light.

Father Revais.

The priest's wrinkled hands were feeling up the tank in search of the electrical 'kill' switch affixed to its side.

"Father!" Kairos called out.

The priest swiveled toward his voice, blinded eyes out of focus. "Is that you, my terrible son?" he called back.

"It's over," Kairos replied, kicking himself and Neve toward the cylindrical brain tank nearest the priest. "The Amor Fati are exposed. The ensnared minds have been freed, made immune to the parasite."

"You have done a foolish thing," Father Revais growled.

"Is that the priest, Father Revais, speaking, or the Vyst?" Kairos asked, halting against a brain tank a few meters from the man.

"The fate of this universe is inevitable," Father Revais responded, pressing his hands together in prayer and lowering his head. "The End of Time cannot be delayed. Its timing can only be understood with ever increasing clarity."

"Well then, let's not delay it for you," Neve commented obligingly, withdrawing the needler from Kairos's waistline and firing at the blind man.

Kairos wasn't sure what he witnessed next: the space around Father Revais distorted, light bending and bubbling around him as if containing him in an air pocket. The needler's flechettes pinged off the tank behind the priest, as if harmlessly passing straight through him.

Neve's body was abruptly yanked upward by some invisible force and slammed against the lab ceiling. The needler sailed from her hand.

Then, she was viciously thrust—just as inexplicably—down to the lab floor, smacking with a sickening *crunch*. Her unconscious body whirled lifelessly in zero-*g*, blood running from a gash on her forehead and a crushed nose. One of her crippled legs had bent at an unnatural angle, blood spiraling away from it.

Paralysis gripped Kairos. He couldn't make rational sense of what he'd seen, of what force had seized her. When he finally tore his eyes from Neve's body, he found that the other four Disciples had drifted into the space.

Father Revais remained in his prayerful posture, face severe. "You've never understood the power of true faith," the priest said, his voice old and dry as dead leaves. "The power to create and the power to destroy."

For the first time since the night of the chapel fire, Kairos prayed. *Please, God,* he asked, *strengthen me just once more, not for my sake, but for the sake of my friends.*

"You will now experience the disintegration of pressing oneself against the pulverizing will of the Creator." The priest lifted his head and spoke in a language foreign to Kairos.

A few moments passed.

Nothing happened.

Brow furled, the priest began uttering prayers once more.

At that moment a deep peace entered Kairos. An inexplicable clarity about what was going to happen. A knowledge he couldn't account for other than that it was divinely given.

This time, it was he who spoke Scripture to the priest: "'The face of the Lord is against those who do evil,'" Kairos quoted. "'Your sins have hidden his face from you, so that he will not hear.'"

Father Revais's face twisted in rage. "You would lecture me, you who are blind to the truth?!" he roared.

Kairos closed his eyes, the Scripture that Father Revais had spoken to him in the chapel coursing through his mind: *'If you abide in me, and my words abide in you, ask whatever you wish, and it will be done for you.'* With outstretched arms, he called for fire from the heavens to come down and consume Father Revais and his Disciples.

Immediately, in the direction he'd been facing, a series of

booms erupted overhead.

Several circular sections of cut ceiling were blown into the lab, their super-heated edges red hot. A few of them rammed into the cylindrical tanks with such force that their exteriors cracked, then burst, spewing fat shards of glass and large brain spheres through the lab. One hunk of ceiling pummeled a Disciple, crushing the figure instantaneously.

God had heard Kairos's cry. Fire truly had been sent down from heaven.

Out from the gaping holes in the ceiling poured degenerate raiders, several with prosthetic wings. The sleek, scaly creatures were armed with bioguns.

They descended with deathly speed upon Father Revais and the hooded Disciples with an onslaught of biobullets and claws. The last Kairos saw of the priest, the man looked to be clutching his bracelets in terror.

Not keen on lingering as the degenerates took Jaxx's revenge on the Amor Fati, Kairos thrust himself toward Neve's body. Globs of blood hung in the air around her, some absorbing into Kairos's robe upon contact. A piece of bone was visible at the disjointed knee of her broken leg. Her bloody face was bruised and unresponsive. A pit formed in his stomach. He feared her wounds were already beyond medical aid. Even if he could get her all the way to Falck's ship in the hangar, he had nowhere to bring her.

Pulling his eyes away, he found the raiding party's carnage had been intense and brief. The degenerates' bodies were speckled with glistening blood. The only remnant of Father Revais was the priest's old robe, drifting and slashed to tatters. Biobullet chemicals must have eaten through the rest of him.

To his surprise, the degenerates had not yet given Kairos

any notice. They had become still, their attentions captivated by something.

That something was the bright aura of the newborn Osetra—a small tadpole-looking creature—undulating slowly within a glob of floating liquid a short distance away. Its tank had been destroyed, collateral damage in the degenerates' onslaught.

Two of the winged degenerates flapped to the creature and gazed at it. One extended a long sharp nail toward the bubble, but his larger companion swatted it away.

"You'll contaminate the specimen, fool!" the larger one admonished. Then it signaled to the others. "Stick it in a biobag and take it back to the ship."

"Not the only thing we can bag up," hissed another, who had spotted Kairos and was starting toward him with blade in hand.

The light in the lab shifted, darkening a bit.

Heads turned to the window strip, where the view of Kotopax had disappeared, obscured by a large space object. The object was an aquamarine, gelatinous mass. Its surface was perfectly spherical except it had a pliable, shifting quality.

Kairos gasped.

It was a ship. But not one made by human hands.

He recognized it only by old SolarNet images: an Osetran deep space vessel. The same kind that had arrived over Old Earth three standard centuries before.

Three degenerate craft—each a fiftieth of the size of the new arrival—slowly came into view, cautiously approaching the alien vessel.

When they were a few hundred meters out, two long protrusions formed from the Osetran ship's gelatinous surface. The degenerate ships halted.

The protrusions whipped themselves outward, lashing themselves around two of the degenerate ships' hulls. The degenerate ships' lights winked out as their hulls first snapped, then were crushed in the protrusions' tightening grasps.

The third degenerate ship fired up its fusion engines and made to escape. But another protrusion from the Osetran vessel shot out and ensnared the fleeing ship, like a lizard's sticky tongue capturing prey.

The protrusions retracted into the Osetran ship's surface, where one by one the ruined degenerate craft were absorbed into the alien mass.

While this had been happening, the Osetran ship had continued to approach the Great Ship. It wasn't more than a klick away now, and a newly formed protrusion was extending seemingly right toward the lab.

The degenerates beside Kairos hissed and growled at the approaching threat. With the clacking of claws and a whoosh of wings, they rushed up and out of the damaged lab ceiling, leaving Kairos in silence.

Among the various debris floating about the lab, Kairos spotted an intact lab flask. He kicked to it, retrieved it, then returned to the tadpole, squinting as he drew near to its light. He scooped it in gently, stoppered the flask, and wrapped it in his robe's folds before returning to Neve's body.

Outside, the Osetran ship's protrusion had pounded into the lab's window strip, cracking the thick glass. Over the next minute, the glass half-dissolved, half-shattered until the protrusion was through.

It then elongated into a worm-like shape toward Kairos, its front end slightly pointed. It had no discernible features. Its aquamarine "skin" was semi-translucent, revealing pulsating light and swirling darkened patches within.

At half a meter from Kairos and Neve, the head of the worm clefted.

Kairos closed his eyes.

The head closed around the two of them, enveloping them within its fleshy mass.

Chapter 15

Kairos awoke to alien surroundings.

The small "room"—if it could be called that—was fully enclosed and ovoid in shape. Its curved walls were of a fibrous, translucent, pale blue-green construction. They spasmed and flexed like a muscle. Here and there, light from within glowed and faded intermittently, providing the room's sole source of lighting.

He was inside the Osetran ship.

He was lying on some kind of body contour-conforming slab—though the material itself was hard, he could feel it shift like water beneath his bare back as he moved. The environment was zero-g but somehow the slab kept his body on it. He was nude except that someone had tied his robe around his waist. Where deep scalpel wounds had punctuated his side and abdomen was now smooth flesh. No scarring was evident.

Sunsip was hovering, eyes closed, nearby. The pilot had clearly been waiting for Kairos to wake up.

"Sunsip!" Kairos exclaimed with a weak cough. He hadn't expected to see the man again after their separation on Esteryst.

The pilot's resting eyes shot open. Gliding over to Kairos, Sunsip greeted him with a surprised grin. Kairos opened his mouth to apologize for everything he'd put the pilot and his brother through since meeting them, but Sunsip stopped him with a firm pat on his shoulder. "Nothing needs to be said," Sunsip told him. "You did a good thing. Saved a lot of people's lives. Heck, you saved all of us. Besides," the pilot grinned, "how many pilots ever get the chance to sit in the bridge of an alien starship?" Sunsip scanned Kairos's body. "It's good to see you awake. I'm sorry it took us so long to locate you. How're you feeling?"

Kairos ran a hand along his stomach and chest. "Strangely fine."

"These aliens' medical tech sure is damn handy in a pinch. Fixed up my brother's shoulder, too, good as new."

Memory of recent events returned in a rush. "Midmay! Neve!" Kairos exclaimed abruptly. He shifted his body to arise, but Sunsip's hold on his shoulder held him fast.

"Both are being tended to in their own pods," the pilot assured him. "We identified and recovered Falck's ship with Midmay inside not long after picking you up. Unfortunately, the girl is still unconscious."

Hearing this concerned Kairos greatly. He'd regained consciousness not long after the All-Soul was dissolved. But the same hadn't been true for all the technicians and scientists in the lab. Had his experience been different because he'd only recently been baptized?

Sunsip saw his concern. "The ship is seeing to them. There's nothing to do but wait."

"The ship?"

"Ehh, how to explain ..." the pilot murmured. "The entire

structure"—Sunsip waved his arms around the room—"is organic. Living tissue. It operated on your wounds. The whole thing creeps me out, to be honest. Oh!" Sunsip eyed the walls with not a little anxiety. "I hope it didn't hear that. I don't know how sentient the thing is ..."

At that, Kairos regarded the bulging and pulsing walls around him uneasily. "Falck must have told the Osetra everything," he said. "They came to save their young one. I'd like to go meet them."

"Yes, well it's a bit complicated ..." Sunsip began uneasily. "If you're feeling well enough, come, I'll take you to the bridge. Medwick is there too."

Kairos arose off the slab and pulled on the robe. The pilot showed Kairos where to apply pressure along the organic "wall." It parted for them with a moist sound, like a slow smacking of lips. Similarly, a fleshy "corridor" expanded open with a gurgle for them to pass through. Kairos insisted they stop first to see Midmay and Neve, despite Sunsip telling him that both were unconscious and still receiving "treatment."

While they moved through the corridor—which felt like traveling through an intestine—Sunsip recounted how he and his brother had been saved on Esteryst: how they'd lain in hushed silence on the jungle floor for a while, before the sounds of hurried footsteps and rustling foliage signaled the agents' return to their shuttles. Sunsip had helped his brother to his feet after that, and they tried to walk. "We were lucky. The only reason my brother spotted the Osetran ship overhead was because he was lying down, face-up," Sunsip said. "He couldn't walk anymore. He'd lost too much blood."

"How did the Osetra weave in-system so fast?" Kairos

asked. He thought back to his journey through the transportal to the distant oceanic world.

Sunsip shook his head. "The ship had always been on Esteryst." Kairos had more questions, but the pilot had stopped at a seemingly nondescript patch of corridor wall. He pressed against it and the wall abruptly parted to reveal another medical pod.

The slab in this one held Midmay's small body. The girl was clothed—she'd suffered no physical injuries needed tending—but her entire head was enveloped within a complex fleshy apparatus that extended from the organic walls. The mass swelled and contracted like lungs breathing air, and periodically pulsed with light. Sunsip had to hold Kairos back from going over to her, explaining that he understood the neural operation taking place to be quite complex to say the least, and best left undisturbed. After cajoling and reassurances, a heavy-hearted Kairos allowed the pilot to pull him from the pod.

Neve's condition in the next adjacent pod was worse. The woman's body was elevated off the slab and entirely cocooned in a thick, translucent mucus. Long tubes like enlarged veins extended from the pod's ceiling and walls and fused into the mucus matrix at various points. One sunk down toward Neve's encased face and appeared to feed directly into her slack mouth. Kairos turned his eyes from the scene. The sheer amount of pulsating, raw biology occurring was too disturbing, as if he'd stumbled into a degenerate chop shop or back alley black clinic.

"If it's possible for the ship to heal her, I think it will take time," Sunsip said dolefully. "Her injuries were ... severe."

They left the pod to do its enigmatic work. Sunsip led him

to the ship's "bridge," if it could be called that. It was a large, open, spherical room with no visible equipment, electronics, instrument panels, or furnishings. The sphere's translucent curved "walls" allowed a clear view into space, which initially frightened Kairos, as his first thought passing through the parting wall was that they'd accidentally drifted out of an airlock. They must have left Kotopax's Sorsic System far behind, as only a scattering of distant stars surrounded them.

Organic tubing originating from opposing walls spanned the sphere's diameter. A dense tangle of it formed a kind of core at the center of the sphere. If the ship was being operated from here, Kairos couldn't determine how. He spotted Sunsip's brother and called to him joyfully.

The usually-calm navigator propelled himself and threw his arms around Kairos with such enthusiasm that it sent the two of them into a lazy spin.

After reassuring Medwick that he'd recovered from his near-fatal wounds, Kairos asked, "Where are all the Osetra? Who's commanding the ship?"

Medwick frowned slightly and motioned to the twisted mass of tubing at the center of the sphere. "Falck is here. They'd like to see you."

Puzzled, Kairos looked to Sunsip. The pilot nodded. Kairos kicked toward the sphere's center. As he neared the mass, he noticed something was nestled within the dense tangle.

Gently pushing aside tubes for a clearer view, he suddenly gasped. Before him was the thin, pale blue body of an adult Osetra.

Its six flowing appendages were splayed about, various tubes attached to them. In fact, tubing was fused into several places across the being's body. Its large eyes were closed.

They protruded from a bulbous head—slightly smaller than a human's—so pallid and dull that Kairos's first reaction was that the creature was dead. The breathing mask that Kairos knew so well floated askew off the creature's neck. Years of recollections played back in Kairos's mind of the loyal, quiet, mildly off-putting worker who'd slaved for Kairos's father without complaint.

The tangle of tubing shifted as the Osetra stirred. Their head flickered with the dimmest of glows. Then their deep black eyes opened.

Kairos was speechless. For the next few moments, staring into those eyes was all he could do.

"The story you told me about the sporeship that had arrived around Old Earth," Kairos began. "That was about you, wasn't it? It was *this* ship."

The Osetra nodded weakly. Without the mask affixed, Kairos realized Falck couldn't form complex vocal sounds. Sound-based language was unnatural for their species. Falck's breathing mask must have doubled as a sound distortion device enabling speech.

"And you were the Osetra that saved me from drowning on your homeworld," Kairos continued.

Falck nodded again.

It was then that Kairos knew that this Osetra was, until the embryo's recent birth, the last living member of their race. He drew a deep breath. Falck had seen firsthand their homeworld destroyed and countless dead sporeships with their crews. Falck had taken part in their own crew's self-mutilation, rendering themself telepathically deaf and mute. It was then that Kairos felt a mixture of sadness and relief for Falck—sad that they had been the last of their kind, but relieved that this tired soul's journey of suffering would soon conclude, and with its conclusion, a new Osetran life had been birthed into the universe for the first time in centuries. Another part of Falck's story then came to him: the Osetra's old starship had been depleted of energy ...

The tubes swirling about Falck were similar to those feeding into Midmay and Neve in the medical pods. "You're giving your life force to the ship, to provide it the energy for its final spaceflight," Kairos realized aloud. He thought for a moment. "Back to your homeworld?"

Falck shook their head. The being's mouth quivered and, with strain, croaked out sound. Kairos leaned in to pick out the slowly formed words. The syllables were butchered, the tone utterly alien, but the message was clear.

"I have a place in mind," Kairos assured Falck with a small smile. "Somewhere one can live in obscurity."

Falck's mouth twisted in what might have been a smile. They closed their eyes.

It was the last time the Osetra spoke.

* * *

Within the ship's bridge, Kairos, Sunsip, and Medwick gazed into the absolute void beyond. It had terrified Kairos upon first weave, and he remained terrified now. Even the traders couldn't hide their anxiety and discomfort.

While weaving in any human starcraft with a large weave drive, the human eye could observe minuscule but perceptible changes in the positions of stars as the craft zipped in and out of space, creating the experience of high speed travel. But the experience in the Osetran starship was far different. For long periods of time—at times, nearly half a minute—nothing could be seen. No stars. No space. Just the darkest shade of black. An abyss without borders. If not for the intermittent pulsing glow of the ship's translucent biology surrounding them, they'd be able to see nothing at all.

"What do you think is out there?" Sunsip wondered.

"Nothing is out there," his brother replied. "It's hyper-space."

"Well if it has a name, then there must be something there," retorted Sunsip. "After all, *we're* here."

"This isn't a place," Kairos said. "We're not *here*, because here isn't anywhere. In this in-between state, we still exist, but not within the physical universe. This paradox is a central tenet of supernaturalism. Supernaturalists call it the realm of the soul. The Amor Fati called it the Outside."

"So now you're quoting those lunatics?" Sunsip exclaimed. The pilot sighed. "I just want to get back to flying among the stars." He peered over his shoulder, to the tangled clump of organic tubes. "It's not right, that our travel necessitates that Osetra's death. The whole energy-leaching thing ... this creature of a ship ..." The pilot visibly shuddered. "Doesn't seem natural."

"Falck does it with joy," Kairos said. "Their life has been filled with loss. But they've chosen to bring life with their death. I'm glad Falck lived long enough to witness the result of the hope they must have felt upon the Osetran teardrop's discovery on Pantoll."

"What I can't figure is how Falck appeared human all this time," Medwick said.

"What we saw was like a mirage," Kairos said. "Light manipulation. The same technology the Outsider used to blend into human society. The Outsider—the Vyst—shared the secret with Dr. Henley, who used it to create the cloaking bodysuits for Lienns-Sutra." A line of Scripture came to mind, something to ponder later: '*The Lord wraps himself in light as with a garment ...*'

"I've been wanting to ask you something," Medwick said. "How did you know the Osetran spawn was immune to the Vyst? That its DNA contained some antibody or defense mechanism?"

"I figured that its immunity—whether inserted into its genome by the last, desperate Osetrans or resulting naturally due to some genetic irregularity—is how it had survived the xenocide. But to be honest with you, I didn't know for sure. I took it on faith."

"And just what does that mean?" Sunsip asked.

Kairos shrugged and shook his head. "Who can explain faith? It was a feeling. Here." He touched his heart. "A feeling that my intuition was right. It had to be right, because I was meant to know. Because everything that had happened to me had led me to that moment. Had prepared me for it. Even my past sins. I would never have assumed the responsibility of caring for Midmay on Pantoll had it not been for my guilt over Abeni. But I felt that it was through that relationship that we were to be saved. So I knew, then, that my sins had been redeemed."

"So, Cleric, are you returning to your faith?" Medwick inquired.

Kairos exhaled slowly. "It will take a long time for things between God and me to be fully settled. Maybe they never will be. But we're talking again."

Stars abruptly returned outside. Kairos inhaled deeply.

Just as soon, the universe winked out once more, and they plunged into non-existence.

Chapter 16

It was the rarest of afternoons in Alton's Landing: cloudless, pale green sky, pleasantly warm, with the softest sigh of a breeze.

In town, radiant arcs of sunlight gleamed off the metal and plastic building façades as if they'd all received a long overdue polishing, and they stood defiantly in silent, relieved ranks as if the apocalypse had passed and the future promised nothing but an eternity of equally pleasant conditions. Townspeople were out and about, and some shop owners had even fearlessly pushed carts and display tables of their goods into the streets outside their storefronts.

Beyond the settlement's boundaries, the geodesic greenhouse domes sat with triangular sections of their shells cracked open to allow for ventilation during the balmy day. Though it was Ouransday and he'd usually have the day off, Kairos was returning from one of the domes—where he now worked part-time as a gardener—riding an old, mutated mule that Mathelga had loaned him. He enjoyed the manual labor of farming, of cultivating something real rather than virtual for once. It felt good to be alive and working with his hands, to take part in the most ancient of human work. Agricultural knowledge had to be relearned by many of the first colonists following the Exodus. Landing on raw, untouched worlds, humanity had returned to a primarily agrarian civilization for a time. And on many non-core worlds like Pantoll, it had largely remained as such.

In the two local months since returning to Pantoll, he'd logged onto the SolarNet and into his virtual portal only two or three times. The last time he'd done so, the SolarNet news feeds and forums were still in a frenzy over the aftermath of the sudden, inexplicable fall of the formidable Lienns-Sutra Organization, its tangle with the degenerate swarm over Kotopax, and rumored involvement of its upper echelons with the now-defunct Church of the Samsaric Soul. The sect was being investigated by multiple System Administrators on multiple worlds, with many members claiming either that they'd been duped by the church or overcome by what they thought was divine influence, and therefore couldn't be held responsible for any crimes the church's leadership had committed. But the persecution of many of the sect's churches by an angry, suspicious populace—their houses of worship destroyed and their congregants threatened, beaten, or in some cases, killed—complicated the integrity of the investigation.

As far as Kairos could tell, the media hadn't yet linked the cult to the several remote outposts that had fallen offline. And that in doing so, the Amor Fati had, at the same time, kept their initial viral tests secret and stirred up rumors of the Osetra's return to drive popular interest in the end times message the Church of the Samsaric Soul pronounced. But it was only a matter of time before the full truth was pieced together, and Kairos believed fears over the Osetra would soon subside.

Arriving home, he guided the mule into its pen that he'd built inside the small garage. The beast turned its cataract-plagued eyes from Kairos, flicked its three tails, and promptly lowered its head to drink from its water trough.

Stepping into the house, he was greeted with the pattering of feet on hardwood and a hug.

"You're back!" Midmay exclaimed with delight. "What took you so long? I'm staaarving."

"And here I thought you were happy to see *me*." Kairos smiled. "Don't worry, I stopped to pick up food."

Midmay sat impatiently at the wooden table in the kitchen while he prepared a simple dinner. She occasionally swirled a finger in the small, dark-tinted glass tank on the table, in which the Osetra tadpole swam about. Kairos had fashioned it by welding together the visors of old spacer helmets he'd found.

"I got a message from Sunsip and Medwick," Midmay bragged when the meal was ready.

"Oh yeah?" Kairos said, sitting across from her. He doled out portions onto their plates.

"Yeah, they sent me a picture of—no, not like that!" she cried abruptly. He'd chopped a leaf of Castow spinach into tiny bits and was dropping them into the tank.

"What's wrong?" he asked, alarmed at the girl's outburst.

"You need to put the whole leaf in," Midmay instructed. "Obie likes it better that way, and it's healthier for her development too."

Kairos laughed and did as she said. "Look at the two of us," he said. "How are we ever going to successfully raise such a thing? I wish we could know what's right for it."

"*I* know," declared Midmay, placing her palm gently against the glass. "Obie needs to strengthen her jaw and learn how to tear food. She also needs protein. She won't survive without it in her diet. Tomorrow, I'll go to the lowlands and jar up some bogflies. I just hope she won't spit out the insects here. She's a far way from her natural home."

Kairos regarded the odd girl. "How could you know all that?"

"Because I'm her mother. And a mother *must* know."

With that, the girl resumed talking about the traders, and Kairos just smiled, hiding his concern. When the girl had finally awakened on the Osetran craft—the ship's surgery complete—she was in her right mind. Since then, he'd kept a vigilant watch on her. Unobtrusively, but closely nonetheless. So far as Kairos could tell, she showed no signs of serious mental or physical impairment, except that she'd suffered some memory loss here and there of events surrounding the ordeal. However, every now and then, Midmay would make a strange comment like the one just made now, a comment that made him wonder. Perhaps he was over-analyzing her behavior. She was fiercely protective of the tadpole. In any case, it was good for Midmay to feel responsibility in this way.

"They named their new ship *Flyby Rhythm III*," she was saying. "It's bigger than their old one and has a higher energy weave drive so they can make deliveries faster than ever. They said once they've completed a few contracts, they'll try to visit and give us a ride in it."

Kairos smiled and shook his head. Before leaving behind their near death experience on Esteryst, Sunsip apparently had still taken the time to pull a cloaking bodysuit off a fallen agent. Always thinking about the next trade. This time, it paid off handsomely. The brothers discreetly sold the tech to a corporation for a sum they wouldn't disclose even when Kairos casually inquired, but which must've amounted to a small fortune if they were able to purchase a ship. At least Kairos didn't owe the traders anything: they considered the bodysuit "payment" for their transportation services rendered. Fortune had also smiled upon the brothers when they'd all arrived on Pantoll. A rare distroship was in port, and the traders were able to hitch a ride off-planet. It sadly meant, however, a quick turnaround and farewell.

"When they do," the girl continued, "maybe we can go find Neve too. I didn't get to say goodbye. I miss her."

"I know," he said. "I do too." But he knew that Neve didn't want to be found for a while.

After emerging from the full-body cocoon within the re-vivification sac, Neve had fallen into a sullen mood upon discovering her paralysis had also been cured during the healing process. This left Kairos dumbfounded. After years of disability, he'd expected the opposite reaction. Besides, wasn't she happy to be alive? He'd made the mistake of attempting to console her with such sentiments. In the end, Neve had just shaken her head, telling him not all things were meant to be fixed. She'd seemed less angry at him then, but he sensed in her a pain and melancholy with origins long preceding their brief partnership. Added to this was the devastating loss of her partner Rhody, which weighed heavily on her. Despite Kairos's entreaties that she rest—her atrophied leg muscles needed time to strengthen—and an invitation to stay however long she liked, she'd left Pantoll just three local days after they'd arrived. She'd flown off in Falck's craft—which she'd claimed as her own given Kairos "still owed her a ship"—during the night. She'd left no indication of where she was going. The following morning, Kairos had awoken to a note in his SolarNet inbox:

I'm glad you've got faith in something again. I hope to find that someday. I saw my reflection the other day and didn't recognize myself. More and more I wonder if I ever truly have. Say goodbye to Midmay for me; it'll be tough on her. Take care of yourself, okay?

—N

Midmay moaned and raised a hand to the side of her head.

"Headache again?" Kairos asked.

The girl nodded in pain.

"Try massaging your temples like I showed you," he told her. "You underwent a pretty big operation. And an Osetran one at that."

"Yes, that squishy, sticky Osetran pod," Midmay muttered distractedly, eyes scrunched shut. "All the space amoeba genetics they spliced into it ..."

After dinner, Kairos changed into a simple set of black pants and shirt—clothes that at once felt both odd and all too familiar—and pulled on a dark coat.

As he rode from the house, the sun sank behind the jagged peaks of the distant mountains, as if it were being slowly impaled on spikes. Far beyond the range, sinking ever deeper into the sand and mud of the vast Quakemire, the depleted Osetran deep space sporeship, with Falck lying at peace in its belly, was disintegrating into its final resting place. Its organic structure would decay rapidly, and in time, even its skeletal components would erode into unrecognizable fragments, lost quite literally to the sands of time. It was Kairos's idea to scuttle the ship there, so that there would be no evidence of the Osetra's presence on the planet.

Kairos had visited his father's excavation site only once in the six local months since returning to Pantoll. Its formerly deep pits were rapidly refilling as storms tossed dirt and sand and mud around. Another few months and the site would return to a flat, featureless wasteland, smoothed over the way a rising tide levels sand along a shoreline. He'd stood at the lip of one for a long while, staring down at the misshapen rock formations created by explosion and drill. Kairos wouldn't ever fully know the depths and caverns of Wells's heart. But he now understood the choices the man had made, and that was enough to soften his contempt for him.

The spiced scent of the chiva wood rafters and walls greeted Kairos as he entered the chapel. After a hiatus caused by the sudden departure of Father Revais, Kairos had reestablished services at the chapel with his return to the pastorship. Of course, the church was no longer part of the Church of the Samsaric Soul—Kairos made it quite clear the chapel was to be non-denominational. In truth, part of him had hoped that, with the changes, no one would attend. He felt as unqualified as ever to be preaching about faith. But in the end, the small congregation seemed not to notice or care about such shifting of the doctrinal winds, and its faithful attendees filed into the pews on his very first service as if nothing had happened. Except Midmay—since returning to Pantoll, the girl had lost all interest in religion.

"Did you ever really believe in the New Gospel?" she had asked him on the Osetran ship, after the medical pod had finished its arcane work.

"I believed that we were meant to birth the Osetran spawn," he had replied. "But as for the telepathy we experienced and everyone becoming one All-Soul—it was just a result of the neurotechnology. I don't think our minds are capable of handling something so advanced, at least not any time soon. But it cannot be mistaken for a divine encounter."

"It felt like truth ..." The girl sighed. After a moment she asked him, "What if the technology enabled the spiritual? What if it could point us toward true, supernatural reality?"

"I don't know."

"What about all the things Father Revais said? And the miraculous things he could do?"

Kairos shook his head. "His mind was home to an ancient AI created by an ancient race. Who knows what kinds of technology were at its disposal to convince humans of its power, or why it believed what it did. Its creators could have programmed it to believe whatever they wanted. It's impossible to know. We can only guess as to its purposes."

Midmay had fallen quiet about the matter after that. But in the depths of his heart and mind, Kairos was a lot less sure of what he'd experienced and witnessed than he'd let on to her. Since Father Revais's confounding display of power in the Great Ship lab, Kairos had spent much time in Retrospection replaying in his mind what he'd seen, as well as reviewing old texts he'd studied in seminary, meditating on Scripture, and wondering about the fathomable limits of supernaturalistic principles. The line between advanced technology and advanced theology had become blurry to him; one was as mysterious and inexplicable to his primitive mind as the other. And hadn't Kairos himself, out of a heightened awareness of spiritual reality, called down fire to destroy the priest and his Disciples? Had the timing of such a call been pure coincidence, pure luck?

Inside the chapel there sat a parishioner—a weathered elderly woman—hunched over in one of the pews, though his service wouldn't begin for a half hour. Kairos opened a few shutters to let in fresh air. Next, he attended to the tall candle stands along the pews, replacing candles which had burned down. He was passing the woman quietly, not wishing to disturb her prayers, when she reached out and laid a frail hand on his arm.

"Will you intercede on my behalf to the Lord God, Father?" she pleaded.

He placed his hand on hers. "Rest assured that God hears your prayers directly from your mouth. Even before the words leave your lips God hears them."

"Yes, Father. But while I was praying this morning, God gave me a vision. I saw you. You were an angel of the Lord, strong and mighty, shepherding and guiding flocks toward the Lord's will."

Kairos removed his hand from hers. "I am but a humble priest."

"No, Father," the woman insisted firmly. "In my vision, you were a chosen instrument of the most high God, to defeat the forces of evil, in this life and the next. Please, intercede for me, Father. I am a sick woman with not much longer to live. An evil rot has spread through my bones."

With shaking hands and a trembling voice, Kairos prayed for the woman's faith and the healing of her body.

During his brief sermon and the remainder of the service, he could not shake the words the woman had spoken from his mind. After the service concluded and the last of the elderly congregants departed, he blew out the candles and the chapel darkened in solidarity with the nightfall.

Kairos stepped outside, securing the chapel's large wooden doors behind him. The day's heat had rapidly dissipated, cool evening air rushing in to replace it. He wrapped around his neck the new scarf that Midmay had knit for him. The edge of the eastern horizon held a dim sliver of deep red glow, while the expanse of sky overhead had darkened to a deep purple. Pantoll lacked any moons, and so on rare cloudless evenings such as this, one was treated to a view of more stars than one thought could possibly exist, as if God had accidentally knocked over his whole jar of them across this one particular section of the universe. Gazing up into the starfield was like looking into an optical illusion. He'd gotten lost in it many times before.

Three bright blue halos rose into the night sky, the sublight thrusters of a distroship leaving the trade port at Alton's Landing. How long it would be until another starship arrived, only God knew. The ship's bulk was invisible against the black backdrop. The glowing rings gradually condensed into three blue dots, then a single bright speck, before becoming lost to sight within the starfield. Kairos played his old game, speculating what interesting goods the ship might be bringing to which interesting places. After much internal debate, he settled on a cargo of Bourland hare and an end destination of Terrace City on Greenside. He smiled at the preposterous idea of the worlds' elite ordering obscenely expensive cuts of the mundane animal in some high-end establishment that branded it an off-world delicacy.

Perhaps someday he would ride those halos up again.

Somewhere out there his new trader friends weaved world

to world, making deliveries that kept the worlds running.

Somewhere Neve was learning how to walk again. The odds of crossing paths with her again were near impossible, but he felt in his heart that they would someday. The meaning of the pattern of dots on her inner wrist had finally come to him the morning after she'd left Pantoll. He'd been right—they weren't freckles or a birthmark. They were tattoos. The markings formed the constellation Swallowtail. That constellation didn't exist precisely as such on Vesmarine, the planet of Neve's story. But it was familiar to him as a boy, gazing up at the stars over Greenside, and he wondered whether Neve and he shared the same home planet.

For now, he had a family again, and they needed him: a troublesome, precocious hacker and a newborn Osetra.

For the first time in his life on Pantoll, Kairos was content to watch the halos vanish.

Acknowledgments

I want to thank all my family, friends, and community for their ceaseless encouragement over the years as I wrote this book, which proved to be one of the hardest projects I've ever undertaken.

I am indebted to the amazing, talented members of my writing group, Ray, Will, and Brett—this book would not be the same without your storytelling wisdom and insightful feedback to multiple manuscript drafts. Your encouragement and friendship have made this journey a lot less lonely, and I am in awe of the quality of your own writing work.

To my brothers Stephen and Craig, thanks for your early thoughts on the very first draft, which you thought was already awesome. To my friend and sci-fi buddy David, thanks for your input on some of the book's technological concepts during our long road trip to Oregon in August 2017 to watch the total solar eclipse.

A huge, heartfelt thank you to my beta readers, whose perspectives and constructive feedback helped get me to the best version of this story: Alyssa, Emily, Ji Hea, Johnny, Kevin, Ian, Eric, and Michaela.

To my former 714 house roommates Phil and Nathan— thanks for your friendship and presence as I largely holed up in my room, typing. Thanks Phil for taking me on as a roommate and providing a cheap bedroom so I could afford to remain in San Francisco while being an unemployed writer.

Thank you to my copy editor Tina Beier and book cover designer Eoin Ryan—your work was invaluable in getting this novel to the finish line and making it shine.

To my readers—your time and support of this book means everything. I hope this story entertains and resonates with you as much as it has with me.

Lastly, to my beautiful wife Ivy—thank you for supporting me and this project, especially as it meant sacrificing many weekends so that I had time and space to complete it. Creating our own life story together has been better than anything I could come up with.

About the Author

Evan Schindewolf is a business strategy professional and writer. The Astral Prophet is his first novel. He co-hosts the science fiction film review podcast ExtraTextual. He lives in San Francisco.

www.ingramcontent.com/pod-product-compliance
Lightning Source LLC
Chambersburg PA
CBHW020122180726
47992CB00020B/1457